QUEER VIEW MIRROR

QUEER
VIEW MIRROR

Edited by
JAMES C. JOHNSTONE &
KAREN X. TULCHINSKY

ARSENAL PULP PRESS
VANCOUVER

ARSENAL PULP PRESS
103-1014 Homer Street
Vancouver, B.C.
Canada V6B 2W9

The publisher gratefully acknowledges the assistance of the Canada Council and the Cultural Services Branch, B.C. Ministry of Small Business, Tourism and Culture.

Cover design by Val Speidel
Cover photography by Daniel Collins
Printed and bound in Canada

CANADIAN CATALOGUING IN PUBLICATION DATA:
Main entry under title:
Queer view mirror

ISBN 1-55152-026-5
1. Lesbians' writings, Canadian (English)* 2. Gays' writings, Canadian (English)* 3. Short stories, Canadian (English)* 4. Canadian fiction (English)—20th century.* 5. Lesbians—Fiction. 6. Gays—Fiction. I. Johnstone, James C. (James Compton) II. Tulchinsky, Karen X.
PS8235.L47Q4 1995   C813'.0108054'08664   C95-910826-2
PR9197.33.L47Q4 1995

Contents

Acknowledgements

We would like to thank Brian Lam and Wendy Atkinson at Arsenal Pulp Press for their belief in and enthusiastic support of this project. We thank friends, mentors and supporters in and around the queer writing world for their advice, ideas and support, especially Davyd Apple, Michael Bronski, Chrystos, Bernard Cooper, Dennis Denisoff, Rosamund Elwin, Lois Fine, Gregory fitzGeorge-Watts, Michael T. Ford, Philip Gambone, Barbara Kuhne, Martin Laba, Sara Leavitt, Bia Lowe, Michael Lowenthal, Mickey McCaffrey, Joan Nestle, Lesléa Newman, Gerry North, Suzanne Perreault, Lev Raphael, Michael Rowe, Robert Thomson, Lawrence Schimel, Wickie Stamps, Keith Stuart, Kate Weck and Dianne Whelan. We would like to thank our trusty postie, Bryan Vipond, for reliably and cheerfully delivering dozens of big brown "do not bend" envelopes every day.

We would also like to thank all those magazines, publications, radio shows, bookstores, community centres and writers' groups who helped publish our call for submissions and get the word out about this project.

We would like to thank Daniel Collins and Val Speidel for their creative genius and patience in putting together a truly wonderful book cover. We would also like to thank our models: Evan Adams, Corinne Allyson Lee, Sam Buggeln and Shirl Reynolds. And last but not least, we would like to thank Jackie Haywood for the use of her gorgeous car, Dolores. Thanks, Dolores!

This book is respectfully dedicated to Joan Nestle and to the memory of the late John Preston, and to all those in our far-flung and diverse communities who work to promote partnerships between lesbians and gay men in political, literary and other cultural endeavours. This book is for you.

Introduction

The idea for this book came together one late summer evening, as we sat at a small round table in a modest, tastefully cluttered, high-rise apartment in Vancouver's West End. Candles were everywhere, their light played on the rain-drizzled window and cast shadows that danced on the art-covered walls. The two of us had just finished dinner, and were somewhere between our last sip of red wine and our first taste of cappuccino. We were toasting the inclusion of our essay, "Across The Lines," in John Preston and Joan Nestle's anthology, *Sister & Brother*. Between mouthfuls of pasta and sips of wine we reflected on the process we had just gone through. Writing about our stormy, intense and complicated friendship had been both painful and healing for both of us.

Writing our piece began in 1992 when we noticed the call for submissions for *Sister & Brother*. The editors were looking for true stories by lesbians and gay men about our lives together. We had only recently begun to renew our friendship after a painful rupture that had lasted more than two years. We knew our experience was important and that we needed to write about it. We met weekly for many months and slowly, honestly and carefully put our story onto paper.

"Across The Lines," our first attempt at literary collaboration, chronicled how and why we became friends, the circumstances that combined to destroy our friendship, and how ultimately we were able to reconnect. Working together on that project, and our ultimate inclusion in Joan and John's Lambda Award-winning book, provided us the inspiration and the impetus to work together on other literary projects.

So what next?

James: I've been thinking of this book project. . . .

Karen: Oh?

J: Yeah, an anthology of snapshot fiction. You know, stories of a thousand words or so each. A gay one—a lesbian and gay one actually.

K: Wait a minute! If you're going to do a mixed anthology, you'll need a lesbian co-editor.

J: Hmmm. Guess so. . . . You know anyone who might be suitable?

One last clink of our wine glasses and that was that. We drafted and sent out our call for submissions the very next day.

Over the following months we mailed notices to over 260 newsletters, magazines and journals in twenty-eight countries around the world. We would have sent out more but many countries did not have any organized gay or lesbian groups or publications to send our posting to. Our first manuscripts came through the mail slot in September and as we began to read through them, we were amazed by the range and diversity of people and places our postings actually reached. Seven months later we had received 581 stories from 337 lesbian and gay writers living in thirteen countries around the world. We received stories from as far north as Orkney in Scotland and as far south as Wellington, New Zealand, from places as diverse and contrasting as the chaotic urban density of Tokyo to a kibbutz on the frontier borders of Israel.

We were excited by the sheer multitude of topics and themes chosen which ran the gamut of first love, supermarket cruising, car sex, love gone awry, change-room sex, dykes cruising drag queens, sex with aliens, surviving gaybashing, fashion oppression, divine sex, cross-cultural pub crawls, unsafe sex, holidays with family, lesbian mothers, breaking up, SM sex, inter-generational attractions, and how to disrupt 12-step group meetings. The tone of the writing was self confident, matter-of-fact, in-your-face, unapologetic, funny, honest, celebratory. Many pieces were distinctly queer, depicting experiences in gay bars, coming out, or homophobia, while others dealt with themes that were more universal, such as childhood memories, relationships and family problems. We noticed several trends within the piles of submissions that would not have appeared ten years ago. People wrote about friendships between lesbians and gay men. Women wrote about sex in graphic detail. Men wrote about long-term relationships. There were very few pieces that were filled with the self-effacing powerlessness of internalized homophobia. And of course, AIDS and its impact on all of our lives was present over and over again.

Choosing the final manuscript was an exciting, challenging and some-times difficult process. It was interesting that we often disagreed about the relative merits of stories written by writers of our opposite gender. It was not rare to hear one of us exclaiming, "No, we've got to put this story in. Gay men will be totally blown away by this type of story by a lesbian," or conversely, "It's so rare for lesbians to see men be sweet and tender with each other. I love this piece." In some cases, one or both of us had negative personal reactions to the content, yet included a story anyway because the writing was strong and the experience reflected a part of queer reality.

We wanted *Queer View Mirror* to include voices from as many social, cultural, racial and class backgrounds as possible. We wanted to have a good balance of published and emerging writers. We also wanted *Queer View Mirror* to include work from as many countries outside Canada and the U.S. as possible.

It is our hope that this collection of queer quickies will provide more than just a glimpse into the worlds we live in and the lives we lead. We hope that this book will serve to introduce readers around the world to the writing of their sisters and brothers in other lands and other social and political contexts.

Our stories, our histories as lesbians and gay men continue to be underrepresented and misrepresented in mainstream commercial media. It is in our own literature that we find true mirrors of our realities as lesbians and gay men claiming our space, surviving, succeeding, and flourishing in a homophobic world. We encourage all lesbian and gay writers to continue writing, continue putting to paper a queer view of the world.

We hope that *Queer View Mirror* will entertain, educate, excite, inspire and entice both readers and writers. We hope reading this anthology will be like driving a car across the country along a seemingly familiar stretch of highway, looking out the window as you cruise past cities and towns, catching a fleeting but lasting sense of a place, a passing glance, a backward look, a flash, an instant that speaks to you, that resonates in your heart.

—James C. Johnstone and Karen X. Tulchinsky
September 5, 1995
Vancouver, B.C., Canada

Keith Adamson

Black Leather Jacket, White T-Shirt

It felt odd, going to stand where he said he'd be waiting, putting himself on display, wearing what he said he'd wear. Well, not quite. On impulse, he'd left the coat in the car; after all, the weather had turned out warmer than he'd anticipated when they made the arrangement, so it wouldn't seem unreasonable that he'd discarded it at the last minute. But it would put him at a slight advantage: to be able to observe without being observed.

There were five minutes to go. Five long minutes, increased by the fact that his heart was beating at twice its normal speed; and he found himself acting impatient, snapping his fingers to the "musak" coming over the station P.A., glancing around him, looking for someone fitting John's description. Black leather jacket, white t-shirt.

At eight his nerves reached jangling point. The minute hand of the station clock swung ponderously into an upright position, and seemed to shudder, as if emphasizing the irrevocability of the hour. A man was walking towards him, thin, too old, surely, to be John; and yet the right height, and a black jacket. And then he passed, thank God, not looking at Ian, who scanned the other occupants of the concourse with nervous anticipation.

The moment moved on; the minute hand swung another notch round the dial. Still no John.

He began to imagine their conversation. Casual at first: "Oh, hi! Have you been waiting long? No, just got here. Nice evening, isn't it? After this morning, eh? Thought the summer was never coming. Where d'you fancy going? I'm easy. A pub? Okay." Then eventually, maybe, having skirted round the real issue all evening: "So, what d'you want to do? Back to my place for a coffee?" Not if he was like that guy a minute ago. More like: "Maybe we'll do this again sometime. Give us a ring." Not bloody likely—and bugger off.

Then he noticed someone else; okay, his jacket was the wrong colour, but maybe he too was hedging his bets. The other guy looked over at Ian, then looked away, keeping his distance. He seemed attractive, but there was no attempt to make contact. It was nearly a quarter past. Ian, in a sudden moment of rash courage, thought, "What the hell!" and marched over to him. "Excuse me. Are you John?"

"Eh?"

"I'm supposed to be meeting someone called John. I don't know what he looks like."

A shake of the head. "Nah."

Maybe this guy was John and didn't like the look of Ian. But he didn't fit, not really: he just looked bewildered. Ian went back to his post, and later watched him depart with a woman who'd come off the train.

Clearly, John wasn't coming. Ian decided to give up and was just about to browse through the magazines in the bookshop when he spotted Tony at the till, buying a newspaper. He breathed, "Oh, shit," through his teeth and wondered if he could walk away without being spotted, but realized it was too late. He racked his brain for an excuse for being in the station, then launched his face into a smile.

"Oh, hi, Tony. Been working late?"

Tony was surprised to see him. Ian explained he had come in to town to do some late shopping, but hadn't bought anything. And now he'd just missed a train, so he'd phoned David to say he'd be late home.

Tony checked his watch. "I've got half an hour before my next train. Do you fancy going for a drink?"

Ian hesitated, shooting one last backward glance towards the busy concourse. "Yeah, well, okay. Why not?"

The pub was quiet. Ian bought the drinks and they shared one of those little round tables, which seemed to throw them unnaturally close together.

"How is David, anyway?" Tony asked. "I haven't seen him for ages."

"He's fine, thanks. Very busy. Works a lot."

And Tony began to talk, openly and effortlessly about himself. How he felt at a loose end; lacking a bit in self-confidence; lacking a lover, and wondering how he was ever going to find one.

"Did you ever think of using contact ads?" suggested Ian, warily.

Tony laughed. "Oh, well. You always think 'what sort of person are you going to meet that way?', don't you?"

"I don't know. Alan and Larry met that way, didn't they?"

Tony nodded, but didn't further the discussion.

As they talked, Ian found himself thinking, as he had before, what an attractive man Tony was, noticing the way his eyes sparkled, the way dimples formed at the sides of his mouth when he smiled. It began to dawn on him that he was quite glad John hadn't turned up and propelled him into an evening of stilted small talk. He was enjoying Tony's company far more.

"You and David have an open relationship, don't you?" Tony asked suddenly.

"Yes, if you can call it that. More 'open' than 'relationship,' I think."

Tony just looked at him quizzically for a moment, then pointed to his glass. "Another whisky?"

"Thanks." Ian watched Tony as he stood at the bar, and thought it was odd how you can find your friends sexy, and never find a way to get to "first base."

"So, how did you mean?" asked Tony, returning. "About you and David?"

"Oh well, you know. We're so far past the romantic stage, we're more like flat-mates, really. Why do you ask?"

"Oh, I just wondered. You know. What do you do for . . . ?"

Ian shrugged. "Just whatever turns up . . . from time to time." He drained his glass, noticing that his heart had started to beat quickly again. "You . . . ?"

"The same, I guess."

Ian thought he detected a blush, which only served to increase Tony's attractiveness—a hint of vulnerability—and he suppressed an overwhelming desire to ruffle Tony's hair.

Tony glanced at his watch. "I'd better get going. I've got exam papers to mark." He finished his drink and stood up to go.

"Well, it was nice to see you," said Ian, regretful the contact was ending so abruptly. "Maybe we'll do this again some time . . . ?"

Tony gave him an odd look. "What, miss our trains?"

Ian laughed to cover his embarrassment, and as they walked back to the station together, Tony bemoaned the state of the nation in general, and the Education Secretary's National Curriculum in particular.

As they went off in separate directions, Ian paused and looked back over his shoulder to watch Tony's departing figure vanish into the crowd. To his surprise, Tony turned briefly and waved. "Yes, indeed," Ian said to himself, "Tony is looking really attractive. And he always makes the most of his appearance." He stopped in his tracks as he realized that he'd never seen Tony looking quite so sexy as he did in his black leather jacket and white t-shirt.

Donna Allegra

Snatched

I've been observing Terry for over a month now and I'm still captivated. She works low-key, methodically, remaining very matter-of-fact with her gestures. During each exercise, she interacts with as much space as her body can fill, like water completing a bowl.

We're not even done with the *tendus* and already she's sweating. After the warm-up isolations are done, she pulls off her black sweatshirt. The clavicles that stand out from her breastplate could be scythes which shave hay within an inch of life. As sweat stains her plain white t-shirt, I observes her musculature come alive to greater clarity, like a photograph appearing in developer.

When we begin the *développés*, the shirt clinging to the shape of Terry's torso looks sinful, elegant. I watch her pull it as if she were removing the plastic wrapping from a slice of packaged cheese. With a single un-dramatic toss, she back- hands it to the corner of the studio where her sweatshirt and sweatpants had gone earlier in the class. She did this without losing a beat between *plié* stretch to *relevé*. The muscles I see revealed on her back display a map of Eden.

As I contemplate this woman, I feel struck by a longing that could shake thunder from a sunny sky. I curse the sprained ankle that has kept me out of dance class for the previous two months. I could have been gazing upon this sleek animal of a woman strong and in her prime. At a guess I'd place her at thirty-two, but she could just as easily be twenty-seven or thirty-six.

With the technique work over and done, Janelle asks us to line up in groups of three to go across the floor for *chaînée* turns. I place myself so as to be in Terry's group, but end up in the row behind. Her turns seem

21

to split the air and stop motion as if she were under a disco strobe. As I prepare with my line to execute our turns, something inside whimpers and feels defeat. I'll never be that good a dancer: and Terry is already on the other side of the room.

After my row has spun across the floor, I say to her, "Those were terrific *chaînées*," my smile like a dog wagging its tail for a scrap from the table. She says "Thank you" in a tone deeper than the heart of winter. Her eyes tell me to leave her alone. She steps away from me to stretch out at the *barre*. I can tell by her studied concentration that I'm dismissed. My hope bursts like a stabbed tomato.

I don't even know this bitch and already I feel like weeping—stung to tears by her disinterest. Her picture is branded to my eyes and I feel as if my soul is the one that's been taken.

From somewhere in the studio I hear Janelle tell the class, "Take a minute and get your jazz shoes on." While the group disperses, Janelle stands studying her body's motions at the mirror, reviewing the dance steps she'll be teaching us.

I try to train my attention on Janelle, but my eyes return to Terry, like my tongue seeking a loose tooth to be sure the pain is still there. A sulking child in me watches as she pulls on her black high-topped Capezios and laces them up.

Janelle plays the first few bars of a club mix of The Police's "Voices Inside My Head," so I know we won't be dancing anything lyrical and soft tonight. I expect the choreography to come sharp, fast, as edgy as the music. No one with any sense ever comes to Janelle's class unless they're ready to be all-the-way-live, as if this were an audition.

I study Janelle with as much concentration as I can muster, but a prowling part of me keeps tabs on Terry. She picks up steps easily and seems undaunted by the challenge of Janelle's fierce moves.

I've been in Janelle's class for over a year now, so I know the style and likelihood of her movement. Her allegiance is more to Black street dance than to *jettés* and *pirouettes*, though she expects us to do double turns and will pull off a triple sometimes. Last week's inside *attitude* sequence finished with a pencil turn stopped a breath short of a dime.

I feel a twinge of panic because Janelle is having us do movement on the floor today. She's also giving an alternative version for the ending of this piece of choreography, in case there's time to do partner work. Rarely is there any extra time. She's so demanding that it takes the better half of class time just to learn her maze of manoeuvres. But I know the territory in this jungle. I'll show Terry she's not the only one who can dance.

We're a small class tonight. Janelle divides us into two groups to work. I'm in one and Terry is in the other. This gives me the opportunity to steal looks at her. In performance she's no less than mythic—a leopard in attack, but she can be as delicate as a cub the moment after a savage pouncing. I witness her become more alive with the choreography—shedding a low-key camouflage for her full intimidating reach, now looking like a cobra hissing.

The gasps and stabs in the music let her lure us to a place where she changes her attitude to embody a sneer and her perfect form plays out the disdain of the righteous. I feel jabbed with her every breath. I find I can't even steal her gestures to use at another time.

I'm a little self-conscious when it's my group's turn to dance. At what point in class had I wet my pants? I don't think anyone else can tell, but shame constricts me from strutting any stuff.

In the last five minutes of the class, Janelle decides to partner us off. I'm surprised when I hear Janelle's melodious voice count off twelve of us all-tolled. I was aware of only three. Janelle points to people at random, "A,B, A,B." I'm an "A," Terry is a "B." Janelle has paired us together.

The "A"s get the floor work and the "B" people have the alternative ending to Janelle's epic-length choreography. We do a trial run-through and, come the floor movements, my back is arched as if in worship to the python that is Terry's torso. I finish on my knees, positioned like a mantis praying before her snaking hips.

Janelle gives us sixteen counts to rest and then we dance it twice more. Each time we dance I feel as if I'm still in a dream I once had of shoplifting a shirt. I beg in prayer for some measure of mercy. But there's no clemency in this store, as in life, where the first people the security guards trail are Black. In the dream my petty theft is treated like grand larceny and I'm swallowed whole in the name of justice.

Finally, Janelle tells us, "Last time around, guys." When we dance, I work as if my efforts will gain me Terry's affection. When it's over, she offers a hand to lift me up from the floor. She then quickly turns away to applaud—as we all do—Janelle, for giving us this class.

Terry then walks up front to speak to Janelle. Once again I've been discarded. At least a scab has formed on the wound I suffer from her indifference. It's crisp, ripe and ready for picking.

I turn to leave the studio. On my way to the door, my eyes fasten on the sweat-marked shirt atop Terry's other clothing. I glance over my shoulder like Lot's wife may have done, bend down and pick up the wet fabric. I'm terrified I'll be caught and exposed as a thief for all the world to see. When I'm outside the door, I feel exhilaration for getting away with it. I can breathe again and I'm not pining. Terry owes me this, and something more. I won't let go until I get it.

Alan Alvare

In the Chapel of the Sacred Heart

The Chapel of the Sacred Heart is not in the main body of the cathedral, but off to the left, among the pillars, quiet and dark as blood. Night has fallen early, as it does in November, the month of the Holy Souls, the time we know we should pray for the dead huddled in the passage between purgatory and heaven, some of them there century after century, clutching their documents, unsummoned by heaven, forgotten on earth.

The cathedral is cold, the priests have turned out the lights, the last Mass of the day is over, the candles are cold at the altar, but the Chapel remains unlocked, luring lingerers. This year Franciscan Friars are preaching a parish mission, sermon after sermon ringing off the ceiling to stir up congealed faith. Some of that leftover zeal, hanging in the air like incense after Mass, has produced a residue of heads and arms scattered among the pews.

Above them all, high above the altar, the statue of the Sacred Heart is suspended mid-air, fixed to the walls by invisible screws. The statue is good quality, probably stone and not plaster, though the Heart on Jesus' white robe is bloody red. The factory imbued this Jesus with the miraculous ability to look neither male nor female, and the hair is so red it should be spiked. There he stands, hands pointing at his Heart, like a drag queen proud of some tomato thrown at her, squashed into her breast on Hallowe'en.

The screws in Jesus are slowly coming loose, and some time in the unknown future (the date known to God, but not yet revealed, unless perhaps to some Italian or Portuguese children), Jesus will come tumbling down on to the altar, amid dust and cracking and obligatory screams. No one, not even Monsignor, knows this, of course, but when the statue falls,

Paulette will laugh, Elise will get dust behind her contact lenses, Robert will ignore it, Victor will have a heart attack, Emma will be crushed, Esperanza will finally feel something, and Martin will take it as a sign of vocation. It won't be the end of the world, or even the Second Coming, but Victor's next of kin will consider a lawsuit.

In the meantime, Jesus stays, fixed, on the wall, leaning, it's true, but to all appearances stable in his inclinations.

The light thrown from rows of flickering red votive lamps almost make him smile, almost make him blush, almost make him blood-warm. Each red spot is a prayer, a love sucking in its nightly breath, thankful for a little oxygen, fearful of mighty rushing winds that might blow them out, waiting to be swallowed up in daylight. 'Til then, all the lovers keep vigil.

So many lovers of the Sacred Heart, all hoping He'll see them kneeling before him, and find them worth a good gossip back home with Mary and Joseph.

"Whom shall I choose today, Mom?"

"I like the looks of young Martin," says Mary. So Martin it will be.

Back in the visible world, or what passes for it, Martin's eyes are fixed on Jesus, wishing he were John, to lie on the sacred breast with the big red heart, next to the stone that can't really be cold, not if he could only be allowed to touch it.

Martin is blond, pimply and eighteen. At home, by a desk lamp, lies an unwritten English essay awaiting a devotion he can only arouse among the flickering lights. But none of the characters in the novel are Catholic, the prof isn't Catholic, the classroom has no cross, and Martin is dying for Catholicism and crosses. He dreams of crosses he will bear, perhaps embroidered on gowns.

Martin is under a vigilant instruction in the faith, as they put it, visiting Monsignor to have the gaps filled in. There aren't many gaps, though. He's been reading about the Church for years, and already has most of it down pat. There is something else, unspoken, between them, which can't be said, a difference too subtle for words Martin or Monsignor can manage. One day, the difference will show up, like a fault in the earth, but for now, the romance is deepening. Not between Martin and Monsignor, of course: Monsignor has no taste for Martin, who (as we said) is blond.

Monsignor Molloy, the Rector of this place, likes his boys as dark as his cathedral. And while Martin kneels here in the shadows, Monsignor is in his room caressing magazines. Boys fucking boys sucking boys rimming boys beating boys kissing boys spreading boys jerking boys coming in boys' faces. He was supposed to meet Martin for more instruction tonight, but the magazines made him stick to his room in the rectory.

Martin has been waiting for Monsignor on his knees for hours. Still, he feels no pain as he looks at the face of the Saviour, and the exquisite Heart that beats eternally for him.

The Chapel of the Sacred Heart is not in the main body of the cathedral, but off to the left, among the pillars, quiet and dark as blood.

Tommi Avicolli Mecca

Angie

from *Libretto for an Italian Opera*,
a performance piece

The senior prom is coming.

Mama and papa are asking me on a daily basis if I am going. I don't want anything to do with the prom. I've never been out with a girl, and I certainly don't want to start now. But there's Angie, who follows me around the neighbourhood and smiles at me in that special kind of way.

I'm in love—with her brother, Guido. *Madon!*

Tired of hearing that if I don't go, I'll miss the greatest experience of my life, I ask Angie. She says she'll go if we double with Guido and his date. I am now into this prom.

The night of the big event. I start dressing three hours before I have to pick up Angie. Mama and papa are real happy, mama's snapping pictures of me getting dressed, shining my shoes, fixing my tie.

Angie's ready when I arrive but Guido's not. He's smoking a joint in his bedroom. "Try it," he says. I take my first toke ever. Before long my head is spinning.

Next thing I know I'm sitting on the sofa in Angie's basement. She's telling me her parents are gone for the night. I don't like that look in her eyes. She tells me to get up. I do and she pulls out a bed from the sofa. Oh shit.

I guess it shows that I'm freaking because she asks, "Whatsamatter, you a virgin?"

"Course not."

"Then come here."

She pulls me down onto the bed and begins kissing me, pushing her tongue inside my mouth. I'm dying. I notice that my pants are open and she's trying to work them down over my hips. I think quickly, and jump up.

"I gotta piss," I announce with an urgency she can't refuse. Upstairs, I see a light on under Guido's door, which is open slightly. And there's old Adonis on the bed beating off.

I must be *stonato* but before I can think straight, I'm on the bed devouring the man like I've never sucked cock before. Guido's so stoned he doesn't know what's going on except he's loving every second of it. I pull out my own cock and beat off. We start coming at the same time, just as—Angie walks in. Guido passes out after he shoots and I'm left to face Angie.

I mumble some excuse, but Angie reads me the riot act, accusing me of everything from being a lowly pervert who's just ruined her brother's life and probably given him syphillis, gonorrhea and tuberculosis, to destroying any chance she has of happiness by totally disillusioning her.

To make matters worse, Guido stirs. "Hey, come on over here and do that again."

Angie storms out of the room.

Always one to help the needy, I jump back into bed.

A few years later, Guido is headed for Nam. Out of work and down on his luck, his lottery number comes up. I show up for his going-away party but don't stay long. Guido comes up to me as I'm leaving: "Hey, come on, you ain't lost your best friend. I'll be home for Christmas."

Guido never makes it to Christmas. But he does manage a trip home sooner than expected—all expenses paid—in a body bag.

I can feel the scream building inside me, but it won't come out.

Damien Barlow

Births, Deaths & Marriages

Deaths

ATTACK PHOSPHORUS TODAY, screams a billboard as we turn off the freeway avoiding Albury and the Murray River, which is slowly dying a blue-green algae death. The Wodonga Hills are baking in the Christmas heat while at the same time coming into a bruising bloom of Patterson's Curse. I am now in the place my parents call "home." I tune into the new FM tourist radio station, "Twin Cities Vacationer," but switch it off, preferring my own commentary.

"Wodonga is a city of decapitated cows, a rural city, a meat-eating city. The abattoir sits on a hill flanked with pathetic saplings, housing frail cattle munching on dry grass. Fumes of their dead bodies (waste as it is called) is periodically released into the air at three—cow spirits ascending to somewhere. The smell is repugnant and slightly intoxicating. After a couple of years' exposure, there is even an inexplicable desire to breathe in deeper at three."

I am not alone in my re-entry. Aaron (a fellow expat) is fixing his hair, rolling a quick last joint.

Aaron: So when's your funeral on?

Me: Tomorrow, after the cremation. When's yours?

Aaron: The day after. Where are they holding it?

Me: At the Albury Botanical Gardens. David always said he wanted his ashes scattered in the Rainforest Walk, among the semen-stained leaves and potent smell of truck drivers on speed being fucked by adolescent schoolboys. He'll enjoy it there.

" . . . Wodonga is also a military city, new recruits arrive every year. Sixteen-year-old rednecks from Queensland cattle stations or small mining communities in western Australia are soon all shorn, branded and trained to decapitate. Teenaged girls scan the shaved-head extravaganza as their future AJ boyfriends (with a wage) are hoarded onto tired interstate buses. This spectacle is also pleasing to the passing tourist who can later find any number of skinheads at the nearby Council-owned and -cleaned toilet block."

Marriages

It must be something in the water (blue-green algae? Sewage? Or maybe some strange coupling bacteria yet to be discovered?), as when I left Wodonga for Melbourne—a young mind desiring with a stale palate the taste of the metropolis, three million new faces, new bodies—I vowed I would never get married. Three years later, I am married, like all good country girls, to a man with rough hands and sun-damaged skin who, also like some of their husbands, has a preference for taking it in the mouth. A cum-kiss is what the bride ordered.

Instinctively, I flip past *The Border Chronicle*'s rendition of "the news," seeking the wedding photos page which encapsulates future lives with four variations: "Allan is the son of . . . the happy couple were married at . . . they will honeymoon at Merimbula, Gold Coast, Cairns, or Nosa . . . they will live in Albury, Thurgoona, Lavington or perhaps Yackandandah." Today I recognize Allison "turn or burn" Mitchell, a Baptist from Faith City, an ugly, ugly, brick veneer place of worship known through whispers to be the centre of cultish practices. Her husband is a cute (Baptist) Italian, apparently packed with plenty of lunch, so Aaron tells me from their adolescent playing-in-the-dark, I'm-pretending-to-be-asleep masturbation sessions.

For us (the expats), Boxing Day is a day to seek refuge away from the now unaccustomed noise and intrusion of "families."

Me: How was the family?

Aaron: All my cousins are getting married or engaged or breeding, even the one I thought was a dyke has some dairy farmer from Tallangatta who is heir to a milking million. My mother even asked when I was going to settle down! I mean, she's gone from supportive but-don't-talk-about-it-with-yer-father to the Faith City catch-cry "turn or burn." I just don't understand it!

Births

Me: By the way, how was the funeral?

Aaron: Oh, okay . . . it was quite horrible, actually. A group of Wodonga Raiders drove past, one of them yelling to Janice, "I'm glad your lezzo cunt-licking girlfriend is dead." Janice and Miriam were like mothers to me, they knew I was gay before I did. They sat me down one day and told me they were lesbians, introduced me to my first lover. They really changed my life . . . gave birth to me, in a proxy queer kinda way. Who gave birth to you?

Me: Well, I feel like I was born on the beats. Little yellow urinal balls and engorged doors with oversized cocks sprouting on them is the backdrop to my first lover, my entry into Albury-Wodonga's *demi-monde*. There is even some of my own artwork still unpainted down over at Willow Park. From my first tentative steps into my first cubicle, I became an all-out slut, devouring my new milieu with the vigour of a just-been-kissed thirteen-year-old.

My younger brother retrieves his homemade Coke bottle bong from its hiding place and starts to cut up the last of his deal.

Aaron: So when are you driving down to Melbourne?

Me: Tomorrow, around lunchtime, maybe.

Aaron: Rachel's prego, she's going to have a kid. My kid!

Me: Do Mom and Dad know?

Aaron: No.

Me: Don't worry, Mom always wanted a wedding and a grandkid before she dies.

West Wodonga, with its brand new McDonald's and university, seems to be bubbling in the heat, plastic slides configuring into unimaginable designs. The "Twin Cities Vacationer" is retelling, in an aloof tone, Wodonga's origins: "Wodonga is Aboriginal for edible nut. . . . It was settled in 1836." What was settled? The birth of Australia's first rural city or that death should be swift for the "natives"? The frequency is now getting faint, I instead tune back to my own tourist station.

"Wodonga is a tourist city, polluting the unseen line in the Murray which divides Victoria from New South Wales. Many things are left unseen here. Aborigines still live in Wodonga, but most have been confined to West Albury (known locally at Vegemite Valley). The Albury-Wodonga Queer Network meets once a month but recently lost its meeting place, while in Thurgoona, residents have halted the building of a mosque. The unseen and unheard in this border city are too numerous to list, but they are here (if you care to listen). As you leave the border, wave goodbye to the algae-free Murray Cod plastered aside the Hume Freeway, who cheerfully bubbles, 'Hope you had a nice stay, come back soon.' "

J. L. Belrose

Shopping

She's a Tart. Posed beside a rack of thirty-percent-off denim jackets. Black mascara. Ruby lipstick. Hair like Cher. Pretending she's a star doing a promo and not a sales clerk in a ladies' wear chain store in a mall.

It's hard not to stare at her. Hard not to look at her pointy tits. Black tank top. She's watching me the same way I'm seeing her, but she's not going to bother coming over. Must be salaried instead of commissioned. Doesn't care whether I want to buy anything or not.

I take my time, letting her look at me. Letting her think about it. I ruffle through a pile of fifty-percent-off sweaters.

Two people wander in through the open store. Mother and daughter, I'd guess. Lost souls. Mother glances around and retreats, daughter following. Little Lamb. Not my type.

The Tart's gone. Damn! Slipped away while I was distracted by the Lamb. I move to the back of the store toward the denim jackets. Her perfume is still there. And so is she, around the corner in front of a mirror. Long fingers, ruby red nails, picking at her colour-enhanced, protein-enriched Cher-hair. Legs apart. Posed. Pelvis pushed forward. She pulls a curl. Eyes focused on themselves. Lips pouted. She pulls another curl.

"Those are mostly small sizes," she says, eyes never leaving the mirror. I look to see if there's anyone else she could be talking to. Her hands move from hair to hips. Black leather mini-skirt. Two inches below her ass. Black leather belt.

She moves toward me, spiked heels silent on the carpet. She's in no hurry. It's a slow night. There's nothing better to do, so she comes over, sticking her tits out. Her bracelets are cock rings. Studded strips of black leather. Silver chains.

She pushes the jackets apart along the rack. "This one might fit you," she says.

"I don't like fringes," I say. I'm thinking about getting into the change room. With her. I see the open door. The tiny pink room. One wall is a mirror. "I need some jeans," I say.

"There's none on sale right now," she says, but motions vaguely to the wall behind us. She's not going to help me. She's settling into another pose. I walk away, pick up a pair of jeans—any pair—and go to the change room.

It takes me a minute to jam the zipper. I open the door. She's still there. "I need some help," I say.

Maybe she doesn't hear me. Maybe she can't make up her mind. She takes a million years to move.

"Okay," she says. Comes over. Leans against the wall outside the door. Arms folded across her tits.

"I can't get this zipper down," I say.

She smiles. Looks down at my crotch. "That's a problem," she says, her eyes coming up to mine. Lips open. Tip of her tongue between her teeth. Our eyes lock. Nobody blinks.

She shoves herself off the wall, comes into the cubicle, pulling the door closed behind her. There's no room to move. Except against each other. I put my hands up under her tits, curling my fingers around to find hard little knobs of nipple, roll them around between my thumb and forefinger, pinching, pulling.

Her hands grab at my arms. There's no air in the cubicle. Just our breath. "Don't crease my tee," she says, and the temperature goes up a million degrees. "Don't mess my hair," she says, and sticks her lip out to blow hair away. She's sweating. "Shit," she rolls her head back against the wall. "I've only got a few minutes," she says, spreading her legs, her skirt up to her waist. I work my hand into her, my thumb flicking at her clit. "Damn you," she says. She loves it.

"You liked it okay," I say, while she's putting herself back together, "and that was just one little buzz. Want to go for coffee later?" She doesn't answer, and then she's gone. Swinging away. Tossing back hair.

I think about leaving the jeans but that's not my style, so I take them to the counter and pull out my wallet.

The cashier is a Puff Pastry. Blonde. Candy floss lipstick. She looks at me. She looks at the Tart who is now standing at the front of the store, posing with one foot upon the base of a display, hands on her hips. Checking out the people in the mall. Then Puff looks at me again. "Hi," she says. I'm really not interested. Fluff. Not my type.

I see the Tart yawn and look at her watch. It's a slow night.

Puff Pastry checks the ticket on the jeans and rings them in. "You used to come into Shirts'n'Skirts, didn't you?" she says. I don't answer but she has my attention. "I used to work there," she says.

I look at her. Soft. Probably has huge pale nipples. She hands me the bag, but doesn't let go of it. "If you decide to return these," she says, "I'm here 'til nine."

She is kind of cute. "I might have to see about getting the zipper fixed," I say.

Michael Bendzela

Titans

Early spring: Awnings drip coldly into open coat collars. Snowpacks the colour of the streets soften and run, releasing their caches of stale dog turds onto the sidewalks.

New pictures have gone up on the billboards crowding around the busiest intersection of the avenue. On one corner, a giant blond man in the baggy slacks that have gone from marginal to fashionable leaps in mid-air, his triumph frozen for eternity; opposite him, a man and a woman gaze at one another wryly across forever-clinking glasses of scotch. These signs of success place silent brackets around the noisy automobile, pedestrian and bicycle traffic melting into and flowing around itself at the corner.

Up the avenue, in front of the gingerbread house built by a late nineteenth century merchant—the addicts long since swept away, the bay windows scraped down and painted multicolours—two women are digging rotted ice out from around their arborvitae shrubs to expose the long overdue tips of jonquil and narcissus.

A few blocks downhill, in a former carriage house honeycombed into apartments, a boy awakens from baseball dreams to water dripping down an already stained and buckled sheetrock wall. He leans over in bed and snaps a cassette tape into his boombox.

One wonders: What happens when such neighbours meet?

Taking a break from their chipping and digging, the women go into their kitchen to discuss over cups of cappuccino what to hang in place of the gauzy material over their big windows. They had hoped the light fabric might let in some sun while screening them from the little windows across the alley—they like to walk around the house in only their sandals—but this illusion of privacy melted away one evening when one of the women, adjusting the bathroom curtain a little, saw how clearly the wife across the alley could be seen, through the lit-up curtains of her own window, receiving a beating from her husband. The woman withdrew from the bathroom window and pulled the shade. Time they went curtain shopping.

The boy carries his booming tape player out to the door stoop where his older brother and several of his brother's homeys are gathered on recently acquired bicycles. He is smaller than the other boys, fatherless, aching for approval. He places the boombox on the ground and turns up the volume, while his brother pretends he isn't there. The others bop to the beats he has brought them.

Something in the clear air makes the homeys hump their newfound bikes over the piles of black snow that still hang around. They pedal and turn and send dirty ice sputtering down the alley. The small boy heaves the big box out to the alley to watch them circle and jump. He shows his adoration by pumping the volume so loud they can hear it on their return runs down the block. With the music thumping, the bass seeming to come from his own chest, it's easy for him to imagine he's somebody, a big star. If only he could be on the pitcher's mound, winding up, the fans holding their breath.

Returning from the store with their new curtains, the women sense the music coming from the alley and stop talking. Catching sight of the boys, they drop their eyes to the sidewalk, experiencing a self-consciousness they loathe. They can imagine what the boys are thinking: *See those short haircuts, those hoops and piercings, those nasty old clothes? They the bitches what came into our neighbourhood and bought the old place where our brothers took a stab at freedom. They might pass quiet on the street, but as soon as you back turned they using they funny money to slide you house out from under you. Pretty soon it all just faggots and AIDS.*

One of the women recalls the comment made by a co-worker they had over for dinner once: "The idea of these mixed neighbourhoods is very nice, but if you had to live with them growing up like I did. . . . " His sentence is unfinished, his thought complete. He lives with his partner in an older, more "settled" part of the city. It was his "them" which pierced the woman: Her partner is a different shade than she. They like to think they can live in a place where there are no thems. They like to look around themselves in the vintage clothing store and see all kinds of people respecting each other's space.

It's what they do now, respect their neighbours' right to play their music loud by remaining silent about it. But who could talk, or even think, in such noise? Why do these kids always have to play their radios so loud?

While preoccupied with the disentombed dog turds on the sidewalk, the women cannot resist a glance at the boys looking at them from the door stoop in the alley. The two gaze down at their feet again, anticipating kissing sounds, whoops, catcalls.

The boys catch this glance which seems to appraise and dismiss them in an instant: *Watch out in Brown Town. The kids there travel in packs and are just looking for an excuse to cause trouble. You try to get along with them, but they're like dogs ready to attack as soon as you step on their turf. Even if you're just driving through, roll up the windows, lock the doors. Keep your eyes straight ahead. Don't get caught in Brown Town.*

The cassette tape reaches the end of its first side and begins to double back. For a moment there is no music.

The white woman and her darker companion pass the stoop without a word. The smaller boy, sensing the glee and hostility rolling like smoke off his brother and the homeys, puts his tongue between his lips and makes a loud farting sound. A spasm of laughter.

The women round the corner safely, relieved, angry that they even need to feel relieved. *Kids.* As the white woman contemplates the sting of her co-worker's comment, a turd-implanted snowball explodes against the back of her head. Her partner turns suddenly. "Did those little bastards just throw something?"

The woman touches the back of her head. Icy water rolls down the back of her neck. Bits of dogshit in her hair. She looks behind her. A small black boy is leaping up and down on the sidewalk, delighted with his accuracy, his second snowball already in mid-flight.

The group is behind the boy. They prop him up and cock his arm. The second snowball blasts the dark woman on the tit. The music going *boom!* behind him. She takes a step toward him. This clears the door stoop. A moment they've all expected, perhaps even longed for. The boy grinning because he has delivered it to them. A scene one can't turn away from.

Lucy Jane Bledsoe

Fierce

I was underage, just out of high school and not quite out of the closet, that hot summer night in Portland, Oregon, 1975. I walked up and down the sidewalk for thirty minutes trying to find the place. From the outside, The Other Side of Midnight was nothing more than a brown, numberless door in a bad part of town.

Once I found it, I pulled open the plain door and faced a hefty woman who stood immediately inside. The bouncer glanced at my fake ID, which I'd spent hours making with a fine-tip black felt pen and an exacto-knife, then nodded me up the short flight of stairs.

I reached the top just as one jukebox song died and before the next one started. In the space of that silence, all the women in the bar turned to look me over. I hesitated, there at the top of the stairs, unsure about what I was supposed to do next. When the music finally resumed, the women went back to their conversations, and I could move again. Feeling as big and obvious as a barge, I made my way to the bar where I found refuge on a stool.

I ordered a beer, but as I tried to drink, my hand shook so hard I sloshed half of it out of the glass. I managed to down what remained of that one and ordered another before turning around to look at the women.

Right away I noticed a table of black and white women sitting together, talking about basketball. One woman popped an imaginary jumper over her head. The others teased her and I figured they were having beers after a league game. I longed to sit at their table.

I began to relax as I noticed these and other women turn and stare at everyone who came up the stairs and into the bar. It hadn't been anything weird about me that had drawn their attention. In fact, I started to enjoy the game, the anticipation, even the seduction, of listening to footsteps on the stairs and wondering to whom they belonged.

Then, I noticed a woman staring at me. She stood by herself, not far away. Her blonde hair frizzed out from her face like a big A-frame roof and she wore loose Indian cotton clothing. Definitely not my type. Still, I loved the attention, any kind of attention.

As I stared back, sweating in the heat of the small, un-air-conditioned bar, wondering what her staring meant, I heard a commotion in the stairwell. Then the sound of feet hammering up the stairs, this time more threatening than seductive.

Four women burst into the bar. They wore heavy makeup, flimsy blouses, polyester hot pants, and high heels. The lead woman marched over to a table of lesbians wearing plaid flannel shirts and short-cropped hair, grabbed an empty chair, and hoisted it over her head. She slammed it down, aiming for the head of a thin woman wearing thick wire-rimmed glasses. Just in time, the woman slid under the table and the chair cracked on the tabletop. A half-full beer pitcher exploded into flying shards.

Another flannel-shirted dyke lunged for the floozy who'd bashed their table and, instantaneously, a brawl erupted. Women threw chairs, overturned tables, wielded high heels and Frye boots, pulled hair and kicked shins. I'd read all the lesbian-feminist theory I could get my hands on, but no one ever wrote about dyke brawls. I crouched down and pressed my back against the bar, hoping no one came for me. The bartender switched off the music and lights, then she and the bouncer wrestled women apart and shoved them down the stairwell. In an instant, it was over.

I left fast. Out on the sidewalk, the woman with the blonde A-frame appeared at my side. "Do you have a way to get home?"

Lying, I nodded yes.

"Listen, you're underage, right?"

I nodded again.

"I thought so. I was about to talk to you before the fight began. Underage women threaten the bar. If you're caught in there, the place will be closed down. Then we won't have anywhere to go."

So it hadn't been my irresistible good looks attracting her attention.

"I'm sorry," she said. "Listen. Before you go home, I want you to understand what happened in there."

She spoke in a low, soothing tone, as if to abate my fear. She explained to me that there was a deep rift between the "old-time dykes," many of whom were prostitutes, and the middle-class "political dykes." Some hookers worked out of the building next door to The Other Side of Midnight. Their pimp often came into the bar to call them for work. One of the "political dykes" had slept with the girlfriend of one of the "old-time hooker dykes." The attack in the bar was retaliation.

When she finished, she looked at me meaningfully and gave me her card. If I needed to talk.

I thanked her and walked off briskly as if my car were around the corner. Once out of sight, I slowed down to enjoy the long walk home in the hot night, and to absorb what I'd witnessed.

The woman with the blonde A-frame was right: I was scared. The fear was nothing, though, compared to the exhilaration I felt. What relief to learn that lesbians hadn't spontaneously combusted from hard thinking and theorizing! I was thrilled to be joining a tribe of women who had a fierce history, one I was only beginning to glimpse. Women who fought hard. Who lusted savagely.

I stopped and threw myself on the grass next to a bronze statue in a small park. Someone had watered the grass earlier and the wet soil seeped into the back of my t-shirt. I inhaled the heady scent of hot summer night mixed with wet grassy earth and fell asleep in a state of pure wanting.

Allen Borcherding

Yente

Today it is only Yente and me. Riding in the spot she laid sole claim to for so many years. We leave without the new dog, the one who bounds effortlessly in and out of the car, who quivers in anticipation of any destination. And without the man. Without them, the trip feels strange. On this bright autumn morning it is only Yente and me.

She lays beside me, curled on the car seat, nose to tail, looking more comfortable than she has for days. Her slender greyed muzzle rests between paws now less than unsteady. Silky black fur feathering out from her body, its fine wheaten tips disappear on the fabric of the seat. She is a tired, arthritic, pained and failing dog, a shadow of the lithe, inquisitive pup of sixteen years ago.

She does not stir from the place where I lay her as we back from the garage. Sunlight streams through the windshield, warms her angular head, warms spots she can no longer reach to scratch.

We drive a route I have planned, without planning, for maybe a week, maybe longer. We loop out and away from home, our first destination that where our destinies merged. My chest tightens as I see again the kennels that held her, ready for adoption. Goofy, gangling, without a hint of the beautiful dog she would become, she waited for an owner. For my wife and me. For a heart's opening.

Next to me lies the pup who reached through that cage, crossed her paws around the wrist of a married man and sent him, blubbering, to the parking lot. Sent him liberated from his composure, his self-control. Karen managed the details, the dog's future secured.

On ancient hips that barely support her, she still draws me in, holds me close, with the same crossed paws.

We follow a highway that arcs past the apartment complex where husband, wife and dog lived, where I played my role, until the dishonesty of it shoved me from the closet. There Yente was my constant, my eye in a turbulent storm when that life exploded, collapsed, crumbled at my coming out. She stayed when Karen didn't, couldn't. From one abode to the next, she performed her dogly duties; moist, frantic greetings, snugly naps, long, contemplative walks.

We drive again the road that took us, a single trip in a loaded-down Volkswagen, into uncharted territory. I packed a futon, a few boxes of books, some hurt, some sadness, and a companion for what lay ahead.

Ahead there is the white, up/down duplex, my first home as a single gay man, where she endured days cooped up on the promise of an evening walk. Yente pulled me, timid, yet inquisitive, persistent, in directions I could not venture alone. As we pause in front of the duplex, a wave of undifferentiated recollection washes over me, leaving me the sense that when I'm ready, I will remember more precisely.

Back toward the lakes we turn, through stop-signed intersections, to a dense and urban neighbourhood, where bohemian is a goal, counter-culture a standard. There she blossomed. Her coat grew long and thick, elegant in her adulthood. Yente the curious, ever eager to explore, to venture forth, leashed and lucky in her endeavours.

I reach over and weave my fingers into her fur. Her coat thicker still, it no longer braids the sun in ribbons down her back. The way it did. The way it shimmered on summer afternoons when we walked up and down the beach, bronzed in the heat of July. She lay shaded nearby, while we glistened on our towels, flipped at careful intervals, and remained watchful.

Yente the furry ice-breaker, who opened doors for me, for the golden boys, the summer sprites, my burgeoning circle of friends. Yente, who waited patiently for my return, from long nights dancing with the uniformed, t-shirt-clad whistle-blowers. Under swirling, scattershot lights, the music thumped in our torsos. The moment hot, alluring and unfettered.

Beside me lies the dignified, expectant dog she became. She insisted that I return each night, my thread of responsibility. She tolerated the occasional catch brought home, but after toast and coffee it was time for a walk. As we matured, she showed me that what we had was worthwhile, warm, secure. Her company was enough to come home to. Desperation didn't make me foolish. We pass another apartment, another duplex.

Atop the hill, we turn and coast down the street where our first house stands, home to successive pairs of men before me, the new homeowner in a struggling neighbourhood. Here she watched a slower parade. Always with enchantment and, now and then, passion. But rule one, no strings.

She saw my aversion to strings fade. Then vanish.

Then came strings. She relinquished some claim to the house, modified her domain for the first live-in boyfriend and his rangy setter, awkward and graceless, his dog, and us. She was lady-like by then. Rambunctiousness no longer part of her repertoire. The backyard evolved into a garden. We settled in.

She consoled me, stayed when Eric left, and left again. Licked the stream of tears when finally I asked him to go. She stayed. At this house she traded insistence for serenity and succumbed to the lure of a place in front of the fire. Where I healed and rallied and fell in love again. Yente adapted to the companions I thought we needed, the temporary cat, the new dog, the permanent-looking man.

This is our status quo, our steady state, where today began. More than half a decade mortared into place. Where some history and memories we share, where a loving if temperamental ear will listen, one more time, to what she was like then.

We're almost there, but early. I drive us around the lake once more. I want her to sit up, to recognize the place, the paths we pounded those many evenings, where we met the boys, where we brought the man. And later still, where three miles grew too long, and she tugged towards the parked cars long before ours came into sight.

I want her to remember the place. But if she did. If she sat up, looked out knowing, I would not finish this trip. I would not leave the lake for the clinic. But I do. And stop the car.

I cup my hand around the back of her head, rub my thumb between her tan, grey eyebrows. The spot for rubbing that pleases her most. I do not feel her sigh. And she does not open her eyes.

Maureen Brady

Intimacy Inventory

In intimacy, one gains the privilege of knowing another's quirks and practices from a close angle. Being mystified by them. Or sometimes demystified. Those things you never know until you occupy a household. Like that Julia sucks her thumb. She is sturdy and self-sufficient, has the carriage of a thoroughbred horse, makes love like a lady, dominates in the bathtub and the refrigerator, but now and then I found her curled fetal on her side, her thumb fully disappeared, her cheeks flexing in a sure, satisfying rhythm. I tried it a few times when she was out. It didn't do a thing for me.

Frankie has a prayer ritual. I never actually saw it. I heard it from the other room at the same time I smelled her incense burning. Three taps on a bell, three clacks of her stick upon the dresser, the mourning cry of an old woman, followed by three shakes of a rattle. Silence for a while, then the series of noises repeated in reverse. Frankie is small and delicate and operates on a standard of worship. She worshipped heroin when she was on it. Shortly after we met, she came to my house and put on whirling Greek music. Dropped to her knees and worshipped my cunt, her tongue imbued with lavish spirit. It was all I could do to receive it, letting the music spirit me a bit out of my body.

I was still reeling from Cristina who had turned me upside down and dropped me on my head. But what was I doing anyway, letting myself dangle on the dead end, the obtuse angle of her triangle, the other points being her and her not-quite-ex-ex? She had an orgasm I envied. She came with screams and a huge gush of fluid spilling out like the water breaking for a baby. Whenever we made love, I felt as if I were participating in a birth of her. My own orgasm became more subdued, despite or perhaps

46

because of my envy. She said I was like a teapot, droning with a low whistle the way it does if you turn the water off but leave it on the burner. I always wanted to try again for seconds and thirds, but she came out of a long history of attempted heterosexuality and didn't seem to believe in multiple orgasms.

Not to get stuck on sex, Laura kept bananas in the refrigerator. Our first date she cooked me dinner—stir-fry veggies. She forgot the rice entirely and the broccoli was raw. "It goes on cooking after you remove it from the stove," she promised with some authority. I thought this strange but didn't rebut—"in my house it doesn't." I shut my mouth and sat at my elegantly laid place at the table and did my best to consume her food, thinking all the while: *This is not going to be a place to get gastronomically nurtured.* Still, I moved in with her a year later. And out the next year, the thinnest I had been in a decade.

Her sweetest quirk was how she laid her clothes out for work the night before she had to teach. Hanging on the wall hook would be a shirt covered by a blazer. A pair of slacks would suspend from breast level down, socks neatly arranged at one end of the slacks hanger, bra and panties at the other. Her shoes would be on the floor, facing out like the clothing. When I woke up to her shower in the morning, I'd see this arrangement and think: *This can't be all there is to her but it's nearly all I've found. Where is she?* I must have been gone too. Otherwise why would I have needed her as a mirror?

I chronically compared her to Sarah (to her great dismay). Sarah was her opposite, which challenged my limited understanding of astrology, since their birthdays were a day apart. Sarah fed me heartily, all the while studying me to learn right portions. They both come from Jewish mothers, Sarah's harsh and brooding, Laura's trim and exceedingly polite, but each said "eat, eat, eat," under almost any conditions. Sarah said, "You take a bite, I'll take a bite. You put your fork down, I'll put my fork down. You push your plate away. I'll push my plate away. Don't mind me if you feel like you're being watched. I'm mimicking. You're my classroom."

"But how do you know I know what I'm doing?" I'd ask her.

"Because you say when you're full," she said, "and this is a condition I'm in search of."

What would they say about me? That I looked over Sarah's shoulder to learn how to study my image in the mirror, making faces at her faces.

Once tackled Julia on the beach, meaning to throw her down with my fury, but then, unable to own it, pretended I was playing instead. Couldn't spank Frankie when she wanted me to turn her on that way. Got hives when I tried to. Shook with terror when Laura threw scissors across the room I was occupying. Have no elasticity when I'm angry.

They'd say I drink coffee in bed in the mornings and sometimes mumble senselessly about what's going around in my head. Find comfort in laundry when I'm distressed. Am easily subdued by hugs and cuddles. Layer butter under my peanut butter and jelly. Have to be told when I'm tired. They'd probably say more, too, things I might not even recognize, given how hard it is to get a glimpse of one's own back.

Beth Brant

Coyote Learns a New Trick

Coyote thought of a good joke.

She laughed so hard, she almost wanted to keep it to herself. But what good is a joke if you can't trick creatures into believing one thing is true when Coyote knows truth is only what she makes it.

She laughed and snorted and got out her sewing machine and made herself a wonderful outfit. Brown tweed pants with a zipper in front and very pegged bottoms. A white shirt with pointed collar and French cuffs. A tie from a scrap of brown and black striped silk she had found in her night rummagings. She had brown cowboy boots that she spit on, polishing them with her tail. She found some pretty stones that she fashioned into cufflinks for her dress shirt.

She bound her breasts with an old diaper left over from her last litter, and placed this under a sleeveless undershirt that someone had thrown in the garbage dump. It had a few holes and smelled bad, but that went with the trick. She buttoned the white shirt over the holes and smell, and wound the tie around her neck, where she knotted it with flair.

She stuffed more diapers into her underpants so it looked like she had a bulge inside. A *big* bulge.

She was almost ready, but needed something to hide her brown hair. Then she remembered a fedora that had been abandoned by an old friend, and set it at an angle over one brown eye.

She looked in the mirror and almost died laughing. She looked like a very dapper male of style.

Out of her bag of tricks, she pulled a long silver chain and looped it from her belt to her pocket, where it swayed so fine.

Stepping outside her lair, she told her pups she'd be back after she had performed her latest bit of magic. They waved her away with, "Oh Mom, who's it gonna be this time?"

Subduing her laughter, she walked slowly, wanting each creature to see her movements and behold Coyote the magnificent strutting along.

Hawk spied her, stopped in mid-circle, then flew down to get a good look. "I've never seen anything like it!" Hawk screamed and carried on, her wing beating her leg as she slapped it with each whoop of laughter. Then she flew back into the sky in hot pursuit of a juicy rat she'd seen earlier.

Coyote was undaunted. She knew she looked good, and besides, Hawk was known to have no sense of humour.

Dancing along, Coyote saw Turtle, as usual, caught between the road and the marsh. Stepping more quickly, Coyote approached Turtle and asked, in a sarcastic manner, if Turtle needed directions. Turtle fixed her with an astonished eye and hurriedly moved toward the weeds, grumbling about creatures who were too weird to even bother with.

Coyote's plan was not going so well.

But Coyote sauntered up the road to Fox's place, that la-di-da female who was forever grooming her pelt and telling stories about how clever and sly she was. As she entered Fox's den, she brushed lint and hairs from her shirt, and crushed the hat more securely on her head. Fox opened the door. Her eyes blinked wide with surprise and admiration.

"Can I help you?" she said with a brush of her long eyelashes.

Coyote said in her new deep voice, "I seem to be lost. Can you tell a man like me where to find a place to refresh myself after my long walk?"

Fox said, "Come in. I was just this minute fixing a little supper and getting ready to have something cool to drink. Won't you join me? It wouldn't do for a stranger to pass through my place and not get a *good* welcome."

Coyote was impressed. This was going better than she planned. She stifled a laugh.

"Did you say something?" Fox was eager to know.

"I was just admiring your red hair. Mighty pretty."

"Oh, it's nothing. Inherited you know. But I really stand in admiration of your hat and silver chain. So distinguished."

"Well, I'm a travelling man myself. Pick up things here and there.

Travel mostly at night. You can find a lot of things at night. It sure smells good in here. You must be a fine cook."

Fox laughed, "I've been known to cook up a few things. Food is one of the sensual pleasures in life, don't you think?" She poured Coyote a glass of red wine. "But I can think of several things that are equally as pleasurable, can't you?" She winked her red eye. Coyote almost choked on her wine. She realized that she had to get this joke back into her own paws.

"Say, you're a pretty female. Got a man around the house?"

Fox laughed and laughed and laughed, her red fur shaking. "No, there are no men around here. Just me and sometimes a few girlfriends who stay over." Fox laughed and laughed and laughed, her long nose sniffing and snorting.

Coyote couldn't figure out why Fox laughed so much. She was probably nervous with such a fine-looking Coyote in her den. Why, I bet she's never seen the likes of me! But it's time to get on with the trick.

Now, Coyote's trick was to make a fool out of Fox. To get her all worked up, thinking Coyote was a male, then to reveal her true female Coyote self. It would make a good story. How Fox thought she was so sly and smart, but Coyote got the best of her. Why, Coyote could tell the story for years to come!

One thing led to another, as they often do. They ate dinner, drank a little more red wine. Fox batted her eyelashes so much, Coyote thought they'd fall off. But Coyote was having a good time too. Now was the time.

"Hey Fox, you seem like a friendly type. How about a roll in the hay?"

"I thought you'd never ask," said Fox, laughing and laughing.

Lying on Fox's pallet, having her body next to hers, Coyote thought maybe she'd wait a bit before playing the trick. Besides, it was fun to be rolling around with this red-haired female. She can really kiss. That tongue of hers sure knows a trick or two. And it feels good, her paw on my back, rubbing and petting. And wow, I never knew Fox could do such things, pulling me down on top of her like that. She makes such pretty noises, moaning like that. And her paw feels real good, unzipping my pants.

"Coyote! Why don't you take that ridiculous stuffing out of your pants. And take off that undershirt, it smells to high heaven. And let me untie that binder so we can get down to *serious* business!"

Coyote had not fooled Fox. But somehow, playing the trick didn't seem so important anymore.

So Coyote took off her clothes, laid on top of Fox. She panted and moved and panted some more and told herself that Fox was clever after all. In fact, Fox was downright smart with all the stuff she knew.

Mmmmm yeah, Fox is pretty clever with all the stuff she knows. This is the best trick I ever heard of. Why didn't I think of it?

Michael Bronski

1995: A Meditation and Litany

Meditation

Question 190. *What must we do to love God, our neighbour, and ourselves?*

To love God, our neighbour and ourselves, we must keep the commandments of God and of the Church, and perform the spiritual and corporal works of mercy.

Question 191. *Which are the chief corporal acts of mercy?*

The chief corporal works of mercy are seven: 1. To feed the hungry. 2. To give drink to the thirsty. 3. To shelter the homeless. 4. To visit the imprisoned. 5. To clothe the naked. 6. To visit the sick. 7. To bury the dead.   *—From the Baltimore Catechism No. 2*

And today? When corporeality is all too real and mercy too elusive?

To feed the hungry.
Walta is strapped to the hospital bed: head half-shaven, stitches red and flared from the wound that allows them to run the plastic tube from brain to stomach to drain cerebral fluid. He is panicked, struggling to get up, out; know who, where he is. Fear of pain replaced by fear of unknowing; terror of death by terror of confusion. I ask repeatedly, hungry for signs: "Do you know where you are?" "Do you know who I am?" A litany of anxiety and hope: "Do you know where you are?" "Do you know who I am?" "Do you know where you are?" "Do you know who I am?" His eyes, uncomprehending, stricken with the impossible: the questions meaningless; his body rigid, shaking with unknowing. Finally a calm: the body

retreats into limpness. Tears appear and he whispers in response to the unspoken question: "Fine."

To give drink to the thirsty.
A year before his death: Walta is helped by my sister, visiting from New York, to get to his aerosolized pentamidine appointment at the clinic. Step by step, legs refusing to move as they should, vision skewered, half-shadowed despite the sheer effort of will to walk and see, see and walk as before. Determined not to use a wheelchair until he has to; defeats occur daily, soon enough. They reach the last of the short flight. She encourages: "That was good, you're doing well." A truth whose very evidence brings pain. Walta: "Oh, Suzanne, I can't even remember what I used to be able to do. When I remember, it's worse." They look at each other, eyes dry; the wetness and comfort of tears superfluous.

To shelter the homeless.
I climb into bed: Walta starts in fright. Dreams of terror fill, flood the room; he yells in fear thinking I am going to hurt him. I reach out my hand. He yells, "Help, help, what are you doing?" Arms that consoled become dangerous, hands that soothed become weapons. "Help," he yells in bed, "help," as he struggles to get away from me. The comforts of bed and home, hands and arms, are lost in panic, discarded in rage.

To visit the imprisoned.
The specialist explains the bronchoscopy: tubes, swabs, lungs, fluid. It is all details and no reality. The words fear, mourning, terror, death, loss, pain are not articulated. "How do I breathe?" Walta asks after being told of the invasive procedure. "There is no trouble breathing," he is told, "you just relax, you'll be able to breathe." The breath of the lungs, even diseased lungs, is not the same as the breath of the quickening heartbeat, the tenseness of the hands, the legs, the neck. The brain races, the eyes dart, the pulse rages. The breath comes from the body like air long trapped in a vacuum; with sound and pain, empty and hollow.

To clothe the naked.
We are in front of our house: Walta, weak and walking with a cane. We meet a neighbour, a noted photographer. She gasps and cries out, "Oh

my God, what happened to you?" The unrehearsed, unadorned emotion jabs like the needle stick I gave myself earlier that day; like the monthly needle in the spine that draws out the fluid flooding and muddling Walta's brain. The illusion of privacy ripped away, the reality of illness exposed. "What happened to you?" It rests in the chilled October air, suspended without a crutch, a cane, a shred of respect or decency.

To visit the sick.
The back is blistered in neat rows: shingles. We both run fingers over the festering. Words go unspoken. Jim is in the hospital; Gerry is just dead. Walta's body is strong, the red, scabbed sores appeared overnight. Rash, hives, sun: to mention alternatives is to imply the reality of the possible: the body has begun to die. The new words go unformed: "symptomatic," "scared," "sick," "embarrassed," "failed," "nothing." Fingers touch skin, pus breaks from sores. The unmentionable seeps into the open; a visitor, uninvited, all too expected.

To bury the dead.
The baths: wordless and inevitably mysterious. Walta and I have just met, bodies in the steam, sex, heat mists about us. Skin and beard, flesh moving and constricting, impulse and instinct join together as if in a dream. The cold, dead night city outside is a grave; the past is gone, we are here now, living and breathing together as if one. The sheer pleasure of flesh and bone, spit and hand seem simple, unpronounced and endless. The body can transcend, the flesh transfigure. For a moment the past, the fear, the outside world, the pain is gone, dead.

David Lyndon Brown

Cracking It

It's just Rita and me in the West Winds. Vera's out cracking it. Vera looks hard case, Rita's saying, in that dress with that haircut. Vera's just got out of the prison farm for selling drugs and he's got this almost shaved head. Rita's painting his nails this sort of brass green that we pinched from the bathroom at Zoe's party and can't stop saying divine decadence and fanning himself with them over the coffee. We're on to about our third cup of Kona spiked with Southern Comfort from Rita's purse, this kind of giant knitting bag full of cosmetics and champagne glasses and some pills we found in Zoe's cabinet and a family-sized jar of Nivea, Rita swears by Nivea as a beauty treatment, when Violet and Virginia and Natasha come in. Violet and Virginia are Glen Innes boys and Violet is the most beautiful boy or girl I have ever seen. He just has to set foot out of the West Winds and about seventeen cars zoom to a halt. Virginia looks a bit like a bony Maori boy in a dress, which he is, but he's got this smart mouth and a lovely, great big mess of real hair which he lashes about. Natasha is about seventeen feet tall on his platties with shoulders out to here and a gravelly voice. Watch out for that one, they said, she can be evil. The first time I saw Natasha I couldn't take my eyes off him; he had on this sort of forties dress and a fox fur and an enormous hat with a veil.

"What are you looking at, bitch?" he screamed, in this big man's voice. "Haven't you ever seen a real queen before?" And then he chased me halfway down Queen Street with a stiletto.

Anyhow, Violet and Virginia and Natasha come in and they're a bit out of it. Natasha lurches over to the jukebox in these black satin hotpants and fishnets. "Girl," he says to us in a loud, out-of-it voice, "gimme some twenties." Rita reaches gingerly into his purse because of his nails and

Natasha spots the Southern Comfort. His long arm snakes across the table and snatches the bottle and he takes a big, long slug and, wiping his mouth with the back of his hand, passes the bottle to Violet and Virginia and they tip the rest of it into their cups. "Thanks, doll," says Natasha and staggers back to the jukebox and plays "Young Hearts Running Free" six times.

Eventually Rita and me go out on to Queen Street. Vera is still shivering on the other side of the street. Every time a car cruises past he sort of sashays over to the curb, but that borstal crewcut is a definite disadvantage and also the prison farm has built Vera a pair of serious shoulders and his biceps and thighs bulge out of this old lace dress he has chopped off up to his bum. Rita goes down and I go up. It's easier for me to walk up in these red plastic wedgies I have cut the backs out of to get my feet into. I station myself in the doorway of the fur coat shop run by this old queen whose party I went to once. The same old coats have been in the window for years and they look a bit tragic. Moth-eaten looking like that old queen's toupee.

I'm watching the cars cruising and keeping an eye out for the cops. Sometimes a car will slow down for a look and then take off and then prowl around the block again and I think they're waiting for more glamorous merchandise to hit the street, like Violet or Virginia or Natasha. And I'm a bit hesitant because this is only the second time me and Rita have cracked it. The last time was when we spent a whole Sunday afternoon getting drunk and drugged and tarted up. I swathed Rita in ten yards of this fabulous black crepe into this kind of draped sari effect held together with staples. I was wearing my red tights and some leather hotpants that lace up the crotch and this little t-shirt with Trash written in felt tip across the front of it. And we kept on putting more and more makeup on and glueing sequin beauty spots everywhere and the drunker we got, the more gorgeous we got. And Rita said let's go out and before we even got to Ponsonby Road we ended up in a vacant lot in the long grass with this Indian hockey team. Naturally, Rita's staples didn't hold out and he was completely unwrapped by the time the team had finished with us.

Anyhow, this car pulls up and the driver says, "Want a lift?" And I say okay and get in and I see Rita and Vera shrieking and waving from opposite sides as we do a U-turn and take off down Queen Street.

"Where to?" he says.

"Where ever your heart desires," I say, from some old movie. He's got this long hair and I think it's a wig because it's hacked off at the ends and he's got these crazy, burnt-out looking eyes and his stiff little dick's sticking out of his pants and he grabs my hand and shoves it in his lap. That's when I think I might be doing something a bit dangerous.

We end up at Mission Bay and the fountain's off but the coloured lights are still on and we're in the back seat sort of tangled up with each other, snarled up in this knot of half-on half-off clothing, not really getting anywhere, and he keeps saying, "Don't touch my hair." Eventually we give up and on the way back up Queen Street, he pushes my face down onto his dick and I give him this semi blow sort of job feeling really wicked in all that traffic and it's not until I'm on the footpath outside the West Winds that I realize I forgot to ask for any money.

Rita and Vera are touching themselves up in an old powder compact from the pile of makeup tipped out on the table. Vera has drawn these eyebrows halfway up his forehead and Rita has gone for a juicy pair of Joan Crawford lips about seventeen times the size of his real mouth.

"Circus back in town?" I say.

"You filthy slut," says Vera, smirking under those alarmed looking eyebrows and Rita says, "How much?"

"Never you mind," I say mysteriously, fanning myself with my last ten bucks.

Doug Browning

Helping Hand

July, 1967

"Can ya give me a hand . . . ?"

I'm digging a change of clothes out of my pack.

"I left my spares at home."

My bathing suit smells mouldy.

"I'll take the ones ya got."

I glance at Devon's arms straddling a chair seat, hooks clinking metal with their reflections in the polished wood floor. Imagining them flailing in the air like the arms of the robot on *Lost in Space*.

Warning . . . Warning . . .

Devon stands in a splash of sunlight, rust-coloured hair a froth of curls, eyebrows the copper of new pennies. When I straighten up he's still almost a head taller. He's just fourteen, a few months older then I am, but already stretched so far that an afternoon with him gives me a crick in the neck.

Rolling my stuff in a ball, I toss it onto the bed beside Devon's ratty cut-offs.

It's weird, without a shirt there's nothing unsettling or odd about his wings. As if sleeves only call attention to the flippers peeking out of them. In just a swimsuit, I see him put together from a different set of plans; not an accident, meant to be what he is. Like an experimental jet.

Devon blinks at me, trying to figure out the smudgy crib notes on my forehead. This is the first time I've had to help him change or do anything else personal. I guess this moment has been on our minds since we started hanging around together, but we've never talked about it. Not even one of those sideways conversations that seem to be about something else. Hell, we've never even joked about it.

Warning . . . Warning . . .

"Still hurt?"

Devon nods at the purple bloom on my right knee.

"A little."

I sidle up to him, exaggerating the limp I got from kneeing a boulder as I swam in to shore.

"You should have it looked at."

Devon turns so we're lapped like a pair of cards with me standing behind and to the left of him.

"You looked at it. I looked at it."

The thumbs I slip into the waistband of his trunks are rubber sausages sewn to my knuckles.

"Can I ask ya something?"

"What?"

"Sorta personal."

"Depends."

His bathing suit's glued to him; I'm pulling it inside out as I peel it off.

"What?"

His cheeks are shallow round-edged bowls pressed together. The pale unsunburned skin reminds me of a film of frozen milk on a strawberry shake.

"Naw, forget it."

"Fraidy-cat."

"Am not."

The bathing suit catches in the notch at the top of his legs. A quick tug and it pulls loose and falls to the floor with a soft smack.

"So ask then."

He steps out of one leg hole then hooks his trunks up onto the bed with the other foot, his left cheek bunching to a perfect half circle underlined by a pen stroke fold through a cluster of small freckles.

"You have dreams, right?"

"So."

"Do . . . d'ya ever have dreams where ya have arms?"

I expect a knife-edge glare, but Devon just looks down at his toes.

"Yeah. . . . Sometimes I can even touch things 'n' feel them, only . . . "

"Only what?"

I bend sideways to grab his shorts.

"Only I can tell something's not right about it."

I can't blinker a quick glance. It pokes almost straight out, a slim pink mushroom with a collar of loose brownish skin behind the head.

"I get that. Sometimes I can tell it's a dream while it's happening."

"Yeah, but this is different."

"How?"

"It's the way things feel that's not right."

I bend down and hold his cut-offs open a little below knee level.

"My sister figured it out before I did."

He steps back neatly into one leg, the other, then I slip them up.

"Janice?"

"Yeah."

The shorts are snug but not so tight I have to struggle with them.

"She says it's because I've only ever felt things with my feet, so that's all that's in my head."

"Guess. . . . "

I picture his skull stuffed full of feet as I reach around to do up his zipper.

"So in these dreams I've got these nice long fingers 'n' everything, but they feel like toes."

His dick's safely under cloth, the zipper doesn't snag, and I get the snap to catch the first time.

"You mean they feel like *toes* or they *feel* like toes."

"Both."

"Weird."

"Yeah. . . . " Devon squeaks around on his heels.

"Thanks."

"No problem."

He plunks himself down on a pillow; I shake out my shorts.

Worming fingers into my trunks, I'm not surprised at how warm I am. My cheeks—both pairs—are probably turning pink.

"Wanna hit the kitchen?"

Devon's eyes flicker to my face then drop to the floor, stalling at half mast on the way down.

"Yeah, I'm starving."

"Me too."

I zip myself up and squeeze the brass button through its hole.

"I haven't got any yet."

He's talking to his knees.

"What?"

"Hair."

He squints up at me.

"Whats that on your head, mould?"

"Down there. . . . "

I can't tell if he's blushing or if it's just sunburn. I almost say I didn't notice but swallow it in time.

"It's no big deal."

"If ya got it. . . . How long?"

"Couple a months."

"I'm still waiting."

"Guess that means I'm gonna look like Sean Connery by the time I'm sixteen."

"Hair everywhere except on yer head."

"Huh?"

"He's bald, dincha know that?"

"No."

"Yeah, he wears a wig for those movies."

"Really?"

"Yeah."

"You're makin' it up."

"No I'm not. I read it."

"Where?"

"Can't remember."

"Yeah, right!"

"It's true."

"No way."

"It *is!*"

Tonia Bryan

Don't Disturb This Groove

A Story of Lust, Music, Fantasy and Obsession

I walked into the joint
The club was jumpin'
people pumpin'
They was groovin' to the sound
Shakin' booties to the ground
I looked up to the booth
to see who was tearin' off the roof
much to my surprise she looked me
dead in the eye. . . .
　　—*R. Charles a.k.a. RuPaul,*
　　　"Miss Lady D.J."

her pussy hovers above me dripping wet just out of reach of my tongue wet wiry black pubies filled with her scent tantalize me she remains just out of my reach her full breasts swing back and forth teasing me luring me i wanna run my fingers through her short braids feeling the rough wovenness of her hair but i can't as usual my arms are pinned down by the strength of her velvety smooth cinnamon scented thighs she looks down at me huge liquid brown eyes hold me in a lust induced trance i'm right where she wants me under the influence of the musk she exudes intoxicated by the closeness of our two bodies. . . .

The scenario is always the same with just a few variations in setting, costume or time of day. These waking dreams, or fantasies if you will, leave me hot, wet and anxious, full of yearning. My desire for her is strong, overshadowing most of my daily activities. The fantasies are so explicit, so frequent and so palpable that I'm convinced she can detect their presence in my mind, in the features of my face, on my breath, in the way that I gesture and move when I am with her. Beyond extremely demure kisses on the cheek, tentative hugs and the few words we have exchanged, I don't think she even knows I'm alive. I don't know her at all, really. She's the D.J. at one of the city's hottest women's bars and I'm one of her regulars.

On what seems to be a typical Friday night, I linger in a hot bath. Languorously I run my hands over my body, massaging scented oils into my skin. From a tape player on the floor Chaka Khan's voice wafts over me like sweet steam from the water that surrounds me. Afterwards I slip into a lacy black bra, matching panties, garters and stockings. Then I pull on a ripped jean jacket, the briefest of black jean shorts and my favourite leather ankle boots.

Twenty minutes later a yellow taxi cab drops me off in front of the bar. I pay the driver and make my way inside, checking first to make sure she's playing. The place is packed as usual. Music is pumping out of speakers placed strategically around the dance floor. Irrationally I refuse to look up at the D.J.'s booth for fear that she might be looking back at me and sense my need for her body pressed on mine.

Instead I move to the centre of the dance floor and begin to respond to the complexity of bass and drums as they play across my breasts, my thighs, my ass and my neck. I imagine that the music is really her fingers and tongue probing, touching, feeling every inch of me inside of my skin. My heart speeds up and a sheen of sweat covers me, making my skin shine like polished ebony. Every part of me is alert, compelled to shake and groove to the beat of the tunes she's spinning.

I close my eyes for a second and suddenly feel arms encircle me, running sensuously up and down the sides of my thighs, hips and arms. I turn around and am met by the sight of Miss Lady D.J. smiling at me. For the first time I experience the taste of her full soft lips on my own.

Then it begins. We move together. I am in front, feeling the grind of her pelvis and stomach as she rubs herself against me. Her hands grasp my breasts firmly. Under the textured cotton of my lace bra, I feel my attention-starved nipples spring to life. I reach back and hold onto her large, firm thighs. She's big and tall like me and our bodies fit like two halves of the same whole as we sway in perfect time with each other and the music. Make my body rock, make my body *rock!*

I gasp as I feel one hand deftly unbutton my jean shorts and slip inside. I continue to move, riding the beat of the drums. I am commanded by a new rhythm. My pussy is wet, drenched with the sweat of exertion and the juices that my lust for her evokes.

Her mouth is on my ear now. Sharp teeth take hold of the fleshy lobe, refusing to let go. I moan loudly then look nervously around. But in such a dimly lit, large space with the hypnotic pounding sound of house music overriding all else, no one seems to care about us or see us as we dance and fuck.

I turn around and face her. Our eyes meet and she presses her open mouth onto mine, snaking a long moist tongue past my lips deep, deep inside. I suck hard and caress its tip with my own tongue and lips. Hungrily I swallow, savouring the taste of our saliva mingled in my mouth.

Inside my panties her hand slides faster, harder over my erect clit. She switches her attentions from my mouth to my neck, biting into the soft flesh at the hollow of my throat where the pulse of my raging blood beats hardest. Her free arm holds me tight, supports me as I lose control. I feel fingers push past my outer labia, delving and dipping into me.

Her eyes are almost closed, her lower lip is pinned as she bites it with force. She looks at me searching for something in my eyes, asking something without words. I feel myself stretch fluidly, encompassing all of her fingers, her whole hand. I scream her name over and over again. My sweat-soaked arms wrap tight around her. My whole body thrusts and pumps madly. The heat is unbearable, the intensity too much. The music intensifies, the beat becomes more insistent. Then. . . .

Everything comes to an abrupt halt. Standing alone and spent I open my eyes and look up to see the goddess still in her booth. Happy to see me obviously enjoying myself with such reckless abandon, she smiles down at me sweetly . . . platonically. Tongue-tied, I stand self-conscious but ready, waiting for the next track to send me soaring, throbbing, pumping over the edge.

Grant Campbell

Inscriptions

1983

Georges Giroux

A pair of blue eyes twinkling out of a suntanned face creased with laughter. Close-cropped graying hair around a bald dome, dense hair on a bronzed chest, faded jean shorts, with the top button undone. The sun bounces off a gold ring on the fingers of a hand that clutches a bottle of Orange Crush. In the background, figures chase each other in the surf, wrestling and splashing in the foamy water.

A man stands before the AIDS Memorial in the winter wind, holding a handful of red roses. Every day, for the last month, he has come with flowers, to stand silently and look at the names. Stepping forward, he wedges a rose under the plaque beside the name of Georges Giroux. Then he moves on, past the pillars, through the years, until another name arrests him.

1987

Gary Rashid

High cheekbones, smooth, dark skin. Brown eyes, warm and inviting, a thin and lanky body with slender fingers that caressed the cheek with feather lightness, that undid shirt buttons with deft facility.

The man shivers as he wedges a rose under the plaque beside Gary Rashid. The wind has risen, and the light is failing. He is finding it difficult to concentrate, to conjure up images. The tiny quarrels of daily life keep intruding on his mind. Timetables and deadlines. Finances. Worry. Guilt.

1994

Antonio Cavellero

The man takes a deep breath, then reaches out and removes the shrivelled, frozen rose from beside the name, replacing it with the fresh rose. He runs his fingers across the indentations of the name on the plaque. Antonio Cavellero. Antonio Cavellero. His favourite name.

"Excuse me."

The man jumps and steps aside nervously, giving place to a tall figure muffled in a coat with a deep hood, who places a white carnation beside another name, higher up on the plaque.

"Sorry to disturb you." The voice is deep, and slightly muffled by the hood. A gloved hand points to the rose beside Antonio Cavellero. "Was he a close friend?"

The man nods timidly.

"I'm sorry."

The man opens his mouth and shuts it again. He wants to speak. The images are there in his mind. A wide grin beneath a thick, bushy moustache, with sensuous curving lips and a fine row of white teeth. Kisses which are deep and soft, full of masculine tenderness and sensuality, broad shoulders in a thick flannel shirt, with dark chest hairs curling over the top button. The images are there, culled from a decade of furtive privacy. They lie hidden in books and magazines, dog-eared and crumpled under his bed and at the bottom of his drawer. They unfold hypnotically in amber lines across his computer monitor, late at night, when his sister and her husband are in bed, and the cat is curled up at his feet.

Not just sexual images, either. The man has thought about Antonio for weeks now, ever since that first lonely stroll through the memorial a month ago. His mind has been hard at work: at the way he and Antonio met at a youth hostel in Switzerland, and travelled through Europe together. How they walked arm in arm through Venice, and swam in the surf on a beach in Portugal. How Antonio called him from New York out of the blue, how he got a job offer in Canada, how he ended up in Toronto. The man's fantasies surround the name on the silver plaque, enmeshing the unknown man in a web of intimate practicalities, scenarios designed to withstand even the most ruthless incredulity.

As the man stands next to the hooded figure, the urge to speak these images aloud grows on him. Even lies, even fantasies, might acquire some solid reality once uttered. Surely, saying something might alleviate his own spreading guilt and shame, at being alive and healthy, at not knowing anyone who has died, at having lost no friends. Surely, he deserves his place in the drama unfolding in the city around him. But before he can commit himself to speech, the hooded figure moves off into the darkness.

The man looks up at the carnation that remains behind, wedged beside a name. Seymour. Roger Seymour. He has never noticed that name before, never made a picture about it in his mind. Perhaps Roger and the hooded figure were lovers. Perhaps Roger had a rich, deep laugh, especially in the warm darkness of the bedroom, late at night. Perhaps they fought constantly during the first few months that they lived together, about things like taking out the garbage and putting the toilet paper roll on backwards. In the evenings, they must have loved sitting down together to an old movie with a big bowl of popcorn. Roger used to read the newspaper methodically from beginning to end, one section after another. After his eyesight had gone, the hooded man probably read bits of the paper aloud, in strict sequence. At the funeral, the hooded man stood beside Roger's parents, holding the mother's hand with careful gentleness, mindful of her rheumatism.

Perhaps all these things happened. But as the man stares at the plaque in front of him, the images fade. The wind moans as it passes among the pillars, now grown shadowy and indistinct in the gathering dusk. The silver facelessness of the memorial defeats him as he stands there in the failing light: the names have once again become mere words, signifying a host of lives he has never known, a community to which he has never belonged.

Julie Varner Catt

Gasoline, Blood, and Johnny Walker Red

My sister's car hurtled into the front yard and exploded in a deafening bomb of rust and dust that rose around us in a brown cloud and for a moment I didn't know what had happened. The girls standing beside me screamed like pigs coming to slaughter. My mother thundered down the front steps, and I remember thinking that I had never seen her run before. The cellulite and loose skin on her upper arms shook so hard that they threatened to detach from her bones and go flying through the air like a liberated pair of flabby wings. The Camaro was wadded up around the oak tree, spilling shreds of glass onto the only piece of green grass left in the front yard. I could smell gasoline, smoke and whiskey, and the funny metallic smell of blood.

I can flick those images through my mind matter-of-factly, as if I were thumbing through someone else's photograph album. The smells, though . . . the mere hint of Johnny Walker Red, the scent of my fingers after filling up my car, the rich thick iron smell of blood (even my own unavoidable monthly blood)—those smells send me reeling, nauseous and trembling. In my twelve-year-old mind, staring at that car, it was impossible that it contained people. It was crumpled so tightly there wasn't room for three people taking up space with flesh, muscle and fat, bone and limbs. I watched the black pool of blood grow under the oak tree and began to understand that my sister and nieces were, for all practical purposes, now one with that shit-box of a car, that steel and glass were stronger than muscle and bone, and that a 200-year-old oak tree was the strongest of all, and wasn't about to get out of the way for anyone.

Mama was grouchy all the time after Karen and the babies died, always hollering at me to sit down, clean up, or shut up, or lying in a motionless heap on the couch, Elvis Presley singing to her through the darkness and dust in the front room. I learned that fixing my own sandwich was infinitely preferable to eating peanut butter out of the jar with my finger, and the less noise I made as I roamed through the house, the less she would scream. I began to anticipate her moods, and to ignore the fear that rose in my throat when I heard her heavy footsteps shake the wooden floorboards in the hall. She developed a habit of surprising me in the bathroom, and I would blush as I answered, no, I haven't been picking my face again, no, I haven't been touching myself down there, yes, I used soap when I was in the shower.

My mother, in the year that followed the accident, dug a hole in me and pushed her sadness and anger inside. I had to wriggle and bend and move my insides around to accommodate her. By the time I turned fourteen I had adopted an arrogance usually borne of emptiness and age and I was often mistaken for an adult.

I sigh deeply and glance at my lover stretched out on crumpled sheets next to me. She is counting the ridges on the ceiling and I know from experience that means she is listening. I watch her carefully, watch her chest rise and fall with the sweetness of her breath, and chant silently, please, please baby, tell me that now you understand why I'm such a shit, why I chase off my friends, why I'm so needy of your fingers on my skin and so rejecting of your heart. I'm already full, see. I'm full of my mother's pain, and underneath that, squashed like my sister in that car, is my own loss, my own anger. So I can fuck you, cook for you, hold you when you cry, but I can't listen to your murmured words of love, can't treasure your quiet secrets. I can hear them—they are overwhelmed by the odour of gasoline, blood, and Johnny Walker Red.

Later in the day we sit in a café. The steam from our lattés rises between us, and we stare out the foggy window at girls walking by. I wonder idly if silence is better than fighting, and peek around the inside of my brain for something safe to talk about so that we don't look like the forty-something heterosexual couples who sit silently in restaurants, having given up on finding any common ground on which to eat their dinner.

Her voice pulls me out of my panic at becoming a forty-two-year-old straight woman, and I meet her eyes with relief.

"What'd you say, darlin'?" Her dark eyes are open wide as she looks at me, and through the hiss of the cappuccino maker I can hear her breathing.

"I'm moving out. My needs are not being met I still love you but I'm not in love with you we are moving in different directions I think this is best for both of us." She speaks in a monotone, and continues with some other words I don't remember, offering up every lesbian break-up cliché I had ever said or heard, with no punctuation, no pauses between phrases. I watch her face as she talks, and for the first time notice the shadowed circles beneath her eyes, the vertical wrinkles between her brows. How much of my pain, I think, does she hold inside her belly, her heart?

I brush the back of my hand over my eyes and swallow the knot in my throat. At some level I must admire her bravery, must appreciate the irony of all those lines coming back around and slapping me in the face, but all I can do is put my spoon down beside my half-empty glass, push my chair back, and walk through the heavy glass doors into the Midwest winter wind.

Lawrence W. Cloake

The Prowling Thought

Tony and Mike slowly drift into post-coital slumber. They snuggle closer together like two question marks.

Tony's sleep is undisturbed in its physical repletion, whereas Mike's is unsure. He groans in the throes of an unsettling dream. Mentally tossing and turning, something shifts and stirs in his subconscious. An inquisitive thought shakes itself from the cloying closeness of Mike's mind. Twisting from side to side, it gets a bearing and moves from the vestiges of the dream. The thought pops from Mike's mind and makes its way to the partly open window, scrambling out onto the ledge in its eagerness to be out in the night.

The thought searches for the after-images of Tony's day. It sniffs the ether of the city's hustle and quickly latches onto an afternoon's vapour. It scuttles across the city's heights and stops above the Oscar Wilde Pub. Peering down to street level, the thought watches a repeat of the episode it has traced.

Tony taps the sweet-sounding six-hundred single into first gear and gently glides around the corner, off D'Olier Street onto College.

A steady throttle and half-clutch pops the front wheel up and spinning. Tony feels the brooding, frowning gaze of Trinity College bearing down on him. He concentrates on his arrogant wheelie and suddenly notices a cycling courier just ahead of him. The front wheel is perfectly lined up with the straining, lycra-clad buttocks. In his mind's eye he imagines the spinning wheel lightly nudging the shifting cleft, and with a light touch to the throttle he can thrust forward again and again.

Tony snaps both the clutch and throttle simultaneously, bringing the front wheel back to earth, up into second. He swings the bike around and passes the panting cyclist, straining to keep himself in check. But as he passes, his bare hand snakes out to cup and clasp the bulging buttock.

Tony snaps back to reality at the sound of the haranguing radio resting on his shoulder, a pickup across town. As he throttles away, he gives the cyclist a wistful look, draws back from the petrol tank, whose vibrations have induced a raging hard-on, and thinks, Another day, definitely another day.

The thought smiles gleefully and suddenly catches a seminal scent, a familiar whiff of Tony. It moves across the rooftops before coming to rest above the corner of Stephens Green and Grafton Street. Tony is picking up a stranded courier.

He quickly moves out into the stream of traffic and, ignoring the cacaphony of blaring horns, nestles into the saddle. His passenger grips Tony's thighs with his knees, hands resting lightly on his thighs, disdaining the sissy-bar for the sake of image.

Tony touches the brake, cranks and flips his machine to one side as he weaves through the traffic. It is only then that he realizes how much fun he could have while carrying a passenger. It brings back fond memories of wild rides in good company. He cranks the bike a little harder, while a smile slips slyly across his face. For once he hopes for a red traffic light, the perfect opportunity for what he has in mind. His luck is in as he spies an amber light ahead. Another blip on the throttle and he suddenly hits the brakes. He is rewarded with a curse and a satisfactory crotch-bump against his backside as his passenger slides forward on the saddle. He feels the guy settling himself against his back, hoping to prepare himself against Tony's erratic antics.

The traffic light changes and Tony shoots away from the green. His passenger grips tighter with his knees, while sliding his crotch even closer to Tony, so that it rubs against his arse.

Tony locks his back brake hard outside the bike shop, eliciting a loud yelp of pain from his passenger as crotch and eager buttocks meet in a final crunch.

"I'm never taking a lift with you again," the courier swears, "you're bloody mad and me poor bollocks is in agony."

"Fine, you can walk next time." Tony pulls away with a satisfied grin and slightly damp jocks.

I hope Mike is home for lunch, he thinks.

The thought grins mischievously and grips itself in a satisfied hug before scampering back across the rooftops to its snug little nest in Mike's mind. . . .

Mike snaps awake and looks at Tony's sleeping form. He thinks back to their fevered passion and realizes that Tony brings more than just love to their relationship. There is a healthy abundance of fantasy, too. If only he could get him to voice his predilections, they could find a deeper understanding of each other.

Mike returns to the world of dreams, safe in the knowledge that whatever happens in the future, they would face it together. Of that he was sure.

Ailsa Craig

Asters & Cigarettes

Rachel took a deep breath and entered the front building. While the attendant looked up her father's name, Rachel made sure she still had the pictures of herself with her lover. They'd had them taken in an instant photo booth at the bus terminal. Kate and Rachel were captured laughing, hugging, and of course, kissing. Rachel couldn't decide which one to give her father. The kiss was her favourite, but she wasn't sure how appropriate it was. She missed Kate, but was glad she'd understood this was something Rachel had to do alone.

The attendant finally handed her some quickly scrawled directions, and Rachel left. She steeled herself as she approached her father's lot.

KENNETH A. MOORE, 1946 - 1980. It was a simple headstone, laid flat into the grass. They hadn't been able to afford anything fancier.

The tears welled in Rachel's eyes and a knot grew in her throat. "Hi, Daddy." The act of speaking destroyed her efforts to hold back tears. They ran down her face, dripping off her chin as she sat by the grave. "I'm sorry, I shouldn't cry like this, I need a smoke, just a second, okay?" She pulled her cigarettes out, lit one, and looked to the grave, "Do you want one?" she asked, and pulled another from the package. She wiped her face and smiled through her tears. "They're not your brand, but I guess after twelve years any kind'll do, eh?"

She pulled the grass away from the edge of the headstone to wedge the cigarette in. "I miss you," she said, and took a long drag from her cigarette. "I just wish I could see you one more time. I want to talk to you, give you a hug. I never got to say goodbye." She looked away, then turned back to her father's grave. "I'm going for a walk, but I'll be back, okay?" She brushed off her jeans and headed toward a patch of forest just outside the cemetery. She wanted to compose herself, and find something to give her father.

Making her way through the brambles, Rachel felt at home. It was like the bush at her family's old farm. Wild asters grew in scattered clumps. "Perfect," Rachel thought, and uprooted them.

It had happened on a Wednesday. The day Rachel took photography class. She was walking home after school, and stopped in the orchard to call out to her father as usual. He hadn't answered when she yelled. Rachel had gone into the house, and watched TV until her mother came in. She was crying.

"Daddy's been in an accident," she said. "He's underneath the tractor." It had rolled over when he was pulling out tree stumps. Rachel went with her mother to the kitchen, and ate chocolate ice cream while a detective with a mean, sad face talked to her mother.

Rachel returned to her father's grave with the asters, and an armful of rocks. "I got these from the bush over there," she said as she put everything down and began digging through the grass with her keys. When the hole was deep enough, she put in the flowers and patted earth around them. They drooped, so she arranged the rocks to help support them until they took root. Pleased with the stone garden effect, Rachel sat back. "It didn't cost anything, but your grave looks as good as the rest. Better even."

She had one thing left to do. Using her keys again, Rachel made an opening along the base of the headstone, and slid the photos in beside the granite.

"None of them say enough alone," she said. "You keep all of them, okay? The other woman is Kate." Rachel paused. "Kate's my lover. I wish I could tell you face to face." She pushed the grass into place. "Mom likes her and I'm happy. I'm not sure what else to say." Rachel stood up, "I have to go. I'll visit again. I love you."

Rachel started walking toward the bus stop. She was half way there when she remembered, and ran back to the grave. "I forgot something," she said, and knelt down. "Kate wanted me to give you this." She pulled a letter out of her pocket, and pushed it in with the pictures.

Kate hadn't let Rachel read it. She'd said it was a letter to introduce herself, and ask for his blessings.

Rachel pulled out a cigarette, lit it, and propped it upright between two of the rocks she'd arranged. "One for the road," she said, and smiled. She kissed the headstone, got up, and left. She had to hurry or she'd miss the bus back to Toronto.

Daniel Curzon

Chickens

Jimmy can hear the chickens, the mild squawks and grumblings. Some-body is in the henhouse. Is it his mother? It must be his mother. No! No! He feels his heart beating in his mouth; it tastes like iron, like medicine, like that stuff that's supposed to be good for him that he hates so much, but his mother gives it to him anyway. He saw her earlier, in overalls, her mouth pulled at the edges, her eyes like BBs because of the sun, her hair uncombed, her hands muddy from the weeds she'd pulled up in the garden.

"We've got to make this place look nice so we can sell it," she'd said, tugging at the weeds—some flowers too. "We're *not* staying."

"But—"

"We're not. That's all there is to it, Jimmy!"

He can smell the damp earth under the house as he sits there. It's time for cartoons on TV, but he doesn't move. Now he can hear the chickens starting to scatter. His mother must be after one, for dinner. The other chickens must know what's coming; they've seen the ax before. But they seem to forget. Yes, they must have short memories, because they get right back onto their nests once his mother has grabbed one and taken it out and cut its head off.

He watched one time, but he doesn't want to watch anymore. The chicken ran around the backyard, blood flying out of its neck, and then sagged down in the dirt and quivered a few times. Later they ate it. He'd had one bite, but that was all. Pam said she understood.

He can hear the chickens squawking loudly now. His mother must be chasing them. But maybe she can't catch them. Jimmy sits in his special space under the house, where it's cool and dark, the place even the dogs don't know about, listening. His hands are hot and his head seems full of sand. The chickens are running, scattering, but they can't go far because his mother has made sure to shut the gate to the pen.

Where's Pam? Has *she* left yet? Jimmy wonders. She was packing her things angrily, then stopped and started cursing at his mother. She was wearing Levi's and a checkered shirt, and her eyes were red and funny-looking, her lower lip all gnawed. "I thought we were all set, Jennifer!" she had cried. "You said we were all *set!* Oh, god, Jennifer!"

Jimmy wants to cover his ears, but he knows covering them won't be enough. The sounds will seep through. Sometimes in his bedroom he tries to blot out the bullies on the bus and the way his little toe is crooked, but you can't stay that way for long. You have to empty the garbage or feed the ducks or go to school or—

One of the chickens lets out a scream. Yes, a scream. His mother must be holding it down with one hand, the ax raised over it. There is the sound of a chop. Then there's no more screaming. Just a flutter of wings.

Jimmy sniffs the damp air. He touches his hair, stroking it just the way he likes, the way nobody else, not his mother, not Pam, knows how to do it. His eyes burn from the dark and the engine that is his heart.

Is it over? The chicken must be dead by now. *Please* be over! But what's that other sound? It's another chicken, begging. It really does sound like it's begging. His mother is killing a second chicken? But why? *One* chicken is enough. Oh, yes, please, one is enough!

He hears Pam's voice falling out of the top-floor bedroom. "How could you, Jennifer? How could you! For Caroline? For *Caroline?* . . . I'm taking Jimmy with me."

"No, you're not," his mother says quietly from the chicken pen. There must be blood dripping from the ax, and bits of flesh.

"He likes me better than you, even if you are his m—"

"You'd better leave," his mother says. "Now."

"We had everything!" Pam cries. "Everything!"

"So you thought."

Jimmy listens. His mother . . . what? Turns away? Stops looking up at the top-floor window where Pam is standing? He hears more movement in the chicken pen. His mother has grabbed another chicken. It sounds like the rooster this time. There is a struggle, a flurry. The rooster is stronger than the hens. The rooster has a sharp beak and big toes.

"Goddamn you!" his mother swears. The rooster must have scratched her.

Jimmy waits, no breath at all, wanting the rooster to get away. Sometimes it flies through the small hole in the wire at the top of the pen they've never gotten around to fixing. Sometimes it—

He hears the fluttering of feathers, the rooster's protests; the nine hens are clucking and running around. The bloodied ax must be in the air. Down it comes. There is a cry from the rooster that tears into Jimmy's heart like the blade itself.

"Oh, Mommy, Mommy, *Mommy!*" Jimmy whispers, digging his hands into his kneecaps, his body bent, rocking back and forth. He tries to make himself into a little ball of boy as the ax comes down again and then again. And then again.

He hears his mother sobbing as she kills the rooster. And Pam is crying and he is crying and the chickens are crying—and flying to the top of the fence and scurrying to find a spot where they won't be murdered. I must save them! Jimmy thinks. I *must!*

But he *knows* what will happen to the chickens.

tatiana de la tierra

Never

She never told me she loved me. she ate my lipstick like it was for her. she used a certain tone in her voice like it was for me. she picked me up and took me with her, brought me back and stayed with me.

the telephone was our heartline. she phoned me at any moment for no reason if only to show me that she would phone me at any moment for no reason. she phoned me in the winter when she wanted a warm bed and a hot woman. she phoned me in the summer when the heat was just right. she phoned me at work to be close to me. she phoned me from another telephone in the same house to seduce me. she took all my calls, returned all my messages, and left on my answering machine words mouthed for me.

she brought me flowers. she opened doors for me. she tucked me and my wavy skirts into her red car, and she closed the same doors that she opened. she perused my perfumed places and encouraged a strut. she pressed my face into her during slow songs, and i visited there with no intention of leaving. she always seemed to know what i wanted. she didn't always give it, but she knew.

the bed was a stage for our drama and the cause of our intimacy. she set the rules and i set the lighting. she whispered vulgarities and i became vulgar. she started and i couldn't stop. she made me do things she'd seen in movies and i responded as if in those movies. i made her do things i'd read in magazines and we responded in a glossy centrefold. i oozed with drama and she licked me up. our names were mantras. our mouths were marbles rolling all over the place. i slept nestled in a nook she reserved for me. i became a piece of gum beside her.

she never told me she loved me.   she never told me she loved me.
she never told me she loved me.   she never told me she loved me.
she never told me she loved me.   she never told me she loved me.
she never told me she loved me.   she never told me she loved me.
she never told me she loved me.   she never told me she loved me.
she never told me she loved me.   she never told me she loved me.
she never told me she loved me.   she never told me she loved me.
she never told me she loved me.   she never told me she loved me.
she never told me she loved me.   she never told me she loved me.

Dennis Denisoff

Fafa Manifesto

Madam Beeman-Popova pours in just enough milk bath to make the cool water the exact same colour as her powdered skin. Once soaking, she unpins her auburn mop and throws it at the collection of wigs dominating one corner of the counter like a pack of alley cats. She can hear the agitated chortling of the grouse and partridges in the garden below, and imagines as well Chappy's slap-happy yips of silence. Soaping her hands, she gently plucks the hefty rings from her swollen fingers, laying the jewels—amber, xanthic, gamboge and ecru—along the edge of the tub where they glitter through the suds like patient goldfish. As she massages her fingers, she watches the swelling go down in the coolness of the fading day.

Something brown flies by the window achirp. Madam wonders how it would feel for nobody to notice what type of bird you are, let alone what specific bird you are. " 'Birds of a feather,' " thinks Madam, "is a cruel assumption to live by." It is clear to her that she is an individual but she is also not so naïve as to assume that her individuality is uninfluenced by context. No, as a self she can only exist if there is a community of others, some collective by which to define her personal characteristics and even the qualitative measures of her worth. Society is, for her, a 3-D diorama, a black forest silhouette enveloping the sharp amber beauty of her character, an oily black night beyond a fake-fur stole as golden as the golden tufts of the bird whose limb-thrilled body has just scattered past her window yet once more.

"It's something like establishing your social ph balance," she thinks, as she gazes at her ghostly legs hovering like well-fed sharks just below the surface of the water. Floundering for the soap which has floated to the other end of the tub, she wonders whether physical traits are as valid as

mental traits in defining the individual. The bubbles of a fart skitter like
new-born hermit crabs up along her inner thighs. "A person defines herself
by what matters," concludes Madam, "not by what matter is." Here again,
she finds herself trying to make a splashing leap from the pool of the
analytic into that of the emotional, and here again she knows that at least
one mediator between the two is the dolphin hoop of aesthetics.

She pries the stopper out of the bottom of the tub with her toes. "Still,"
she goes on, now rubbing a mint balm along the chafed folds of her belly,
"we can't throw the analytic out with the bath water. It's too much a part
of the netting that's trapped me into thinking this way; to cast it aside
would be to cast aside the source of my thoughts and so, I guess, my self
as well." She considers the poor dolphins drowning in those tuna nets,
and then considers momentarily the poor tuna. "No," she continues
(noticing the sound of the puff of talc—"fa fa"—against her fleshy
shoulders), "what we need is some sort of aesthetic model that recognizes
the limits of its own assumptions without getting pretentious about this
recognition. *Fafaism* won't appear in a void, but that doesn't mean it can't
demand that we recognize art's freedom from the artist." "Fa fa fa," agrees
the puff.

"The most important community for aesthetics," she concludes, dab-
bing a finger tip into the pot of Egyptian ash nestled in one corner of the
tub, "is transhistorical, a community through time." Again something
golden-brown dives past the open window and Madam consciously
informs herself that it is that same bird that had passed by before—the
one and the same individual, struggling creatively against the assumptive
powers of the mind. As the last of the water swirls away with the dingy
grey scales of her own dead flesh, Madam lifts what is left of herself and
heaves it out of the tub. She finishes powdering her body, arranges a pale
yellow towel on her head, and opens the bathroom door to the succulent
smell of trout frying with basil and just a bit of dill rubbed vigorously
along the inner spine of the fillets. Chappy is sitting on her bed licking
himself intently, but even more disturbing for Madam is the golden flying
squirrel that hovers cautiously at the open window like a corrective
endnote to her thoughts. The squirrel licks a bit of foam from its lips.

The realization that she has not only got the type of animal wrong, but
even the species, makes Madam lightheaded, and she sits down next to
her dog to regain her bearings. These sorts of coincidences make her feel

sure that she is destined for fame, if not as a philosopher of aesthetics, at least as the neighbourhood clairvoyant. So often she forgets that the mind works on more than one level simultaneously. It is clear to her now that while she has been formulating her notions of a transhistorical, self-corrective aesthetic, some other part of her brain was off not only defining all birds as birds but defining even squirrels as birds simply because they fly. "When one says 'bird,' " she notes to herself, "one thinks 'flying animal dot dot dot'," but even *that's* invalid. Even if every bird one ever sees is a flying bird, flying doesn't name a bird. Being netted doesn't name a tuna. Nothing names anything really. How to incorporate this self-corrective into an aesthetic so that it'll deny its own superiority, mock its own validity? The new aesthetic will have to be a reactive aesthetic, an almost flagrantly reactive aesthetic that will let no one forget her lack of originality while still somehow keeping individual diversity in the foreground." The little squirrel, seeming to understand that Madam is feeling crushed and humbled by its presence, crawls onto the bed and hovers about two feet from her ample limbs, its black, nutty eyes swirling cautiously in their loose sockets. "Fa fa fa fa fa," its chompy little teeth mutter through the foam.

Phillippe H. Doneys

Anarchy for the Solitudes

I had never met an English Canadian or an American before the age of seventeen. To go across provincial boundaries into Ontario or the United States always seemed like an adventurous excursion into the unknown. And as other *Québecois* teenagers at the time, the sense of contrast became an easy claim to common identity. We would troll our way up to the Parliament, branding our new found verve with the *fleur-de-lis*, a joyous excuse to skip our Friday afternoon class.

That's why my encounter with Dan was both thrilling and intimidating. Dan was driving from New Brunswick to Regina, Saskatchewan, and on his way, stopped to visit the old city of Québec. He was a student at the University of Saskatchewan and spoke as much French as I did English. I met him on rue St-Jean, the main street within the walled city. In fact, he accosted me asking for directions. He was struggling with a map that fluttered in the heavy crosswinds which often envelop the city. I didn't need the map to figure out that he wasn't from here. He had the lightest blue eyes and he parted his hair far on the side in a meticulous way only English people bother to.

"*S'il vous plaît,* where, *où venir tu?*" he stumbled.

"Trois Rivières," I answered, guessing at his intended meaning and attempting an English accent. The oddity of the question caught me off guard.

He looked at me in puzzlement, then smiled warmly. Shivers of excitement shot up my spine. I don't know if it was from the manifest intimacy of the moment or the tepidity of his taffy candied breath.

"No, I mean . . . me . . . *moi,* where . . . *où est-je?*" he stammered, pointing to the map.

I reddened in embarrassment which appeared to please him, causing me to blush even more. Before I said anything he stuttered another Creole sentence from which I understood that he wanted to go someplace. I assumed he was asking what to visit in this city. Unsure of my version of his comments, I followed him to a café across the street. We ordered some *crêpes Bretonnes* and then laid the map across the small table.

As our fingers crisscrossed over the narrow streets of the city, I kept looking at his square jaw and the delicate glaze of his lips. The perfect symmetry of his face was striking. He seemed to notice my fixation, but I was not sure until I felt his knee press against my leg. I desperately wanted to know more about him, but felt powerless without a shared language. I'd never regretted so much all the broken pencil tips I forced into the door lock of my English class. I used to tell my teacher I had no interest in trading languages. I always thought that learning English was the first irreversible step toward assimilation, and French being relegated to the inscriptions on the tombstones of our past. But at this moment, a sense of ridicule pervaded, boundaries disintegrated and the fears sang a tune I was too far from to hear.

A few minutes later, we were on the Plains of Abraham, at the edge of Cap Diamant, overlooking the St. Lawrence. Dan, a history student, managed to make me understand he knew all about the battle which turned North America into an English haven. We found a place niched among the wind-blown shrubs at the edge of the escarpment. It was a striking view. The wind blows under the old Québec bridge that stretches above the St. Lawrence and battles with the ships returning to the sea. The serene Ile d'Orléans, a long witness with Gross Ile of the passage through the delta of Irish immigrants longing for a new world, now was facing a contemptuous urbane Château. In front of us, the tip of Lévis stood defiant, as if it could have baffled an astute Wolfe.

The gusts were getting chilly at this time of day. Dan sat up closer to me and put his arm around my neck. We were silent. Well, we couldn't really say much. I felt his warm finger against my forearm which gave me more goosebumps. Not a word was mentioned. Then, I felt his warm lips against the side of my mouth. We took our clothes off in unison, piece by piece. A heat emanated from his soft skin, permeating through me. Our feet stuck out over the edge of the cliff. And right at that moment, with bodies tangling, skin rubbing and hips thumping, I thought of the Battle of the Plains of Abraham. At the very spot where French and British armies fought, I felt we were righting the wrongs of the past. We didn't say much after our bodies collapsed on each other in exhaustion, sealing the zillions of struggling seeds, but we paced our breaths and hummed a sound that it seemed we had shared before.

Later on, I saved a lot on pencils. We met a few other times, Dan and I. We still really didn't say much to each other, but we knew it was okay.

Nisa Donnelly

Epitaph Undone

If we had met before, when you were still beautiful and I was not yet mad, before your purple splotches and night sweats and my whisper-perfect demons, would we still have been friends? Or only casual acquaintances walking the same wide road, nodding to each other as we passed: you happy, me angry? That's how it was supposed to be, wasn't it?

"You dykes," you would say, rolling your eyes, "you're always pissed off about something." But by then you were angry, too. Not just about some thing, but about every thing, about that skin that drew too close over the bone, exposing your veins like fine blue satin cords fraying, about hair that fell away, betraying terrible secrets. You had such beautiful hair, pale and fine as summer sand.

The first time I saw the truth, we were at a crosswalk. I turned to hear your words. Some thought, lost, no longer important. The inevitable gust of March wind caught your hair, lifting it a few millimetres, exposing the lesion no larger than the nail on my little toe. And I looked into your eyes, pretending not to have seen. (Such a little lie. So many big ones were waiting for us.) You pulled a cap from your back pocket, one of those ugly knit things that sailors and poor boys wear. Dark blue. The colour of lesions. You would tell me later that you knew I'd seen, that you were thankful I didn't flinch, didn't look too long. I have a strong stomach; only my mind is fragile.

You did your best to hide. The world saw and turned away. You saw and could not. Turn away. From what was happening. You sometimes asked me about hell, the private part I've mapped. "Is it beautiful or horrible?" you would ask, as if we were Hansel and Gretel and I was the one who knew where to scatter the crumbs. "No, not beautiful. Not

88

horrible, either. It just is." I lied, I had to; I have not yet been where you were going.

Long letters connected us, wandering back and forth between the coasts, flying over the common land we had known but had left unclaimed, except as children. Black midwestern soil, rich from rivers passing wide, wider than any of us have ever seen, ten thousand years old, surely more. Now the land sheds its richness, the way it sheds us, its outcast children. That summer, after you died, I watched that same river, wild and angry, broken free like an untamable mythological beast, claim everything for miles on either side. It raged from being held too tightly by men who did not understand its true nature. Would you have smiled? Have said it was the devil's due, for all those good Christian foot soldiers who had cast their children out for being different. Hard people, with hard lives and harder tears. Those were our people. You refused to claim them; they refuse to claim what I am.

"I hated that place, those people," your last letter said. "We tried so hard to rise above all that, to forget what they are, what they've done. Did we succeed? I think so. I hope so."

And I was reminded of a poem about another young male artist who had run away once, too, from the banks of the Spoon River all the way to Paris, only to have those who stopped to look upon his work see it in the eyes of Lincoln, the hint of the despised homeland. It fascinated you that I know Edgar Lee Masters' poetry more intimately than that of any of the real masters. And why not? Look where I'm from, I told you. I've washed my feet in the Spoon River, hunted cattails by its marshy shore, tossed pebbles and my childhood dreams into its green shallows. You and me and Edgar Lee Masters. The river followed him, the way it followed us, leaving traces of mud between our toes, beneath our nails that we could never quite carve out or chew out or brush away. So deep, so old, so unforgiving, it became part of our skin. Of us. Of only me. Now.

The way they told me you had died.
I went to the mailbox. It was summer. Or early fall. That odd, in-between season that only those who have lived a long time in a climate as self-sure as San Francisco can discern easily. I inserted the long silver key into the squat brass lock. I need to remember, you see, the small glass window,

the etchings of leaves on the little door, the number so even, so plain. How the hinges make no sound.

The envelope was square and white, so white it glowed in the California sun. You hated the California sun, the enforced casualness, the forced gaiety. There is no room for this kind of sun to shine in Manhattan. Manhattan is real, you said, as if California is not. The paper ruffled a little as I ran my finger beneath the seal. Good paper. Only the best. But you could no longer afford the best, had long since sold off your treasures one by one until you were left with the computer you could not sell and your books that you would not.

The card, stiff and sharp-edged, cut my skin when I pulled it free; it fit that tightly in the envelope. You would have been pleased at that little bit of perfection. Automatically, I slipped my finger into my mouth. Bit down. Sucked. It wouldn't have been right to bleed on your letter. You were afraid of blood by then. Strangers' blood. Strangers who were more afraid of yours. And I was just afraid.

The card was simple, a few printed words, elegant type. I don't remember what they said, only that they said too much. Someone whose name I will never know had gone through your Rolodex, typed each stranger's name, affixed each stamp, carried the small square pile to a post box on some Manhattan street corner and walked away without looking back. We cannot risk looking back.

And I sat, in the California Technicolour landscape, a place more beautiful than I ever dared to imagine as a child, and felt the knowingness of death slam against me, knock the breath from me, the feeling out of me. And I waited, while the world exhaled.

My doctors tell me that if I am ever to be well—odd, they do not often use that word "again"—I must learn at such moments to feel. I do not want to feel. Not that. I have lost too many young men who laughed because I know Edgar Lee Masters and not Keats, who pulled on ugly knit caps the colour of lesions, who saw the truth and called it God, who trusted me to scatter the crumbs, never understanding that I don't know the way back, either. I take comfort in those moments of numbness. Sometimes, it is all I have.

Marianne Dresser

A Queer Night in Tokyo

I'll see you in Roppongi at 11:00," Ulrike said and hung up the phone. I hurriedly wrote down the specific instructions—which corner of the train station, which exit: north or south, the nearest architectural landmark, and what commercial logo to look for on which neon billboard—all necessary reference points for successfully arranging a rendezvous in the vast urban chaos that is Tokyo. After two and a half months in Japan, I was at last going to sample some of its hidden *rezubian* subculture.

Well, perhaps "subculture" is too grand a term, implying a more obvious presence, a recognizable community. There *are* lesbians in Japan, but unlike the flaming gay boys who throng the streets of Shinjuku, Tokyo's oddly antiseptic "sleazy" quarter, they are well hidden to the point of invisibility. Hardly surprising, given the patriarchal cast of Japanese society with its feudal cultural and gender codes still firmly in place underneath its outward appearance of cutting-edge modernism.

So I was delighted that my intrepid friend, a Dutch lesbian photographer on a year-long student exchange program, had managed not only to find a real Japanese *rezubian* bar, but had also acquired the personal contact there that would allow us access. Without a preliminary introduction, a *gaijin*, or foreigner, would never get past the elaborate politeness that masks the iron-clad impenetrability of Japanese society.

After another typically confusing day at my job serving as the token *gaijin* in a small, hip architectural firm, I negotiated the clockwork commute from midtown Tokyo to the tiny, pristine apartment in a northern suburb that I shared with my girlfriend. Janet had been here for over a year, engaging in a well-paid but ultimately futile attempt to teach English to Japanese teenagers at a private school. Following my fervent but terribly misguided heart, I had relocated to Tokyo to be with her. Although neither of us was willing to admit it, we were enacting an expat queer version of a "Can this marriage be saved?" scenario.

Worried that she might lose her job, Janet was emphatically *not* out; we played our public role as two Western women "friends" living abroad. But no foreigner in Japan has any real privacy, and every shopkeeper within a mile knew exactly where the two strange American women lived. Although I was too obedient to ever say so, I thought our precautions were ridiculous. We were incontrovertibly *gaijin*, and secretly I was beginning to enjoy my newfound capacity to elicit squeals of fright from small children or whiplash-inducing headspins from blue-suited *sarari-men*. We were already seen as particularly interesting specimens of alien creatures, freaks of nature, so I didn't see how any other "queerness" on our part could possibly matter. In the end, Janet's paranoia and her mastery of passive-aggressive control tactics won the day, and so we carried on with the transparent pretense, fooling no one but ourselves.

But after-hours and away from the incessant curiosity of her students, Janet was as eager as I to check out the *rezubian* bar. So, after our evening rice and miso, we began the important work of planning our respective costumes for the night's outing. After some deliberation, we both ended up in the little-boy drag that was the current unisex fashion rage for trendy Tokyoites. Maintaining the conventions of heterosexual femininity to which she would eventually revert, Janet tipped the scales of her gender-bent image with eye shadow and lipstick. Bravely we ventured out in our baggy black Comme des Garçons suits, downscaled men's shoes, and short slicked-back hair. The subway ride was no more nor less alienating and hilarious than usual. We received the requisite ambiguous stares and were correctly identified by two kids shouting *"Gaijin-san!"* (roughly translatable as "Mister Foreigner"). Thankfully, no one attempted to practice their English on us.

Our Dutch friend met us at the designated place, her solid northern European body stretching the contours of a dark-blue Japanese schoolboy uniform. With Ulrike in our midst, looking like a Eurodyke version of an obsessed Mishima character, any notions of blending in with the crowd were discarded. We three unlikely pilgrims set off on the convoluted back-alley route to a nondescript bar tucked between a *yakitori-ya* and a *karaoke* place emitting a thin stream of heartfelt (if off-key) wailing.

Ulrike knocked on the door, and conducted the elaborate display of baroque pleasantries, roundabout introductions, and name-dropping that allowed us entry. We were ushered into a narrow room veiled in cigarette smoke. A long, dark wood bar paralleled the left side of the room. Leaning against it were five or six grey- and blue-suited businessmen carrying on with one another in the characteristically gruff, casual speech reserved for Japanese males. A few women clad in frilly pastel dresses were seated demurely at the tables in the no-man's land between the bar and the entryway. The exaggerated birdlike tones of *onnakotoba*, "women's speech," floated toward us from their conspiratorial conversations.

I was seriously confused, certain that there had been a mistake. This was just another typical Tokyo dive filled with *sararimen* and bar "hostesses" whose job was to make sure their male customers' glasses were never empty and provide inane, ego-stroking conversation at their whim. Our arrival had caused a noticeable ripple among the inhabitants; we were being thoroughly scrutinized with dozens of brief, oblique glances from every set of eyes in the room. But no one approached us, and we made our way to a deserted corner table. Ulrike went off to the bar for drinks, for once amazingly preempting the instantaneous service that is standard in Japanese public places. Janet and I gazed at the scene and each other and laughed incredulously.

When Ulrike returned with our drinks, I accosted her immediately: "I thought you said this was a lesbian bar. What are all these guys doing here?"

"It took a long time to find this place. Let's just stay for a while. *Kampai!*" she toasted, and drank.

We drank, looked at each other and at the other patrons, while they appraised us with intense sidelong glances. I sensed an imminent approach; the knot of excited voices at the bar signaled that someone was screwing up the courage to cross the great cultural divide to actually *talk* with the strange trio holed up in the corner. After about fifteen minutes of mutual inspection, two self-appointed emissaries swaggered over nervously. They wore the uniform of the thousands of corporate drudges and petty bureaucrats who elbowed me in the subway every morning: blue striped suits, stiff white shirts, perfect replicas of British club-striped ties. It was only when they began to speak to us in their heavily-accented English that I realized these garden-variety businessmen were in fact women. Despite the flawlessly executed, typically male manner in speech, stance, and gesture, their voices heard up close, pitched higher by nervousness and coerced bravado, revealed an elaborate gender ruse in progress.

Our new friends exchanged a few rapid-fire salvos with their compatriots at the bar and we were soon faced by a phalanx of extremely curious, extremely "male-identified" Japanese *rezubians*. Summoned by their dates, a few of the flashy femmes joined us, plying us with bottomless glasses of *sake* and *shochu* while their masculinist counterparts proceeded to grill us about Western lesbian habits. Our bizarre conversation, conducted in a mixture of broken English and equally maimed Japanese, ran the gamut from what kind of underwear we wore to whether our wives were pretty.

Our wives? In her serviceable Japanese augmented by a few crude gestures, Janet explained that she and I were "together." This was met with utter incredulity. None of our eager interrogators would be caught dead going out with their "wives." The other women in the bar were either their "mistresses" or a queer variant of the bar hostesses I had imagined them to be. Like typical Japanese married ladies, the wives waited patiently at home, kept dinner warm, and would, on their return at 2 or 3 a.m., get up immediately to prepare a meal or a hot bath for their "husbands." Didn't we have wives too? How could we two "boys" be together?

By now an alcoholic haze was descending, and the verbal exchange was reduced to monosyllabic grunts and headshaking incomprehension at our mutual strangeness. Janet, Ulrike, and I managed to extricate ourselves from our hosts' inexhaustible hospitality and stumbled out. We walked back to the train station sharing our bemusement, smug in our notions of cultural superiority. In a twisted parallel to the youth culture obsessions currently sweeping Tokyo—James Dean, rockabilly rebel posturing, and completely unattainable *Route 66* road trip fantasies—Japanese lesbians seemed to be living in a slightly twisted version of '50s butch/femme universe. We Western dykes were *far* beyond that. We weren't internalizing our homophobia, participating in our own oppression, or reenacting the patriarchal heterosexist model. We didn't have "wives," we had partners, colleagues, sisters in the struggle, fellow radical lesbian feminist separatists. Right on!

And yet, all the way back to our tiny closet in Takinogawa, I kept thinking about the *rezubian* bar and the women we had met there. Those passing Japanese androgynes, their "wives" and "mistresses," were negotiating a particularly virulent form of *samurai* patriarchy. In a society that gave its women up for lost if they weren't married by age twenty-three, a few lesbians had found a way to be together. The "businessmen" in the bar spent every day of their lives conforming to the corporate monolith in order to support themselves and the women who depended on them, and who loved them. Some part of me recoiled from the oppressive gender-coded social mimicry in which they lived. But even though it made me uneasy to admit it, I found these women oddly beautiful and brave. And the more I thought about the fallacious equality of my relationship with Janet, the more I envied the clarity and brutal simplicity of their tyrannical coupling. While we Americans hashed about in mushy realms of "compromise" and "process," those *rezubians* knew who wore the pants and who steamed the rice.

I never made it back to the *rezubian* bar, and after a few months I left Tokyo to pick up the shreds of my abandoned life in San Francisco. It took another year and a couple of long-overdue affairs, but eventually I left Janet as well.

J.B. Droullard

Contact

It was a warm night and the air conditioning wasn't very effective in removing the tropical moisture from the heavy air in the busy bar. Corey was glad he'd opted for the tank top after all. Usually he was inhibited about exposing too much flesh in public, but he'd been working out lately and felt confident about the way his arms had picked up some attractive bulk. There were distinct new bulges in his biceps when he gripped his beer bottle, and the tan he had worked on in his time off lounging at the pool, brought them out to the best advantage.

It was only eleven, but there was already a crowd. The unusually warm evening had brought the boys out early. Corey was chatting with a new acquaintance, Alvaro, the Cuban bartender, when he noticed a new blond guy at the other end of the bar. He seemed to be preoccupied, staring out at the dance floor. Even though his brows were knit in concentration, his seriousness couldn't disguise a friendly profile. Corey couldn't help but notice that the blond stranger already had exactly the physique that he was aiming to attain. He admired the way his bleached-out jeans moulded his ample crotch.

Corey hadn't been laid in a few months. Even though he'd promised himself to get out of the rat race and get out more often in this new job, things hadn't quite worked out exactly as planned. He thought the move to Florida would be more exciting. He missed his friends up north more than he had anticipated.

All too quickly after the move, the old job stresses had reappeared and despite the cowboy clone get-ups there in central Florida, most of the guys he noticed in the bars down here were just as queeny as back up north.

He didn't feel like he was expecting the impossible. Just a nice masculine guy who liked to do it with other men. More to the point, who liked getting it on with one particular man—i.e., himself. Ever since he'd moved, Corey had a lot of difficulty sleeping in the new apartment. At first, he thought it was just because the new place was empty since his furniture hadn't arrived. Anyone'd have trouble sleeping on that make-shift air mattress, Corey told himself. But the insomnia continued even after things were set up just like he wanted.

That dream last night shows you just how horny I really am, he mused silently at the bar while Alvaro was busy with other customers. The previous night he had a wild dream—a combination of science fiction and pornography. A dense black orb had touched down on the roof of his apartment complex, bringing a handsome, well-built, bald alien with rainbow-reflecting skin. The unearthly guest was polite enough to ring the doorbell before walking right on in through his front door.

At first Corey was petrified, almost peeing in his light cotton boxers. But the apparently friendly male alien sat on the couch next to him and quickly established a soothing mind-link. Corey quickly understood that the handsome extraterrestrial meant no harm.

Corey offered him a beer and they watched some television together. The alien had a little trouble drinking from the can, as foam leaked from the corners of his small mouth. A short while later, Corey noticed that the iris rainbows in the alien's skin had suddenly became much more intense—it was especially apparent at the top of his smooth bald head.

The alien moved closer to him on the couch and his smooth skin rubbed up against Corey's arm. He expected the skin to feel rough and scaly, but it was wonderfully soft and silky smooth. He felt a moist tingle on his arm where the alien had touched him. It grew warm and pulsating and spread quickly. The tingling sensation moved directly down to his crotch and he instantly had a raging hard-on, but not one like he had ever experienced before. He looked over at the alien and noticed that, since he was completely without clothing of any form, he was also sporting a large erection.

Suddenly, the alien was levitating horizontally about a foot off the couch and inviting Corey to climb aboard. Corey's raging hard-on made it fairly ridiculous for him to pretend he wasn't interested. He appreciated the alien's down-to-earth honesty after the snotty pretensions of the bar scene.

The twin pulsating patterns on the alien's perfectly-shaped hard ass signalled just how turned on he was. Corey instinctively pulled the floating alien closer and poised his rockhard erection close to the pulsating psychedelic love-portal. Just as Corey began to think "lubrication," his cock slipped effortlessly inside. Throbbing peristaltic motions pulled Corey's in further and with barely any effort on his own part, Corey began to feel hot love juice mounting pressure in his loins.

Suddenly there was a new sensation. The alien's prehensile prick had worked its way around in back and was circling Corey's own asshole, begging entry. It secreted a silky warm gel and pushed its way inside, like it had a mind of its own. Once there it instantly assumed the exact form of Corey's insides.

The pulsating tugging motions on the alien's ass drawing him in further and the throbbing motion's of the alien cock pushing him in further were soon too much and Corey came explosively in an hallucino-genic supernova deep inside the alien's greedy ass.

He felt the alien's sphincter grab him for all he was worth and noticed a white blinding flash as the alien also came. But Corey felt no liquid ooze from the alien's stiff cock, just warm gently-coloured pulsating light.

They fell together in a rumpled pile on the couch. They embraced each other, earth-style. But after a few minutes the alien transmitted a message how imperative it was that he leave. Atmospheric conditions were rapidly changing outside and the light-absorbing properties of his black orb parked on the roof would be impaired if he didn't leave immediately. He risked detection by Air Force radar if he waited any longer.

But I am leaving you with something special to remember me by, was the next thought that popped into Corey's mind. The alien had already absorbed enough human culture from Corey to know to kiss him on the mouth before he drifted back out through the door. Corey fell into a deep refreshing sleep on the couch. It was the best sleep he'd had in over a month but in the morning the dream was simply too wild for him to dare to believe true. Besides, the following day there no evidence of "the gift" the alien had alluded to in the dream.

Corey broke off from his daydream at the bar. It was just in time to notice that the blond guy at the other end of the bar had shifted his attention away from his direction. So, he *was* looking at me when I wasn't looking, he thought. Maybe he's just as interested in me as I am in him.

Nonchalantly, yet deliberately, Corey made his way down to the other end of the bar, but the blond was making animated conversation with an obvious acquaintance, doing his best to ignore him. Corey was close enough to detect the sweet lingering fragrance of Bain de Soleil that perfumed the boy's skin.

Corey felt down. When he'd caught the guy looking his way he figured he was interested. A wave of dejection swept over him. He turned to leave, but accidentally brushed up against the blond's nicely-shaped arm.

The boy's skin felt warm, smooth and inviting. "Not meant for me," Corey sighed to himself. Yet, he noticed even in the dim light how the guy's skin briefly flushed iridescent where he had touched it.

The blond turned around, rubbing the spot on his arm, and flashed a big warm smile directly at Corey. "Hello there, stranger," he intoned invitingly, still rubbing his arm. It was as if some irresistible organic agent of sexual arousal had been transmitted from the surface of his skin like a dermal pheromone, a cutaneous aphrodisiac.

So the alien left me something after all, Corey thought to himself, noticing the blond boy's basket grow stiff with desire. He winked suggestively, and they left together without further ceremony, each knowing exactly what was on the other's mind.

Annette DuBois

Michigan

The road stretches to the place where earth and sky meet, blurred by twilight and the snow that clogs the wipers. We have been driving through the storm for hours, heading home. It is late November, central Michigan. We have been together for three days in a cabin on the lake, with four other women from ACT UP. In the close quarters tempers have flared, and sexual tension has been pervasive as smoke from the wood-stove. The snow began the evening we left Ann Arbor, and hasn't stopped.

The diffuse light and silence are familiar to me, and the open spaces feel like home. Kari doesn't share my comfort: her knuckles are white on the steering wheel as she coaxes the Toyota forward, and we're hearing the same tape for the fourth time. No one speaks. Snow falls silently over rolling fields, sparse trees, and a few farmhouses where solitary lights glow.

"Look!" Michelle says suddenly. "Farm stand half a mile ahead—hot cider. Wouldn't that be good?"

"Just the chance to stop for a while. Kari must be tired. Right, Kari?"

Kari nods, reluctant to admit her fatigue.

"Let's see if they're still open. I could use a stretch. Okay? Judith?"

"I guess. Let's."

We see the farmhouse now, a simple box-shape sheltered by ever-greens. The attached barn is of course red to the house's white, and there are lights within. We pull into the driveway: it's been plowed, though the drifting snow is reclaiming it.

Five women pile out of the car and into the cold, each in her own direction, each careful not to look at the others. Squares of warm yellow light draw us through the snow. I know what we will find before my mitten touches the door: it is so like places from my childhood. Weathered wood, fruit and preserves stacked carefully among hand-lettered signs, quilts and dried flowers and wooden animals on the walls. The scent of apples and wood smoke welcomes us, and the woman who sits beside the fresh-baked breads feels like home. I feel myself relaxing for the first time in too many days.

She is maybe fifty, with a bandanna over grey-streaked hair and a bulky sweater like the one she is knitting. She greets us almost too effusively, with the awkwardness of one too often alone. As the others examine fruit and cookies, she asks me about the weather, and where we've come from. Are we students? She has a daughter at the university, though not the big one in Ann Arbor. And what do I study? Her daughter majors in English, and she'll be home soon for the holidays, with all her books. Her isolation is painfully clear, but the warmth is real. As I sip mulled cider I find myself telling her about my home town where they grow apples too, where my friend Sarah from high school runs another farm stand with her husband and son.

Someone clears her throat.

"Liz?" It's Judith. "Are you ready? Let's go!"

I don't understand her impatience, but I take leave of our hostess. As I follow the others to the car I see her watching from the window, and I know she is thinking of her daughter.

The door slams heavily, and the car and the silence close in again. We drive on through the blizzard, this time without even music for distraction.

Finally Judith speaks. "God, people like her piss me off!"

"Why?"

"All that bullshit about her daughter. Can you believe that?"

"Judith, she misses the girl."

"Can it, Liz. She's so sure we're nice young ladies like her precious daughter."

I can't see her, but her voice is distorted with rage. "What do you think she would have said if she'd known her barn was full of lezzie perverts? Do you think she'd give you the time of day if she knew you eat pussy?"

"Judith. . . . "

"Don't 'Judith' me! Do you think she cares, anyway? It's so fake it makes me sick. I want to take the damn apples back and . . . "

"And what? Judith, how the hell do you know what she might say? Maybe she's a bigot. Maybe not. There are a few decent human beings in the world, you know. For all we know, she could be a dyke!"

"Really likely. You know, Liz, someone's really going to hurt you one of these days."

"Andrea, the woman didn't say a word about queers or politics or anything of the kind. Apples and the weather and the English department at CMU and you have her figured for Jesse Helms in drag." I've turned in my seat. "And since when is there anything so terrible about quote eating pussy unquote? Happy fucking 'Womyn's Weekend.' Happy fucking gay pride!" Judith looks away, and for a very long moment no one responds.

"Could you believe those quilts? And those animals? Back in New York . . ."

"Back in New York, where everyone's so evolved that bad art doesn't exist and no one gets queerbashed? This is all rather incredible. Speaking of Jesse, he might as well retire. He isn't needed any more. Listen to us. ACT UP's finest—and we're sure we've got enough queer cooties to drive away the whole Midwest!"

Images come as no one speaks. Judith, telling us WCBN has given her an hour every week for a queer show. Andrea, addressing the board of regents about the university's bathroom-sex crackdown, conviction powerful in her voice. Kari, standing up to her ROTC commander at the cost of her scholarship. Michelle's infamous safer-sex demonstration with a melon. And one shy middle-aged woman who talked to me about apples and English departments in spite of my nose ring and the "Dyke to Watch Out For" pin I realize I'm still wearing.

It is dark now, snowflakes crowding into the headlight beams. Kari turns on the stereo, and Tracy begins to sing about a revolution.

Gale "Sky" Edeawo

When Willie Mae Goes

That Willie Mae is one good time gal. She still hanging with the best of them. I'll soon reach age sixty-seven, so that makes Willie around 'bout sixty-eight. Don't tell her that though, 'cause she still puts fifty candles on her cake. Life to her is one *big party*. She says she was only born to hang loose, drink booze, chase women and kick back to the blues. She danced before she could walk, she was cursing as soon as she learned to talk. Made love to her best friend Jenny at age three. By ten she knew exactly what she was going to be, and that was a woman's woman. Don't nobody bring no tears or sad faces when Willie Mae goes. Bring liquor, beer and reefer. Laugh and dance 'til the wee hours of the morning, 'cause that's what she always did.

She seldom held down a job, said they were too confining, always managed to have some type of income though. Went through all types of women, sponsors she called them. Fine women, homely women, women on welfare and money-making women. Women with degrees, and others who could not read. Never was able to keep any of them long, she was the life of the party, but hell in a relationship. Too self-centred, but damn good between the sheets. Sure, I had her. Our dyke circle, as we were called in those days, was small, limited and gay, and our one initiation was to sleep with Willie Mae. Hell, the woman turned out and brought home over half of our community. She's still bringing them in. Guess you only as old as you feel.

When Willie Mae goes, she'll probably be out dancing with some young Barbie doll at an overcrowded disco. Perhaps she'll be shooting pool at Tommie's, or at some backyard barbecue telling jokes and playing cards. Or maybe she'll be at home on top of some new woman, trying to prove how she acquired and plans to keep her Casanova status.

I know she won't leave here attending a political rally, or teaching gay awareness. An activist she ain't, and a community liaison she'll never be. She finds that part of life quite boring, finds reality depressing. Charmed her way through high school, never touched a piece of literature since. Hates reading, does not own one book. Not the Holy Bible or the Satanic Ritual, not a comic book or magazine.

But she claims a record collection that will blow your mind. From Bessie Smith to Whitney, and all the Divas in between. She also has an accumulation of porno films that belong in a sexual archive. Sister Willie is just one get-down, good-time, game-playing, woman-chasing type of gal. Don't nobody bring no tears or sad faces when Willie Mae goes. Bring liquor, beer and reefer. Prepare to boogie 'til the wee hours of the morning as she always did.

She danced before she could walk, she was cursing as soon as she learned to talk, made love to her best friend Jenny at the age of three. To Willie Mae St. Vincent, life has always been, and always will be, one *hell of a party*.

Lois Fine

So Unexpected

Josh pulled off his running shoes too quickly, taking his socks off in the process.

"Pee-yoo. What stinks?!" his brother Abe held his nose as he walked by. Josh reached out a leg to trip Abe. But instead Abe caught his leg and bent it upward so that Josh's toes were sticking in his own face. "Here, take a whiff, sucker. Or should I say, stinker. When's the last time you showered, Chanukah?"

"Ow, ow, okay, okay, I give I give. I'll do anything." Josh was yelping as his brother held onto his leg, twisting it and making sure that Josh's toes were right up against his nose.

"Anything?" Abe asked, applying a little bit more pressure.

"Ow, ow, anything, anything. Just let go, asshole."

"What was that you called me?" Abe wasn't letting go.

"I mean brother." Josh knew his lines. It was just a matter of playing out the script before Abe let go.

"What kind of brother?"

"Oh, mighty, wonderful, super brother."

"Anything else?" Abe couldn't resist giving a final twist.

"Ow. Kind. I said kind, didn't I? I meant to say kind." And with that last invokement, Abe let go. Suddenly and completely. As if it had never happened. Abe continued on his way to the kitchen and Josh was left rubbing his ankle and fishing his socks back out of his runners. He had to admit they did smell pretty bad. But, what did they expect? It's not like there was anyone around to remind him to take a shower. He tried it on Abe.

"Well, whaddaya expect. It's not like she's ever home anymore to remind me to take a shower." He yelled it into the kitchen. Abe had started frying onions, the loud sizzle filling the room. Josh went in to talk to his brother.

"It's not like she's ever home to remind me." He repeated.

"What are you talking about, Josh?" Abe looked bemused.

"You know, she's never here anymore."

"She? Oh, you mean Mom."

"You know who I mean, asshole. How am I supposed to get any proper nutrition? All you ever cook is lousy home fries."

"Ahh, but that's where you're wrong, my boy. These are not just lousy old home fries, or any old home fries. These are the Abe Cantor special home fries, learnt from our dear old dad, *halev b'shalom*, may he rest in peace, who learnt how to make them from his dear old dad, Zayde Issie, *halev b'shalom* too."

"Will you shut up, Abe. Do you have to be such a goody-goody? Doesn't it bother you that she's never here? I mean, come on. Isn't there a law about leaving your kids alone?"

"Josh, you're seventeen years old. I'm nineteen. I hardly think she's a felon." Abe carefully added the boiled potatoes from the fridge to his onions, pressing them down into the pan ceremoniously.

"Well, I don't care what you think, Mr. Independence. I feel abandoned."

Abe pointed across the room with his spatula. "There's the phone, kiddo. You know where she is."

"Forget it. I'm not calling her there." Josh started wiping at himself, as if he was shooing bugs.

"You're a baby, Josh. I can't believe you're such a baby."

"Whaddaya mean? Just because I happen to miss her. Maybe I love her more than you, did you ever think of that?"

"Did you ever think you're narrow-minded and you can't deal with your mother being a dyke, and getting a new lover?"

"She's forty-eight years old, for god's sake."

"What's that supposed to mean?"

"Well, she's old. What's she doing staying up all night and never coming home? And she sleeps 'til two or something."

Abe got out two plates for the table and placed them on either side of the ketchup bottle. "Josh, last I looked, you were sleeping in 'til four in the afternoon."

"But I'm a teenager. I'm expected to do things like that. She's not."

"Wash your hands, they're filthy," Abe said. Josh didn't move. "I mean it, Josh. Go get washed." For a minute Abe thought Josh was going to lay in on him with all the usual stuff, the you're-not-my-father-why-do-I-have-to-listen-to-you stuff. But he didn't. Abe watched as his little brother washed his hands at the sink, got two forks from the cutlery drawer, and sat down to his dinner.

Luc Frey

Remembrance

I have been loving the nights. Quiet, soothing, embracing nights breathing with excitement. Warm nights in the summer, wind caressing bare skin, laying side by side in the sweet early morning dew of a lakeside meadow. Cold nights in the winter, frosty breeze dodged in a doorway, seeking each other's warmth in embraces, lost in a hundred arms. Dark nights, brightened with flickering lights of the bars, the sparkle of the stars, the gleam of a smile. Promising, shielding. Long ago.

The phone rang in the night. How are you? Not bad. What's on. *I've got queer-bashed.*

A flash. Empty brain. Numbness. Sudden remembrance. Things long forgotten. Buried deep inside a barrier of unshed tears. Hidden away, out of sight. Images like daggers, cutting apart the leather-turned feelings. Memories oozing out of open-cut wrinkles of a silenced soul. Night—the doorbell. Wide open eyes in a flour-pale face. Trembling hands grabbing my arm and shoulder. A voice so flat. Come quick. He's in hospital. Got queer-bashed in the park. Just heard it. Oh God, come.

A wave of nausea, the stomach a clenched fist. First heat, then hate, so cold it turns to icicles, slipped on with the jeans like a second skin. Why? The dark night—bright lights of the hospital's emergency ward—clean, white, antiseptic. Grey faces, tired, no words. No purpose. A black leather jacket, dirty, blood-stained, cuts in one sleeve. More ice builds up inside, mounts like a wall against the false glances and words cast upon a dying soul. Now and later on.

Hours? Time is no longer measurable. The coming and going of figures clad in white and green. Unconnected scraps of thoughts in numbed brains, torpid rough-rubbed surfaces of feelings in what were once warm and loving bodies. Kaleidoscopes of images behind sightless eyes.
"Miss . . . ?"
Have I been sitting here? Alone? With others? "Yeah?"
Green uniforms united—law and medicine.
"There was a note in his belt. Are you . . . ?"
"Yeah—how is he?"
"Serious. They slashed his face—couldn't save his eye, I'm afraid. . . . "

The bright lights—white gauze gleaming, leaving uncovered half of what was once part of his face. Out of shape now, out of colour. An eye, half-closed, staring, not seeing—for months. A bloody ragged line, a mouth once, swollen, sore, not speaking—for months.

A life between. Between here and elsewhere, life and death, madness and sanity. A life between. Work, hospital and home. Home—no longer a place for rest, peace and joy. The bright lights of the night—flashes of memories. Restlessness, sleeplessness, helplessness. Friends—words—tears. Why? Months.
He can't stay alone. Doesn't react to anyone of us. What can we do? A refuge in which to hide—a bedroom with an open door. A ghost, the face—or what is left of it—gaunt, grey, silent. A scar—red like a cane mark on pale skin—from brow to chin cuts not only a face apart.

A routine to keep sane:
Washing, shaving, dressing, feeding, *silence.*
Loo, chair, table, bed, *silence.*
I speak to you. I read to you. *Silence.*
Silence. Silence is more than no words spoken.
Silence like an empty space—not to be filled with a heartbeat, the blink
of an idea.
Silence like a cave—not to be lit by a torch.
Silence like an empty ocean—not inhabited by life.
Silence like a deafening din, cold embracer, fierce tormentor.

Bright lights in the night become a cry.

Exploding in the head, deafening the ears, last stone in an icy wall surrounding what were once feelings.

Cry—first sign of life in a newborn. Cry—newborn? Out of death? Back in the land of the living? Living? The cry cuts through the night like a knife cuts a face to pieces. Dripping wet with tears and sweat. My arms around you. Trying to hold together what seems to break apart. Hours. Hoarse words in my ear, difficult to understand them under the suffocating shroud of a cry that covers every cell inside with cotton-wool-like density that leaves no space for words to be squeezed through.

The phone rang in the night. Again. Years, a lifetime later.

The ring becomes a cry. Remembrance like a bright blinding flash lights the night, cuts through dreams and hopes.

I have been loving the nights.

Once.

Gabrielle Glancy

Withholding

My grandmother saw the sparkles, she said, shooting in front of her eyes, when, moving to the outside of the crowd, she passed out on the provost's lawn which was really meadow overlooking Monterey Bay. As, ten years earlier, my grandfather had suddenly wilted down and died in the middle of a crowded dance floor at my uncle's wedding, I thought for sure this was it: my college graduation would be how my grandmother's life would end.

I held her hand as the paramedics carried her on a stretcher into the provost's house where they laid her down before asking me to leave. In the hallway under weavings, baskets, and dark carved African art, I cried soundlessly into the wall.

Minutes before I had left her arguing with my lover, Sharon, whom she had met for the first time that day. "She should have married him, what was his name, when she had the chance," my grandmother was saying. They were discussing *The Portrait of a Lady*. Purist, and completely unforgiving, Sharon had no appreciation for how my grandmother was reading the book not as a novel, but as a biography, and how sad she thought Isabel Archer's life had been. Sharon couldn't see the absurdity and sweetness of it—how far this eighty-year-old uneducated Russian woman who had read all of Jane Austen, all of Thomas Hardy, all of Virginia Woolf exactly the same way, had actually come. And neither could I. I was embarrassed, and so left the two of them alone to talk.

Earlier that day I had tried to tell my grandmother what my relationship with Sharon really was.

"Of course," she said. "You like each other and you live together. That makes sense."

"And we sleep together," I said.

"And you sleep together," she repeated. Then she thought about it.

"*That* I don't understand."

That summer I moved back to New York.

I can't remember now how exactly it came up, but at some point in one of those conversations I often had with my grandmother in which I asked her to tell me stories I already knew—how she came to this country, how my mother met my father—the kind of stories which, for some reason, I remember less the more they're told to me—my grandmother made reference to my mother's first husband.

"Oh, my father, you mean."

"No," she said. "I mean, your mother's first husband."

"You mean my father," I said again.

When she realized what she had said, she put her hand over her mouth.

Later, when I asked my mother why she never told me she had been married before my father since I already knew she had been married twice after, she answered, characteristically, "I lived a whole life before you were born. There's a lot about me you don't know."

Which made me remember how as a young child I was convinced my mother was keeping the truth from me—that what she wasn't telling me was that I was half of a pair of twins, that the other twin died inside her before it was born, that we had grown in there together, the two of us, but that I, the lucky, or the stronger, had been catapulted into life, leaving the other somewhere, mysteriously, behind. Of course she tried to convince me, but there could be no proof and although the idea eventually, though imperceptibly, lost its power, as much as she reassured me, I never believed it wasn't true.

Six months before my grandmother died, the three of us sat at the kitchen table sorting through old photographs. "Who's this, Mom?" I kept saying, passing pictures to my mother almost faster than she could answer.

"That's Mel," she said. "That's Stan. That's my cousin Lenore."

It had become a kind of game.

Then we got to a picture I had never seen.

"Who's this, Mom?" I said. It was a man in uniform, a blond soldier, holding his hat. My mother held the picture a long time. Then she said, "Who's this, Mom?" to my grandmother, exactly as I had said to her.

"Who's this, Mom?" my grandmother said, automatically, taking the picture from my mother.

For a moment she looked confused. She squinted and held the picture closer to her eyes. Then she lowered her glasses and looked at my mother.

I knew this must be the man.

mu groves

what a drag

Me on the cracked cement. Lloyd is leaning over to give me a skinny hand up, he's falling on top of me with his blue toothbrush poking out of his shirt pocket. We're half off some sidewalk. It's wet and dark and middle of the night blurry. We stumble around like dogs on ice for a while then get some forward momentum, up Davie to where food is, he says. I think I have to puke. Lloyd is laughing, shrieking, but doesn't have a camera.

He steers me into some place with weird things hanging everywhere, dolls, toys, tricycles, plants, birds. There are so many colours my eyes hurt, but I can walk now and Lloyd has quit with the hyena laugh. We get a table on the side where it's not so bright and 8x10 glossies of movie stars stare down at us. Lloyd says I'm going to love this.

Lloyd orders coffees and I'm gawking at the legs inside the fishnet stockings that are taking our order. I must be grinning drunk because she turns to me next and whispers, "You like what you see?" I smile some more, so I don't blurt out anything stupid, and notice she has lashes out to here. "Yeah, I guess you do. You might not like what's under here though." Lloyd starts to giggle. I want to kill him, but I can't be bothered because she's lifting her very short mini up at the front and shoving her crotch into my nose. His crotch, excuse me. Lloyd almost falls in his coffee. She gives my nipple a quick squeeze and blows me a kiss as she flounces off to the kitchen. I'm still grinning. What else is there to do?

A drag show starts up on this weeny stage across from us. Our waitress person is on and she's wafting around lip-synching and gyrating herself into my shoulder. People are yelling and clapping and I almost forget again that she's a he. Then Lloyd starts flicking his tongue at her and I want to be sick. Just as she's finishing her number, this woman walks up to our table and squeezes Lloyd so hard I think he's going to pop. She's enormous, not fat, just big, with long stringy hair. Lloyd introduces her as Michelle something, but all I can think of is Janis Joplin. She sits down, leans over and pinches my cheeks. "She's so cuuuute," she's yelling and I'm sure everyone in the restaurant can hear her.

Her eyes are glassy behind her shades and she's blabbing about the great drugs she just did. Lloyd is giggling sometimes but ignoring her, watching the show. I'm just sucking her in like she's an angel sent specially to me. She keeps touching my face and saying, "I can't believe how cute she is." I don't believe it either, since I just emptied my stomach into a doorway and almost picked up a drag queen, but I like her saying it just the same. She's beautiful too in some way I can't quite figure out. I don't take my eyes off her.

Lloyd and Janis are dragging me away from the show. The waitress is waving and blowing kisses. She runs over and gooses me when I wave back. I guess I'm still smiling. Out on the sidewalk Lloyd looks really sickly and I probably look the same, except whiter. Janis is almost leaping up into the awning with her beret sliding around on her stringy hair. With no warning she grabs me around the waist and plants a wet tonguey kiss on my mouth. I kiss her back. It only lasts a couple of seconds but it feels like I've touched royalty.

Lloyd and Michelle start to look important and I figure they're going to score. This leaves me in a bus shelter, no roof, a wet bench and a wet cold guy on it. He lurches around and jams a finger under the tab on a beer can, almost weebling himself over. Then he smoothes a paper bag into a can collar. He pulls a plastic bag out of his pocket and a plastic bottle out of the bag.

I'm noticing this sideways, watching for the bus. I'm thinking how somebody might get off and sit on the bench and turn the old guy's life around. Me, I'll just get on and go home. "Hey, honey, canya gimme a hand here?" I turn around and he's wrestling the lid. It's Value-Pack Vitamin C. "Bloody safety top. You got nails fer gettin' this off with?" He swigs beer while I snap the seal.

I hand the bottle back to him. He's shaking as he digs out a couple of vitamins and stuffs the bottle and bag away. He pops the pills. "Really need these. Yup. Really needed these," he's slurring, beer dribbling down his chin. The bus is floating into view. The old guy is guzzling now, rocking back and forth and humming. He's not waiting for the bus, he's not waiting for anything. I'm on the first step up when he yells, "Hey, take yer vitamin C. It's good fer ya." The doors slam shut and all I can do is give him the thumbs up sign through the glass.

The next time I see Lloyd we're both sober. Me in just brushed teeth. He tells me Michelle dove off a seventh floor balcony a month later. I think Michelle who? Then I'm seeing angels. Hey Janis. . . . Is it a party up there or what?

J.A. Hamilton

Trifles

Jeannie said *Take me* and I found it hard to resist. I was her mother's friend, her mother's long-ex-lover, visiting and hard-pressed against my carnality, clamped vice-tight down on it and wanting.

Little girl, little girl, I repeated to myself and watched her from across the kitchen, watched her root determination tough and sinuous across the linoleum between our feet.

Take my picture, Jeannie said, her voice throaty. She was tall with angles perturbed by softness. Her face was a cameo. She smiled. *Outside, where you used to take my mother's. I want you to.*

Jeannie wanted me to take her, take her hand, take her out to the pocket below the mountain behind their house where the waterfall is a slut and the mist is the coming apart of a thousand erotic ghosts. There to photograph her, thieve her wobbly adored smile and all the juices of her girlhood. A series of those pictures of her mother established my career.

What about— But I couldn't say it.

Don't mind Mom, Jeannie said and reached for an orange from the earthenware bowl on the table, not taking the blue of her eyes from my face. She dug her fingernails through the fruit's skin, parted pieces and took them in her mouth. I watched her lips open and moisten.

The air was the hot and pulsing yellow of August. When I was Jeannie's age, twenty-two, I wanted girls of seventeen and sixteen, schoolgirls carrying books and snapping pink gum. Jeannie was a baby with folds of fat on her tiny arms and thighs, two teeth, a scrap unable to propel herself across a room.

The scent of Jeannie's insistence was the stinging chemical smell of my darkroom. It mixed with earth, steaming and fecund, tart and daring.

I can't photograph you, Jeannie, I said and lit a cigarette.

She wrinkled her nose. *You always take my picture when you visit,* she protested and ran her tongue over her fingers.

Not since you were small, not in a decade, I said, deeply inhaling and blowing smoke at the ceiling.

You don't think I'm pretty anymore?

Jeannie, no.

Well, then? Jeannie stood, her roots swelling up my legs, twisting. She pulled her bathing suit down from her shoulders and the sweet rounds of her breasts licked into sight.

I turned away.

She crossed to me and pressed against me from the rear. *You know what I want,* she said.

I shook my head.

Pictures of me naked and wet.

Jeannie, don't, I whispered.

By the waterfall, under it. I know you want me.

During my childhood I wanted a girl in a yellow dress across a classroom.

My back was scorched. *I don't,* I said. *You're wrong. You're letting your imagination run wild.* But I stayed put, didn't move away or turn.

Her young right hand slid down my side and around the top of my thigh below my shorts. I watched it, knuckles and tendons. I said, *I'm old enough to be your-*

Mother?

Bente Hansen

Just One of Those Days

I'm not sure how it came to pass that I became "Heroine of the Week." I certainly wasn't trying to win any popularity contests, nor was I attempting to garner any amount of attention. All I meant to do was appease my growling tummy and was, in fact, in search of a quick fix snack—preferably a cheeseburger. Instead, I became the saviour of a group of sophisticated (if not somewhat gaudy) ladies—just because a rude, crude and remarkably ugly dude in a souped-up El Camino (that's right, *El Camino*) was being a jerk.

I don't know what got into me, really. It had been one of those days right from the get-go. I woke up late and slammed my toe into my idle exercise bike in my mad rush to get ready for work. I almost broke my neck in the shower and since the scum bucket I have for a landlord never fixes anything, I ran out of hot water while rinsing the soap out of my hair. The bus was running early, which never happens except for when I'm late, so I had to spend my "fun" money on a taxi. Of course, I ended up with this smartass cab driver whose "shortcut" became a "longcut" due to some road construction that he'd conveniently forgotten about. He drove me all over the damn city before finally dropping me off at my office. Now here's the kicker. When I arrived, I discovered that I'd forgotten that it was Heritage Day and I actually had the day off.

What the hell am I going to do now? I thought, seething at my utter idiocy. It wasn't just that I'd nearly killed myself getting to work on a national holiday; it was that I was sure I had made plans to do something that day, and for the life of me, I couldn't remember what it was. Oh well, considering how the first part of my day had gone, this was about par for the course.

I decided to walk the sixteen blocks to where my car, a slightly beat-up Toyota Celica, was being repaired. Luckily Janice, my mechanic (and one-time lover) didn't believe in all these ridiculous federal holidays and was tooling around her rebuilt-from-scratch '56 Corvette (a beauty to behold).

"Hey, girl," I said, grinning at the sight of her. She was in ripped overalls, a cut-off t-shirt and a pair of old Nikes. On her head sat a Hard Rock Café cap, backwards, of course. Even dressed like that, she was an incredibly sexy woman. *Um um,* I thought to myself appreciatively. However, now was not the time and truth be known, I was still a little pissed at the whole morning thing.

"Hey, babe! What brings you out on a holiday Monday?" she asked, tinkering with the engine (or maybe it was the carburetor?). I just shook my head, made a face to show my frustration and ruefully replied, "You wouldn't believe me if I told you." I recounted my morning of insanity and ended up sitting on the floor with Janice, laughing at the absurdity of it all.

"That must be why I came to see you, Jan. You always make me feel better. So is my beater going to live to drive a few more miles?" I glanced at my old Celica. It wasn't much to look at, but it was a great car. I got it when I was sixteen and I had just turned thirty-two.

"Hell, that vehicle's good for another 10,000 clicks. You just have to remember that it's old. You have to be kinder to it." Me! Not kind to my car? Well, okay, maybe I forget to check and change the oil regularly, and there was that thing with the brakes, but besides that I cherish the little beast.

Anyway, the car was ready to roll, so I paid Janice for her trouble, got into my baby and left. Her engine roared to life. For being so old, she still had exceptional pick-up. I took off out of the garage and down the street. It was as I was tooling down Main that I realized I hadn't eaten all day. My tummy was rumbling and for reasons unbeknownst to me, I was craving a cheeseburger, never mind that I had been faithful to my diet for a whole week (a record for me), the image of a big, juicy cheeseburger sat in my mind like a blazing beacon, calling my name.

I turned down Mulroney Drive, a nasty one-way street with used car lots run by rip-off artists, an antique furniture store and a cheque-cashing store that charged forty percent of the cheque's amount. It also had the best damn burger joint in town.

I signalled to change lanes and that's when it happened. This nasty looking man in his El Camino had been sitting in my blind spot for the last two and a half blocks. As I attempted to change lanes, he sped up so he was parallel to my car and leered at me with a look that suggested he hadn't been laid since the Berlin Wall came tumbling down. He whistled appreciatively, which, I suppose, could have been taken as a compliment, but I was too tired, cranky and hungry to be amused. I was about to step on the gas and be rid of this loser when the only set of lights on the God-forsaken street turned red. Oh God, I thought to myself, how can my luck be so bad? As I came to a stop, a loud, braying sound filled the air and the cretin pulled up next to me.

"Hey honey," the jerk said, "I think maybe you should stop and take a look at the merchandise before you take off." He had a sex-starved look on his weasel face which, quite frankly, I found revolting.

"You're not my type," I replied, trying not to look this creature straight in the eyes.

He laughed scornfully. "And what is your type, girl?" Just then the light turned green. As I tore off the line, I shouted back, "That's right—girls!!" I roared up the street and, seeing the burger joint loom on the horizon, I signalled to get in the other lane. That annoying, braying sound filled the air once more, and much to my dismay, the fool in the El Camino pulled up again.

"Hey!" he shouted. "I bet all you need is a good fuck. That'll cure you of your sickness."

Well, that was it. All the anger and frustration of this totally fucked-up day rose like bile in my throat. I screamed something which, to this day, remains incoherent in my memory. I'd like to think it was something like, "Die, you scum-sucking, three-legged, poor excuse for a human being." I then proceeded to sideswipe his beloved El Camino. The last thing I saw was the utterly surprised and somewhat terrified look on his face as he veered off the road, over the sidewalk and smashed through the doors of the burger joint, running over three or four tables before crashing into the grill. Luckily, the only person in the restaurant was the owner and he was in the back room, but not for long. He and the jerk came running out of the joint.

"Get back! She's gonna blow!" the owner screamed at us.

"*My car!*" the jerk screamed to no one in particular.

Oh God! What have I done!? I screamed to myself.

Before that frenzied thought could even be completed, the top of the burger joint was blown about 150 feet into the air. Then the strangest thing happened. It started raining hamburger patties. *Cooked* hamburger patties. One landed right in my hand, so I ate it, thus quenching my desire for a burger, even if it wasn't a cheeseburger. About ten minutes later, the RCMP showed up.

On the way to the cop shop, I found out that the jerk was named Big Bobby Lee (strange for a man who only stood about five-foot-four), who was wanted in connection with pimping and selling girls into white slavery—he was the sleaziest of sleazoids! However, the fact that I'd just helped the cops catch a felon didn't appease the owner of the burger joint. He wanted me arrested and locked away. The cops took me down to the station, just for questioning, they said, but I still ended up in a holding cell.

But boy, what a holding cell it was! I've died and gone to heaven, I thought as I was escorted into a small room containing seven of the most beautiful women I'd seen in a long, long time. Finally, I thought, my luck is improving.

As it turns out, these seven luscious ladies were going to be Big Bobby's latest shipment of white slaves. They were picked up when the cops received an anonymous tip cluing them in on his activities. Now that Big Bobby was in custody, they could give their statements and go home. As they left, they approached me, one by one, and thanked me for helping them get their freedom. One went so far as to hug me and tell me I'd saved her life. Not bad for a day that started out so shitty. Later that week, I received a phone call from the local paper. The ladies had nominated me for the "Heroine of the Week." It was an honour the paper gave to women who performed exceptionally heroic acts. Considering that all I'd really done was lost my temper, I felt a little strange about the award, but what the hell, I accepted anyway.

When I returned home from the cop shop, that little red beacon on my answering machine was blinking like crazy. It was my mother. "Hello, dear," she said. "Are you going to show up for dinner? Everyone's here but you!"

I *knew* I had plans for today!

Neil Harris

Strangers in a Strange Land

Reserve duty again. It feels like it's never going to end. Every year a new rumour about lowering the age when we will be discharged, but whichever way you look at it, it's still a long way off.

For the first time ever I'm going to the Gaza Strip. Up until now, I've always managed to avoid the situation, always managed to find a way around it without breaking the law. This time I knew I had to go. After all these years of occupation, we were finally giving it back to the Palestinians and in my head there is this absurd political gesture—"I want to be part of the withdrawal."

Our bus pulls into the tent compound, our home for the next thirty-four days. The men we are replacing have a weariness in their eyes. They crowd around us as we emerge from the dusty red bus, eager to get back to homes and families, eager to get the hell out of here.

We all know the score—foot patrols in the refugee camps, night searches, road blocks. Maybe just one point of contention. Who is it more humiliating for? The oppressor or the oppressed?

As the light fades, the previous unit completes its hand-over to us and they start loading up and moving out. I stand outside my tent watching them leave and I'm engulfed by a wave of jealousy. A slow and heavy fog is moving in on us, given a strange sheen by the sea of dazzling floodlights which encompass us. The main road outside the compound is buzzing with vehicles urgently making their way home before the curfew. The last part of the set is completed by the wail of the muezzin from the mosque in Bureijh, calling the men to pray to Allah for the fifth time that day. That day and every other day.

How have I ever let this happen to me? Just a ninety-minute drive from home and yet so far removed from Tel Aviv, the gay coffee bars and clubs, our beach by the Hilton, my friends who know who I am and what I am.

This is the man's world that only appears in my nightmares. When we sit around the glass-top tables of Shenkin sipping our double espressos, we pretend that reserve duty is heaven on earth—thirty-four days of men, men, men. But the 'girls' haven't come close to an army uniform in years.

I'm the only one still too proud to use the old queer line to get me out of this. I continue to do my bit every year, avoiding the jokes about the women at work who always give in if you charm them enough. Everyone in my unit just assumes that I'm in between girlfriends. Let them assume. In Shenkin they continue to compare notes about the waiter who wears particularly inviting jeans, while I tighten the guy-ropes of my tent, check the night duty-roster and discover that I have nothing until four in the morning.

Sleep evades me. The sleeping bag is prickly, an awful irritating nylon weave. I stroll across to the kitchen where thankfully the cook has left some coffee simmering on the gas. I take a sip from the ladle. The thick black mixture soothes as it slides down my throat. I take a jug, fill it with steaming coffee and start walking back to my bed. Maybe I'll read for a while.

Half-way across the compound I hear muffled shouts through the fog. I hurry in that direction, trying to discern what I am hearing. The coffee laps the edge of the jug and splashes my trouser leg. The sudden stain of heat is a shock.

The shouts are curses, accompanied by shoves and light blows. Nothing damaging but enough to scare the prisoner who is blindfolded, kneeling, with his hands tied behind his back with nylon cuffs. "You fucking shit," the guard seethes, and he knees him once again in the back. The young Palestinian keels over, only to be ordered to get back on his knees by the bored guard. He awkwardly regains his position, his shirt covered in wet mud.

"What the hell are you looking at?" The soldier on duty takes me into focus. He's about to make some smart remark when he remembers me getting off the bus in the afternoon, and the memory includes my officer's rank. Suddenly less heroic.

"We brought him in an hour ago. He was in the street after the curfew." He avoids making eye-contact, knows that I'm less than impressed by him.

"So what are you knocking him around for?" I stare hard, wait, but receive no answer. I dismiss the guard—I'll deal with him later.

The kneeling youth is shivering. I find a blanket and begin to unbutton his wet shirt. The moment I touch the first button, he flinches, expecting another blow, clenching his teeth in anticipation of the pain. Slowly I remove his blindfold, crouching in front of him. His eyes are lowered to the ground, scared of what will happen next.

"What's your name?" I ask in Hebrew, unsure whether he will understand.

"Rafiq Kuttab." His voice is deeper than I expect, much fuller and rounder. I can't help but stare at him, his clear lines, jet-black hair, eyes so dark I'm not even sure what colour they are. I stare silently. His eyes slowly move from the mud and dust to find me totally absorbed in him. "I did nothing. I was in the alley outside my house. I did nothing." The anger wells up in the veins around his neck, bulging through the dark skin, crossroads of defiance. His dark eyes smoulder. I am overwhelmed by his beauty.

"Rafiq, listen. You're wet and cold. I just want to help you, don't be so scared." As I speak I feel panic well up inside, an illogical overwhelming fear seizes me. He now stares at me as if he is running the show. His hands are tied behind his back, he's kneeling in the mud and yet I'm the one who is now subservient. I move again to unbutton his shirt, but this time he doesn't jump. His eyes follow my fingers and then draw me once again into a stare, our faces inches apart. His shirt unbuttoned, I suddenly realize that with his hands cuffed behind his back there's no way I can remove it. I feel foolish. For the first time he smiles, his teeth glowing like ivory spears. The shirt drapes across his arms revealing a body beautifully defined, not something he has worked on, simply a natural and stunning gift.

His chest is splashed with mud, black on brown. My hand moves to scrape the drying mud but my head knows that something else is really happening. He shows no resistance to my hand as it moves across his chest, revelling in the stark contrast between the hardened mud and his smooth, perfect skin. His stomach is rock-hard, barely moving as he breathes. And all the time his eyes follow my every move.

There is no longer fear. We know nothing about each other, and yet we know everything that is happening here and now.

Wes Hartley

Anarcho-Queer Guerrilla Treespiking Ecobashback in the Clayoquot

On our way to the Clayoquot to spike trees we stopped off in Port Alberni to check out the illegal picketline encampment of certain overpaid wildcatstriking so-called forestworkers to sort of "join" with (sort of) fellowhumanbeings in ironic and kinky videodocumented "brotherly" solidarity against our now-jointly-hated corporate enemy hydraheaded Mac/Blo the Undead.

We arrived proudly decked-out in our biker-black shitdisturber QUEER TREESPIKER sweatshirts bearing totally queer gifts—sugarcookies and fudge.

A former Port Alberni union shitworker (now a crossdressing confectioner in Kitsilano) had donated pans and pans of uncut fudge, scores of Nanaimo bars, and twenty dozen dayold bakery cookies, all the kinds badboys like best.

Our queer Gang Of Four had a lot of fun distributing the fudge and got off on getting to gladhand and cheer-on certain tuffy sexually repressed bluecollar milltown chunks. One could almost imagine being almost on the "same" side, homosexually speaking.

We did eyeball one disingenuous fellowqueer (totally closeted, his babyblues averted, passing under macho picketsignage) who very quickly fucked off. (We had been assured by a wellknown South Island radical faerie that yelling "Mary!" in a crowded bar in Port Alberni on a Saturday night would for sure result in dozens of sprained necks.)

After portioning-out our highcalorie queer communion goodies we had quite a bit of fudge left, so we decided to pack it, and we were presently surprised when a couple of chummy picketers said they wanted to pack fudge with us in the back of our van.

What delicious ironies we kept tasting there on that illegal picketline under the downpouring late autumn rain.

How do you tell which one is the groom at a logger wedding? Easy. The drunk one on the left is always the groom, except in Port Alberni.

When we arrived at our carefully chosen offroad jumping-off-point (on the south shore of Dead Kennedy's Lake) we launched and loaded up our twoholer oceangoing queer kayaks Thunderbuns and Wavehumper then stashed our escape van under camouflage tarps in a dense salal thicket under scrubby hemlocks.

We paddled northwestwards across the lake towards the so-called "cutblock" we had targeted to steal back from the corporate ripoffs. This isolated community of sacred groves was tucked away in the upper reaches of Clayoquot Arm on the Western shore up a creek in that "light grey area"(the so-called "integrated management zone") behind the so-called "scenic corridor." We had reconnoitered most of this supernatural terrain in an exploratory foray during the summer.

The ballast stabilizing our trusty kayaks consisted of a week's supply of vegan bush cuisine, all the makings of wintertime treespiking camp, and eight antique canvas backpacks loaded with four thousand sawblade-mangling seven-inch tempered steel spikes (with their dime-sized heads nipped off so they could be countersunk deep).

Our ecobashback High Way Men (Green Boner, Rainbow Cheeks, EcoBear Witness and The-Wildboy-Of-The-Woods) were fully equipped and itching to spike some butt.

It took half a day to lug all our kayakballast a considerable distance into the bush (through that narrow so-called "scenic corridor") to our hideaway campsite inside the cutblock.

We used up all our spikes in six days, rescued fifty-seven oldgrowth sacred groves, and chainsawproofed several thousand giant spruce, fir, and red cedar oldtimers.

Our illegal mission-of-mercy was carefully documented on video fea-turing us hardcore queer method actors glaring (sort of) menacingly out from behind our sissy warsurplus balaclavas, Oka-style-outlaw queer bandanas, and fruity wraparound desert freedomfighter headgear. It is our deviant intention to collage these liveaction treespiking instantreplays with apocalyptic nightmare footage of the worst recent clearcuts, interweaving these with pirated newsfootage exposing fatcat corporate executives boozing-it-up with political hacks and so-called "forest alliance" sellouts, augmented with soapopera outtakes chronicling the mass arrests of generic masochist neo-hippie treehugger martyrs, spliced-in with our homemovies of wildcatstriking milltown picketers grinning at the camera like shiteating hyenas with darkbrown chunks of something stuck on their teeth.

As we broke camp and hefted our gear back through the so-called "scenic corridor" towards our kayaks, we erected biodegradable warning signs notifying potential pathogenic invaders that these groves have been spiked and are now protected for all time.

At around three in the morning guerrilla-in-a-black-skimask filmed a balaclava-and-toque brigand supergluing a diatribe and a greenscribbled map onto the front door of the socalled "forest alliance" in Ucluelet-Where-The-Sun-Don't-Never-Shine, claiming our Gang of Four just spiked ten thousand trees with ten inch spikes! (What hyperbolical anarcho-sizequeens we almost sound like, eh?)

Bashback Treespikers Tactical Mission Reportsheet

Since any and every recourse to "The System" reinforces it (such as sober ceremonial submission to stylized arrest for socalled "crimes of conscience") treespikers will never go along to get along.

Uprising from sound irrational bases, our anarcho-critical activities are not mediated by any socalled "alliances." They are completely outside "consensus reality" and will always be dispersed, decentralized, unpredictable, and therefore out-of-control, just like we are.

We don't give a fuck whether generic politicians, corporations, or policestate enforcers reform their laws and regulations or even erase them, since our anarcho/eco direct response both to them and to their system steals all its power and effectiveness from flaunting and breaking their herd rules, escaping undetected, then flooding their socalled media with firststrike newsreleases and cleverly composed video documentaries.

It is our kinky pleasure to administer this antiauthoritarian icewater reality enema. We stand up to bullies and we insist that they have our shit and eat it too.

What we do is what bashback means.

We are not idealists. Idealogue pathology makes us Thoreau up. We never mistake words for reality. Our real spikes defend real trees from real chainsaws. We are Riel outlaws, *eh tabernac!*

We plot and conspire to cultivate and nurture virtue, not law. Our masterplan is to inoculate all our sacred groves with antibodies specially designed to protect them from the fatal disease of logging. This is what we have now done here.

A respectable beginning. . . .

—Spiker Jones and his Sissy Shitkickers

Matthew R.K. Haynes

Night Soil

I remember frequenting the park during daylight. Before school. During lunch. After work. It seemed to take up more time than I wanted to allow. Nonetheless, I gave in. To a hunger? Perhaps. More to fear. Fear of being alone or never having been loved. I would get a blow, give a blow, fuck or be fucked. It was simple. It was something I held onto. I honoured it, almost. Any time of the day I would go to the park and get something, a hand job at least. There was always someone there. Someone to give something.

I would see them moving behind the bushes. I would hear them playing games behind tinted windows. They would sit side by side for a few moments and then leave. No parting glances.

It was autumn. The leaves were blowing and the rain was pounding hard. It was easy to overlook the cold when you longed for some sort of warmth or gladness. It was easy to suffer through anything if the reward was great enough. I always found the reward to be nothing absolute. A quick orgasm. A twittered feeling. A sweet sweat. Nothing absolute. The autumn nights were wicked. I was told by more experienced homosexuals that the night life was much better than the sorry-ass daytimers who needed to get home to their families. I thought they were okay. Not a ten. But not a zero either. The thing about the daytimers was that you could see their faces. You could tell what they wanted. Their eyes would shine on you. They would even make you feel good about yourself with all their trashy talk. Like a star, but only a porn star at best. But I knew who I was with. In the night it's tough. You never know. You can never tell. You drive by, shining your lights in the windows of vehicles, hoping to get a glimpse of what you were going to bring home. I never played night games. I was too afraid. I had this insane fear that someone would kill me or something. But I always wanted to. Because I figured if the night life was better than the daytime then I could maybe, hopefully, find someone I could really relate to. Not just a quick whatever. Because it seemed that the night life housed those kinds of people. And if you had the guts and if you were lucky enough you could find exactly what you were looking for . . . or close enough. Something more. Something outside of a car. Outside of a public restroom. Outside of all the same old shit. I thought that maybe I could be the lucky one. The one to find it all. Maybe.

The days were getting shorter then, and the nights seemed to creep up on you. I found that I couldn't rest easy knowing that there was something going on out there and I wasn't involved in it. I had to know. I had to find out.

I went to the park one night when the wind was calm and there were no rains and the sky was lit bright with a near-full moon. I was comforted by the starry sky and its compassion. I drove along the two-way half around the park, until it turned into a one-way. I felt like I was driving an ice-cream truck and there was this loud music playing from the truck, only I couldn't hear it. But everybody else could. It was like a call or something. Like an owl in the middle of the night. They make these love calls out to wherever. And the entire forest hears these calls, but I don't think the owl really does. But then these owls reply, and it is like a mating ritual. And playing out a call like an ice-cream truck. Hoping that they all come running to buy something. I turned around and made my way back to the entrance. Nothing. No one. I thought that maybe it was my unlucky day. But as I turned around to make another go at the night life, a vehicle pulled up behind me, and I looked in my rear-view mirror. Its lights were dim, and I could see that it was a truck. I was scared. The truck was beat-up and old and jacked-up, and I couldn't imagine any homosexual driving something so . . . I don't know, "manly" maybe. I kept moving forward. I would speed up a little to get some distance between us, but the truck would move close to my ass. We were halfway around the park, nearing the one-way. I clenched my teeth. Entering. Knowing that there was no turning back. I came to a stop. The truck came to a stop. I heard a door open and boots hit the pavement. I looked to the rear-view. I only saw pants. White pants. There was a knock on my window. I was afraid to look. Another knock. I swallowed and looked out the driver's side window and saw no one. Another knock, louder this time. I turned my head towards the passenger side, and there he was. His face in my window. I really couldn't make it out. I thought, This must be the one. This is the one. I unlocked the door and let him in. The light from my dome lit up his body. Tight, white pants that showed me everything. I smiled when he got in. I really didn't get a chance to see his face, but I thought it must have been beautiful. He unbuttoned his pants, and I immediately got an erection. He started to moan, and I just went down. Easily. Smoothly. He came. I looked up from his crotch, and I couldn't see his eyes from under his baseball cap. But I could see his lips pucker and his teeth grit. His hand flew to my face, and my head hit hard against the window. A blow to the stomach and blow to the face. I fell to the steering wheel. I think he called me a fucking faggot as he left the car. I heard his truck leave. I got out. Stumbling to the grass, I collapsed to the earth. The blood from my face dripped calmly into the soil.

I wondered who had been here before me. I wondered what had grown from their blood.

Jackie Haywood

Sole Brothers

In subservience to my ever present appointment book, I dutifully sit in yet another waiting room (aptly named). To amuse myself I observe the other patients' shoes with vicious sociological critique. The diversion fills the time and I'm able to stare covertly from under the pages of the outdated, family magazine without seeming too curious. Looking down at my own feet I smile in solitary appreciation of the recent, non-distinguishable resoling job on my Italian leather ankle boots.

I gaze around the office, noting that the wallpaper doesn't blend properly and the light fixtures need dusting. The opening of the entrance door prods us all to a state of alert. Ah, beige Hush Puppies, topped by light brown cuffed cotton pants. I listen closely when the receptionist asks prying questions of the new patient, relieved it's not me. He's attempting to answer in low tones, yet still be heard above the blustering of the office staff. The sounds of my grumbling stomach seem to resound over both the whispering young man and the office personnel. Does the fellow wearing the battered high-top running shoes next to me notice the offensive ventriloquism? Frequently my stomach lashes out acoustically because I am unable to eat. This unwelcome intestinal display is usually due to fasting for an upcoming invasive medical test, or the lack of interest and energy needed to cook for myself. I can't seem to keep weight on, but continue holding onto my vast collection of oversized clothes, hoping there will be a change and I'll be myself again.

The guy across the aisle wears ill-fitting sandals on severely swollen feet. Unable to latch the buckles, his feet painfully bulge within dusty socks. (The tired sandals are probably the only footwear he can use out on the street.) I fleetingly ache with sympathy and recoil in fear at his disability. The battery powered scooter parked outside the door with the sappy neon-coloured plastic flag flying from the back undoubtedly belongs to him. Poor devil, that'll never happen to me. If caught in a similar unfortunate circumstance, I'd be carried in on a chaise lounge by strapping bacchanalian dancing boys. "When I go I'm . . . going . . . like . . . Elsie," I sing to myself, arms imaginatively thrust forward, long painted nails clawing Liza Minnellishly towards the spotlight. God I'm losing it, right here in the Midtown AIDS Clinic.

To prevent a display of uncharacteristic queenly madness I focus on the remainder of the room. The routinely placed magazines, weathered and worthless, are only interesting to a clandestine footwear critic or the extremely bored who haven't thought to bring their own diversion. To a creative observer it could appear that we silent men on the naugahyde and pine chairs comprise an audience at a very off-Broadway theatre. We all sit quietly while the white-clad performers, outfitted with varying props, bustle behind the counters. They follow ingrained stage directions; carrying clipboards, vials of liquid, and stacks of files containing our secrets. I suppress an urge to say something out loud, a joke or a crude comment like, "Camp it up girls, show us your tits." I need to have some degree of control, to be seen as an individual (even an obnoxious one), not continue to just sit here like a docile sick person waiting for another dreaded needle or a piece of bad news.

It can't be much longer before the resident nurse, dressed in synthetic material from foam-core shoulder pads, to her orthopedic-like shoes (caked from frequent hasty polishing), crosses the footlights and calls my name. She will make eye contact, flash a perfunctory smile and lead me into an excessively illuminated examining room adorned with more ancient magazines and gleaming metal objects waiting to pierce my skin. When it's my turn I will recklessly toss my mangled magazine back on the sorry stack, glance triumphantly towards the sea of solemn faces and stride off behind her. I will swiftly leave my battalion of diseased comrades eager to be closer to the elevator and getting the hell out of here. On the way out I won't stop at the counter to tussle for another appointment, but will phone from home, prolonging the frustrated struggle between the overbooked doctor's rigid schedule and my appointment book full of countless health-related commitments. Exiting stage left, I will sweep past the gauntlet of undesirable footwear as if onto much more interesting things.

Five years ago in less frequent sojourns to medical waiting rooms, the shoes I observed were similar in fashion: well-polished rich leather loafers and boots that grew out of the hems of denim. If you followed the creased denim legs upward they would belong to a well-built man wearing the obligatory black leather jacket and full moustache, a regular Castro Street poster boy. These days there is a shortage of recognizable tribal footwear. The well-worn floor showcases running shoes, suburban mall replicas of Eddie Bauer models, and scuffed generic lace-ups. Is the demise of my health destined to be chronicled by the changing tide of accessories chosen by waiting room companions?

At last the nurse calls my name. Rising unsteadily, the cruel, familiar pain in my legs relentlessly threatens to push me back down into the seat. (I'll fall on my face before I'll use a cane!) Swaying like an intoxicated rumba dancer, I try to balance. With arms pumping to a non-existent beat, I feverishly grasp at the back of my designer blue jeans which now hang vulnerably low from my hips since my once tanned, round, desirable ass has disappeared.

The man in sandals with swollen feet moves forward unexpectedly. In a mute offering to join the dance, he reaches for my arm. With gratitude, I accept his strength and caring, avoiding the knowing look in his eyes.

Like a sedentary chorus line, all heads turn in our direction as we awkwardly promenade behind the white-clad one as she moves down the corridor leading me to a bright sterile cubicle and yet another wait.

Christina L. Hulen

Keeper of Hearts

When you asked for my heart, I gave it to you. No one before had ever asked, and I had never offered. So when you asked, I was both flattered and a little frightened. You asked without affection or tenderness, but matter-of-factly, as if there should be no question, no hesitation. Yet there were questions. I wondered how I would survive without it. Because I had never before parted with it, I wondered if somehow I would feel different without it. Though you convinced me I could give you no greater gift for Valentine's Day than my heart, and you promised you would take care of it. So I gave it to you willingly. After all, I loved you and trusted you.

The first week without it was difficult. There was pain when I changed the bandages and when I moved too quickly. I had to take care when showering because too much soap and scrubbing made the fresh wound sting and grow pink and puffy. Sweatshirts to obscure the scar and lack of a bra became my daily attire. Still I endured the discomfort because I loved you and I knew the pain would subside.

What I found most difficult to deal with was its physical absence. I missed the strong hard pounding I felt after running and the rhythmic surging that overwhelmed me when we made love. My heart was gone, and I began to wonder if I should have given it away so hastily. Yet you assured me that everything would be fine. So I took to laying my head on your breast at night and allowing the steady beat of *your* heart to lull me to sleep.

When you displayed my heart in a lavender jar on the coffee table next to your *Architectural Digest*s, I didn't say a word because it seemed to please you. Though I didn't like eating our TV dinners in its presence. It was too raw, too naked. And the jar you placed it in was too small. The tissue pushed up against the lid and pressed itself against the glass, as if it were trying to burst out.

After some time, I got used to it being there. I barely noticed it. Then you started inviting friends, relatives and even strangers over to see it. It became the centre of attention at parties. I no longer existed. It was that jar they looked at or the scar that rose from my blouse. They never looked at me. It would have been unbearable were it not for the fact that you were so proud.

You kept it immaculate. When guests littered every available flat surface with empty bottles and half-eaten plates of food, you said nothing. However, when an unfinished hor d'oeuvre found its way on top of the jar, you hunted down the offender and chastised them in front of everyone.

Although it embarrassed me, you took to carrying it around with you when we went out. Dressing room clerks at department stores asked if they could keep it behind the counter for you while you tried on clothes. You always refused. You said it was precious, that no one could touch my heart but you. And, because you were happy, I was happy.

After a year had passed I noticed a change. Rather than rushing home to be with me as you usually did, you came home later and later, smelling of cigarettes and scotch. My heart started to gather dust. When I asked why you hadn't cleaned it, you said you were too busy and told me not to nag at you anymore. Several days later, I came home from work to find my heart was no longer on the coffee table. I searched all over the house and finally found it, in the closet, on the bottom shelf, between the sweater your mother sent you for Christmas and a pair of old shoes. When you came home from work I asked why you moved my heart, but you didn't answer. You left abruptly and didn't come home until late that night and the following night you didn't come home at all.

I began to think you might be hurt because I'd never asked for your heart. So the following week when Valentine's Day came around again I planned and prepared all day. I took my heart out of the closet, polished the jar, and placed it back on the coffee table next to an empty jar of the same design and proportions. I prepared your favourite meal, lit candles, and played seductive music.

When you came home I couldn't contain my excitment. I asked you for your heart. The colour drained from your face as you looked past me to the jars on the table. You turned and walked out of the room. I followed you to the bedroom where I found you sobbing. I didn't know what to say. I didn't want to fight. I said nothing. That night I laid my head on your breast. There was no sound. You were hollow, empty. A puckered ribbon of red was peeking above the bodice of your nightgown.

Welby Ings

The Bachelors

I've just turned onto the main road. Through the rear-vision mirror I can see the swirl of dust rolling out and resettling over the long grass. Nobody mows the roadsides in Pukeatua.

I'm tired.

I've been down here for Murray's twenty-first. One of those compulsory returns to the district that you are forced to make because your brothers have stayed behind with the family.

Coming up here, on the right you can see the Conways' place. The old house up behind the plum trees. The one with the broken gate and the cattle-stop full of thistles. There's a sign on the letter box.

Maurie and Jack Conway
NO SHOOTING

Ever since I can remember they have lived here. Their farm marks the dividing line between the north and south of the district; the last stop before the school bus winds its way down into the dust of the Acacia Gulley.

They are strange guys, part of the tangle that makes up the fabric of this community. They moved up here from the King Country years ago—not long after their father died. They bought forty acres but since then it's just run down into ragwort and thistles. "They are terrible farmers," Dad says. "A bit simple—shut up there away from the main road." He reckons they only have one brain and a smart dog to share between them—poor buggers. Their stock are always out on the road. I remember when I was a kid, it was a standing joke to see how many chooks you could run down when you drove past their gate in the morning. There was always something dead and lying in the gravel.

139

I guess, like most things in this district, their place is part real and part legend. The boys still judge the calf club and dress up as Santa on alternate years for the local school Christmas party—they still remain unmarried, despite the rumour concerning them and the local post mistress. "Gay bachelors," they call themselves. They'd have a fit if they knew what the term meant.

You know, I remember one summer, when I was in form four, they rang up Dad and asked him if I wanted to earn some extra money helping them put in hay. They were mean bastards. I biked five miles up through the Acacia Gulley on my sister's bike, slogged my guts out stacking their bales full of chopped thistle and all they gave was a box of bloody biscuits.

I remember standing there in the headlights of the tractor, after we had finished up and Maurie—that was the eldest one—telling me what a hard worker I was and how they couldn't have done the job without me and asking if I'd be available again next year . . . and then he hauls out this fucking biscuit tin, wrapped up in Christmas paper and shows me how to strap it on to my carrier. They said that they had made them themselves. I couldn't believe it. They thought they were being bloody Santa Claus. Shit I was pissed off.

It's probably still back there, somewhere down in the Acacia Gulley, rusting away in the bracken fern I threw it into on the way home.

"Tight as a ram's arse," Dad said, "exploiting young kids." He wanted to go up there and punch their lights out for them, but Mum reckoned that they didn't know any better. They lived in another world, she said. They thought they were being generous.

Generous!

I bought her a balloon and a packet of liquorice for Christmas to show her what it felt like.

Mean buggers.

I didn't stay at home much longer after that. When I got my School C. I moved down to Wellington and went to work for the Post Office. I heard bits and pieces about them, dotted through letters about noxious weed inspectors and my sister's calf club prizes—but you lose interest after a while. I guess they became a dog-eared sort of joke.

Wellington consumed me. It had pubs and clubs and a night life that didn't shut down at eight-thirty. I got myself involved in gay politics—

found out how oppressed I was and illustrated it all with badges. I hit the big time. I was on marches and TV and appeared in the crowd scenes in the papers. Mum and Dad even saw. I was wearing my "op-shop" jacket. It only has a small pink triangle pinned onto it now, but once it was ablaze with messages. In its time this coat has saved the whales, reclaimed the night, supported Nicaragua and Maori sovereignty and halted all racist tours. It has also, single-handedly been smacked over by a gang of street kids in Cuba mall. (This coat has a loud mouth for something that was bought from the Salvation Army.)

I don't know why I did it, really. Showing off, I guess. Sort of Flaming Faggot comes home. Show Pukeatua a thing or two.

It went down like a lead balloon.

When I arrived at the hall, Murray and all his mates were over in the corner, slinging back the Steinies. The place hadn't changed that much; the curtain on the stage was still torn, the cut-down car-tires had had another coat of white paint on them and had been stuffed full of toetoe and hydrangeas. Someone had sprinkled talcum powder on the floor.

Maurie Conway was up on the stage playing the piano, while some of the local Young Farmers helped to set up the stereo system. It was just as I had imagined it: Wild Time Pukeatua—disco dancing to the Bee Gees, with half a dozen farmers' wives reeling themselves like a combine harvester across the floor at you. . . .

Staying Alive—Staying alive . . . uhh huh huh huh. Staying Alive.

God!

And you're in the corner there, trying to be chic, dancing discreetly with some girl who looks like Alison Holst, who keeps telling you how some of her best friends are gay and asking what you think about the AIDS problem.

And then at supper-time, Maurie Conway climbs back up on the stage and breaks into "The Days of Wine and Roses."

It's all the same. It never changes.

The kids I grew up with have left home, bought their second hand Cortinas and hooned around Te Awamutu, and now they're married and back on the farm again.

It's like a kind of pattern stamped on these places, part of the patted and approved process of growing up in Pukeatua. You look around and you can see their parents watching you now—cold eyes and smiles.

"That's Jean and Bevan's eldest boy—you know, the homo. He's come up from Wellington."

At suppertime I sit with my brother's mates, slinging back Steinlagers and laughing loudly. Telling jokes and calling across the hall. I have an *Introducing . . .* sticker stuck over my pink triangle. Maurie Conway is up on the stage thumping the guts out of the ivory keys—you can see him watching you out of the corner of his eye.

Days of Wine and Roses . . . Days of Wine and Roses.

When the evening is over and the few remaining family are left behind to sweep up the hall, Dad comes over to me and tells me I look like I had a good time.

"Yeah," I say, "I had a good time." We pick up the glasses and take them out to the kitchen for washing up. Mum asks what should be done with the old hydrangeas and we decide to take them outside and throw them over the fence. She gathers them up and gives them to me and then goes up onto the stage to close the lid on the piano.

When I get outside it is quite dark. There are only three cars left in the carpark; Mum's, mine and somebody else's.

I take the flowers over to the fence and throw them in a bundle on to the other side.

Pukeatua.

From behind me someone comes walking. At first I think it is my brother, but I turn around and it's Mr. Conway. He's a little bit drunk.

"It's a nice night," I say.

There is a pause.

"It's a nice night."

He looks at me.

He looks small.

"I . . . I never thanked you for the box of biscuits. . . . " I laugh, but then I feel awkward.

He looks over the fence at the hydrangeas I have thrown there, and then gazes up into the night.

"You found the note in the bottom, then," he says.

I laugh. I don't know what he's talking about.

"I hear your brother's gone back down into the King Country," I say. "Back to the old farm . . . to your mother."

He stands up and holds on to one of the battens and I think that he is angry with me. I shouldn't have mentioned the biscuits. I've put my foot in it.

"My mother is dead," he says. "Jack has gone down to his own mother. . . . We're not brothers."

The car has just turned out onto the western bypass, somewhere halfway between Wharepapa and Arohena—somewhere miles from nowhere. Through the window here, the farms file past in smooth succession, small towns and small people just like my own.

I unpin the pink triangle I have attached to my jacket and carefully let it fall onto the seat beside me. It rolls out of sight between a Just Juice carton and a pair of sunglasses.

Around a corner I pass the Whakamaru hall. Some guy is outside straightening up the crates, waiting for his mates to come and pick up the empties. One of the local boys, I guess.

I wind down the window and shout out to him, parping the horn and waving. He waves back and then stands up and looks at the car in confusion.

I feel good.

I turn on the radio and drive back to Wellington.

Kevin Isom

Tongue in Cheek

As an attorney, I try never to get caught with my pants down. But sometimes it's unavoidable, and you just have to stand there in the cold wind, very much surprised.

As when I recently learned of a Georgia Court of Appeals decision holding that, without being tongue in cheek, rimming is not a crime under the Georgia sodomy law. It seems that the esteemed court reads the sodomy law as applying only to oral-genital contact (in addition to genital-anal contact, the usual thrust of the statute). Since the court does not view the dark side of the moon as "genital," oral-genital contact does not occur when the tongue does go a-traipsing. The tongue is free to explore, with the sanction of the court.

I wondered, as I read the decision, has the whole world gone mad, or is it just me? Am I the only one who finds this decision incredibly absurd? The pragmatic lawyer side of me realizes that this case is a step forward in narrowing the antidiluvian Georgia sodomy law, and it enlarges the rights of tongues throughout the state of Georgia. From Dalton to Valdosta, people are probably enthusiastically cleaning their kitchens right now (for those of you not familiar with Southern expressions, I'll let you guess from context what that one means), all with the approval of the Georgia Court of Appeals.

Mind you, I mean no disrespect to the Georgia Court of Apeals. That court is one of the finest in the land, and they clearly made the right decision under the law as it is written. But I can't help wondering what those briefs must have been like. Or the motions that preceded and followed the submission of the briefs. I would particularly have enjoyed witnessing the oral arguments in the case. They must have been real

humdingers. It all turned on the definition of "genital." Where did the
State find its definition of "genital"? Webster's? And where did the
Defense look to rebut? Or did the State argue legislative intent, asserting
that the original legislators intended the statute to include what had
happened here? That is one argument that must have gone lickety-split,
because I cannot imagine that the original legislators could have given
much thought to the matter. The court probably shafted the State on that
one.

I used to think the only humour I'd find in law was in the limited
rations that were doled out in law school. Like my classmates' t-shirts that
read, MAKE LOVE, NOT LAW REVIEW (very neo '60s). Or the time that the
professor in Business Associations spoke about agents engaging in bond-
ing activity, and I was laughing hysterically in the front row—no one else
found it funny. The classmate sitting beside me was straight, but because
we spent a lot of time together, everyone thought we were a couple. So I
bought a t-shirt that read, I'M NOT GAY BUT MY BOYFRIEND IS, and he had
one made that read NOT HIS BOYFRIEND. His wife, not to be outdone, made
herself one that read THE LESBIAN WIFE.

Classic humour, the likes of which I never thought I'd see again outside
of law school. But then the Georgia Court of Appeals goes and decides
that under Georgia law it's hunky-dory to send your tongue where the
sun don't shine. Now, that's legal humour of the sort befitting the best
legal minds of yore, like the famed Judge Learned Hand (swear to God,
that was his name). Which just goes to show that in Georgia, at least,
vigilance is the order of the day. Because if you're not always on guard,
it's easy—and legal—to get licked.

Faith Jones

True Confessions

1: Straight

I was in this phase of reclaiming language. We would be having sex and I would say, "My cunt hurts," or "Get your prick out of my face, I'm not going to suck you off." He liked this, even though, as you might gather, I was a selfish lover. He liked the words and got off on me saying them. I felt uneasy with this: if I was reclaiming language for female power, how come he still had orgasms two-to-one over me? Okay, this I could live with. Then one day he said it. "I'm sorry I came all over your cunt," he said. I got up quickly and went to the bathroom. Sitting on the toilet (I didn't have to pee, I just sat there to lend verisimilitude to my errand) I worked out a plan. I went back into the bedroom and told him I hadn't realized how late it was, I had to go somewhere, could he leave now? When he was gone I had a bath. Then I took the sheets off my bed and washed them. I waited in front of the washing machine, smoking a joint. I put them in the dryer and smoked another joint. I remade my bed and got into it.

The next day I saw him at the bar. I smiled but didn't go over to his table.

2: Bi

I found out by accident that she was sleeping with her ex-boyfriend again. Although we had not discussed it, I realized right away that Doreen would simply claim that we weren't being monogamous, and she had been clear all along that she was bisexual. So I never brought it up. I just started being as mean as I could to her on-again off-again boyfriend. This wasn't hard, as he was younger than me and insecure. Actually, I think that's

146

what Doreen saw in him. He was very easy to boss around and would retreat whenever either of us snarled at him. At a party at her house I "accidentally" fell asleep on the sofa. He went home because he was trying to be sensitive. In the morning I woke up on the sofa, got up and crawled in with Doreen. We didn't have sex but I wanted her roommates to think we had so they would tell the boyfriend. (They had been my source of information when she'd started seeing him again. I assumed the information flowed in both directions.) Actually, we hardly ever had sex because she was more interested in being surrounded by adorers—of whatever gender—than she was in "the act." I know this because years later the boyfriend and I compared notes. We had become good friends by then. My relationship with Doreen had lasted a few months, his had lasted two years on and off. Recently, he picked up a bisexuality anthology in a bookstore and saw that she was one of the contributors. He was too freaked out to buy it; he didn't even read her article. I really wonder what she said.

3: Lesbian

Linda and I dropped acid in the kitchen of her Gastown studio. Then we walked over to John Barley's and staked out a corner table. It was early, not too many women there yet. The waitress came over and took our order—two dry ciders with lime and ice. I drank cider because that was the non-beer lesbian drink that year. Linda ordered the same as me because she was too stoned to make a decision on her own. In fact, she'd lost her entire capacity to think the moment we'd stepped into the bar. Maybe it was all the flashing lights. When the place started to fill up she felt better and danced. I was unsure I could look cool dancing, so I just sat at the table. Janet came in, and after talking to me for a minute, said, "You're on chemicals, aren't you? It makes me wish I had some." Then we watched Janet's ex-girlfriend necking with another woman. A woman I didn't know came over and she and Janet complained together for a while. I gathered her ex was the woman Janet's ex was necking with. At closing time, Linda and I got a ride home in the back of someone's pickup. We went to my place. Linda discovered she'd started her period and it had soaked through her pants. We took a bath together because I couldn't stand the idea of her being somewhere I wasn't. Then we tried to order a pizza. It turned out there weren't any all-night pizza places in Vancouver. We sat at my kitchen table and wrote a poem about it. I think that's the closest we ever came to sleeping together.

M.S. Kershaw

Paradigms

anon

you remember it like this: new york and four-four forever. accusations.
with a laugh. *you've been goin' too hard, guy, so sure, you're tired; take a load
off gettin' yer load off!* you had to hold on to the back of a chair at work and
the thought occured: mortals merely fall or faint or pass out but celebrities
collapse. isn't that what happened to lola falana, the papers said? she
collapsed from exhaustion at caesar's palace. straight drop. had to be
helped from the stage. glamour. no one helps you but, hey, it's just some
bug you nabbed from thetubstheparkthatboybarsweetness last week. and
at the hospital they say you've got pneumonia, the doctor says, *you've got
pneumonia, son*. son son son. of course you're twenty-two and this can't be
'cause you're bronze burnished of the fire isle, but you're fading and they
won't say why can't say why can't say die— never say die. but you do.
and you're not a target because history hasn't stirred. you're so early—pre-
cede even the blame of poppers and lube—that you're forgotten, because
despite the bracelet you have no name.

guts

at first it seemed implausible because of the stink of male shit and because
you were clumsy and because the urinals were as cacophonous as angel
falls (before bed, mum running the tap so you could pee, you blushed;
she might sneak a look at your thing) but hell, counting yourself lucky
you're not fucking pee shy; can stand and piss and glance and size up, rub
yourself up. but it seemed implausible: your ass bare on the toilet seat;
the pacing boots outside the stalls; dreading the heels of security guards,
hidden cameras, plainclothes, and him: all desire and no language, no

nursery rhymes to cajole your child, just the empty mouth you must fill. red grotto. he'd slipped away from work, a lexicon of odours (turpentine or cologne or deep fry grease) and it seemed implausible his fingers could open you, that you wouldn't whimper, that there could be a righteousness of skin against the stink of male shit. your lips were on the nipple, hand sliding under belt to ass crack, the other cupping his balls, and in the sudden silence at last it seemed plausible. you waited to disappear.

betrayal

if it weren't for the weather you'd quit this westcoast bullshit. you were just reading the travel section in *playguy/mandate/blueboy*; all montreal men look gay: a sweater tied round the neck and the pants—you can never find a pair—that make a butt so fine. still, there's the language. well, one needn't do all that much talking. DANCE! DANCE! *voulez-vous couchez / avec moi / ce soir?* (or australia, dead-headed with eighteen hours jet-lag and sydney burning around you bright as beetle shells, how you hung with reg and sean, hung sean, narrow nasalities, mate. bugger the queen and bugger all and bugger me. oh, sweet tanned ass island empire! macho thong boy continent!) *no assflossing in montreal*, say the westcoast friends, *only snow. you'll miss the beach.* never the twain. (if more distant, trade winds and shield between, reg and sean would send you postcards, guffawing as their g-strings hit the tile. *so where ya ridin' ass, mate? downside-up in canada, you say? pity.*)

drumstick

you give yourself the go ahead. *go ahead.* so you're thirty-six and no one calls you *boy* anymore (not even in old photographs). so the answering machine doesn't blink as much or blinks too much with the domestic traumas of friends. so you only order the alfredo small portion. *go ahead, show a little leg.* so they think you're not trying because you've never embraced lycra; you're happy in your navy rugby shorts. *show a little leg.* it's the first sunny day of the year and you're pumping the new mountain bike through the ghetto, past the smokey hangouts. rainbow flags curl on a breeze. guys at the outdoor tables. *show a little leg.* you've got pretty swell gams—and the moxy to brandish 'em while the western world's still clothed to the ankles. *now!* flashing past and your leg bending up, pushing down, max. torque on the pedal and they're sipping, smoking, smiling

behind their *vuarnet* shades. the long hollow of muscle in your mighty
swank thigh; you know they'll swivel a glance, so you stand on the pedals,
show your buns, where your crotch creases darkly to perineum. and you
swear you hear a whistle. yes, yes, the goddamn wind is in your ears and
is lifting the rainbow flags but surely, yes, surely someone whistled.

pastoral
if you'd just had a book published (pink trivia, the films of brenda vaccaro,
lo-fat slavic cookery), the back blurb would say, ———— *lives on a farm
outside* ———— (the napa valley, the eastern townships, new mexico)
with his lover, two dogs, and a plethora of irritable barn cats. and suddenly he's
framed, warbling in the slow-ooze pane of the old window, like you're
squinting through heat. he's unearthing turnips: ink blue leaves, blood
lavender stalks, the bulbs wan as stained teeth. those incredible fingers
brushing soil from the turnip nipple (these incredible fingers you never
stop reading when he's curled them around a coffee mug, lately more hair
on the knuckles). a dog bounds through the carrots. *sophie!* he's yelling.
sophie, get outta there! but is crouching, is scented textures—flannel and
wool, is rubbing behind her ears. *yeah, there ya go, girl. you like that, hunh?*
you're taking notes (the films of lorna luft) but his things are among your
things: a recipe on your work table for mexican pan bread, the knees in
the four-poster, in the yard the old citroën he's named *snazz.* you look up
from the recipe, hoping to see him, square teeth, waving, a finger behind
sophie's ear; but he's gone. you hear the wheelbarrow. in the barn the
plethora of irritable cats is tensed to pounce.

Mara Kinder

Life Before Lesbianism

The baby has on temporarily clean diapers and second-hand clothes. She puts it on the damp grass outside the back door of the rundown house which leads to the furnace room, which in turn leads to the basement suite they live in, and struggles with the heavy baby buggy. It catches on the boots and bicycles in the narrow entrance. She tugs on it impatiently, tiredly, and yanks it over the too-high ledge. While unfolding the buggy she notices the baby putting dirt into its mouth. Oh well, builds the immune system, she thinks. She picks up the little love of her life, her reason for being, and gives its little body a squeeze, kissing its dirty mouth, before putting it into the stroller. The baby, who never, since conception, stayed still for a single moment, starts kicking its legs and bouncing. On their journey, the full seven blocks to Safeway, she has to periodically stop because the baby has pulled itself into a standing position. She fights the little body, gently but insistently repositioning the baby's limbs, and carries on.

This little daily excursion allows her time to dream, albeit intermittently. Her dreams are of escape, this particular one made possible by the lottery ticket in her wallet. With a mere hundred thousand dollars she could leave the man with whom she shares the basement suite. She would buy a big house, divide it up and rent out suites to single moms and lesbians. She would go back to art school, have more babies; and in the summer she would write on a new computer, one with a colour screen and a hard drive. She would live happily ever after, have friends and occasionally lovers (none of whom would ever live with her) and a car too, a Renault or a Volkswagen bug and a driver's licence. At Christmas break she would take her babies down to Mexico and they would sleep in hammocks on nude beaches. Happiness was a lottery ticket away.

They reach the corner where the second-hand bookstore is and she wonders if perhaps the baby would tolerate an unmoving buggy long enough for her to browse through the psychology section. Of course, sitting still does not interest the baby in the least. It starts reaching out from the buggy and pulling books off the shelf. The aisles are narrow and she can't position the buggy far enough from any shelf to prevent this, so she replaces the fallen books and, awkwardly manoeuvering the buggy, makes her way out of the store and towards the too-bright Safeway with the wide aisles, thinking that a hundred thousand would also buy her a babysitter.

It's not that she doesn't love the man, she thinks, simultaneously wondering if the pizza crust she is holding is too expensive and if she can stand another rice and vegetables meal. It's not that at all. He's a very good man, as far as men go. It's hard to explain about the man. She used to need him, depend on him. On his strength. On his stability. On the walls he put up. Walls she could lean upon, walls she could bounce against so that she no longer bounced into outer space. But now she has her own walls. Now her priorities have changed. Now she depends, knows she depends on herself. Now she has the little bouncing bundle to fill her voids. She is no longer afraid of being alone, only of losing her baby.

Something happened that spring night eight months ago. Something happened with that final scream when she felt she was going to split in two and she saw, in the mirror her midwife held for her, the furry ball, the top of her baby's head, emerging from part of her body distorted beyond recognition. Something happened when she held the little wrinkled person who pooed on her hand while she sipped champagne and murmured "My baby, my little baby, oh, my beautiful baby." After that she knew she could do anything. She was strong, powerful, and there was nothing she could not handle. There was nothing she would not do for her baby.

She'd held the baby forever. She'd smelled the baby's brand new breath and licked the inside of its little mouth. She nursed it, held it and gazed at it for months (and then she got worried). She cried for the women in war-torn countries who could not feed their children, she hurt with the imagining of their desperation and despair. She started taking part-time courses. She cooks and cleans. Feeds, changes and bathes her baby, does endless loads of laundry, nurses the baby several times a night, and when the man comes home, she listens to him talk and gives him dinner. Somehow in between all of this she studies, writes papers and exams, driven and determined to receive perfect grades. Driven and determined to one day provide security, a little townhouse and piano lessons for her baby.

The man wants time and attention too. The man wants sex. The man wants too much. The man who once taught her to say no, at the time a concept new to her eighteen-year-old mind, now tries to push her to meet his desires, desires she does not share. She dreads the nights of feeling that hard thing pressed into her back. She won't, can't, let it inside of her; but sometimes, for the sake of peace, she agrees to lie close to him and kiss him as he thrashes it about with his hands. The man has big hands and a hairy body. He has strong smells and takes up too much room. She wants to be alone with her baby, with the baby puke smells and the baby hands which reach for her; the baby mouth that tugs at her nipples and the baby body which she holds close and sometimes falls into an exhausted sleep with in her hammock strung across the room they used to use as a studio, where she now studies, and where the baby things are kept.

Walking back from Safeway with a bag of groceries jammed into the rack under the buggy and another hanging from the handlebars, she looks at the big fancy houses where people with a lot more money than she has live. She looks at her baby whose diaper now needs changing and who is starting to complain and she wonders what options a twenty-year-old mom with two years of fine arts education and a man she doesn't know what to do with has. The lottery ticket, she knows, will remain only a dream.

Jeff Kirby

Cockaholic

This is my first meeting, so, you know, it's difficult and all, so bear with me. Breathe. Okay. Hello, my name is Jeff K. and I'm a cockaholic. I admit that I'm absolutely powerless in the face of dick. I can't help myself. I see a guy's bulge and everything comes to a complete stop. I lose it. All control. In awe, like being slipped some stuff, the world gets into a poorly lit soft focus, leaving this hard fierce radiant object that drops me to the ground on a crawl, lips reaching—suddenly I remember the first time I wanted something, anything in my mouth: my fist, daddy's finger, a blue rubber ring, Jesus, *anything* just fucking stick it in front of me and please don't try to make me fucking walk yet, give me a few more months for chrissake. "That's my big boy, come and get it. . . . "

There must have been some pivotal moment when not just anything could appease my taste buds. I just knew my mouth wanted dick. No substitutes. It helps that I'm gay. And I don't know why, didn't care really, but everybody around me wanted to know why, except for the thousands of married men I sucked off, they didn't care either. "Boy, if my wife could do this. . . . " Look, you're not proving anything by having a wife or girlfriend, I mean, I believe you're straight, I can taste Brut, but don't compliment me by comparing me to your wife. Of course I'm going to suck your dick better, because I want to. I'm not obligated to servitude like your spouse.

And after meeting hundreds of thousands of dicks, you'd think I'd have grown tired, despondent, "you've seen one, you've seen them all," right? Whoever said that must not have been looking. Millions of dicks and never one the same, even on twins. Each guy wears his differently. Like snowflakes. Absolutely magical. It still seizes and moves me, the mystery of arousal. What have we here? Hello! To see his meaty piece rise to the occasion. I know it's just filling with blood, but I continue to marvel.

So, when's the circle jerk start? Recovery? Recovery from what? What's that . . . can I go a day without dick? Why would you want to, man? Wait a sec, you want me to abstain from cock for how long? Three months? I'm not vegetarian, Cher. You trying to kill me? And no jacking off? Get real, I'm here because I thought you guys liked dick. You love cock but you should be able to not have any. Give it to me! *There's more to life than sex.* Ain't that a kicker? I fucking hate that, like it's some profound truth everyone subscribes to in blind faith, "the final word" that stops talk-show hosts dead in mid-sentence. "White Men Can't Jump," "Jesus is Lord," "Toronto the White, I mean the Good." "Mommy, why can't I have all the dick I want when I grow up?"—"Because I said so, now stop all this dick talk and eat your Kraft dinner and canned peas like a good boy." There's absolutely no data to substantiate that there's more to life. None. In fact, I'm willing to bet all of life that really matters comes from unceasing, limitless creative acts of sexual delights, and everything else is a facsimile. Sure, there's work, but why do you think they invented work? To keep people like us from pleasuring ourselves all waking hours. Now we just have sex in the workplace and they're trying to criminalize that. *Aren't you afraid of AIDS?* No, I'm not afraid to live. *It shouldn't rule your life.* Man, I could think of worse rulers: Reagan, Mulroney, the Pope. . . . The Pope goes around pretending he doesn't have a dick, look how fucked up Catholics are. If you guys are religious, why don't you simply worship what you say you love. My dick could use a little. Hey! What happened to that crosstalk rule, it's my turn to speak. You want me to leave. What, you scared of a little dick? Me, too! Okay, I'm going. You guys abstain yourselves until after the meeting. I'll be in the park seeking rulers.

Catherine Lake

Chambers

Ten minutes before the bell and she sits leaning against the giant garage door in the jutting-out corner where the wind swirls past. Even on the coldest days, the wind never reaches this area, or at least she's not yet felt it. She signed in early and now sips her coffee, slowly mediating with drags of her cigarette. This way, when the buzzer goes, she can take those extra sixty seconds to complete her morning solitary ritual.

Another company's Mack trucks are lined up on the other side of the fence. These cement trucks foreshadow hills of gravel and sand stockpiled in their yard. One morning, she thinks, I should come before light, grab some tools and hop that fence. Steal one of those bulldogs that ride high upon the front of the trucks. Take a hacksaw to it if I have to. Take it home to Kate. Have something to show for a day's work.

She thinks that she has stopped feeling the need to wonder if they're going to give her any real work today, any day. She might as well be mopping up the shop. She calls it housekeeping, what they do give her. Completing maintenance checks on the guys' power tools or the shop machines: the drill press, band saw, sandblaster, whatever needs a touch of oil and a quick checkover with the wipe of a rag. This wouldn't be a problem if she was ever given the opportunity to hold worn or broken parts in her hands, assess the damage and create the remedy. But the men fix their own or the shop's or deny that a small welding is needed if it means they can do it themselves, later. Even though there might be enough work for all, the men hoard work like their own stockpiled jars of spare fasteners, always trying to appear indispensable. She knows now that she'll have to wait for one of the old guys to be forced into retirement or one of the younger ones to get hurt on the job—pull his back or get caught in a chamber with toxic gas and drop dead on the spot. A few of them she's been known to wish this on, but this or a chamber explosion is extremely rare. The city does well in preventing lawsuits.

For three months last fall she was down in the chambers, inspecting pumps, grinding off gears, shutting down water lines. Dismantling the main valves, five feet in diameter and hundreds of pounds. Using her arms, legs and shoulders, using her tools, knowledge and hands. The cool wet of the chamber; another wind shelter, another confined space. Fifteen feet down in maybe six-by-six or eight-by-ten feet. She could scurry better than the men, bend into tight spaces under pipes because she is shorter and thinner and more agile. Some of them, their guts barely squeeze through the manhole. They failed to take note of this fact however. Nor did she receive any payback for her quick willingness to lay on her back beneath a pipe or crawl on her side to inspect a pump in the wet, thick grunge of the chamber walls and floor. Her back would seize with the shock of cold water leaking out and down her neck. It was an underground oasis to her. The gears, the water, the grunge.

An apprentice's injury had allowed her to fight for the stand-in position. And so she was briefly elevated away from her usual bland labourer status, to lower her hips to the chamber's tunnelled entry so to practice, at last, the truth of her mechanical license. Kate was an ardent witness to her happiness. They spoke of babies and mortgages. She thought she had maintained most of herself and finally won—earned what she had been craving for over two years. For over two years she had swallowed her pride, washing it down with the fluidity of silence and avoidance. Skirting those boyfriend/husband questions, she ducked and shuffled past those "what's *she* doin' here" comments, thinking that her flexible endurance had finally prevailed when she was rightly chosen to join the crew whose mechanical work takes them down into the chambers.

For three glorious months her layered back sweated while her fingers reddened from the wet as she welded or grinded or simply prodded at a valve. Even when it was her day to stay up above retrieving the required tools from the truck and relaying them down, she felt proud and useful. The bright red cones diverting traffic created a border for her as she stood listening intently for calls from below while watching back the stares of passing people. Any stranger could discern her iron spine whether she was sitting on her tool box, or leaning against the truck, or especially when, with a sinewy grace, she would climb in and out the chamber's circle entrance. And in those months of evenings she had the power in her hands and the strength coursing through the whole of her body to make love with a vigorous passion. She had to scrub herself well, though, since Kate said that she could smell the chamber all over her. So first thing home, she would shower or soak. But even though the fragrant soap or bath oil could mask the scent for others, she knew herself, if she took her palms to her nose and inhaled deeply, the chamber was there—its presence deep in her pores as though that underground rush of water had always been there. She had just never known what to name it. A wet iron scent. And she loved it.

Joe Lavelle

Two Mums

It was noon when they phoned me. Their usual child-minder had been taken ill. They had to be at the workshop for 1:00 p.m. and everyone else they had contacted couldn't do it. So, reluctantly, I agreed. Anna and Peta would drop Zach off at 12:30 and collect him at 4:30.

"Thanks," said Anna, her voice slowing down, the relief audible. "He's had dinner. He'll be no trouble at all, honest."

"I hope so," I said. "What kind of things is he into?"

"Oooh, whales and dolphins, ice cream, Gerald—his teddy bear—and asking questions."

I dreaded that, the whys, hows and whos of a four-year-old. Why had I agreed? I convinced myself that it would be fine, it would be a learning experience. And, anyway, it's not as if I hadn't met Zach before.

Presumably Zach would bring along Gerald and some other items of interest. In case he didn't I looked around the house for anything that might grab a four-year-old's attention. All I came up with was a copy of *Free Willy* that John had brought from a video-tape sale at Woolworth's. That proved to be enough.

Anna and Peta showed up at 12:30 with Zach clutching Gerald and holding an ice cream cone. He kissed his parents goodbye and, after waving them into the distance, sauntered into the house. He demanded an orange squash and announced that he would be glad to watch *Free Willy,* though he had viewed it before.

I sat on the couch and he lay belly-down on the floor looking up at the TV, clutching Gerald. The opening images of the movie, orcas swimming and flipping out of the water, mesmerized him. "Wow, there's a big one," he said in his squeaky high voice. He momentarily turned around to look at me. Smiling, he returned his gaze to the TV screen.

Minutes later he jumped up and sat beside me on the couch, putting an arm around me and covering his face with his free hand. "I'm scared of the scary bits."

The soundtrack to the film became ominous and a "scary bit" ensued. When the scene ended Zach remained put.

"It's over now," I said, trying to sound comforting.

"There's another scary bit comes on again," he whispered.

"Is there?" I asked, cuddling him.

Pulling himself away slightly, he said, "Yeah, another scary bit comes on again in a minute."

He was right.

His attention to the film then waned. Sitting up and looking at me he ventured: "Joe, do you have two mummies?"

"No, Zach, unfortunately I don't."

"Why? Was one of your mummies shot dead on Aigburth Road?"

"No, Zach, I've only ever had one mum," I replied, smiling. "I know you have two mums, but I have a mum and a dad."

He looked puzzled, then said, "Like Robert. Robert has a mummy and a daddy."

"Yeah, that's right, like Robert."

"Robert said if I got two mummies who gets the spider out of the bath. But I told him. I told him sometimes Anna does it an . . . an . . . an sometimes . . . sometimes Peta does it." He smiled. "That's right, isn't it, Joe?"

"I don't know, Zach, it sounds right, though."

After a pause, he said, "It's not nice not having two mummies."

I found myself briefly fantasizing about how things would have been if Mum had taken up with her best friend Ethel or dad had eloped with Mr. Dexter, his boss at the post office.

"You're right, Zach, it isn't nice for a lot of people."

Zach changed the subject. "I'm gonna go to school soon." His voice was excited and even more high-pitched than usual.

"Is that right?" I said. "You know you'll meet lots of other children with parents like Robert's at school?"

Zach's voice metamorphosed from excitement to disbelief. "But . . . but won't there be other boys and girls with two mummies like me, too?"

"Well, yes, there'll be children with two mums or perhaps two dads too."

Zach looked confused. The tone of my voice didn't encourage him. I felt awkward. I drew his attention to the TV screen. Thankfully he duly became engrossed in the the movie. Later he requested another glass of squash and fell asleep on the floor. I carried him to the couch along with Gerald. At 4:15 he woke up. Sleepy and confused he became tearful. I gave him a hug and explained that his two mums would be there for him soon.

Anna and Peta arrived shortly after 4:30. Before departing Zach kissed and hugged me, then demanded that I kiss and hug Gerald. Gerald at least didn't complain about my facial hair.

Denise Nico Leto

Macaroni

I used to grate the cheese on Sunday. It was my job. I'd take the chunks of hard cheese—romano, parmesan, asiago, provolone—and place them in the grater my ma had clamped on the side of our kitchen table, and turn the handle on the grater over and over again. One revolution, then another. The handle was long and heavy with a wooden grip that was painted pale green. I used to have to stand on a chair to reach it. For hours I stood at the kitchen table turning that handle until mounds of snowy white cheese stood on plates and in bowls. All the women in the family would be in the kitchen making macaroni. They'd pat the flour, roll the dough, cut it into strips, and then drape the strips over the tables, the chairs and sometimes the window sills. One time after a long grating session, I wandered out of the kitchen and fell asleep on the couch. When I woke up and went back into the kitchen, it seemed like the room was covered from floor to ceiling with thin strips of fresh dough and I said dreamily, "Oh, macaroni." And that was my nickname from then on. It just stuck.

See, we didn't call it pasta. It wasn't until I moved away from the old neighbourhood that I found out what other people called it. We just called it macaroni or spaghetti, but never pasta. And my family never called me by my real name after that dreamy day in the kitchen with the long, thin noodles everywhere.

After that day everything shifted. Some unseen elemental force crept into the kitchen, swept through the rooms of the house and took us all by surprise. It started with Aunt Maria dying of cancer. Her little terrier, Leonardo, barked every day for hours and got thin and stark and never again ate much. Then he'd just curl up in a ball and shiver. Dad lost his

truck-driving job and had to start working at a gas station at night. My
brother Sal sat for hours in his bedroom doing drugs and listening to Bob
Dylan. The social worker came around and took notes with her brown
clipboard, her ruled paper, and her ball point pen. Ma stopped Nairing
her moustache because she was too worried about "making ends meet"
and "the government lady" to bother with the dark, errant hairs that
seemed to dress her upper lip for battle. There were no more lush, crowded
Sundays full of noodles and women and sauce. We ate mostly pepper
sandwiches and minestrone soup. Even the basil and oregano we grew in
old olive oil cans dried up and fell away. No one realized how much Aunt
Maria had held the family together. Without her we unravelled like a
blanket too worn and frayed to keep anything warm again.

I took to the garden. It was overgrown and dry. I weeded and shoveled
and fertilized. I knelt in the dirt and sweated over earthworms and husks
of old garlic, piles of dead things and the bright, new seedlings waiting
to be planted. I knelt in the dirt and sweated over the changes in me.
Things that were somehow familiar but unnamed. Things my family
noticed but pretended not to. I moved toward the name anyway, the fact
of the word *lesbian*. I sweated over that word. I went over every inch of
it. I dug it up and looked at the root. I liked what I saw. I saw *me* there.

While my family came undone, I came out. They thought this was part
of the unravelling, another disaster like losing a job or dying of cancer or
shooting drugs. I saw it as part of the whole, a thing beautiful and
frightening, but not disastrous or separate. Not separate from the delicate
strands of cheese falling softly into bowls or the thin strips of noodle
draped over chairs. Not separate from the opera on the radio, the
conversation always at a boiling point, the peppers crackling, the din and
swell of passion and pain around me. Different, but not separate. My
family didn't see it that way. So I had to tell them. I had to remember
everything about *our* family for them. If I could remember, wouldn't that
mean I had been there, a part of it? And wouldn't that mean I was a part
of it still?

I remembered the details, the sinew and grit of a day, the pulse and
circumstance that make up a life. Details that seem to glide by and
through, seem to be merely routine, but really are at the centre, the heart
of it all.

The way my cousin Dominic stood in the living room with his dark, thick hair falling forward as he bent over the violin and with exquisite timing played a piece of music so fierce and beautiful no one knew where it came from or what exactly to do when he stopped. The way he'd put the violin down and look up, eyes softer than mink but with a terrible, unsettled brightness about them. The way Aunt Jo and Mrs. Conti said, "bool sheet," in perfect unison when watching the evening news. The way Dad took an old beat-up, rusty wagon and washed it and painted it bright red and straightened out the long black handle and fixed the tires so we wouldn't be the only kids on the block without one. The way he came home from work angry and tired and yelled for us to get him "a cold one from upstairs, now!" We'd grab a beer from the fridge and pour it into the frosty glass from the freezer and watch the layer of white foam slowly recede into a bright gold colour. The way Ma never touched us delicately or affectionately but handled us in broad strokes and strong physical gestures. We stood still while she combed and picked and bathed. Her love hurt like the skin of a rough hand caressing the soft part of a child's cheek, but that same hand held us up and took us in so that we became as necessary to each other as food. The way Aunt Maria took to my nickname:

"Ah, Macaroni," she'd say, "you know what that means, don't you? *Ma Caroni! How very dear.* You should remember that. How dear you are. How dear this life is even when it plucks the tears right out of your eyes. The world may never know you or care like I do but *you* should always know and remember."

These are the things that never made it into the social worker's notes and these are the things I remembered while sweating and digging and planting. While my family came undone, I prayed with the dirt and the things underneath and I began to sift out the bits of bone and blood, to connect the shards of new breath, to go up from root to the damp new air. To go from little Italian girl in the kitchen turning that long, heavy handle to a young woman in a garden planting and sweating and dreaming of other women to a lesbian who could also be Italian who could actually love another woman who could love me. *A long time.*

All I could see was her mouth—round and purple and full. I was sitting in the garden in the dirt sorting and counting seeds and she was walking up the path. All I saw was her mouth. It made me think of the redness of tomatoes mixed with the strong green of the vine. It made me think of kissing and sucking, of putting her lips in my mouth and how sweet it would be. I thought of the way we used to eat tomatoes, right off the vine, and then we'd shake a little salt on the warm fruit and bite into it. I thought of what it would feel like to kiss her, to bite a little on her full lips, to taste the sweat of the salt there. I kept counting, "one, two, three, eighteen, sixty-five." I stopped.

"You must be Mac," she said.

"Yeah." I knew who she was too. Carmela Rizzo. Her family lived in the east county and had some land out there. Her Aunt Rose was about ninety now and still lived there. Carmela and I played together at the Rizzo's when we were little, but I hadn't seen her since.

She stared. I stared. Finally she said, "Where's your ma? I got something from Aunt Rose for her."

"I don't know," I said.

And she left. That was it. All the threads stopped unravelling. The tiny, fragile seeds were what suddenly made the most sense to me. And I dreamt Carmela. I ate her for breakfast. I watched her at the movies. Her image stole into my optical nerve and sat there unmoving. I took the seeds and planted them. I gave them perfect food, water, and light. Purple and green tendrils like tender strips of noodle came up and curled toward the sun.

I found Carmela at the Rizzo house standing in the kitchen. She wasn't surprised to see me. Her dark hair was short and wavy, her eyes like two olives: black and shiny. Her skin was brown with a hint of green, the colour of tree bark. She turned her head to see me and she didn't smile in the usual way, her mouth didn't turn up at the sides, it just became fuller and she moved toward me and we stood there together until I lifted my hand up and touched her shoulder. She lifted her hand as though to put it over mine, but she didn't and we stood there damp and terrified, knowing and not knowing.

This is how we were for awhile. Suspended in the heavy air of the kitchen, that central room in our lives. For us, it wasn't the closet, it was the goddamn kitchen. It kept us hovering, faithful to an idea of ourselves until that idea proved false and we were left standing in the kitchen, in love.

What kept us apart at first was the fear of a special kind of unravelling. The way the family comes apart thread by thread, flesh by flesh, bone by bone, when lesbians spring forth, push upward, come out. But the family can dry up and fall away and there will still be lesbians. They will come together and lay beneath blankets made warm with the fresh heat of their bodies and they will know. The way Carmela and I *knew* each other. The way we kissed a dark mediterranean kiss. The way we came apart and held together. Tender and purple and strong like wheat. Semolina: the heart of durum wheat. *Macaroni.*

I wonder about my Aunt Maria, about whether she would curse Carmela and I or give us her blessing. I don't know. What I do know is what I remember. The spirit of the matter. The dreamy day in the kitchen with the long, thin noodles everywhere. The smell of pungent cheese. The grater turning, always turning. Watching my Aunt Maria, once thick and round as a meatball, turn wispy and dry like a thing the wind could crush. And the wind coming in and crushing mercilessly. Leonardo barking. Months in the garden turning the dirt over and over. And Carmela who finally knew. Carmela of the mouth and the land and the sweet wheat sea. Her mouth on my mouth, our skin the skin of wine barrels, our feet tough as the hooves of a goat, our hands bare and ripe and covered with dirt, our lives spreading upward and outward. *How very dear.* I can never forget.

Shaun Levin

Inner Organs

It's so warm in here. So good to have my own place at last. No matter how small and rundown it is. I don't care how noisy it gets outside or how bad the neighbourhood is. This is mine. All mine. Must be somewhere around noon by now. The light under the door makes the cat a shadow across the room. I could lie here forever.

"Isn't that right, kitty-cat?"

Now all I need is a man who'll love me like crazy. Someone who'll wonder to himself where I'd been all his life. And say things to me like, oh, I love everything about you. I'll take care of you and be with you until the end of time.

"Happy there in the dark, kitty-cat?"

I'm all sweaty behind the knees. I could open the shutters and let in some light. I could get up and have some coffee. I could make myself useful. Don't think I make a habit of lying around here like this. I'm up at seven every morning and off to work. Cleaning houses. But it's Saturday today, so I'm entitled to my rest.

"Isn't that right, hey, cat?"

"Waa," the cat says.

"You silly thing."

I should have gone straight home after work yesterday.

"I know, I know."

Just like I planned. I should have listened to my intuition. But no. What I went there for, I don't know. I was feeling tired and hungry. I thought it'd be nice to relax and have a beer. After having spent the whole day mopping other people's floors and cleaning their shit. You've got to give yourself a treat after a hard week's work. So I went to that place.

Because I like it there, with the two regular old fogies in the corner staring into their beer bottles like crystal balls.

And there in the corner he sat. Like a king.

"Like a king, kitty-cat."

It's not like I wanted anything from him. I could have sat there just looking at him. Feasting my eyes, you could say.

"Feasting my eyes, kitty-cat."

There was something about him. The way he just sat there. Regal as anything. Made you feel it was enough to be near him.

"Hey, kitty-cat, know what I mean?"

And then they came in for coffee, the two prostitutes, like they always do.

"You know."

They nod at me and I nod back. It wasn't as if it was my first time in that place. I knew the regulars. The thin one in a tight black mini-skirt and a bright red fur coat. And it was freezing outside. And the fat one. Big meaty thighs, trudging along behind her.

"Honey," the thin one says to the guy.

He, calm, so calm, lounging there with his eyes on the TV screen. That male laziness that makes you feel weak all over.

"You're looking good," she says to him. "God, I love you. Give us a kiss. *Mpwa*."

They got comfortable. Off comes the red coat. Tug at the stockings.

"God, what a night," she says. "Dry as a pita. Cold as a witch's."

The fat one empties three sugars into her coffee.

"Honey," the thin one says to her. "Baby!"

The man is tall. His legs stretch out in front of him like he owns the place. Maybe he does. And his dark hair and his shirt bright paisley and tight. Open to the belly with a chest so muscular, laced with soft curls below a dark chin and between his nipples.

"Oh, kitty-cat."

I so wanted to feel them brush against my skin.

"Yossi, honey," the thin one says to him. "Give us some loving."

And there was something about him. Something that reminded me of my dad. I could tell he had the same. The same. Oh, he would touch me the way my father did. Hand around my shoulder. Hug me. He'd let me come up to him and he'd hold me.

He turned.

"Hey, Yossi," they called to him.

He turned his head and scanned the café. He let his eyes linger. Yes. And then away again. He'd spotted me. Seen me. I know he had. He'd looked my way. And then turned back again. But he had noticed.

"He had."

He sipped his beer. And then turned around again.

"Didn't he, kitty-cat?"

The way he turned. The way he held his beer. I just knew. The two of them following his gaze. Fat one smiling. Definitely. And he let his fingers linger. They wanted us to be together. I knew they were smiling for us. He'd let his eyes linger for longer. I could tell he would be different. He would dance with me when they played our song. He would sit on the edge of our bed and tie his laces and lean towards me before he went to work and kiss me on my forehead. My boy, he would say.

And then it all got so ugly and I wanted to get away. To get as far away as I could from that place.

"Hey! What you looking at?" he said.

"Yossi," they call to him. "Hey, Yossi!"

No one moved anymore. There's still some beer left. Just below the label. Some beer left. The bottle's covered in sweat, dripping wet. But if I moved, if I budged, he'd see my knees. See my legs shaking. Almost done. Ah, refreshing beer, cooling the insides. Better be off soon. Feed the cat. Must be hungry by now. Probably missing me. One more sip. Stop shaking. Stop stop shaking. Up up up.

"Give the guy a break," the fat one said.

It's so warm in here.

"Isn't it?"

I could stay under the covers forever. Maybe I should. Maybe I should. It's getting darker outside too. The cat finds his way easily in the dark and cuddles up closer.

"Nnnn," the cat says.

His fur up against my sweaty back.

"Yes, kitty-cat. Come to Daddy."

Judy Lightwater

Heywood Park

A large woman in a stained flowered skirt and long hair explains my past lives as we sit in her crowded house trailer, amid bric-a-brac, cat hair and dust from years of incense. A house cleaner she's not. She calls herself a psychic. Her candles, quartz crystals and faith in herself convince me this is true. In this tattered part of town at the ocean's edge, crowded with discarded washing machines and clotheslines, I don't need persuading. I want my eyes opened, my sight extended. Her trailer sits on a cement pad surrounded by old bikes and rusty car parts. At each window a clay goddess figure rests amid the clutter of better things to do.

"For centuries anger has burned in you. You were a Roman soldier who refused to fight. You killed a man as he tried to rape a woman. You have fought injustice in many forms." She looks at my face. "You and your mother have met in other incarnations. You were enemies then as now."

Her words take me back to the fifties and sixties, when knowledge was deciphering *shleppers* and *schmendricks*, and the rest of the Yiddish my parents used to disguise what they were saying. Analyzing the hierarchy of grown-ups, rated by religion and income, wasn't much of a challenge for a twelve-year-old. It all seemed very simple. Only non-Jewish men drank or were unfaithful to their wives. Of course I had no source but my relatives for such information. Poor taste in clothing, inability to get ahead, children who married badly, all these were the fates of Gentiles.

These stereotypes could have been true. Not because our Catholic neighbours threw beer cans on our lawn, but because all those Jewish people I knew appeared perfect. Even the most recent immigrants, those with accents and numbers on their arms, whose children my parents didn't want us associating with, seemed upwardly mobile and fashionably

dressed. Like us they were well-behaved, university-bound, and not overly
religious.

Appearances were the number one industry in Heywood Park. One
had to be silent, crazy, or both in order to live there. The myths of
happiness, mother love, absent but gentle fathers, and marriages made in
heaven were alive and well on those quiet streets. Green lawns, quiet
sprinklers, and the smell of steaks on the barbecue are the first things I
remember. Our house at 1770 Birchmount always had red geraniums.
They circled the shrubs and occupied orange clay pots along the window
boxes, the same every year. Our brick and shuttered home, custom-built
with post-war dollars, looks exactly as it did in 1950. The oak trees are
bigger, the elm trees have died, and the school looks smaller to me now,
but I still expect to see my pink and white bicycle in front of the house.

Each home in Heywood Park had its secrets; a web that baffles
now-grown children living out their lives in other cities. Alone at night,
flipping through picture albums that don't match their remembrances,
they wonder. Did Scott Deder ever come back? Did Denise Pinnick's
eyebrows eventually grow in? How could Paul's brother kill himself and
was he really gay? Some parents meant well; others did not. Some families
healed their sorrows. Others were not so lucky.

I was the black sheep, the dyke, the one who told the truth. I ran away,
learned to laugh, and refused to pretend. I'm the fearful one, the pene-
trated one, the outcast with whom aunts and cousins now cautiously tell
their secrets. There are many refugees from Heywood Park and I'm proud
to be one of them.

I turned forty. I owned a home and knew the price of my parents'
cranberry leather furniture. As a child I thought my family and our
furniture were middle-class. And in Madison, Wisconsin in 1959, we
were. An ordinary family with dyed-to-match carpets, a black ironing
woman, an Italian cleaning lady, one son in private school and a stay-at-
home mom.

Many were richer, much richer. There was old money, too, clubs we
couldn't join, streets we couldn't live on. Our club, the only one for us,
had a big blue pool with low and high diving boards and a quiet green
golf course. My father played twice a week, Wednesday and Saturday.
Every three years he and his golf partners traded their Oldsmobiles and
Cadillacs for new models. They parked in the driveways of Heywood Park

in the summer, one shiny car after another as I rode my bike down the hill. When the snow and cold began, they put them in double garages, shovelling their way out until their wives began to worry about their hearts.

In my fortieth year I lunched with my Aunt Loretta in a brown-panelled pancake house in downtown Palm Springs. We hadn't seen each other for five years. At sixty-five, she looked younger than my mother by more than the three years separating them. She still dyed her hair the same shade of brown and pursed her lips in exactly the same pattern she did when I was five. She hadn't tanned for the last twenty years so her skin looked like skin, not the tight drawn leather of many of her peers. I wanted to stroke the wrinkled softness of her arms. She asked if I still bit my nails or wore a bra. My answers, like our conversation, remained eternally the same.

"Are you really going to write about this?" she asked, as if I was thinking of describing my bowel movements in the *Jewish Post*. "This" was our family, the drama Loretta had been part of her whole life. She fiddled with her fork, moving around the julienned ham and cheese cubes of her chef's salad. The air conditioning was on so high I'd forgotten we were dining in the middle of the desert. She hated the dress I'd worn to impress her, but didn't say so until later in the week.

"I don't know anything about your mother. She never talked to me about anything then and we barely see each other now." She shook her head. "I always knew something was wrong at your house."

"This lifetime finds you timid compared to former selves," my psychic explains, "these protests and placards a mere trickle of a deep red rage. Your eloquent speeches and sharp wit are whimpers of an ancient knowing. Beware. You may erupt. Rivers of revenge flow through you. The evils of injustice be warned."

I walk home, filled with wonder at the knowledge of my beginnings. I drop a postcard to my Aunt Loretta, thanking her for the *mandel* bread and telling her I'll see her for Thanksgiving. On this sun-lit autumn day red geraniums still bloom in my neighbour's gorgeous garden. I nod at them—pretty in their own way, but forever destined to be my least favourite flower.

L.D. Little

First Love

Graham first fell in love on the morning of his fifth birthday. Beneath red circus-train wrapping paper, inside a just-right box, nestled a set of handsome books. "With love from Mommy and Daddy." A hard shiny cover, a waft of new ink. Graham stared at the delicate line drawings of a boy in a summer camp hat, short pants and reaching-up socks.

"Who is this boy, Mommy?"

"That's Christopher Robin, dear."

Graham would collect dandelions to plant in a pretty garden in his sand box or make a nest in the garage, hiding from the bad boys up the street. He would look up to see Christopher Robin, blue eyes under a halo of curls, asking in earnest courtesy, "May I play, too?" Graham would stand and extend a hand (palm up, as his mother would) and say, "Christopher Robin, I'm so glad you've come. Please, will you stay to tea?"

With his sister's doll china spread out on a towel on his bedroom floor, he and Christopher Robin would offer each other peanut butter sandwiches. (Often, they would invite Graham's bear, Winnie, to join them, he being a mutual friend.) And they chatted about the best colours for weaving construction paper mats and what a good idea it would be to have a real live kitten.

Or sometimes they would visit the zoo animals who lived beneath the backyard elm and feed biscuits to elephants and pandas and saucy parrots, brighter than whole baskets of crayons. When Graham was sad they would curl up and whisper secrets until the sadness grew soft and warm.

Sometimes after dinner Graham and Christopher Robin would hide behind the big chair in the living room and peer out at Graham's father as he sat with his newspaper and his coffee. Every now and then Graham got near enough to his father to smell the sweet lingering peppermint of his breath. Graham would suck the sweet breath deep into his lungs and hold it, as if it were a gift, until he felt lightheaded.

Walking home from school, Tommy Harper and his friends jostled Graham off the sidewalk and yelled "fairy-boy" in his ear. They punched him and when he fell to the gutter, scraping his arm and cracking his lunchbox, they ran away, laughing.

In his room at home, picking tiny gravel teeth from his palms, Graham sobbed and hugged Christopher Robin. "Daddy says we have to be tougher." He struggled to speak sternly to Christopher Robin. "We must be 'proper' boys," he said. Then Graham put his lips next to Christopher Robin's ear and whispered very quietly, "Daddy doesn't like us."

One snowy afternoon he and Christopher Robin arranged his sister's dolls into a choir on the rec room couch, propping songbooks in their laps. "Now, girls," explained Graham, "Christopher Robin will play the piano and I will direct you in a beautiful song."

Graham's father filled the doorway. His eyes seared through the line of dolls and bored into Graham. He gripped his son's arm, shaking him. His eyes spit anger and something else, sharper and deeper, Graham did not understand. Graham's knees wobbled.

"Goddammit!" he hissed. "Play with the *real* boys!" Winnie the bear went crashing into a porcelain lamp. Emptiness exploded in Graham's chest. Christopher Robin ran and hid in Graham's bedroom closet. He would not come out.

Graham tried hard, all the time, not to think about Christopher Robin. He sat on the little stool in his room, with his fists pressed against his eyes and tried until his head hurt. At night when Graham cried into his pillow Christopher Robin would sneak out of the closet and slide silently into bed beside him. "Christopher Robin, please don't go away. Please go. Don't. Please? Please?"

Michael Lowenthal

Day of Atonement: Confessional

For the sin we have committed before thee by unchastity:
And for the sin we have committed before thee with utterance of the lip:
And for the sin we have committed before thee by deliberate lying:
For all of these, O God of forgiveness, forgive us, pardon us, grant us remission.

It wasn't deliberate lying. Nothing passed through my lips that was specifically untrue. It's a distinction, okay? Omission and commission. I'm *not* living with a lover right now.

So what if Randy's due back in three weeks? The kid didn't need to know.

I didn't lie to Randy, either. Not that I feel great about the phone call, because I don't. But he's the one who set his own trap. "Did you have sex last weekend?" Correct me if I'm wrong, but Sunday night is not the weekend. Sunday night is a school night. It's the first night of the week.

And that's the whole thing: it was just one night. Big deal. Who said we had to be monogamous while we were apart? I don't remember signing that piece of paper. Randy said it would make him more comfortable if we didn't sleep around, and I told him I wanted him to be comfortable. That's true. I don't like to see him upset. But I never said I wouldn't do it.

For the sin we have committed before thee by impurity of the lips:
And for the sin we have committed before thee by folly of the mouth:
And for the sin we have committed before thee in meat and drink:
For all these, O God of forgiveness, forgive us, pardon us, grant us remission.

All right. I did promise Randy I wouldn't suck anybody without a rubber. But let's be real. The kid was only nineteen. He just came out a few months ago. *He's going to be positive?*

Besides, he dove right into my crotch before I could say anything. I would have told him about our ground rules, but he was already slurping away, darting his tongue into my hole, everything. After that, it would have been rude for me to say I couldn't do the same thing. I'm not into all that top and bottom crap. If he sucks me, I'm going to reciprocate.

I didn't abandon all of my senses. I would never have put it all the way in my mouth if there had been a lot of precum. But there was hardly any in the beginning. Maybe one drop at the tip. Usually if people are leaky, you can tell from the start. He didn't start dripping until he was all the way down my throat.

In an ideal world? Sure, I might do it differently. It probably wasn't worth the risk. But do I believe for a second that Randy hasn't done the same thing? One little suck without a rubber? How long can you go without the taste of real meat?

For the sin we have committed before thee by violence:
And for the sin we have committed before thee in wronging our neighbour:
And for the sin we have committed before thee by association with impurity:
For all these, O God of forgiveness, forgive us, pardon us, grant us remission.

First off, the kid *asked* me to be rough. I would never do that kind of stuff unless a guy asked me to. He kept begging me to do it harder, harder. Make it hurt, he said; he said, I can't feel you. I'll admit I got off on it. Randy never lets himself go like that.

After a few minutes of really pounding him I pulled it out as a tease, to make him want it even more. I love to see a guy's hole pouting like that, like a baby's mouth when you take the pacifier away. That was when I saw the streaks of blood mixed with the smears of shit on the rubber. I would have stopped if he wanted me to. I don't want to kill anybody.

"What if there's blood?" I said.

The kid got this intense ecstatic look in his eyes, like a teenager hitting the bonus round on a video game, his eyes focussed on the lights dancing across the screen. "Make it bleed," he said. "Make it all come out."

So I shoved it back in, even harder this time. I pulled his ankles tight around my neck and lifted him off the bed. Then I fucked him straight down, imagining my cum flowing all the way into him, through his bowels, into his stomach, right up into his throat. I was filling him up all the way.

That's how I came, and it was one of those totally smooth orgasms, none of that shuddering and stuff. Which is how I could feel that the cum wasn't pooling in the tip of the rubber the way it's supposed to. You can feel it when it does, that body-warm wetness on your skin like pissing in a swimming pool. I hadn't seen the rip in the latex when I'd pulled out earlier. I guess the blood and shit had masked it with their messiness.

I had to tell him right away. That's some pretty heavy stuff. He looked at me strangely for a second before he spoke, and I actually knew then what he was about to say.

"What do I care?" he said. "I'm already positive."

When I got home, somehow I forgot about it enough to sleep a few hours. But then I had to get dressed and rush here to the synagogue. I had promised Zaydeh I'd stay with him while he prayed. I hadn't really planned to fast; I haven't done that in years. But I forgot to grab breakfast before I left, so I haven't had anything to eat. All day I've been tasting the traces of precum in my mouth, bitter and rancid, like pennies dipped in salt water.

I can feel the place on my cock where the rubber must have pinched too tight. There's a tiny blood blister that popped and is oozing stuff. I can't remember if it burst open during the sex or after. My throat is sore. It feels like the lymph nodes, but it could be just from chanting all the Hebrew with its harsh consonants. I'm dizzy, too. Is it the fasting, or the beginning of something much worse?

I just hope I make it through until they blow the shofar. Not that I really believe in this religious stuff, but it's kind of like an insurance policy. If I last until sundown, maybe that proves I mean it when I say I'm really sorry.

For the sins for which we are liable to the penalty of death by the hand of heaven:
For all these, O God of forgiveness, forgive us, pardon us, grant us remission.

Lori Lyons

Flesh

The yellow incandescence of a forty-watt is a poor approximation of the pulsing white light of a dance floor. Still, she practices playing seductress in the bedroom mirror. Beside her a heap of rejected images twist in a pile. Slinky silks and kinderwhore cottons mock her attempts to cast a spell that will carry her confidently into the world of waiting women. Flesh pressed to overflowing in black nylon, she poses trying to believe her provocative stares. Wanting to create a seductive image, she settles for a cute one, then settles again for one that doesn't make her cringe at a ridiculous fat woman daring to dress for seduction. She needs to believe tonight. Believe that the women she watches, watch back.

She is not stupid to the game. She knows that the women she watches are not perfect. Knows that she is lured by quick smiles and confident flirtations more than perfect breasts or lithe bodies. Knows that the women she wants most, most often resemble the woman she loves last. Wants them, lusts for them, because their angular faces remind her of Angie sighing and thrusting above her. Wants them because memory mixes with imagination when she imagines nuzzling the soft curve of their bellies as they lay sprawled before her. Her desire is motivated by memory and by soft secret glimpses of possibility, but her desirability? That springs from different memories.

Grade school taunts and teenage rejection. Well-meaning adults who talked about her pretty face. The gym teacher (classic dyke icon) who said she did really well for someone her size. All the people who never thought she was lesbian, who never wondered why she didn't have a boyfriend since it was obvious. The ten-minute workout women on TV doling out guilt and arousal in a vicious mix. Dykes in the bar hitting on Angie because they must just be friends. Not to mention all the friends who could never consider being her lover.

Stuff it all inside. Pressed as tight as breasts in a bustier with just enough exposure for alluring vulnerability. Find the attitude, the desire that is strong enough to mold her wounded self into a seductive form. Fat girls understand that the sexiest thing a dyke can wear to a bar is an air of carefree resilience. There is no pay-off in showing too much hunger. Lesbians are strong and rebellious and powerful. We take enough shit living day to day. There are therapists to tell your troubles to. In the world of the bar, love thrives on a fuck-you attitude. There is no room for her daylight vulnerabilities.

Two quick strokes of black and eyes flash defiant in the reflecting glass. Soft smooth exaggeration of the mouth and lips glisten a seductive red. The masquerade is beginning. Tonight, the hurts of a thousand other nights are buried. The shy hesitations of being too fat, too ugly, too mediocre are buried deep inside the flesh she so often despises.

Smile at the mirror and catch a cab, darlin'. It's the witching hour. Wrap yourself in the cloak of dyke magic, flaunt the illusive power of sex and rebellion. Try to forget that witches frequently get burned.

Judy MacLean

Tee Attempts to Break Up with Me for the First Time

She waited until after dinner to tell me. A good dinner, too, that she had cooked, pasta with a spicy eggplant sauce. Tee was not a vegetarian, but I was, and she had learned to make some wonderful things for me. Now, she was saying she wanted to split up.

"It's not you, it's me. You're older than I am, you're a more experienced lesbian, you're more athletic, you're smarter, and people look up to you."

She had often said those things about me. I always answered, "People who are older, more experienced lesbians, and more athletic deserve to have a lover, too." I wasn't going to concede smarter. And the part about people looking up to me was an exaggeration.

I was a disc jockey at a rock station and I had a women's music show on a little non-profit station. People at the rock station knew I was gay, but I never mentioned it on the air. I *did* mention it on my other radio show, and once, when I gave a speech at the Gay Freedom Day Parade, I got introduced as "the only out lesbian disc jockey in the whole USA." But people looking up to me? Lots of people think disc jockeys are superficial.

"I'm still in love with you," she said. "But if I were a man, I'd say I'm becoming impotent. Being with you, I feel worse and worse about who I am. I can't let it go on. I'll fade away to a nobody."

I was her first woman lover, her first lover of any consequence. Tee had strong features, decisive black eyebrows. She should have been able to tell she was a dyke when she was thirteen, just by looking in the mirror, instead of having to wait for me to teach her ten years later. Now she looked all sparkly through my tears. When we met, her name was Tammy. I thought Tee suited her better. It was stronger, had more *panache*. It was definitely more dykely. So then she was Tee to everybody.

I couldn't believe she wanted to leave me because of my good points. I told her how illogical she was being, but I couldn't seem to change her mind. Finally I said, "All right, all right. I guess I'll go home now."

"No, you can stay. It's late. It's too far."

It wasn't. I lived four blocks away.

We went into her bedroom and undressed silently, on opposite sides of her bed. It was awkward in a way it had never been, not even the first time we made love. Then, she had been clumsy, but avid. I lay down stiffly, close to my edge of the bed.

Tee rolled over and folded her body around me, her breasts against my shoulder blades, her knees nestled behind mine, her nose in my hair, like she had done hundreds of times before. But now it felt strange.

"Tee," I said, "Tee? In your definition of splitting up, do we still get to do this?"

William John Mann

Tricking

It's such a queer word: tricking.

As if tricks were the opposite of treats—unpleasant, distasteful, toxic to the system—instead of what they are. Tricks are the caramel on the apple, the cinnamon in the twist, the cotton candy on the stick when all the ducks have been shot down. Tricks are how we treat ourselves. Not that all tricks are always so delectable: some of mine have been the proverbial rocks in Charlie Brown's paper bag. But most of them are sweet: Hershey's Kisses. Milky Ways. Almond Boys.

Tonight, it's his nipples that enthrall me, little pink cones in relief against sweat-dappled copper skin as he moves in a rhythm that seems to ignore the beat on the dance floor. He wears cut-off shorts but no belt, a vest but no shirt, boots but no socks, a grin but no smile.

It has been a summer of random magic, of surprising spirits conjured up between the sheets of my bed in my room overlooking Provincetown Bay. Strangers' kisses have exposed souls to me. The uneven scar on one boy's abdomen and the crinkles at the corners of another's eyes have revealed more truths than I could have ever discovered in a more consistent lover.

It is the last summer in which I am to be young.

"Going tricking?" Javitz had asked me, earlier tonight, in that voice that knew the answers to its own questions. I just laughed.

Tricking. Such an odd little twist of a word. As if I would take one of these boys home with me, and rather than sex, I'd pull a rabbit out of a hat. As if we'd get to my door and I'd refuse to let him inside, instead turning to him with a maniacal grin to say, "Tricked ya!"

Tricking.

Do gay men still trick? someone asked not long ago. Don't be absurd. This is the way it is.

"Hi," he says to me.

He strokes his stomach idly; little beads of sweat, succumbing to gravity, leave shimmering trails down the smooth brown flat plain. He can't be more than twenty-three.

"I've seen you around," he says. "I'm here for the summer, got a job until Labour Day. You work up here?"

"No," I say, which is a lie. Mystery helps in this town—especially when you're no longer twenty-three. "Are you a houseboy or a waiter?" I ask, knowing the options for a boy his age.

"A houseboy," he says.

And so, the script stays on course—except for the brief flutter of my eyelids at that precise moment when I catch the eye of a man across the dance floor. My breath catches, and I worry that the houseboy notices. But he doesn't—of course not: he's deep into character. To acknowledge my distraction would be akin to an actor on stage responding to the laughter of the audience in the middle of a scene. He carries on, as is proper, but I stumble, drawn by the man across the room, a man who isn't really there.

Now when I was just a boy, my mother told me a riddle that terrified me. It went something like this: "A girl is put in a room with no windows and only one door. That door is locked from the outside. There is nothing in the room with the girl but a radiator. Later, when they open the door, the girl is gone. What happened to the girl?"

The answer: "The radiator."

The radi *ate her.*

Somehow that riddle has popped into my head now, sitting here on Javitz's hospital bed, the snow rattling the windows. Javitz is my ex-lover, and he's sick. You know what from. He's forty-seven—a terribly old age for me to contemplate ever being (I'm thirty-two). Yet the alternative remains much more disturbing.

I'm sitting here now, on the edge of his bed, remembering my mother's riddle, and Javitz asks me if I'm going tricking tonight.

"The snow's too bad," I tell him.

"Never stopped you before," he says, and he's right.

"What's your name?" he's asking.

"Jeff," I tell him. "And yours?"

"Eduardo."

We shake hands. Our eyes hold.

And so, another one.

Loving strangers is a heady mix of romance and reality, the sordid and the sublime. I have returned this summer for that dapple of sweat across a boy's bronzed back, for the magic that happens when the two of us marry eyes across a dance floor and become forever young.

"Can I still get away with it?" I'd asked Javitz before I left, as I always do.

He laughed. "Maybe for another year."

"And then what?" I asked, trying to mask the honesty of the question.

"You're full of riddles," he said.

"Here's one for you," I offered. "A girl is put in a room with no windows and only one door—"

Javitz doesn't go with me to the bar. Not since he witnessed one man—near fifty, near bald—asking me if I wanted to go home with him. "No," I demurred.

"No," he echoed. "Of course not. Nobody cares about an old man in this town." He visibly slumped, shoulders sagging, like a tire slashed.

A boy beside us began to giggle. "They're going to find him washed up on shore in the morning," he whispered to me.

And they might as well have. The man was already dead.

Growing old is not for sissies, Bette Davis once said. But sissies *do* get older. All of us sissies here tonight, with the hot juice of youth in our veins. Some of us are already well on our way. Some of us are going to die, long before our times. But what does it matter, Javitz says. Get old or get AIDS: take your choice. The end result is the same. Especially here, in this place: this place of smooth pectorals and shaven torsos, heads full of hair and bodies jumping with T-cells.

"How old are you?" Eduardo asks, as if it were the next logical question in our conversation.

"How old do you think?"

"Twenty-eight?" Last year, it probably would've been twenty-six, but it's good enough; it's what I want to hear.

"Around there," I lie. "And you?"

I can feel the eyes of the man across the dance floor, the man I spotted earlier. He is from my class: those eager-eyed young men ready to embrace the world with their feathered-back hair and wide ties whose faces, even now, stare eternally in black and white from the glossy pages of our yearbooks. He can hear my conversation with Eduardo. I'm certain of that. I wonder what he must think of me, out here as he once was, like they all were, pumped from the gym, lying about their ages, ready to fuck. That's what the fear has become: not that I too may die, but that I'll go on living, by myself. Except, of course, for the children. And always, more of them.

"Twenty-two," Eduardo responds.

And every summer, a new crop is twenty-two, standing on the cusp of the dance floor as if they were the first ones ever here.

The snow blasts the windows again. Javitz is asleep now, and I'm still trying to figure out why my mother's riddle so terrified me all those years ago. I think it was because it didn't make any sense, and mothers were *supposed* to make sense. The riddle was utter nonsense, and that's ultimately why it scared me so.

I mean, if what happened to the girl was that the "radi" ate her—what is a *radi*? If those syllables had had some double meaning—like, for example, slang for rhinoceros—it would have carried some logic that, in my opinion, would have made the riddle much more clever. But "radi" means nothing, so how could a "radi" eat her?

Thus I had this image of this malevolent radiator coming to life like some mad creature dreamed up by Stephen King. Its hot burning iron would have elongated into claws, straining against its bolts. Breaking free, it would have pounced upon the girl, looming over her just before consuming her with its steaming mouth.

But now, as I sit here and watch Javitz drift in and out of his unnatural sleep, I think that the reason the riddle so frightened me was not so much the monstrous radiator, but the image of the poor girl being shut up in a room with no windows, with nothing to do, with no way to get out—abandoned, left to die, forgotten. They put her in there and left her all alone, defenseless, against that evil radiator. And my mother had the nerve to ask: "What happened to the girl?"

Hah. As if she didn't know.

David May

Died of Love (An Excerpt)

Ron Phelps is used to casual discussions about death. He is even used to speaking in normal tones instead of whispers, whether on street corners or in the gym, about the subtle nuances of his own health status: T-cell counts, ratios, tiders, prophylactic treatments, antivirals. Even at parties he and his friends discuss the latest experimental treatments with the same enthusiasm they once had for hallucinogens. But Benjy Bentanno's insistence on asking Ron pointed questions about which support group he has joined while they are at this particular party, which is nothing more or less than an orgy (condoms required), seems somewhat out of place. Still, he answers Benjy as casually as he might answer any other question, telling him not only the support group's name and location but the facilitator's name as well. Benjy, who Ron knows has been widowed twice, nods sagely at this information. Where Benjy's life mission had once been (in his own words) to "collect husbands," it is now to assist other men, whether or not they want his assistance, adjust to widowhood. He does this by encouraging the partners of ailing men to join support groups to prepare themselves for the inevitable, after which he promotes grief groups with the sort of passion Ron generally reserves for an exceptional pizza.

Ron has known Benjy for something like fifteen years, since that long ago era Ron wistfully alludes to as "the Party." Benjy had been famous then for being both beautiful and sexually available. He is still handsome, Ron now notes to himself, though heavier. But like many great beauties, Ron knows from personal experience that Benjy is a boring bed partner, one who passively waits to be pleased, challenging his lovers to impress him. Initially flattered at the attention, Ron was like most of Benjy's playmates, eager to please the god-like beauty he had unexpectedly found himself in bed with; but just as quickly, he lost interest in Benjy's languid kisses and bored caresses. It was then that Ron decided that a man's kiss told him all he needed to know in terms of sexual compatibility. Bobby's first kiss, for instance, had been perfect. Six years later, Bobby was still Ron's favourite kisser, even if they seldom kissed anymore.

Bobby was also invited to the party, had even planned on coming tonight, but had felt too tired, too weak from days of constant diarrhea. Ron was glad that he could come himself, that Bobby hadn't insisted on him staying home (as he knew the ailing lovers of some of his friends had done) to share his misery. Bobby will be asleep when Ron gets home, he knows, asleep under more covers than Ron needs himself, with the cat and the dog nestled on either side of him.

"This is your first time, isn't it?"

At first Ron thinks that Benjy is talking about the party, an odd assumption considering their shared history. Then he realizes that Benjy is talking about losing a lover to AIDS. It's disconcerting to Ron to think of his dying spouse as one in a series.

"First and only," he answers. "I never lived with anyone before Bobby."

Benjy nods, suddenly and obviously distracted by a man he sees across the room. Ron decides that the moment is not to be wasted and makes his escape with a "See you" and heads downstairs to the basement where the action is.

This particular safe sex party is a monthly event in the home of someone Ron knows only slightly, but has nonetheless known for years. He guesses that they had sex at some point, but so much remains unclear from those years called "the Party." Or perhaps the two of them only assume they've had sex since they saw each other everywhere they played before 1982, and so began greeting each other in the street with a nod and a hello that implied more than either of them actually remembered. Even now, Ron is unsure of his host's name, though this knowledge is less relevant than his ability to chip in five dollars at the door and bring a six-pack of his choice.

In the basement, on piles of pillows, sagging couches and old mattresses, or standing in dark corners, groups of men are engaged in the sort of explorations they once all took for granted, but now require so much extra paraphernalia. Condoms (both lubed and unlubed) are everywhere, in candy dishes and ashtrays; rubber gloves lay neatly in their boxes on tables along side spermicidal jellies and clear plastic wrap. They are taken as much for granted now as cans of Crisco and bottles of poppers had once been. These changes are remarkable, Ron is well aware, but more important to him is the preservation of this society of men, men who seek comfort and pleasure in each other, men who touch and are touched, who can reach across the chasm that separates them to kiss and be joined for however many moments it lasts. Bobby calls it "making new friends." Ron smiles to himself as he thinks of it, smiles and makes eye contact with another man who smiles in return, thinking the smile is for him. And then Ron realizes who he is.

"Hi, Ron."

"Hey, stud-muffin! You've grown a beard. I like it."

The beard in fact had kept Ron from recognizing Ken immediately, and it was his tattoo (the name of a now deceased lover etched forever across his right deltoid) that alerted him to Ken's identity.

"Yeah?"

"Yeah," says Ron, stroking the new beard.

They kiss.

They haven't seen each other in months, and that had been at this very place. They'd met as soon as they'd made eye contact that night and were rolling around on a couch a minute later. So shamelessly had they coupled on that couch, so oblivious had they been to anything but each other and their mutual desire, that Benjy had dubbed Ken "Mr. Couch," and has referred to him as such ever since, but only when there is an audience to regale with fabricated details of Ron's brazenness.

They collapse onto a nearby mattress amid their own laughter, kiss for a very long time, and strip off each other's clothes. There is no negotiation, no question as to who will do what to whom. Their bodies collide. Ken fucks Ron. They come together. Covered in each other's sweat, they remain lost to the world, kissing each other often, laughing out loud. What neither recognizes just yet is that they are both relaxed, completely at ease, for the first time in months.

Ken wrestles Ron down, both of them laughing. Still damp with sweat, they slide against each other easily, indulge in prolonged kisses, and begin again.

It's almost a shame, both think, that we didn't meet before. I could've been just as happy with him. Maybe. . . .

But neither dares to finish the thought, even privately. Instead their bodies speak for them, frightening them both with their intensity, but not frightening them enough to keep them away from each other.

Later they kiss goodbye, each calculating in his head just how soon he can arrange another meeting without appearing too needy.

Tom McDonald

Louis & Willie

Louis is banging on the bathroom door, loud and steady.

"Come on, Willie, he says, "I ain't playing around now."

I don't think he's gonna try to knock it down or nothing. He ain't that mad. He just wants to slap me around a bit, show me who's boss. But I ain't in the mood for his shit today. I keep an extra pack of cigarettes in here so I can at least smoke. He'll get tired and go away, but it's hard to tell when. Sometimes he gives up real easy. Other times he keeps banging and banging. Now he's telling me he's gotta go to work and needs to shower. I don't believe him. Just last week he used the same line and I got myself a black eye from it. Looked real stupid. Even yesterday I was sitting at school with a fat lip 'cause I mouthed off to Louis and he just backhanded me.

"Come on, baby," Louis says to me in a deep, sexy voice he knows gets me going inside. "I ain't gonna hurt you. I just wanna talk to you, Willie."

I smoke and wait.

"Come on, Willie," he says. "I gotta piss real bad."

He can use the sink if he wants, like I've done lots of times 'cause he's in the bathroom being stupid. One time he got me in the kitchen and kept tickling me and jabbing at my sides 'til I pissed right in my pants. His friends were over hanging out, getting high, and they kept laughing as I cleaned my piss off the floor.

I hear Louis pee in the sink, a real long piss. Then he yells, "You gonna have to come out sooner or later, Willie, and I ain't gonna forget this time!" I hear him mutter, "Make me piss in the sink, motherfucker." Then everything's quiet. I wait a long time still, just in case.

Today's fight was dumb 'cause I didn't do nothing. Angel's right when he says we gotta put college first or else we ain't gonna get no place. So I stayed all night at Angel's studying, which is cool, 'cause it's just his moms and his sister and her two kids, and they all went to sleep early so we got to hang out all night and work 'cause I need lots of help with my writing and Angel needs lots of help with his math. We fell asleep on the couch and when I woke up I realized I forgot to tell Louis I was spending the night, not that he cares half the time but this time he sure did, 'cause when I got home he was still up, drinking rum and acting real stupid, macho and shit.

"Where you been?" he says to me. His jeans were loose, down around his thighs, the tops of his boxers showing. He didn't have no shirt on, turning me on 'cause his chest and stomach is so fine. But he had crazy eyes from coke and he was drunk but too wired to sleep.

I tell him where I been and why. He don't like that. Now he don't like none of my friends, but Angel he really hates, 'cause Angel don't take no shit from him. And Louis hates me being in school. He tells me when he ain't drunk or high that he's proud of me for going, and he helps me out with the bills 'cause I only work part-time. But he's scared that the academy won't call him and he'll have to be a security guard the rest of his life and I'm gonna be a doctor and he don't like that at all.

Ralphie, who lives in the building I grew up in, told me Louis was no good, but Ralphie likes my shit. Not that I don't like his, but Louis, man, let me tell you! Angel says I just stay with him 'cause he's so good looking which nobody can say he ain't 'cause he is fine, fine, fine, but I love him and he loves me and all this crazy shit between us ain't gonna last 'cause I know it's just 'cause he ain't got called to the academy yet and he's just partying too much and it's gonna work out 'cause you got a feeling inside you when you know something's right between two people and I got that feeling.

I flush my cigarette down the toilet 'cause I can hear him snoring. I open the door and sure enough, he's in bed, asleep, in his boxers, his cock hanging outta the fly. I undress and climb into bed. I give the head of his cock a kiss 'cause I love his cock just like I love him and then I kiss him on his lips. He don't know what's going on 'cause he's out for the count. But I do it anyway. Then I just crawl up next to him, pull up the sheets, and hold on tight.

Susan B. McIver

To Leave and to Cleave

a woman shall leave her father and her
mother and shall cleave unto her wife
—Genesis 2:24 (paraphrase)

Breaking up required twelve years, four continents, one poet, and Rebecca's dream. All in all it was quite an undertaking that left us well travelled, older, and not a bit wiser.

I was thirty when we met. Rebecca was forty. I'd always thought that forty was the prime of a woman's life. Rebecca was certainly in her prime: cute as a button, peppy, with enough of a past to be enchanting, and brimming with possibilities of the future.

At the time I was a professor. Rebecca was a student who had come back to university for a year's refresher course. She dropped by my office one day after returning from a weekend's visit home. "I brought you some of my homemade jam," she said, handing me the jar. It was the first time I had noticed her warm brown eyes and generous smile. A few months later we became lovers.

At the end of the school year Rebecca left to resume her job and former life in a rural community amidst a large family composed of an elderly father, brothers and sisters, and their children. That summer I made the first of many visits to her home.

The next summer we went to Europe. It was then that I recognized the first two of what would become the three axioms of our relationship. Axiom No. 1: Rebecca was an excellent travelling companion. Axiom No. 2 was the inverse sex: home distance ratio, that is, the farther away from home, the better the sex. Together these two axioms made for great memories.

Axiom No. 2 had a shadowy corollary, namely, sex happens only in the dark and is never mentioned the next day. I certainly wouldn't have instigated this arrangement, but I could live with it. After all, it's easy enough to go to bed early and it's a heck of a lot better to do and not talk than to talk and not do!

It was the last one that got us. That was the 3-F axiom: Family, First and Foremost. The idea that life didn't have to revolve entirely around your biological family had never occurred to Rebecca. When I suggested that we could establish our own home, she replied, "Are you crazy?"

Our lengthy break-up started the first time I was confronted by 3-F. That was well into our third year. By that time I'd learned not to talk about what we did in bed and since what we did kept getting better, silence was indeed golden. So, as we lay satiated in Rebecca's bed one morning, I was surprised to hear her say, "I can't go on. It's not normal." I snuggled closer. She pushed me away. "What will my family think?" she said, jumping out of bed. "I want to be just friends." We were friends all day through the evening. Then we went to bed and I touched her breast. Suddenly I had a whole new appreciation of friendship!

The next twelve years were a tug of war between No. 3, Family, First and Foremost, and my ever hopeful persistence in trying to convince Rebecca that she could have a life and a love of her own. We continued to travel. Somehow though I seemed to lose ground with each trip. I stopped tugging in Hong Kong. We were sitting on the balcony of our hotel room, sipping gin and tonics, and watching the sun set in the harbour. "It's been a wonderful holiday," I said, reaching for Rebecca's hand. "It has," she replied. She gave me a tender bittersweet look and right out of the blue said, "You should find yourself another lover."

By the next spring I was madly in love with a flamboyant young poet. I called Rebecca to tell her what I assumed would be welcome news. There was a long pause. "You must be glad I did what you wanted," I continued. Silence.

My poet phase lasted two years. Afterwards I reflected on what to do. Perhaps Rebecca had changed? Would she now be willing to enter into a committed, guilt-free relationship? Familiarity does have its attractions, so I picked up the phone. Rebecca was delighted.

For a while I had hopes for our reestablished relationship. Rebecca was as good a travelling companion as ever and she had lost her inhibitions:

we made love day or night and even talked about it. Then while basking in the sun on a California beach I leaned over and nuzzled her neck. "What would you think about a visit from the Christmas fairy this holiday season?" I asked, and blew teasingly in her ear. "Me." Her jaw tightened. "But how could I explain to my family why you were coming around again after being away so long?"

Late that fall Rebecca visited me. Upon waking one morning she said, "I dreamt we were going on an extended trip to someplace really foreign. Saudi Arabia. We'd planned the trip for a long time and the night before we were to leave I told you I wasn't going." My stomach knotted. Her dream was our relationship. She gave a little chuckle and said, "The funny thing was I knew all along I hadn't intended on going." I thought I might retch over the side of the bed. "Do you realize the significance of that dream?" I asked. Hopping out of bed Rebecca quipped, "Significance? It was only a silly dream." I looked at the ceiling. No. 3 was up there smirking at me. I knew he'd win. And he did.

It's been over twenty years since Rebecca gave me that first jar of jam. She has yet to leave her family.

I now live an open life and cleave unto my wife, Anne.

Ian-Andrew McKenzie

Songs and Gardens

I used to play the William Tell Overture for him. I never really cared for
Rossini, but the song was one of Noah's favorites. He said it made him
feel rugged, young and happy. To me, he already was quite rugged, with
his masculine good looks and wild, thick hair. He looked like a rogue,
and he carried himself with confidence and health. Whereas I was
generally quiet, Noah made his own vibrant noises: my name shouted
raspily through the house upon his arrival, or his boots on the hall floor
as he marched toward our bedroom. When I was strong enough, I would
answer his hearty sounds with the Tell overture and he'd smile and nod
appreciatively.

Noah told me one night that when I die he would sell my piano. It hurt
me greatly, the thought of someone pounding away at the keys without
appreciating their value. Noah tried to explain that without me there
would be no music left in the piano and it would be painful to have it stay
in the house. But I did not want to listen, so I started playing Handel
loudly. There was no heart in my playing and the notes marched out like
ruthless soldiers, orderly and devoid of emotion.

A few days later I was sick. Each breath was a challenge and I felt too
weak to practice. I found the strength only to rise and retrieve some bread
and a grapefruit from the kitchen. I took my food to the night stand by
the bed, placed it there, and climbed back in under the covers. Noah was
pulling his clothes on. I could see by the lines in his forehead that he was
deep in thought. I asked him where he was going, but he ignored me. He
pecked me on the cheek and swept from the room, his footsteps heavy on

the wooden floor of the hall. When I heard the front door slam closed, I started playing a weak sonata, but only in my mind.

The following week, my strength continued to elude me. I lay in the back garden on a blanket I had dragged out with me. A breeze stirred the air and hinted that autumn was on the way. After sitting in the late afternoon sun for awhile, I heard Noah arrive home and call for me inside the house. I called back to him, but my voice did not carry beyond the garden. I figured Noah would deduce where I was and come to me, so I sat and waited.

I hummed and watched a worm writhe across the cobblestone walkway and burrow into the black dirt under a small red verbena. I watched a butterfly reject a geranium, a marigold and the proud, hearty gazanias before throwing itself ecstatically into a bank of impatiens. I lifted my chin to the moist, pungent fragrance of generous petunias. But Noah did not come.

The sky was beginning to grow dark. No familiar noises came to the garden from the house. No boots on wood, no loud, deep voice. I stood in the garden and started walking toward the back door, pulling my blanket over helpless white begonias and colourful yet masculine coleus.

I pulled open the screen and strained to hear Noah moving about inside the house, but all I heard was the old wood breathing and the doves cooing under the eaves. I was alone.

I met Noah at a costume party. He was dressed as a pirate, complete with sash and scabbard. As he spoke to the other guests, they would look at his handsome mouth and white teeth. They would scan down to his sinewy neck and his open collar, observing his dark, smooth skin and his virile chest. He caught me staring and strode up to me. "Dance with me," he said, and wordlessly I followed.

As I walked through the house, I remembered the sensation of Noah's sword handle pressing against my hip as we danced. With each step we took, it would press into me, hard and without apology. I ached at that memory and I wished not the handle but the blade had pressed into me when I found Noah's note on the piano:

"My darling,

"I have gone and will not return. I am leaving because it hurts so much to love you. I am watching you as I write this. You sit surrounded by your flowers and birds, and you watch a butterfly. I can hear you humming a song you've played for me.

"You wait for me, I can tell. But I can't bring myself to go to you. I can't stand the thought of that garden without you. I would rather leave now and remember you in the garden or at the piano. I cannot bear to watch you fade away and die, just like the flowers around you.

"I am no brave pirate. I am just a coward, so please do not be insulted when I tell you that I love you and always will.

"I'm sorry."

I looked out the window. Darkness had fallen just enough so that the flowers in the garden had lost their individual colours. I turned to the piano and pulled down the shelf so the keys could rest for the night. There was little music left in my heart, much less my hands, as I folded Noah's letter and placed it on the bench beside me. The doves' noise outside, usually melodious and warm, had lost its rhythm. I heard a gentle flapping against the window pane and looked to see a moth or a butterfly throwing itself against the glass, then it fell to the sill in exhaustion or death.

I don't know which it was, exhaustion or death. I hadn't yet discovered the latter so I didn't know how different it would be from this terrible fatigue. But I knew that as night always falls and gardens die, so soon would I.

Michael Gregg Michaud

Mad About Dietrich

Francis calls. "I need help." It isn't a question.

"Oh. Well. Okay."

"Bye." The conversation is over.

Steven's house is brightly lit, surprisingly clean, and seems to be filled with flowers. Large vases stuffed to overflowing with tuberoses in the saffron orange living room. White azaleas on either side of the hearth. And a massive arrangement of assorted, candy-coloured flowers, suitable for a winning race horse, leans against the Tibetan altar in the dining room.

Francis is standing in his jockey shorts and bare feet in the kitchen, fumbling with plastic IV bags, a syringe, and a cellular phone cradled against his ear. His skin is silky smooth and blacker than usual, set against the lemon yellow walls. The tea kettle whistles.

"Make coffee now," he says. Then he hurries around the corner into Steven's bedroom.

I heap two teaspoons of sugar into a mug of instant coffee, and step into the hall. Steven is sitting up naked in bed, watching television. Francis kneels over an end table, arranging pills on a faux silver tray.

"Hi, Steven," I smile.

He looks up, grins widely and waves enthusiastically as if trying to get my attention.

"How ya doing, doll?" I ask.

"Pretty good," he says, but he sounds out of breath.

"Thanks," Francis says. He stands up, and clicks off the phone.

"Put these on." He sounds exasperated as he tosses a pair of undershorts at Steven.

"How's he doing?" I ask Francis while he steals a quick sip of coffee in the kitchen.

"Nurse said the test was okay, but his dementia is making me crazy."

"What do you want me to do?"

"I've got to give him a bath and the food will be delivered before noon so I need you to take care of that. It's paid for, so just put it away, and we'll set it up later before anybody starts coming."

"House looks nice," I offer.

"Help me get him in the tub, okay?" He looks like he's ready to cry.

I follow Francis into the bedroom, and walk into him when he stops short at the foot of Steven's bed.

"What are you doing?" he exclaims.

"Watching Betty Grable," Steven says. His undershorts are on his head at a jaunty angle.

"Your underwear's on your head!" Francis sounds mortified.

"You told me to put them on." Steven is confused, and pouts.

"And that's Joan Crawford, not Betty Grable," Francis states, shaking his head.

After the food is delivered and put away, and Steven is bathed and put back to bed, I take Francis' hand in the hall and tug him toward his room.

"Come on," I offer, "he's asleep."

"No he isn't."

"Yes he is. Come on."

Francis is on top of me, and in me at once. His reluctance quickly disappears, and he begins to pound me, slam into me relentlessly for ten or fifteen minutes. The comforter and sheets are kicked to the floor. When he comes, he rolls off me and sits on the edge of the bed with his head in his hands for a moment.

"I'm sorry," he mumbles. "Did I hurt you?"

"You needed it."

"I guess so," he mutters as he walks slowly to the bathroom.

While we are drinking coffee and eating cold chicken wings on the patio, I hear Steven shuffling through the house. Suddenly, he appears in the doorway wearing only his diaper. His hair is standing straight up in the air. Tubes are hanging from him, and he's carrying his portable IV suitcase.

"I'm ready," he says. "When will the taxi be here?"

Francis rolls his eyes, and sighs, "I'm so tired."

I get up and lead Steven back through the house.

"We need to get you dressed, doll," I say while I'm holding him by the arm. "Tonight's your birthday party."

"Oh, really?" Steven sounds happy.

Steven doesn't know anyone at the party. He claps and sings "Happy Birthday" along with all of us, and struggles to blow out the candles on the cake. I help him open his presents, though he really doesn't understand what's going on. I sit beside him at the dining room table which is decorated with candelabras, and laden with a beautiful buffet.

Steven leans toward me and whispers conspiratorially, "Can we take some of this food home with us?"

"Sure, honey," I say, "I'll fix a bag."

After everyone leaves, and the house is oddly quiet again, Steven seems ill at ease in his surroundings while Francis struggles to unbutton his shirt. He looks desperately around the room.

"What are we doing here?" he asks.

"You're going to bed," Francis states flatly.

"How did we get here?"

Francis becomes rigid, and drops his arms to his sides. "How did we get where?"

"Paris!" Steven is now impatient.

"Paris," I repeat.

"In Marlene Dietrich's apartment. Where is she?"

"Oh, Steven," Francis sighs, "snap out of it."

I help Francis undress Steven, who pouts and laughs until we ease him into bed. Then he pulls the covers up under his nose.

After he separates that evening's pills into little rows, Francis picks up Steven's juice glass. He looks at it a moment, at me, and back at the glass. Then he smells it.

"What did you do?" he snaps at Steven. "Did you piss in this glass?"

"Just a little," Steven answers after a moment.

"You can't do that!" Francis is stern.

"Oh, it's not so bad," Steven sighs.

After Francis returns with a fresh glass of water, Steven sits up, takes his pills, and studies the room carefully.

"I can't believe this!" Steven exclaims. His mood suddenly turns to one of anger. "She's stolen all my decorating ideas!"

Merril Mushroom

At Yalla's Place—1960

My Mama's the one taught me how to do 'em," Yalla says to me. "She did eleven of 'em on herself. She always said she'da done it when she was pregnant with me, but she didn't have the thirty-five cents for the catheter." Yalla's telling me how she does abortions, one of the ways she makes a living. Nineteen-sixty was a hard time for getting abortions or birth control, either one.

Yalla works at the girl's place or in a motel room. She never works at home. She charges a hundred dollars. "It's safe enough," she insists. "There's no need to have problems. I'm clean and careful. Everything is sterile, and there's no cutting. The hard part that's so painful is getting the catheter through the neck of the womb. That lets air in. Mama says the air kills the baby, and you pass the whole thing out together, tube and all, like a miscarriage. If there's ever a problem later, the girl can go to the hospital with a miss. I do it for these girls all the time. Keeps 'em away from the butchers." The girls were glad for Yalla, too.

About then, Butchie comes strolling into the room. Just got outta bed. She tends bar all night, sleeps late in the morning. "Hey, you," she says to Yalla, walks past her.

Yalla leans forward and pops Butchie on the backside. "Hey, baby."

Butchie turns fast and yanks Yalla up out of the chair. Yalla's a big woman—tall, fat, big tits and ass. Butchie's tall too, and square built, short hair, men's clothes, of a size to look Yalla right in the eye. She does; takes Yalla under her chin with her thumb and first finger, puts her lips up to Yalla's, and kisses Yalla solid right on the mouth. Then she goes to the Frigidaire.

Yalla sits down again and looks after Butchie with her eyes all soft. I

like seeing them lovin' like this instead of fighting. Butchie bends down
so she can see inside the little, short Frigidaire and opens the door. The
top rack is all beer in bottles, lying down. The middle rack has a few more
beers standing up. That's all that's in there. No food. Butchie pulls out a
bottle of beer and pries the top off with her back teeth which makes Yalla
frown, but you could tell she's keeping quiet about it, maybe said it too
many times before and maybe Butchie hit her, told her to shut up about
it already it's her own frigging teeth.

Now Kate comes through the room from the back hallway, dudded
up, too much. "Goin' to work," she says. She grabs the bottle Butchie
holds, takes a long swig off the beer, and sets the bottle on the floor next
to the door on her way out.

"Where's she goin'?"

"Turn a trick. She be right back."

"Boys inside?"

"Watchin' TV."

Right then comes Davy, the three-year-old; Anthony's seven; Yalla's
boys. Davy picks up the beer bottle Kate left by the door, puts it in his
mouth, turns it up. "Give it here, squirt!" Butchie bellows. She grabs the
bottle away. "Can't stand when folks let a kid get the brew. I think that
is real degenerate. How about I go down and get us some Castleburgers,
huh, Dave?"

"Me too! Me too!" Davy runs in a circle around Butchie.

She snatches him up onto her shoulder. "Let's go!" Then both of them
head out the door.

Yalla and I listen to the rest of one side of "Lady in Satin," and I get
up to turn it over. "Bleee-ooo-ooo-ooo. . . . ," Yalla sings. She sings good.

Knock on door. Yalla gets up and goes over, puts the chain on. "Never
know," she says. "Who's there?" she asks, louder, at the door.

"Joan and Jennie. We met Butchie buying burgers. She says come up
and get a beer." Yalla opens the door, in they come, grab Yalla, hug her
hard, each one. "Hey, baby," Joan and Jennie say to me.

"Hey," I say back.

"Where's Kate?" Jennie asks Yalla.

"Trickin'."

"Where's Lonnie?"

"Sleepin'."

"Where's the boys?"

"Anthony's watchin' TV. Davy, he's with Butchie."

Joan opens up the Frigidaire, gets a beer, hands it behind her to Jennie. "Here, honey." Gets another, closes the door, stands up straight. She makes a prying motion with her fist next to the bottle cap.

"Over there," Yalla points to the coffee table.

Joan picks up a beer opener from the table and pops the cap off her beer, trades it with Jennie for hers, pries the cap off that one, and takes a slug. Jennie looks at her bottle, then puts it in her mouth, tips her head back, and chug-a-lugs. She hands the empty to Joan. Joan gives Jennie the other beer. "I'll get me a fresh one."

Now Butchie comes in with Castleburgers, a bagload, and Davy beside her carrying a bag of doughnuts. Butchie gives out the burgers, one for each of us. She gives two to Davy. "Take one'a these in to Anthony." Davy disappears into the other room with the burgers and the bag of doughnuts.

BANG. BANG. CRASH. BANG. People next door fighting again, Patsy screaming and cursing: YOU GODDAMN SHIT SUCKING PIG FUCKING BASTID GETOUTTA GET OUT YOU FUCKER!

"Here we go again," says Jennie.

"Old man beats her," says Yalla.

"She don't do so bad herself," says Butchie.

CRASH. BANG. CRASH.

"Lookahere." Yalla has something to show. We go in her room. There's her easel, paper on it, pastel chalks on a board next to the easel. She is working on a portrait of Butchie, and it's beautiful. It's fucking gorgeous.

"Woman's a fucking genius. . . . "

"I could *never*. . . . "

"Oh, Yalla, ain't that something!"

"Ooooooooo. . . . "

SLAM. Door slams. "Hey!" Here comes Kate back, finished working. She has Pat, Dionne and Frannie Lee with her. "Looka who I found!" They have more beer. Dionne has a reefer.

First thing Frannie does is turn up the record player.

Hot damn! We're having another Saturday afternoon party at Yalla's place!

Adrienne Y. Nelson

Neighbourhood Watch

A bonsai tree crooks its neck at the entrance gate like a nosy wild-haired woman peeping out her window. Apartment E is at the top of the stairs. I am a single woman with no children, moving in. My love life is non-existent.

A circle of black women buzz around my apartment. They offer me housewarming gifts of wooden coasters and crystal trinkets. Shirley, the radius of the circle, assures me she'll be a good neighbour. "I'll watch your back," she says. "I live next door if you need me. Never know when some crazy might be in the shadows, eyein' you. Can't be too careful."

Shirley tells me she and the others keep their men in check. Her circle glares at me sideways, making sure I get their drift. I nod, "Uh huh, I know what you mean," but go about my business, ignoring them. I have no time for heterosexuality. I long for a female lover. This longing has lasted over a year.

I decorate my apartment in purples and blues, then go to the thrift store and purchase a few pictures. The owl hanging over my stove is named Olivia. She is a stained-glass woman with wisdom. I believe she has the power to find me a lover.

After two weeks in my apartment, the doorbell rings. It is Shirley. I glance around her, looking for her circle, but she is alone. She invites me to a lingerie party. Her press-on nails flip through the pages of a catalogue, pointing out the latest in bikini underwear. She shows me a see-through teddy she'll win if she's the best-selling hostess.

"May I come in?" she asks. Her eyes squint over my shoulder, trying to make out the bean bag in the corner of my living room.

"Can't right now," I say, "I have a date."

Shirley's eyes become well-heated swimming pools, open for the summer. She looks at me as if I'm her favourite cousin on vacation, eager to jump into warm water and tell her my business. But I nudge her elbows and tell her, "Sorry, I have to go."

It seems a woman named Rachel has been eyeing me and was bold enough to ask me out. Our dinner date at a seafood restaurant turns into a midnight movie rendezvous, *The Rocky Horror Picture Show*. I have never met a black woman who knows how to chuckle, especially at silly white stuff. Rachel really turns me on. My panties moisten when I see her head cocked to one side, highlighting a seductive widow's peak.

An actor in the theatre sprinkles confetti in our bucket of popcorn. The show is almost over. I wonder when I'll take Rachel to meet Olivia.

We spend almost every day together, playing checkers and giggling at *Get Smart* episodes. Rachel and I are meant for each other. She even loves the sound of wind chimes tinkling in open doorways. Olivia smiles whenever she enters my apartment. One day, I had to wash Olivia's mouth out with Windex because she said something dirty about Rachel and I making love.

Shirley doesn't say "good morning" anymore. She stopped speaking to me after seeing Rachel kiss me. I think Shirley thought the moment our lips met was the missing piece in a jigsaw puzzle, finally forming the sky's horizon. Shirley doesn't invite me to lingerie parties anymore. She lost the way to my apartment after Rachel and I slid along each other's thighs.

I think Shirley knew the moment my drought was over, my mouth drinking from Rachel's mountain spring, making her come. I heard a casserole dish shatter in her kitchen when Rachel began to moan. Her meatloaf was probably ruined.

One morning, when Rachel and I emerged from my apartment, Shirley slammed her screen door, pretending not to see our smiles beaming, "Yes, we're lesbians." My neighbour doesn't nod her head in acknowledgement anymore. Whenever I pass by the laundry room, she forgets to scoop and measure soap powder, pouring it wildly into the machine, gritting her teeth.

Her circle has turned into vipers. Whenever they think I'm within earshot, they whisper loudly to each other, things like, "Girl, I didn't know she was funny." Rachel and Olivia hear their whispers too, but we pay them no attention and go about our business because we have no time for ignorance. Rachel and I are too busy moving her furniture in.

Lesléa Newman

The Bear

Amy bought Esther the bear in the first throes of passion, when she longed to give her the moon, the stars, the sun and the planets. What was a $200 bear compared to the entire solar system? A mere drop in the bucket, especially given the fact that it was fifty percent off at the time, and Esther was quite taken with the life-size monstrosity; the soft white fur, the big brown eyes, the pointy nose, the cute, rounded ears. So Amy dragged the bear home and propped it up in Esther's favourite easy chair in front of the fireplace, only too glad to give up half their collective furniture for a toy, if that would make her honey happy.

And it did. Esther adored the bear and fussed over it endlessly. In summer, she draped a hot pink bikini top across the bear's chest and put a beach ball on its lap. In winter the bear hibernated in style, warmed by a set of maroon and white striped mittens, hat and scarf, knit by Esther's mother. On Hallowe'en the bear wore a tall witch's hat, on Yom Kippur an embroidered cap, on Christmas Eve a long white beard.

Years passed, and passion waned, as it will. The bear now acted as a barometer: when Esther was in the mood, she dressed the bear in a see-through, lacy negligée; more often, Amy would come home to find the bear in an old, ratty sweatshirt, a bowl of popcorn and the TV *Guide* on its lap.

Time went on and things did not improve. Now, most days Amy would enter the apartment only to find the bear with its back turned toward her, and Esther's door closed. Any day now, Amy feared she would come home and find the bear gone altogether, but that never happened. What did happen was far worse: just yesterday, Amy unlocked the door to find the bear sitting in its chair with its head sliced off with a butcher knife, a steady stream of ketchup matting its lovely white fur. And Esther was gone.

Lesléa Newman

The Saviour

She fell again." The man stops walking and looks over his shoulder at a screaming pink snowsuit lying prone on the snowy sidewalk.

"Oh, for Christ's sake." The woman stops too and readjusts her bundles, pushing aside a long tube of red wrapping paper with an impatient thrust of her chin. "Can't you watch her?"

"I thought you were watching her."

"How can I hold onto her with my arms full of presents for your mother, your father, your brother, your Aunt Edna, your Uncle Charlie. . . . "

"All right, all right." The man repositions the huge box in his arms as the child continues to howl. "She wouldn't be so tired if we hadn't had to look at every single goddamn toaster oven that's ever been made. Only the best for your charming sister."

"You know, you're impossible," the woman says. "I ask you to help me with the Christmas shopping for one day. One lousy day. Now you know what I've been going through for the past two weeks."

"Well, if you wouldn't wait until the last goddamn minute. . . . "

"Well, if you didn't have so many goddamn relatives. . . . "

"Jesus, that's my fault, too?"

"I'll get her. Just hold this." The woman thrusts one of her shopping bags at the man.

"I can't. Just put it down."

The woman puts the bag down, then moves it to the edge of the slushy sidewalk, out of the path of an approaching shopper. The bottom of the bag gives way and bright red and green bundles spill onto the grey sidewalk.

"For Christ's sake, now look what you made me do."

"Jesus H. Christ." The man bends down to help the woman retrieve her packages. Neither of them see me pick up their child, hoist her onto my hip and steal away. She stops crying immediately. We turn a corner and the shrill voices of her parents fade. I think I'll name her Christie. For Christ's sake.

Laura Panter

One Bed, Two Bodies

The orgasm stays in my head like a hurricane. Its beauty and its destruction so indelibly entwined. The brevity of emotion. The way we curled into each other as if we were frightened of our own power. In one pure, perfect motion I saw love and fear, passion and death, dancing like children in soft flannel nightgowns, naïve to anything but the joy of the moment. A link to everything I had ever known. The way the complexity of my life in her became as simple as the quivering of her thighs. The way fluid ran across my cheek like an answer.

I wanted to tell her that I understood. I wanted to tell her before the vision became clouded by appointments and time. I wanted to say that I searched for her mother in dreams. I wanted to say that sometimes I saw sorrow so great it lay over her like a thick blanket, and that all I knew was to pull at the corners of its fabric. That if I couldn't take it off her, I would climb in under and lie with her. That love wasn't a big enough word for us. That the word alone is relative. That being alone just stretches distance between us, while that moment of hers stays tucked beside me; with its own heartbeat, its own life.

I wanted to tell her that I was scared. That I was giving up resistance. That death in that moment seemed simple; that forever was just the next second. That a car hurtling off the highway is just an analogy to sex. In that orgasm there was finality. That we swerved off the paved white lines and threw ourselves into the crashing dark. There was an end to what I know. What I have known. What I have ever imagined knowing. There was finally no context. There was a bed, and two bodies.

A bed, and two bodies, and nothing else.

One bed, two bodies, and everything.

Christopher Paw

Rediscovered Skylines

Thanksgiving Monday I cleaned the windows. It surprised David as much as myself when I slipped on a pair of track pants and trekked to the corner store in search of Windex. He watched in awe when upon my return, I stripped down to my Kleins, rifled through the rag pile under the sink and went out on the patio. First, I saturated the five-foot pane, wiped it down, and did it again until I discovered glass where there had only been soot. All the remnants of the external forces that had tried to penetrate our home, dissolved on contact with the blue liquid. The white rag turned black.

To do the outside of the solarium, I squeezed between the half-metre space of glass and railing. The railing was rusted and although the building inspector assured us it was well anchored in the patio's concrete, I still worried. But I was so tired of looking at the urban skyline through a film of car exhaust that I checked my fear and didn't think about the ground below.

I rearranged myself inside my grey underwear. I was wearing the metal cock-ring that keeps me in a state of preparedness. That and the sight of my David. I looked into the apartment through the sullied glass and saw him watching me. I imagined he held his breath as I leaned over, testing the limits of the rusted railing.

Below, faggots and students walked by, returning from or going to this city's gay ghetto. Although there was a cool October breeze in the air, the sun beat hard on the patio. I felt its heat on my skin. The warmth inspired erotic fantasies and I pretended that I looked as good in my underwear as I did at the dawn of the rave age. Sure, there was a little more paunch where muscle used to be, but from four floors up, no one could tell. Sucking in my gut enough to squeeze into the space, I pulled the trigger on the bottle and continued my housework adventure.

Wedged in that little space, my body responded to the imagined stares of men who passed below and the real one from my lover inside. As I leaned backwards, putting more weight on the aging rail, I smiled to myself. I remembered the time, years ago, when David and I argued. We argued a lot then, each testing the other's limits. This time I had left angrily, intent on showing him that I wasn't stuck with him. That I could do better. My rage directed me toward the bar around the corner. A couple of drinks later, it pulled me into the back room. I remembered the mixture of relief, release and remorse that accompanied the foreign blow job. I couldn't help but think of David. Though shrouded in darkness and seething with anger, I could still smell his cologne. Even the way the stranger nicked his teeth on the underside of my cock reminded me of my lover. As he led me from the dark environ, I tried to figure out how to ditch him. I wanted to run home to David, apologize and make the feeling of betrayal go away. I didn't want to be there. My judgement had been poor. I knew it. When we emerged into the relatively well-lit bar, I saw it was David who held my hand.

Luckily, he knew me well enough to anticipate my actions. His eyes had long since adjusted to the dark by the time I entered the hole. He knew what I would do. He knew how I would feel. He'd found a way to bypass my irrationality and leave my emotions intact.

By the time I finished the outside windows, my arms ached from the repetitive motion. David had moved our potted tropical forest from the windows' edges, leaving me easy access to the interior glass.

Inside, the grime was different. The glass was coated with cooking grease, dust and pollen from the plants, but mostly the windows were stained with residual cigarette smoke. The new rag turned a nicotine-stained yellow. The inside filth was more subtle than outside, though the windows were as dirty. No matter how frequently we opened them to let all the crap escape, some of it was always trapped inside. It had to be forcefully removed with glass cleaner and an ancient tattered, Golden Gate t-shirt purchased on a solitary visit to San Francisco.

I knew the shirt was bought before David and I met, but I couldn't remember whose it was. Whichever one of us bought it, I was sure it came from the Castro. Probably purchased one morning while returning to a hotel, or friend's house, having hastily left the previous evening's trick. Leaving a shirt behind because it was trapped under his legs and there was no desire to speak with him . . . to wake him up. To face the reality of what was considered the fast lane.

As I finished a pane, David trailed behind me, replacing plants to their position of optimum sunlight. Contrary to Murphy's Law, although the rag was saturated and next to useless, the last three panes, the sliding doors to the solarium, were the cleanest. The panels that move, allowing us to put one foot in the exterior world while remaining in our carefully constructed cocoon.

The rose bush, the pot plant and the Boston Ivy have climbed the one solid wall of the solarium, giving it the appearance of a green house. Somehow, in the midst of all the concrete, steel and glass, we have created a living, breathing oasis.

That night, we sat for the hour between required viewing for television addicts and rediscovered our skyline. It was brighter with the layers of smog and nicotine removed. We could clearly see through what was a blur of dirt and debris only hours earlier. We each lit a cigarette and exhaled the smoke in tandem. I watched the clouds drift to the window pane, sucked away by a tiny draft that wouldn't be noticeable until December winds would whip through the city. On the street below, a transport truck backfired. I pictured the cloud of exhaust as it rose silently, invisibly to the outside window, depositing itself on my newly cleaned world.

Rebekah Perks

Baby Wakes Up Angry

I have learned to kiss the soft skin of her sleeping face and move gently over and away from her. I sit on the couch, my breakfast balanced on my knee. I watch her sleep as I chew bites of banana and little rings of cereal. When she opens her eyes she will be at her most solitary. Bitterness will rise from her vulnerable body like steam. I wait until she comes to me, after layers of clothes and cigarettes and coffee, to speak.

I wonder over what grey landscapes she flies at night to wake with a mouth full of such salt. Maybe it is her mother's cluttered kitchen where she spends her nights smoking cigarettes and fending off armies of bleeding babies and bird-beaked men. I don't know where she goes at night, but she wakes back in her soft fleshed body with crusty eyes and blood on her cracked lip. She wakes back into her butch body and it is her anger that wakes up first. Her gentleness comes later—comes more slowly and with careful hands.

I am glad her anger has not been beaten out of her. She is a fighter still and maybe always will be. I struggle with her sometimes to find a place where we are both still soft and innocent as we once were, as we never were but wish to be.

I don't wake up angry, but I have my own schedule of rage as regular as clockwork. We are making love. I come hard and resentful and put my head unconvincingly on her shoulder (she always knows when I fake affection). I move down her torso with a cold empty head—only my lips alive. I know where she is vulnerable and I am heading there. In that moment, I have forgotten who she is. I think she means me harm and I have taken her punishment and am smug in the knowledge that she has not reached me.

She pulls me back up her body by the shoulders. "Wait, wait, what's wrong?" I am silent but finally admit when she pushes me that I feel like I have been fucked, fucked over, fucked as punishment, fucked like "take this, bitch." I watch her animated face turn blank and still. I have seen this same expression once, a curling in around the pain, when she fell and tore her shoulder. She says she felt only tenderness toward me. "I believe you," I say, although it is a long time before I really do.

On another day, I am all gentleness and desire. I glide my hands softly to her belt, trying to keep my movements slow and soothing like she is some skittish horse; like my approach will make all the difference. Her strong hand trails after mine, traps my hand on her buckle. I watch her face as she measures the forces of pleasure and shame, control and vulnerability. The mix is too strong. She gathers both my wandering hands and tucks them safely under her arm, "No, baby, no, shh, shh."

When she moves into me with her fist, into such a deep private place, and I open to her, spread my legs as wide as they go, welcome her in, it is a triumph of trust. When she presses her cock into my cunt, and her head wet with sweat falls against my face, she whispers, "Baby, I love you," and means it. These are things neither of us were raised for. We come together against the greatest odds—against everything that tried to break us. I reach for her in ecstasy and she is there with me. She is there with me. We are a fucking miracle.

Felice Picano

Matthew's Story—1974

If I lived this close I'd probably come here every day," Matt said. We were just leaving the Japanese Tea Garden, slowly walking along a loop of asphalt embedded in lawn, headed for the front of the de Young Museum. We'd been on our feet for several hours and I was beginning to worry about his leg.

"I come here whenever I can," I admitted. "And did so more before I became gainfully, tragically, employed."

Matt looked at me in a way that showed he appreciated that I was "using" language, i.e., doing something with it to please him.

"I'm beat!" I added. "Let's stop."

It was a late Sunday afternoon, and solidly sunny and warm for San Francisco. Despite the day, a school bus was lined up in front of the museum. We'd been inside earlier, looking mostly at the Oriental Arts collection ("Shoji-screen for weeks!" my old pal Calvin said after his one visit. "And enough fans for every Madama Butterfly that ever trod the boards!") but we'd not seen any kids. Maybe an older tour group was using the bus. Now I dropped my jacket onto the lawn and fell atop it. Matt looked hesitant, until I reached up and pulled him down next to me.

"What's that?" he asked, just now spotting through the trees another building.

I told him it was the California Academy of Sciences, "which no living human has ever willingly entered."

Matt laughed. "You're funny."

He put his hand next to mine as we looked up at the small, dappled clouds. San Francisco is generally lousy for cloud-watching unless maybe you go to Lands End just before a major storm arrives. But for high whites, the east coast is superior, and the midwest best of all. So while he watched clouds, I watched Matt.

I still couldn't believe he was here with me, next to me. Still couldn't believe he'd been with me nearly a week, or that he was so astonishingly good looking. In fact, every time I looked at him, I kept finding new aspects of his beauty.

"You know what that little pagoda in the garden reminded me of?" Matthew asked, suddenly sitting up.

It was fruitless to guess. In the few days we'd known each other I'd already learned he might say virtually anything after an intro like that.

"This temple in Danang," Matt continued. (See what I mean?) "The funniest thing happened when I went inside."

"Oh?" I encouraged him.

"Not funny, ha ha, but . . . " Matt looked at me. "You don't want to hear this."

I grabbed him around the neck, baring my teeth. "Kill and eat!" I threatened.

"Well, okay, I'll tell you. But I warned you, it's really dumb. . . . When we were stationed there, I used to go around Danang. You know, like a tourist, with a camera and all. I guess I shoulda' been a little afraid. The VC were all over the city, as we found out once it was retaken. And there were incidents—delivery boys riding up on a bike who'd assassinate you—that sort of thing. But for some reason I never felt afraid in Danang. I'd leave the guys at a café or restaurant and go wandering on my own. I liked the place. It was more, you know, *Asian* to me than Saigon, which is sort of like Paris done up in chopsticks.

"So this one late afternoon, I'm wandering through the back alleys of town and I see this . . . it looked like a lion. A female lion. Not with a mane and all. But the biggest damn cat! Just walking around. I couldn't believe it. So I follow, like at a distance. And it walks on, sniffing here and there. No one in the alley. I turn a corner and it's gone. Then I see its tail just going in some doorway. Up some stone stairs. Very old looking, covered with, what do you call it? Verdigris? I'm thinking this must be a really old building! But it's hard to see it all, hidden among all these Danang-type wooden shacks and houses made of particle board and aluminum. At any rate, I still can't believe a lion lives here, so I go up the stairs and into this dark old doorway.

"I find myself in the middle of a temple. Gongs are going off and the place reeks with incense, and there are candles and statues everywhere and it's huge and dark and empty. No lion anywhere.

"I'm about to go back out, when I spot this old guy in a yellow robe. We've seen these yellow robes all over the city, naturally, and since they're against us, we're never too happy to see them. This guy however is really old. And skinny. Just a bunch of bones. He's pulling up the yellow cloth around him when he spots me.

"He stands up and comes over to me asking me something or other, walking with difficulty. I see he's like really arthritic, his arms and legs are bent and the joints are swollen. Very pathetic, the way he looks, the way he moves. Yet he's smiling and happy, and his old eyes are like really bright.

"So I ask him if he saw the big cat. My Vietnamese is shit, but that much I know. 'Where's the big cat?' He laughs. I tell him I followed the big cat inside. He laughs more, covering up his toothless mouth with his yellow cloth. I'm about to turn and leave, when he says it's him. He's the big cat.

"Obviously he's loony. But then so am I if I saw a lion wandering around the back alleys of Danang, right? So I say okay, and I give him a few coins, some piastres. And I say Amida Buddha and I keep smiling and I back away until I'm about out of that room.

"I turn to leave and suddenly, I don't know, I feel something behind me. I turn around and . . . I don't know, maybe it was power of suggestion or hypnotism or the smoke and darkness, but I swear to you, Rog, I saw that lion there inside that temple room. And I didn't see that old monk anywhere.

"I high-tailed it the hell out of there! But for the next coupla weeks I couldn't stop wondering about it. These monks are supposed to, you know, gain powers. What if that rickety old man, who could barely move around inside that temple because of how ill and deformed he was, what if through the power of his mind, he became that lion and in that powerful, healthy body, he walked the alleys of Danang?"

Victoria Plum

Sweet Nothings

Once upon a now-ish time there was born a cute and highly desirable baby girlie named Sweet Nothings.

From the time the midwife smacked her newborn pink little bottom and the darling murmured "mmmMM-mmm!" instead of wailing, Sweet Nothings knew she would be a lassie's lassie.

This was long before the Gay Gene Report of 1991 followed on the heels of the Gay Brain Centre Report of 1987.

She was nurtured in a happy, warm-hearted household with a Real Mummy and Real Daddy who had Great Hopes for Sweet Nothings, and there were no problems. All admired her singularity when from an early age Sweet Nothings chose jeans and leathers instead of frothy rainbow-coloured frocks as party gear. They applauded when Sweet Nothings went for round things like jam donuts and burgers to wrap her little mouth around while her friends chose hot dogs and chocolate-dipped bananas.

Objects of the phallic kind inspired her not: the neighbours played King of the Castle, but you'd find Sweet Nothings in the library happily constructing caves with beanbag cushions. Most pointedly, in light of her future career, she distinctively preferred the round buttons on the typewriter Mummy bought her for her sixth birthday to any projectile exuding its lead onto paper. On this machine she wrote her first short story, which began with a wish:

When I grow up I wish to be grate. I will be a book writer and make magic words about the heart. I won't never ever marry a man because I want to live with my mum. She's luvly and makes me Cambridge tea.

The former wish would come true, the latter she would outgrow. Sweet

Nothings did grow a bit but she was not always appreciated at school due to being small and her brows meeting in the middle and having squinty eyes. This disapproval simply toughened her.

She set her sights on Dreaming Spires where blissful words dance on the horizon. There she moved, to love words all the bright day long. Night times soon found her fucking her gorgeous English professor, Emily Strimleep, deep into the dark hours.

Emily Strimleep happened to be a Very Married woman who gave away her attraction to Sweet Nothings at one-on-one tutorials by unbuttoning her chambray shirt a button too far. Very soon, they both became all unbuttoned and oh my dears very sweetly wrapped in one another. Dr. Strimleep's husband didn't mind one bit. He only tried to kill Sweet Nothings once, and soon her first story was published in *Strimleep's Anthology of Young Writers*.

And so the happy tale of celebrity lovers progressed. Sweet Nothings was never possessive after Dr. Emily; she picked her lovers as punctiliously as one chooses intimate undies and she always got what she wanted. Success fell into her hungry, loving hands like ripe fruit. Her career took off in an alarmingly phallic way but there was no stopping it. She even starred on Melvyn Bragg. Her stories grew longer and more daring, the lovers infinitely more powerful and fewer of them Very Married.

Then one day Sweet Nothings awoke to discover that although she was now rich and famous there was a Hole in her Heart needing a plug. Lovers of the past had generously provided building blocks to success and quite right too; who'd not give half a kingdom for good passion? Yet something was lacking.

Sweet Nothings lost her appetite. She pined. In her search for PR (permanent relationship) she found herself addictively attending literary lunches and searching with a naked aching for Ms. Right. Then it happened. . . . She saw her Desirable Lesbian across a crowded room. Their eyes met. They approached. Sweet Nothings' pink button turned somersaults in her panties as she noted the circular tattoo on Des's wrist: *Refuse to Live the Little Life!* She was tall. Her name was Paco Rouge. "Paco Rouge," said Sweet Nothings breathlessly, "I always get what I want, and I want you, Paco."

Off she swept Paco, and together they still reside. During the festive season you may find them walking the cats on the heath or making Whittards tea for interviewers and admirers. And, though you may feel free to substitute the end of this tale, I am quite certain that they will live happily ever after-ish.

Cynthia J. Price

Chromosomes

The lab is cool, sheltered from the outside tropical humidity by venetian blinds which filter the sun through to shine in stripes on the white sterile walls. The gentle hum of the air conditioning unit sustains life of the two cool-headed scientists who work within these four walls, systematically checking blood samples for Down's Syndrome, Kleinefelters and XO's.

In one corner, the fat test-tubes sit brooding in a humid steambath for three days and three nights until the chromosomes within the white cells have grown sufficiently for me to study them.

I drop these little cells from a height onto clean microscope slides so that they split open and spread their chromosomes for easy viewing. Once stained and fixed I can count each group under the binocular microscope and photograph them. I cut them out of their photographs and arrange them in pairs on a piece of white paper and check that there are no pieces missing and no pieces left over.

Jill is in charge of the lab and she has taught me all these techniques. In my days of training she would sit on her lab stool in front of the microscope looking for a good grouping to show me, then call me over to take a look. She never climbed down from her stool but just leaned to one side so that my arm would have to touch hers as I looked through the double eye-piece. Two arms side by side like a pair of chromosomes. And I would feel the electricity jumping across, backward and forward, between our two limbs.

My feelings for Jill multiply and grow in the sterile atmosphere of the lab. I take every opportunity to call her over to verify what I see, and just as she had done in training, I lean over to one side so that we make chromosome arms together. (Only it's harder for me to lean sideways as my growing belly tends to make me top-heavy and I have to make sure I don't fall off the lab stool and make a fool of myself.)

Jill drops an excerpt from a medical journal onto my desk and says that she wants me to play around with a new technique. Banded chromosomes! Each little cross and Y have little zebra stripes, making it easier to pair them off and see what is wrong. All this can be achieved by using a different dye. But the article is not clear on the optimum length of time that the slides must stand in the purple dye to get the striped effect, so I must set up rows of slides and leave them standing for different time spans. This will take time and patience.

I am overworked and tired because of my pregnancy but throw myself into the project with enthusiasm. I must use volunteers for my batches of tests and so it is easy to slip my own sample unnoticed into the groupings.

I would do anything for Jill, and not just because she is my boss. I am happily married. No, let me rephrase that. I am married. I am incubating my own chromosomes to form my first child, but I like Jill more than I should. Much more than I should! And some days when we work together, the air conditioner can hum itself hoarse but the humidity of the water-bath permeates the whole room with its jungle-animal moisture.

I wait on edge for the three days and three nights to pass while my chromosomes are hatching. Checking under the scope, I can count forty-six in every group I look at, but cannot yet tell how the pairs will match up. I take snaps of the tangled sets of limbs indulging in an orgy on the glass slide and then must wait another agonisingly long day for the photographs to come back from the processing lab. At last I may have absolute evidence with which I may convince myself that I am normal and squash those funny rumours going around in my head.

I hold my breath while I sort out the pairs. (Here I am, four months pregnant, obviously fertile, but I still feel this stupid need to check). This pair goes here, that pair over there, nearly finished. Thank God—the last pair are both X's. I am officially what the geneticists call a 46XX, with nothing missing and nothing left over. The proof I was looking for. I am pure unadulterated woman and can stop these silly thoughts that maybe I find Jill attractive.

Jill walks into the lab and leans over to see how the zebra stripes are coming along. With her arm against mine we both study the pairs of linked chromosomes pasted onto the white paper, and the sterile laboratory turns into a steamy incubator once again.

Jim Provenzano

Split Lip

You never forget the moment when you did nothing. You never forget how his skull would have looked had you owned a gun. You never forget the glint of joy in his eyes as the blood flowed from your lips.

You're surprised at how the plainclothes police are oddly polite. They drive you around the neighbourhood looking for their faces. You know they ducked into a straight bar or down the hole to the PATH train. The police won't follow up too hard. After all, you fought back. You got a few punches in. They like you for that.

The surgeon at St Vincent's, where you expected to be treated cruelly, is tall, Asian, handsome and gay. He jabs your mouth with a needle full of anaesthetic, covers your face with surgical paper, and sews into your lip. You remember an episode of *China Beach*.

You go to work on Monday, rationalizing that the reason you spent the entire weekend in bed was simply because you were tired. At your desk, you run your tongue over your stitches about four hundred times. The plastic thread juts up from your skin.

You remember little details in your nightmares. One had an earring. Another's sneakers were red. The third wore a Georgetown baseball cap. The dreams make you lose sleep. You snap at everyone at work. You even cause a guy to quit his job. His desk is cleared in a week.

No one knows how much hate got into your veins.

You try to be nice to your sort-of boyfriend later that week. He holds you and strokes your head. He can't kiss you because your lip is still swollen. You can't suck his cock because your mouth is puffy and raw. The have succeeded in preventing you from making the soft form of male-to-male contact they so despise. Three weeks later your boyfriend starts cancelling dates because you've been so *negative* these days.

You go shopping for weapons with your straight cousin who lives in the Bronx and got shot on the subway. He gives you his *nunchackus* and suggests you buy a hunting knife. Switchblades are too tricky. Instead you get Mace and a whistle—maybe you'll go back and get the knife. The *nunchackus* hang on a wall, becoming more decorative than functional.

You walk by the bar where it happened. You see the sidewalk where your bloodstains have been trampled away. You see the boys inside watching video clips of Joan Rivers. They stand in their J. Crew slacks and Perry Ellis sweater vests. You remember how they shrivelled out of sight when the fighting started, how you shouted back, defending this bar and your right to stand in front of it, the look on the gay men's faces, stunned at the blood spattered over your Read My Lips t-shirt and black leather jacket, being suddenly embarrassed for looking like such a clone, then more angry at the simpering manager who gave you a paper towel. Your friend, when he asked to call the cops, was told to use the pay phone outside.

Looking around at the silent drinking men, you wonder what you thought was worth defending.

In the morning, weeks later, while getting dressed, you think through your day's plans: "Do I wear the Doc Martens (for kicking back) or the Reeboks (for running away)?"

You walk the streets, wary of every corner. Your hands grip whatever pocket weapon you brought today. You see the crazy people on the street and now know how they got that way. You wonder how long it will take before you act like them.

Wearing a whistle on a chain around your neck, you feel safe, sort of, trying not to think that blowing a whistle might merely call attention to your beating, inviting not assistance, just an audience.

You become extremely comfortable with your heterophobia. You learn to admire drag queens and prostitutes. You begin to travel exclusively in packs of large, muscular gay men.

You break into tears for no apparent reason. You spend hundreds of dollars on cabs. You no longer have second thoughts about the execution of certain criminals.

Andy Quan

Bald

Gay men were shaving their skulls, their pates peeking out into daylight. Some had blue veins, some had razor cuts, others had odd bumps and lumps. If they were not shiny bald, then at least, hair was short. Short, short, like crew cuts. A military allusion. Or impossibly stylish. Short everywhere except for a cowlick that would rise up from the brow, like the Belgian comic book character Tintin.

I considered this trend seriously. After all, it had been four years since I had seen my hair short, and I was admittedly tired of the long black hairs that would appear everwhere, thick Asian strands in the carpet, in the sink, in the shower and on bathroom tiles. I wasn't tired of the attention, but I was tired that it only came from women. There was, I have to recount, a roughly drawn poster I had seen up outside of Toronto's Glad Day Bookstore that advertised a club for gay men who had long hair or who loved long hair. But to me, it seemed no different than the specialty classified ads that appeared in the back of the community bi-weekly requesting submissive types or water sport fanatics. To the mainstream gay man, I was definitely out of fashion.

Still, it was not an easy decision. When I told friends of the idea, most lamented what a shame it would be to lose such hair. Some thought that it might be a good change. Perhaps something clicked when I spoke with Ronnie, an actor friend of a friend. People always told me how intelligent he was but I could never tell. He seemed to express only mild interest in me and we only made idle chit chat when we met. Besides, I was jealous. I was deeply attracted to his physical form, a blond boy next door with a handsome rugged face, a football player's physique—a body that somehow avoided looking too planned and precise, unlike those of so many others in the community.

"Don't listen to that crap," he tossed, his eyes elsewhere, sneaking a look at who his ex-boyfriend was talking to in another part of the bar. "Why would you follow some stupid trend? Why would you need to follow the crowd? Gay people can be so superficial." His attention altered to watch a tall brunette cross the floor. "That's not a comment on you, it's just, why would you need to?"

I adjusted my ponytail, my hair drawn back and held by a thin black elastic. It's a game, I thought to myself. Checkers, Parcheesi, poker. I want to play, and how can I play if people won't even let me into the game? I got up to leave, and felt a flash of anger. I swallowed it. Heat bounced uneasily against my interiors. Ronnie could wear whatever he wanted, the most out-of-style clothes, the most garish colours. He could grow his hair into a river of blond lengths. He could keep his chest unshaved if it wasn't already (shaved chests having become a trend as well). He would still be pursued as he probably had been pursued all of his life, men buckling at the knees at first sight. And he would never know that he did not need to play the game because he was in it. He *was* the game.

When I shaved my head, I felt glorious. It was a nice surprise to learn my parents had gifted me a strong round skull. I sent my braid to a Chinese-Canadian artist friend who thought he could work it into his next piece, a pseudo-museum display on the cultural artifacts of a composite Chinese-Canadian family. I showered and felt the hot spray directly on my head, my hair did not need drying, the number of hairs in the carpet slowly diminished.

Most importantly, I walked along sunny Church Street and felt the weather on the very top of my body, and amazingly, like a miracle predicted but not believed in, heads swivelled, other eyes caught mine. If one has never swam in the ocean, there is no way to describe to those with no experience of it how the salt smell rises into your head to the heights of your senses, how every inch of what surrounds you feels alive and in motion, how the salt leaves its traces on your skin as you leave the water. Ever since I had come out of the closet, I had long hair, and I had never known what it was like to be close shaven. More accurately, I had never known what it was like to be recognizably gay, and to walk on a gay street on a hot summer day. With all that mess of hair, the narrow-visioned denizens of my gay world saw only an exotic creature with foreign roots. They could not see my desire through the forest of hair, could not name me as one of them. For with my skin already a different colour, they needed another signal to call me their own. Shaving my head, I had learned to play the game I wanted to play.

How many of you have ever seen your head bald, seen the lines and veins and patterns of the skull, to see how nature has formed that skull without the adornment of hair? That summer, I saw it and it was a revelation. Its round form showed me the shape of the world in which I was learning to take part.

Shelly Rafferty

In the Market

My nephew BJ is generally a pain in the ass, but since my sister was in labour again, I decided I could put aside my "I'm single, again" depression and babysit. And he's not bad company for a five-year-old.

Surprisingly, I found myself more interested in the Mighty Morphin' Power Rangers than he seemed to be, when he decided that his nourishment should take precedence over my couchbound hangover.

"I want some cereal," he said, kneeling on the floor. His little brown face was unnaturally close to mine. I ignored him, but he put his hand on my chin and turned my face to his. "Do you have any cereal?"

"Michelob Light, Zima. There's probably a splash of Dewar's left. What's your pleasure?"

His face registered his lack of familiarity with the brands I had suggested. "I don't like that kind," he admitted sheepishly.

"Never mind. Get dressed. Let's go to the store. How 'bout that?"

An hour later we were loaded down with supermarket fixin's for staples like French toast and chocolate milk, when I suddenly remembered the focaccia at Grimaldi's on 87th Street.

"Hey, we gotta make a detour, Beej," I said. BJ was holding my hand and twisting his baseball cap from side to side. "That okay with you?"

"Do they have cereal?"

I took that for a rhetorical question and dragged him around the corner.

Of course, I had an ulterior motive for going to Grimaldi's, although BJ's presence was sure to undermine my plan. I looked at my watch. 10:45. I hustled BJ along. If my calculations were correct, the woman after whom I had been lusting for several weeks would already be in the check-out line. Damn. This was not going to be the week in which I'd get my chance to strike up a seductive, casual conversation. Oh well.

But there she was. Weighing grapefruits. Looking gorgeous.

"Get a basket," I instructed BJ, jostling him toward a stack of square plastic boxes. If he struggled, I didn't notice. I was too busy trying to make my cowlick lay flat.

The basket thunked clanking at my feet. "I can't carry it," BJ complained.

"Don't worry, sport," I said, grabbing the rattly handle. "I got you covered."

"Ooooh, apples!" he suddenly exclaimed. He made a beeline for the Granny Smiths.

This presented a small problem: I couldn't quite keep an eye on both my nephew and my future girlfriend with each of them wandering to opposite corners of the produce section. Across the piles of mangoes, papaya and passion fruit, I let the woman whose slender hands, narrow waist, and startlingly short hair had dominated my recent sexual fantasies distract me. She was decked out: Sugar Daddy-coloured corduroys, a pale, cream cotton shirt under a loose-fitting, boxy plaid jacket. The fact that I didn't know her name did little to dissuade me from knowing that I was definitely in love. How was I ever going to get to talk to her?

She had just moved to the bananas when I remembered my nephew. I twisted toward the apple bin. I couldn't see him.

"BJ!" I called. "BJ!"

No answer. I careened around the pineapples, angled around the onions, looked under the green peppers. Where could he have gone?

"BJ!"

"Aunt Katie!" I heard his voice.

"Where are you?" I was panicked. "BJ!"

"I'm on the phone!"

Strange, his voice seemed to be coming from the shopping cart parked next to the object of my affection. Her back was to me, her profile in a three-quarter turn.

I knew he was near.

"Excuse me," I said abruptly. "My nephew. . . . "

The woman suddenly stepped backward and turned to me with a smile.

At her feet sat BJ, cross-legged, cradling a banana to his ear.

My hands flew to my hips. "What do you think you're doing, buster?" He and the beautiful woman exchanged a look.

"I'm talking to Susan," he replied solemnly.

Curious, I looked at the woman again. Her left hand pressed a banana against her shoulder. Suddenly, Susan put her banana to her ear. "Sorry, BJ," she said gently. "I think you're in trouble."

BJ's expression was concerned.

"Sorry," whispered Susan to me. "We were just . . . "

BJ was on his feet. He tugged at Susan's jacket. "I'm not supposed to talk to strangers," he said. "Don't hang up." He thrust his banana into my hand. "Here, Aunt Katie."

I took the banana. "What am I supposed to do with this?"

His toothy grin was full of wisdom and mischief. "It's for you!" he giggled.

Faustina Rey

The Truth

Did she put her tongue in your mouth?"

The question crossed the urgent distance between my father's thin lips and my own inoffensive ear. It pierced its way into my brain through my eardrum, trying to find the private core, the secret intimate place where the truth is kept. My father's question filled not only the inner cavity of my mind but swept out into the room. Standing by the kitchen door with a tray of tea, my mother heard it. Sitting grim and grey in the chair by the chimney, Isaura's mother heard it. Pacing back and forth across the jute rug, hands stuffed into his jacket pockets, the headmaster heard it.

I had been safe asleep in bed when the noise of the engine woke me, and I saw the lights of Isaura's mother's Citroën coming up the mountain from the main school toward the rondavels. If Nina Portofino had driven all the way over to Mbabane from Mozambique, it had to be bad. I slipped out into the thick bushes in the valley of the stream which we called "the secret garden," and planned to hide there all night, until Isaura's mother was gone. But it was cold and the rocks were damp.

"Did she put her tongue in your mouth?"

The question came again. Why had my father come to get me and not my mother? I lowered my eyelids and glanced across at my delicate mother, standing like a frightened creature in the doorway, unable to put her tray down, unable to either come into the room and assert her presence or to leave it and slam the door. Why hadn't they sent her in to talk to me on her own? She would have settled down on my bed, as though she was going to read me a story. And I would have told her everything and she would have understood. But perhaps she didn't want to come, had refused to come. Perhaps she found me disgusting now, after what Nina Portofino had told her. My mother didn't love me any more.

"Did she, Tikki? Did Isaura Portofino put her tongue in your mouth?"

Isaura's tongue in my mouth. Isaura's enormous, wet, red tongue pushing its way insistently between my lips, flicking over my teeth, filling my mouth. Isaura's lips on mine, kissing me, her cheek against my cheek, her mouth on my eyes, my nose, her fingers on the back of my neck. My fingers in her long thick black hair, my hands stroking her pale olive skin, her eyes gazing at me. And the feeling of wanting, of pushing, of something hot between my legs, moving my whole body closer to Isaura's. That tight, prickly feeling, as though I were wet and turning to water, it thrust me toward Isaura and her warm skin, her breath on my cheek, the electric flesh of her bare arms touching mine.

"Tikki, this is a serious business. Mrs. Portofino has driven all the way over from Maputo. The headmaster has been woken up in the middle of the night. It is not right for an eighteen-year-old girl to be kissing a twelve-year-old."

The eighteen-year-old was Isaura. The twelve-year-old was me. But it wasn't like that. We were the only girls at a boarding school of a hundred and sixteen boys and Isaura was in love with the art master. The art master was Zulu, Isaura was Portuguese. That was what upset Nina Portofino. That was why she had driven all day from the coast of Mozambique to the Swazi mountains. The school was multi-ethnic, multi-racial, multi-denominational, but Isaura's mother did not want her daughter marrying a Zulu. Friends was fine, friends was super, but not sex, not marriage, not babies.

I knew this with a dreary clarity of which my father seemed incapable. Isaura had told me about kissing Dan Kuzwayo, the art master, and I made her kiss me that way, in exchange for not telling on her to my mother. An inquisitive twelve-year-old learning about sex from an older girl. But I was in love with Isaura. I loved her with all my heart, and when she kissed me, I believed it, I savoured it, I relived it as though she had meant it, as though she had loved me too and later, when we were older, when I had passed my exams, I would get a job and take care of her, and we would be together forever.

My father cleared his throat as though he was going to ask me once again, but the headmaster and Mrs. Portofino took this as a signal that they should take over the questioning. The headmaster stopped his pacing and turned toward me. Mrs. Portofino got out of her chair and strode over to the table where I was standing. Their eyes glared at me. The pupils had constricted to tiny pinpricks which could bore a hole in my head and get at the truth. Only my mother stood apart, with the tea tray.

"Oh, do put that down," snapped my father.

And she turned away toward the kitchen, turning her back on the scene going on in her living room, but before she turned, she looked at me, and the corners of her lips moved and she smiled. A sad, thoughtful smile. And I looked back at her and I knew it was all right.

"No," I said, clearly and calmly. "Isaura did not put her tongue in my mouth."

The pupils in their eyes relaxed, dilated. Their bodies moved backward, their hands reached up to their faces, touching hair, mouth, cheek.

The truth is precious, a precious gift. In southern Africa you do not wear it on your sleeve, you cherish it to yourself and offer it only to those who value it as you do. My mother knew. It was enough.

Jeff Richardson

Say Uncle

I can tell you about the first time I was fucked, if that's what you want to hear. I was eight years old and he was my uncle, my mother's brother. He made me lick his cock first—he was babysitting, they were at a movie—he made me lick his penis, and then he said to put his balls in my mouth. I could only get one in at a time, but he wanted both, so he slapped me hard on the back with the palm of his hand. Even through my shirt it stung. I managed then to get both balls in my mouth at once and he said, "Good boy." I was choking and my eyes were blurry—he started to purr like a contented kitten.

He made me lie on my back on the floor then, and he shuffled his jeans down lower and squatted over me until his ass was in my face, and I knew I was supposed to lick it. It was so hairy I felt my mouth was filled with some coarse-furred animal, and again I started to choke but he didn't care. "So pretty," he kept saying as he stroked his hand along my belly. He'd pulled my shirt up almost to my neck and then he undid my pants and put his rough hand on my penis. All the time his butt was pressing down on my mouth and I was afraid he was going to lose his balance, fall out of his squat full down on my face. He's a heavy man—he would have snapped my neck in two.

When he turned me over, his purring grew louder. He pushed one finger in—it seared me. Two fingers, three, then his cock. I must have passed out, escaped into blackness, for the next thing I remember was feeling something warm and wet on my bottom. I moaned a little and reached one hand back to feel it. He swatted me. "Don't touch that!" he shouted. "*Don't you ever touch that!*"

I cried then. I couldn't help it if he punished me, I had to cry. But he

234

didn't. Instead he stroked my back and said, "Shh, Puppy, it's not that bad," and, "Next time it'll be easier." I kept on crying and he just sat beside me, watching for a long long while. Then he started up suddenly and tried to put his thing in me again. It was soft now and wouldn't go in. I could tell he was trying to make it hard with his hand, yet every time he pressed it against my hole, it bent over. Finally he picked me up in the air and held me facing him. He stuck his tongue in my mouth. "Sissy boy," he sneered. "Makes men kiss him." Then he dropped me to the floor.

"Put your pants on," he ordered. I did. "If you ever mention this to your mom or dad," he said, "I'll kill you." I knew he would. "Your bum will be sore for a few days—don't let anyone see it. Don't let anyone see any part of your body. You keep covered up. You dress yourself alone in the morning—you put your pyjamas on in the bathroom at night."

"Yes, sir."

"Next time will be easier. I told you that."

"Yes, sir."

"It's going to be fun, Charlie. Believe me—you're going to like it."

If I hadn't been fucked by Uncle George would I have become what I am today? Or did Uncle George fuck me because the mould was already set and he sensed it: here's a little fairy boy, he'll enjoy it? What came first, the chicken or the egg? I was certainly chicken, though I felt for weeks—*years*—afterward that I was an egg, ever so fragile, that had smashed on the hardest pavement, never to be put back together again.

But I am together, today, in my own way. I'm stronger than I ever imagined I could be. I'm a Pretty Boy, a Fairy Boy—Uncle George's secret favourite—but I'm also the man who took George to court. Twenty years later. I lost the case—on a technicality. He lost his job, his wife. I cried on the witness stand—just a little—and it was all planned, all rehearsed. I would never cry in public the way I cry at home, alone. It made Uncle George break down to see what he had made of me. It made the judge stop breathing as I recounted step by step what happened: first time, second time—all the times until Dad found us. Dad wouldn't testify—said he didn't remember. Mom said, "Don't make him, Charlie. It'll kill him," and I said, "Don't call me Charlie. You know I'm Cherry now."

"Cherry," she said quickly, and I could tell the way she looked at me that she's afraid. My mother, afraid of me. My father, afraid of me. All of them, afraid of me. Who would believe that a silly queen could make them quiver? God, I think, I might as well have been straight—some macho wife-beater striking fear in the hearts of those who love him best.

So it's come to this: strength and fear and revenge—and I know who I am. That's the best part of being queer: you know who you are. You simply can't help but. . . .

Uncle George, I wonder—does he know who he is? I can't afford to care—not for too long—can't afford to worry about it. But did he know who he was when he called me Puppy? Did he know who he was when he pulled on my penis, trying to see if he could make it grow?

I never fantasize about him—some victims do—and yet, when I'm ready to come, if I say his name to myself quickly, just his name, I come a lot more strongly. "Uncle George," I whisper in the dark. Or, better yet, just *Uncle*.

Michael Rowe

Princesses

When I was very young, we lived in Beirut. These are my earliest memories: the hot desert sun, and the black wrought-iron railings of the balcony which opened our apartment to the street far below.

I would sit in the shade of the balcony's awning and look at the picture-books my mother purchased on her many shopping trips home to Ottawa. She never took me with her, but when she returned, she brought me presents, books wrapped in blue and silver paper.

"Look what Mommy's brought, Hugh!" she would cry as she swept across the marble floors of the living room. She'd pick me up, and kiss my face. I'd smell her perfume and stale cigarettes. "Did you have a nice time with Daddy and Eliza? Were you a good boy for Hengameh? Be a little man, now, Hugh. Look what Mommy's brought! Storybooks! Isn't that nice? Look!"

On rainy days, I would lay with her under the covers of the bed she shared with my father. My mother smoked endless French cigarettes, lighting them with a heavy brass lighter from Syria. It looked like a lump of molten gold. She used a tortoise-shell cigarette holder to smoke them, and their scent clung to her like incense.

Mother read me stories of fairy princesses, and trolls, and magic waterfalls that became raging torrents. The spell of her voice took me into the world of the book she was reading, as magic as the story itself. When she read about the haughty princess who had been tricked into the red dancing shoes that eventually danced her to death, I took it as a warning.

I imagined the pain of dancing into the dark night, through filthy streets, endlessly whirling, unable to stop, while no one even knew I was gone, much less dancing a mad tarantella to an invisible, merciless

237

orchestra, to an agonizing death. My mother would never know I was gone. I saw her in my mind's eye, desolate at her loss. And somehow, terribly, wondering if I had gone on purpose, just to hurt her.

The story terrified me, but fascinated me as deeply as it repelled me. It became my favourite. My mother would indulge me, but only up to a point. Then she would want to read something else, like "Clever Gretel" or "Snow White and Rose Red." But my favourite was always "The Red Shoes."

After story time, Hengameh, the maid, came to take me away for my bath. Often, when I was in clean pyjamas, I lay on my parents' bed and watched my mother get dressed to go out with my father. She would spray on Joy. The heady mist of it reached me on the bed like a cloud of flowers. She stroked on black eyeliner and blue eye-shadow. In her shimmering evening gown, she looked as beautiful as one of the princesses in my books. The last touch was always the jewels, the diamond earrings and brooches that sparkled in the lights of her vanity mirror.

My breath would catch in my throat, and I wished I was as beautiful as she was. In my storybooks, beauty was always a hallmark of virtue. Virtue was always rewarded with happiness and love. She kissed me lightly as she swept out of her bedroom, telling me to be good. I promised to be good. It seemed a small enough price to pay for watching this miracle occur on the nights she went out of our house to be beautiful for other people.

My father was largely invisible to me, but this did not lessen his power in our home. His presence was felt everywhere. Sometimes when I spent afternoons with my mother, I would sit at her vanity table and touch her perfume bottles when she wasn't looking. They were beautiful cut-crystal flacons that had belonged to my great-grandmother, heirlooms with sterling-silver tops, filled with amber and gold. In our family, enormous value was placed upon objects which had been owned by the dead.

The rim of the bottle carried the scent of the perfume, and when I closed my eyes, it evoked any number of memories. My mother wore perfume every day of her life, but the lusher, richer scents were the ones she used before she went out with my father. These, in turn, invoked my father as well.

In the left-hand corner of the vanity table was a silver-framed photo-graph of my father in his R.C.A.F. uniform. My father is young and dashing: tall and powerful, with a dazzling, confident smile. Whenever I looked at that photograph, I felt a fluttering in my stomach. I knew he was handsome. I knew he was strong, because when he picked me up and played with me, I felt secure in his arms and I knew I would never fall. He would swing me through the air, and I felt weightless as a bird. I would press my face against the soft cashmere of his sweaters, or the white cotton of his broadcloth button-down dress shirts if he had just come from work. I would trace my small index finger over the discreet navy-blue W.P.S. monogram on his breast pocket. When I buried my face in his neck, he always smelled like aftershave and pipe tobacco.

I would giggle wildly, feeling that I could fly if only he wouldn't put me back down on the ground. To have my father home with us before I went to bed was a treat unlike any other. On the nights that he came home after I was in bed, I could always count on a kiss in the dark that woke me, sometimes long after my bedtime.

The ghostly scent of him would announce his presence, and moments later he would lean over and say, "Goodnight, Scout." He would hug me, and I would hug him back and say, "Goodnight, Daddy, I love you."

Hengameh called him *Monsieur*, Mother called him *William*, Eliza called him *Father*. When I spoke to him, I called him *Daddy*.

Where my mother was remote and cool, as I imagined a queen would be, my father was fire. He was all that was masculine in my world, which was composed of women. When my mother read me the stories out of the books stacked in my playroom, the handsome prince who saved the day was always my father. And when the prince carried the princess off to his kingdom, where she would become a queen, and rule justly and kindly for all of her days, I knew that she felt the same way I did when my father picked me up in his strong arms. I knew that as the princess pressed her face against the prince's scarlet cloak, and they rode off on his gallant steed, she smelled his aftershave and pipe tobacco, felt the smooth cotton broadcloth of his monogrammed dress shirt, and she knew that nothing would hurt her ever again.

I sometimes wondered what princesses did when they grew up, and decided that when the time came, I would find out.

Sandip Roy

A Walk in the Park

I saw him within ten minutes of walking into the park. Like me he was standing quietly under a tree, his face hidden in the dark shadows. Near him on a bench overlooking the lake sat two couples trying to ignore each other as they doggedly pursued romance. I noticed him when the tea-wallah came by with his big metal kettle filled with sweet milky tea.

"Chai, chai," he intoned walking up the path and stopping near the bench.

Getting no response, he started to move on when a man emerged from under the tree. As he stood near the tea-wallah getting his little clay cup of tea, I saw him glance at me. Our eyes met and then skittered away.

"Careful," said the teawallah, "it's very hot."

He raised the cup to his lips and blew on the tea as he took a tentative sip. Twentyish, moustache, not bad-looking. I slowly walked past him and turned around. He turned around too. I stopped ostensibly to stare at the glassy dark surface of the lake. I heard him walking towards me. He stopped near me and then cleared his throat.

"Do you have the time?"

I looked at my watch. "8:05," I answered.

"That's right," he concurred, looking at his.

We proceeded to stare out at the water in companionable silence.

"Hot night," I tried.

"Should rain soon," he replied.

A man walked by with a dog. I heard the sudden rustle of wings as a crow shifted in its sleep.

"What's your name?"

"Abheek," I lied.

"Mine's Arun," he offered. He moved closer so his hand lightly brushed mine. I made no attempt to move. His fingers got a little bolder touching my hand. I cautiously rubbed his palm with my fingers. Neither of us were looking at each other. We both kept our eyes on the path. A man and a woman with a cycle were coming towards us. We moved apart slightly.

"Do you have a place?" he asked softly.

"No."

"Neither do I." He sighed. His hand was now gently rubbing my thigh. I moved away as a group of schoolboys singing Hindi film songs came clattering down the path.

"Let's walk," he suggested. As we walked off we saw another man glance at us and walk away.

"You have to be careful," he said. "Lots of police harassment these days. In case anyone catches us I am Arun Biswas from JD Park and you are my brother Asu's friend from H.J. Birla College."

"Okay. And I'm Abheek Bose."

The park, which looked so dark and quiet from outside, was teeming with life on a summer night. Retired old men dressed in white. Young maid servants sneaking a moment with the neighbourhood swain before running home to cook dinner. College students discussing exams, films and football. Everywhere we stopped someone would come along. We found an empty bench and sat down. Keeping a careful lookout on both sides we started to rub each other's crotches through our trousers. At the first sound of footsteps we sprang apart and fell to contemplating the lake.

It was hot and muggy—even the leaves were still. His shirt was unbuttoned and I could feel the sweat beading the hair on his chest. I edged closer to him on the bench. He took my hand and placed it on his crotch. I realized he had unzipped his pants. I put my hand inside, feeling him through his underpants.

"Do you suck?" he whispered.

"Not here," I said.

"I'll keep watch. Please."

But before I could, an old man came down the path, coughing and hacking. He stopped at our bench, scratching his protruding stomach.

Then with a heavy sigh he sat down beside us. I glanced at Arun. He had pulled his shirt down to cover his crotch as he discreetly tucked himself in. We got up.

"I know another place," he said.

"It's no use," I muttered. "There are too many people."

"It gets emptier after nine-thirty."

"I can't stay that late."

He nodded. "Well let's just walk to the gate. Maybe we can meet another day."

We walked down the path in silence. I was wondering if I would ever be able to have sex here without being interrupted by all these people.

"Wait," he said and went behind a tree.

I heard him peeing. I stood there watching the tea-wallah go by again.

"Well," I said as he emerged, "I guess I should go."

And then the first drops of rain hit me. Fat warm drops of summer rain. First a drop, then two, then suddenly someone seemed to gash the pregnant dark bellies of the cloud and the rain came down in sheets. Everyone started running helter skelter towards the shops and bus stands outside the park. The schoolboys rode by on their bicycles, pedaling fiercely. The courting couples held books and newspapers over their heads. And suddenly we were alone—alone with the steady drumbeat of the rain and the rich smell of wet earth. Like someone just reached out with a wet rag and wiped all those people away.

I looked at him—his carefully coiffed film-star hair hanging limp and wet over his face. I could see the drops of water on his eyelashes and moustache. He was grinning at me. I smiled back and put out my hand to touch him close up.

And then we kissed—long lingering kisses with our eyes closed, no longer looking out for who was coming up the path. As he moved his body into mine the rain seemed to come down even harder.

And it surrounded us like a protective wall as we stole time fiercely and sweetly under the gulmohar tree.

Calvinism

As I knelt before the crucifix, I couldn't help noticing that Jesus wore Calvin Kleins instead of a loincloth. I quickly stared down at the floor, embarrassed, but I stared up at His crotch a moment later. I was curious if He hung to the left or the right. To my surprise, He had an erection, which was pointing down his right leg like a Muslim bowing down to Mecca.

It was so incongruous, I thought, staring down at the floor again but seeing His pale and wasted body before my eyes. His cock was swollen with desire, so vibrant, so alive, despite the debilitated state of the rest of His body.

He wasn't my type at all. I prefer a powerhouse of a man, well-built and with a chest like a barrel. But I wanted Him, Christ, wanted to feel Him inside me, reaching, probing, filling me with His god-hood. He wanted me, too. I could feel His eyes on me, and deep inside I felt a sense of pride in my body, pleased that the Lord wanted me. Was this pride sin? I wondered briefly. No, I decided, I was one of the chosen. *The* one He had chosen.

I looked up at him again, and He smiled as our eyes met. I smiled back at him, feeling like I could hardly believe my luck, like being in a bar and having the man I wanted want me back. He shrugged, a movement that looked as if He were lying in bed and had tried to rise. He stepped away from the cross, then crumpled to the floor, His limbs too weak to support him. I lunged forward to catch Him. Shame burned through me at the thought that I might have caused Him to harm himself. I cradled His body against me, protectively, as if He were a child. He shuddered and shook uncontrollably for a moment, and I was overcome with a feeling of wanting to do anything to make His pain go away, to make Him well. But at the same time I could not help noticing the feel of His cock pressed against my leg as the seizure twisted His body.

I helped Him to His feet, and He leaned heavily on me. One arm was thrown around my neck for support, the other out-thrust in a wild gesture, pointing towards the confessional. The stigmata was plainly visible on His palm. I looked at it more closely. It wasn't a stigmata, but a lesion, large and purple, making him look as if He were a scholar who had accidentally spilled ink into His cupped palm.

Before we had made it completely into the confessional booth, He began reaching for me, His fingers weakly fumbling at my belt as He groped. I shut the door and then helped Him, undoing both the buckle and my zipper, letting my pants fall down around my knees. I was wearing a pair of ordinary white briefs and the head of my cock poked above the elastic band, swollen with desire and anxious to get a look at our Lord. When I felt the first touch of His trembling fingers on my cock, even through the white cotton, a thrill ran through my body unlike anything I had felt before. I burned with ecstasy, feeling almost luminous myself. This is the Passion of Christ, I thought briefly, before the passion overwhelmed all thought.

Hardly able to control myself, I knelt before Him and tugged His underwear down. Freed from His Calvins, His cock rose, tall and majestic, a divine ascension. I paused as I bent towards Him, marvelling that I was about to service Christ, son of God, who died in our stead, for our salvation.

"This is my body," He whispered, pulling my head towards him. I didn't mind His impatience; He had died to save me. I opened my mouth, and took His cock between my lips, letting it rest on my tongue like the wafer, tasting, savouring. His head rolled to one side as I began to work my tongue back and forth. Soon His mouth opened in a small gasp of pleasure. "And this is my blood," He continued, and came in my mouth.

Craig J. Simmons

Shopping

The extraordinary almost always happens during the performance of the ordinary.

I am a happily married faggot.

On Thursday mornings I go grocery shopping.

Sammy and I are wakened at seven o'clock by the obnoxious buzzing of our alarm. Sammy gets up immediately and jumps in the shower, as he has a meeting at eight. I get out of bed a few minutes later and begin to slice fruit for our breakfast.

Sammy finishes his morning beauty regimen and comes to join me in our usual morning meal of cereal with fruit, an English muffin, and freshly-squeezed grapefruit juice. Our dog Hubie begs for morsels at my feet but he quickly moves on to Sammy as he is a much easier target. Sammy gives Hubie a piece of his muffin.

Sammy gets dressed in the executive drag which he hates but I love. I think it makes him look sexy. He thinks it makes him look like he's stolen clothes from his father's closet.

"What are you doing this morning?" Sammy asks as he plays with his hair, pulling pieces this way and that, searching for the right combination of wind-blown-casual and glued-down-formal.

"What day is it?" I toss back from the bathroom door where I am standing watching Sammy perform his final touches.

"You know I hate it when you answer a question with a question."

"Yes, I know," I say, and I start to laugh because this is all so familiar and usual. It makes me happy to have these little rituals which create such an insular bond between the two of us.

Nonetheless.

"What day is it?" I repeat.

Sammy has had time to think. "It's Thursday, which means that you're going grocery shopping."

"Baby gets a gold star." I lean over and give him a kiss on the forehead. "Is there anything special you need?"

"No, just the usual stuff."

Sammy is ready to go.

He ties his shoelaces, debates whether or not to take an umbrella, checks his attaché case to make sure he has everything he needs, searches frantically for his wallet, keys and sunglasses, kisses me whenever he passes within range of my mouth, and pauses when he opens the door.

"Two things."

"Shoot."

"One. I can't take the dog to the meeting so Hubie is yours for the morning. I'll pick him up later when I go to the office."

"No problem."

"Two. We need paper towels."

"I've already got it written down."

"I love you."

"I love you too."

We share one final kiss and then he is out the door and I watch his beautiful ass as he steps into the elevator.

He stops the door from closing.

"Three."

"Three." I laugh because there is always a three or four from the elevator. It is in Sammy's nature to remember things at the last minute.

"Get fresh flowers from that place on West Fourth. They're better than at the Safeway."

"Got it."

"You work at three?"

"I work at three."

"Bye, baby."

"Bye, honeybuns."

Hubie and I take the van to the Safeway on Broadway because it is the best one, based on the exhaustive research Sammy and I have done on all the grocery stores in our neighbourhood over the last four years.

Hubie sleeps in the van. He is the laziest dog I have ever met. He doesn't even have the energy to look out the window when we are driving. Sammy already had Hubie when we met and, even though I am not a natural dog person, Hubie and I have carved out a certain camaraderie over the years. He likes me because I pet him, which is something Sammy rarely does. Sammy feeds Hubie continuously, which is something I rarely do. Hubie seems to like this balance of things.

I park the van and head for the store. Hubie doesn't even lift his head when he is locked in the van. He doesn't mind. He just wants to sleep, warmed by the morning sun shining through the window.

I am quick at the grocery store. I know where everything is. I know the lay of the land. I do not waste time and am rarely tempted by bright flyers announcing in-store specials.

I get my grocery cart and head towards the first aisle which has toiletries: soap, toothpaste, and hopefully the thick hair mousse which is the only kind Sammy will use. The mousse is in so I pick up four cans. It's always nice to have extra.

I zip through the next couple of aisles, picking up boxes of cereal, long grain rice, fresh pasta and a case of Diet Pepsi. I do not forget the paper towels, and in fact pick up three packages on sale. I know how much Sammy loves his paper towels. To Sammy, paper towels are one of the necessities of life.

I arrive at the produce area. The bananas are looking good, but the strawberries are terrible, which is too bad since these are Sammy's favourite and he loves them in his cereal. I get butter lettuce and fresh peppers, both yellow and red. I get celery and carrots and on a whim I pick up an eggplant. It is a quick and easy dinner, just slice it and coat it in breadcrumbs.

Someone bumps into me as I am poking through the tomatoes. I turn to look. It is a thirty-something gentleman wearing jeans and a sweatshirt. He has brown hair, ears that fold over at the top which make them look like they have been accidentally shaved off, a vein that runs up along the right side of his face which pulsates as he tries to pick the correct tomatoes, and a nose too large for his face, forcing the rest of his features to struggle for the room remaining.

All of this I notice immediately.

He looks up at me and I see that he has brown eyes. He sees me, his eyes widen, we fall in love with each other and he looks back down.

The loved man picks three or four large tomatoes, places them in a bag, turns, places them in his cart, walks a few paces, looks over his shoulder at me, and then moves out of the produce area into the cereal aisle.

I turn back to the tomatoes and pick out three large juicy ones.

I move into the dairy area. I am constantly aware, as I pick out skimmed milk and low-fat cheese, that there is a man I love moving through the store. I can sense him in the centre of my back, his movements tracing a map up and down my vertebrae. I know when he pauses and sorts through the fresh chickens. I know when he is at the deli counter. I know when he queues up to pay.

I move quickly through the rest of my list, slowing only when I come to the bakery to check and see if the scones are good. They are, so I buy a dozen of the raisin variety. These are the kind Sammy and I prefer.

I sense I am being watched as I am paying and I turn to see my possible lover staring at me. I smile, trying to make it look bittersweet, trying to make it say, It would have been nice if the timing were different. He looks away for a second and then back at me.

He understands.

Joe Stamps

Who Am I Now?

Back in the sixties I wore my hair long and grew a beard. People used to say I looked like Jesus.

When I was stoned people said I looked like Rasputin.

After the Sharon Tate killings people stopped commenting about who I looked like.

But I knew who I really looked like, the moment I saw the poster in the subway. Al Pacino as Serpico was a dead ringer for me. It irked me that no one else ever noticed the resemblance.

Years later, after putting on some unwanted weight, and with my hair prematurely streaked with grey, I went through my Grizzly Adams period.

By the eighties, my hair and beard were quite grey and I suddenly became Kenny Rogers.

Eventually my hair and beard were completely white and I was bordering on being portly. I accepted the seasonal Santa Claus jokes.

I've even been taken for Jerry Garcia from the Grateful Dead.

I never really minded any of it, until about three years ago.

I was in a bar, drinking my bourbon on-the-rocks. I wasn't cruising anyone, just minding my own business. In the mirror, I happened to notice a young man staring at me. We made eye contact and he didn't look away. He smiled. I smiled back. He came over.

I was flustered. People don't approach me much anymore. I offered to buy my new young friend a drink, but he insisted instead on buying me one, which I thought was even better.

He was young, with a number of years to go yet to be half my age;

cute and scruffy in a 'Bill and Ted' kind of way. We drank and chatted. He told me about his Spiderman comic book collection.

I admitted to having a thing for Wolverine, especially in the Weapon X series in which he was mostly totally nude. "He can scratch my back with those retractable metal claws anytime," I said.

He smiled and signaled the bartender for two more drinks. He brought up the EC Classics of the fifties: *Tales from the Crypt, The Vault of Horror.* He read them in reprints. I grew up with the originals.

I was able to hold up my end of the conversation quite well, better than I was able to keep holding in my stomach, though if he noticed it didn't seem to matter.

He started telling me how much he really loved *MAD* magazine and that he had almost a complete set of issues all the way back to the sixties.

"That's really terrific," I said. "Though I have to admit I've outgrown *MAD* magazine."

"Outgrown *MAD*?" He stared at me wide-eyed. "What are you saying?"

"Just that the only time I ever bother to even flip through the pages anymore is when I'm sitting in my dentist's waiting room." I shrugged. "It's really for kids. You'll outgrow it."

"I can't believe I'm hearing this." He shook his head in amazement.

"Oh, you can believe it all right. . . . I'm hot for *Wolverine*, nostalgic about *Tales from the Crypt.* I wonder what else we can find that we might have in common?"

He ignored my lame overture. "What would you do without *MAD* magazine?"

I looked at him over the top of my spectacles. "How do you mean?" I wondered if the kid was weird. Serial killer material. He was beginning to make me nervous. He had bought me two drinks. That was weird in itself.

"Well. . . . " He shrugged. "I guess you can do anything you want when you're famous."

"Famous? I'm famous, am I?" I smiled, finally catching on. "So . . . you recognized me?"

He nodded, grinning at me, basking in my imagined celebrity.

"I'm not who you think I am." I shook my head. "I'm not Kenny Rogers."

He burst out laughing. "Kenny Rogers! Hah! That MAD sense of humour!"

He wasn't one of those who thought that I look like Kenny Rogers. I wondered hopefully if he thought I looked like Al Pacino. It would be a sign, that this was the one I've been waiting for. The one I would be spending the rest of my life with.

"Kenny Rogers!" He shook his head trying to contain his mirth. "You're too much. . . . " He chuckled. "Would it be okay . . . umm . . . can I call you Bill?"

"Bill? Why Bill?"

He stared at me as I lifted my glass to my lips. His smile faltered. "Aren't you Bill Gaines?"

I nearly choked on my drink. I threw a furtive glance at my reflection in the mirror behind the bar.

"Bill Gaines!? You mean the publisher of *MAD* magazine!?" I was really shaken. "He's got to be close to seventy years old by now! Do I look seventy to you? Do I!?"

"I'm sorry. . . . I didn't mean to upset you, it's just . . . " He shrugged. "You look just like him."

I signaled the bartender for a refill, even though I wasn't done with the one I had in my hand.

My young friend began searching the crowd for an avenue of escape. "I'm supposed to be meeting someone here. I think I better go look for them."

"Yeah, I know." I smirked into my drink. "I just saw him go into the back room."

"What?" He glanced over his shoulder towards the open doorway leading to the darkened recreation area in the rear of the bar. "Who?"

"Alfred E. Neuman."

He blinked, then chuckled. "Guess I deserved that one."

"Guess you did."

He paid the bartender for my drink, but indicated he didn't want one himself. He stood there for a couple of seconds, but then turned and moved off into the crowd.

"Thanks, anyway, for the drinks!" I called out, making sure everyone heard that he had paid for my drinks. I hoped it embarrassed him.

I sat alone, drinking my bourbon and ruminating. I really thought that for a fraction of a second he actually considered staying with me. After all I had managed to hold my own in a conversation about comic books, that had to be a plus in my favour. I seriously doubted that there were many people in the bar, even half my age, who could have done any better. A case of mistaken identity. Relationships have started with less.

"I could be Captain America," I thought wryly. "And he could be Bucky."

I consoled myself with the idea that to somebody that age anybody over thirty probably looks like they are seventy.

"It's no fun being famous," I thought as I signaled the bartender for another drink. "What's left for me now? Walt Whitman?"

Wickie Stamps

Fine Lines

We are engaged in our regular play: bondage, cutting and whipping. Thoroughly wet—and enraged—I decide to fist her. I release her restraints. I kneel over her. With ankle restraint in hand I hit her. The buckle of the restraint slams into her ankle bone. As soon as it lands I realize I aimed poorly and had, perhaps, really injured her. I look down. My lover, who immediately cried out in pain, has placed her hands over her head and curled up into the fetal position. Slightly stunned or perhaps high from the scene, I stare at this human being that lays whimpering before me. Unconsciously, my hand tightens around the restraint. I think I mumble a feeble apology. But, I am not sure, for at that moment, a new-found sense of power is spreading throughout my body. A terrified woman lays cowering before me. Although a small part of me is horrified at my inadvertent act of brutality this fact was lost in my desire, actually my compulsion, to again *really* hurt this woman. I wonder if she has safe-worded. Probably so. Hopefully not. My breathing quickens. I envision myself rolling this woman—my lover—over onto her back and smashing her in the face. With each blow I'd tell her what a fucking miserable cunt she is . . . just like . . . just like. . . .

I stop myself; stop my thinking; I stop this fantasy which is propelling me back into a world I know too well.

I breathe in and suppress an urge to vomit. Mechanically I reach out my hand, turn over my terrified lover. Gently, I pry her arms open and pull her close to me. I sweep her tear-stained hair off of her face.

I begin to rock her in my arms. In the silence, broken only by my lover's muffled sobs, I am forced to understand that the huge divide that I had so smugly carved between my father and myself is really nothing more than a fine line that exists within my mind.

Christina Starr

Girlfriend to Girlfriend

In 1989 I loved a woman. For the first time. She was a teacher of languages. When we met, we spoke always in French. She spoke easily. I imitated. I wanted to copy her words and learn from her tongue. I wanted my mouth to fly through the language like hers did. Like her language. Like her tongue.

I adored her. For what she could teach me. About her. About me. For the straight blunt swing of her dark brown hair. For the quick generosity of her smile.

I craved her. Because she was bright and political and honest. Because she gave laughter and words.

She never knew.

I lived with a man. She'd recently left one. I didn't know any lesbians, including myself. *If I were a man,* I wrote in my journal, *I would say that I am in love.*

Our lessons ended and we became friends. Still speaking only in French. The allure of the foreign, for me. The adoration of a disciple, for her. We went to movies and drank coffee. We talked late at night and drank wine. We built trust and affection. We discussed and debated. We confessed.

She told me there'd once been a woman. Who taught her things on her body but did not make her a lesbian. I was afraid to ask what she learned. I was afraid to know what sex with a woman might teach me. I was afraid to tell her I loved her.

We did not kiss. We did not hold hands. We did not make love. We were friends.

Three years and one baby, for me. Three years, one marriage and four miscarriages, for her. I came out.

She faltered, felt angry. *Here goes another one off to the lesbians and we won't have anything to say.* She did not say she was angry. I did not tell her I had wanted to love her.

I told her instead about the women I met. The new things I learned about bodies. The inestimable bloom of desire. The sprout of new life from breast down to thighs. The touch of fingers hot as new leaves. (*Daphne unpetrified.*)

Safe in continuing friendship, she said that she had been angry. Safe in continuing friendship, I said I had no plans to let go.

I am lesbian. She accepts. She is not. We are friends.

1994 I write an article. *Making a sexual choice.* A coming-out story, accepted for print. The words define sexuality as choice. My sexuality. My choice. How I nurtured courage to use it. How I taught myself out of compulsion. How I loved a woman and never told her.

Publication date nears. I decide that it's time. Everyone knows, except her. *I have this friend, the first woman I loved. Consciously. The first time.*

I print a copy to take her. On a visit, out of town. I expect her to be touched, flattered. Warm. We will hug. There will be closeness and sharing. Our friendship will deepen. And I will come home, with no more secrets.

She does not read it, distracted. I worry she won't and consider disclosure. I leave it one more day.

At night we are reading. She in her room, I on the living room futon. We have said *goodnight*.

She calls between walls. Suddenly and with the confidence of trust. *Who's the woman you loved and never told?* Deep into *Saturday Night*, I am stunned. The answer, in casual calling across the thin wall, girlfriend to girlfriend, in our pyjamas, impossible: *I didn't know you were reading* that.

A secret? Who? I can't guess. But she does. And runs. As if towards an accident. With a single response. *No!*

Then sits, by instinct, on a chair. Reads again the revealing paragraph. Asks again to confirm.

And I feel like a magician unschooled in magic. My trick's been too good, the deception too thorough. The audience now won't believe me.

And I am wordless, embarrassed. *It's like getting a present,* she says, *five years too late. It's like finding all the flowers are dead.*

I have nothing to say. I am surprised by the impact I've made. Surprised how I want to avoid it. How I want the rabbit to get back in the hat so we can say the trick never happened.

We don't say much more about it. Somehow we get back to bed. Somehow we say a second goodnight and turn out the lights, again.

In her room perhaps she is dreaming of me. In mine I am chasing rabbits.

Matt Bernstein Sycamore

How I Got These Shorts

It's my fifth trick. He calls around eleven, says do you go to Concord. I say 100 an hour, 250 for the night, wash up, catch the last train, and of course he isn't there. So I'm standing there waiting, thinking he's not going to show up and there isn't another train 'til morning and what the fuck am I gonna do. Finally, this man comes up in Speedos and a windbreaker, says are you Tyler like there's anyone else around with pink hair. Then we're driving along, he's pushing my head to his crotch saying *suck my cock suck my cock* and I'm sucking his limp cock, he's doing Rush every few minutes and squeezing my balls and we're driving in the pitch dark—I don't know *where the fuck* we are. Tells me he's been up all weekend on crystal, met these two straightboys and don't I want to fuck these straightboys. I say yeah, I really wanna fuck those straightboys. Says he gave the straightboys his Mercedes and they're gonna show up at his house, I'm thinking hell yeah the straightboys are gonna show up with your Mercedes. We get to his house and he's flying off his ass, chasing me around, trying to get me to do crystal. Then this straightboy shows up—but he's by himself—and he's some *flaming* fag, just flaming. I pour him a drink, I'm standing there in my boxers sort of flirting with him. The trick comes in, I'm sucking his cock and the straightboy's watching, I'm kind of embarrassed. The straightboy takes out his cock and I'm thinking that was easy so I suck his cock and then the *real* straightboys show up, turns out the other guy was another whore. The real straightboys aren't so cute—one of them has a potbelly and he's only about eighteen. I say you wanna drink. The trick takes me in the other room, says you like ecstasy does it make you horny. I say X *oh* it makes me *so* horny. I take the X and I've already smoked a lot of pot and had some Xanax and

Valium and Niacin and a few drinks. So I'm Xing my brains out, hiding
in the kitchen. The straightboy with the potbelly comes in, says are you
watching a video. I say *you* wanna watch one and I turn one on. He watches
and I squeeze my cock, he gets scared and runs into the other room. I go
in the bathroom to take a shower. I'm spacing out in the mirror and the
straightboy comes in, looks both ways, locks the door and says shh. . . .
Takes out his cock and pretends he's gonna piss, starts jerking off. So I
help him. He comes twice, says keep this between us okay. I say don't
worry *honey*, go into the bedroom and the trick says did you make any
progress with the straightboys. I say I just jerked one off. The other whore
is trying on all this underwear, it's like everything from the *International
Male* catalogue and more. He's trying on this leopard print metallic thong,
swinging his hips in front of the mirror, saying things like shhh*wank*. And
that's when I put on these shorts.

Sherece Taffe

The Club

As I enter The Club I'm greeted by loud pumping Soca music. The air is thick with the smell of sex and my hormones begin to overtake my dyke senses. All around me is a sea of the beautiful bodies of pretty young gay men. They cause this dyke to harbour thoughts that might get me into trouble with the radical dykes who believe they are the keepers/guardians of dyke etiquette. If they knew that deep down I desire the bodies of gay men they would surely revoke my privileges. I long/yearn for a pretty little gay boy. Not an underage gay boy. The gay boy I refer to is a gay man that is little and pretty and fresh and sweet and eager and controllable. The gay boy I refer to is one whom I am bigger than so that I have all the power. So that I can corner him and demand that he bend over and then I can do him with a dildo the way I've always wanted to do a gay boy.

The boys in The Club assault the place in my mind where I keep these fantasies. The boys in The Club awaken the urges I protect. How do I, a conspicuously large black dyke, ogle gay boys without being noticed by the other dykes that populate The Club? Will it look suspicious if I approach one of the pretty boys to dance? These thoughts are running through my mind as I enter The Club. Then, without warning, the sweetest boy I have ever seen crosses my path. All thoughts of appearances leave my mind as I follow him to the bar. I catch the eye of the bartender and ask the boy what he's drinking. After the drinks arrive, I escort him to a quiet corner of The Club and proceed to slip him all of my best lines. While I'm chatting him up, I'm aware of the stares we are getting. This excites me. There are men around who seem to be wondering if I'm a man in drag or if I'm a straight woman in drag or if the two of us are

259

role-playing dykes. The attention that we are getting is putting me in a hell of a mood so I drag him onto the dance floor. As the music pulsates through my aching body I pull him closer and suggest that we leave The Club.

In the taxi, I push him away as he tries to kiss me. He tells me that he has never had sex before and this elates me. The driver watches and I know he's wondering what to make of us, but that doesn't concern me as much as the fact that I'm beginning to realize that this boy thinks I'm a man. He tells me that drag queens have always fascinated him. He tells me that he jacks off in the men's room after he sees a show. He tells me that I'm the first drag queen he has seen who dresses "down" instead of dressing up like a "Glamour Girl." I grab his face and kiss him hard on the mouth then push him away again as he tries to touch me.

When we reach my place, I instruct him to sit as I enter my bedroom. I go to my nighttable, pull out my dildo and harness, and strap it on. Then I go and stand in front of him. He asks me to put the lights on so he can see me. I tell him where the switch is and as he walks towards it, I grab him from behind and push him over the couch so that his behind is up in the air facing me. He lets out a startled little squeal that gets my juices flowing. As I rip his pants from his butt, he tells me to slow down because this is his first time and he wants to savour it. I tell him to shut up and memorize the moment so he can savour it later. I tell him that he will keep quiet except to voice his pleasure. He nods his head and I ask him to nod in response to my future questions because I'm in charge now and if I hear his voice before it is orgasmic I will cease the festivities and send his ass home.

To this he agrees and I proceed to put a condom on my dildo, gloves on my hands and lubrication on his waiting trembling eager ass. This sensation alone causes him to moan with pleasure so I ask him if he likes how that feels. As he begins to nod I slide my finger into his quivering hole and he chokes back a scream. As I guide my finger in and out and around, he arches his back and moans again. Louder. I pull my finger almost completely out and attempt to insert another one inside him when he lets go of a scream so filled with the double edge of pleasure and pain that I falter and my hand slips away from him, which causes him to collapse in a heaving mound on the couch. I wait until he is about to catch his breath before I jam three lubricated fingers into his ass and cause him to yell out in pain and beg me to be more gentle. To this request I slap his butt and tell him since he has broken the rules he must leave.

While he begs me to please don't send him home unfulfilled, I take the opportunity to lubricate my dildo then plunge it into his tender fresh virgin exposed hole. This pretty little gay boy lets out a scream so piercing, it stops me in my tracks. This action, or inaction, drives him wild and again he's begging. To hear this boy begging me to fuck him urges me on and the butch in me finally takes complete control. Now I'm sure I can really feel my dick penetrating his tender flesh. As I ram him deeper and harder the power of the situation wells up inside me and I begin to spank his soft supple ass. This drives him into a wild frenzy and his voice rises at least three octaves. Plunging my dick deeper into his flesh I feel him about to explode with an orgasm, so I slow down my rhythm just enough to decrease the urgency and prolong the experience.

My boy is now thrashing about wildly, begging and begging and begging and begging. He screams and thrashes and begs and cries and laughs and screams some more. The boy is bathed in sweat and his black body glistens in the moonlight. He can barely contain himself as I initiate him into the world of pure lust-filled, mind-altering, sensory-overloading, inhibition-depriving, body-draining, dream-making, fantasy-fulfilling sex. Feeling my orgasm about to overtake me, I return to the deep rhythmic pumping strokes that threaten to drive my boy over the edge into the land of orgasmic madness. On the edge of my own descent into this same madness, I'm suddenly transported back onto the dance floor of The Club where I have been dancing with the sweetest prettiest boy I ever did see. As I'm about to proposition him, I see a woman who makes me abandon my fantasy for the moment, thank him for the dance and head toward this butch-looking, femme-acting dyke dressed almost identical to the pretty gay boys.

She is fierce on the dance floor and we approach each other without exchanging any words. After the dance I buy her a drink and she tells me that she has been watching me and my boy. She asks me if I'm bi and is relieved to know that I am not. This discussion reveals our common interest in doing a boy and we agree to cruise together. Watching her scope out the boys brings on a rush of desire so deep I must fight the urge to grab hold of her and do her right there in The Club. It is at this moment that I begin to think maybe my fantasy can be fulfilled by this woman who looks so much like a boy. Thoughts of seeing her naked flesh draped over my couch begin to creep up on me and my cruising becomes a cloak to shield the wanton lust beginning to replace the need to live out my fantasy.

At the end of the night we negotiate a rendezvous to meet the following week and continue our cruising for pretty fresh tender boys. In the meantime we watch The Club empty and speculate on which boy we would be able to do easily, which would require the use of force and which would take us both on. On my way home, alone, in the taxi I rewrite my fantasy so that my butch-looking, femme-acting fellow boy-craving dyke replaces the boys who were there before her. Perhaps this is a fantasy I can share with those radical /political dykes without the fear of expulsion.

Cecilia Tan

Larceny

Sarah shouldered her pack. Now was the good moment to leave.

Not like one time five years ago, when she got caught stealing peaches from the widow Johnson's tree. Riper and sweeter than any she'd ever had from a store, Mrs. Johnson used to bring baskets of them over in neighbourly kindness when Sarah was small. But she hadn't done that in a long time and Sarah had grown tall enough to pick the fruit for herself. It wasn't stealing that first time, because no one had told her not to. But after the old widow bitched about how she didn't want "that girl" in the yard, then it would be stealing. Mrs. Johnson deserved it, Sarah decided, for all the things Sarah overheard her say to other neighbours over the back fence, things she would never let Sarah's father hear, like "that tramp of a girl, growing up to be as rotten as her mother, the no-good hussy, running off like that." And so Sarah had snuck into the yard when Mrs. Johnson was trimming her weeds around front.

There it was, the sweet taste of revenge, lascivious flesh, the deep bite of satisfaction as she sat in her own yard and licked the juice from her fingers. That was the good moment, when she was so full, and before her father found out, and beat her with the flat back of the hairbrush that her mother had left behind. It might not have been so bad if she hadn't shouted, "You don't care about the fucking peaches! I know you just want to sleep with the old hag!" She would have missed the whole ordeal, the humiliation of being fourteen years old and bare-bottomed over her father's knee, if only she had gone.

Then there was the time two years ago, when she'd gone to the prom without a date. In her second-hand white heels, she danced with one boy after another and stole their wristwatches, just because she could. The ones with leather bands, with tiny buckles like belts on the wrist, those were easy. Some of them were still stiff, brand new grown-up gifts, and she pocketed them with special glee. At the end of the night she'd stood on the curb as she watched tuxedoed, gowned bodies make their way to cars and limos. That was the good moment, knowing she had all their petty little happinesses tucked away in her rhinestone purse. But then it was gone, as they were all gone, to parties, to lose their virginity, to start their adult lives. She ruined her shoes walking in the grit along the golf course, and, cursing her blisters at the top of her lungs, heaved the watches one at a time into a sand trap. She limped home to find the lights in Mrs. Johnson's bedroom burning bright and her own house dark and for the first time, empty.

And now, now she stood at her bedroom door, with her hand on the knob and her pack on her shoulder, heavy with things: a pair of silver sconces (wedding gifts to her parents), her mother's jewelry (from the ivory inlaid box that her father had never touched), that hairbrush, a novel she'd found (on the bus, next to a sleeping woman), her father's wrist-watch and wallet (which he always left behind when he went next door) and room for plenty of peaches. The good moment upon her, she stole into the night.

Robert Thomson

Recipe for a Merry Christmas

Take one deepening economic depression and couple it with your low paying, hateful part-time job. Add a dash of shitty weather and an impending mutated flu virus spreading rapidly through your friends and relatives, remembering that it will only be a matter of time before you too are stricken.

Add two second cousins that you've only seen three times before and for whom you've had to purchase presents. (Oh yeah, *teenaged* second cousins.) Blend in one great-aunt who can't dress herself in anything other than polyester pantsuits, in which she looks surprisingly pregnant at age sixty-four. Being careful not to disrupt her really really big tall hairdo, gently remind yourself that her ability to buy gifts for others is as well developed as her fashion sense. *(Last Christmas? "Here you go, honey, I hope you like it. What is it? Well, it's kind of a bag, I guess. You could use it as a make up bag.")*

Combine with the two acne-ravaged second cousins and the one Wal-Mart-inhibited Aunt, her three chain-smoking daughters, their boyfriends, lovers and/or new friends. Sift in twelve pounds of denial, three quarts of verbal abuse, eight cases of alcoholism and one fully stocked bar. Sprinkle generously with rumours of unspoken abortions, private adoptions, HIV infections, cocaine addictions, lengthy hospital visits and a hush-hush affair with a noted politician and let boil for several hours inside the house of the deceased relative who links all the above together, the same relative who left her vast fortune to an operator at a psychic telephone service.

For those desiring a more lively gathering, consider introducing to the proceedings an exhausted three year old with good lungs whose favoured method of communication is crying.

Wrap the proceedings in a thick coat of repression and serve immediately.

At the end of the gathering (provided that all assault charges have been dropped) hug and kiss affectionately goodbye and part with warm wishes for the next gathering at Easter.

Robert Thomson

Just Best Wishes

A birthday card arrived for me in the mail yesterday. From Mother. From beyond the grave. Or at least from postal purgatory. And only six years late! Now I know that the dead can communicate with the living.

On the card is a painting of a small lake with still waters and a family picnicking off to the side, waving in the direction of the card holder. The family members are smiling, enjoying a peaceful lunch, a peanut butter and jelly sandwich and chocolate milk picnic. There are no tears or tantrums. It's all smiles and God.

The son is wearing a blue and white striped shirt and sailor's cap and is missing his two front teeth. He looks all of ten years old. He will probably grow up to be a doctor, perhaps a vet. There is a squirrel staring at him from a nearby tree with an odd, seemingly knowing smile on its face and you can never overlook the foreshadowing nuances of greeting cards. The boy is oblivious, however, to the squirrel. He is too busy waving and smiling. Perhaps he'll become a proctologist or maybe a politician. Same thing. Whatever he becomes is not the point. The point is that he is supposed to be me. Or rather, I was supposed to be him.

This card was chosen cleverly by Mother before it was lost in the mail six years ago. And even though it says HAPPY 24th BIRTHDAY! in large carnival yellow lettering, what the card is really saying, or wants to say, is, *What happened to that little boy?* My mother wants to know. She feels she has a right to know. I don't think Mother's version of him ever existed outside of her own head. Perhaps he drowned. Maybe it would have been easier that way if I had. It would have been less traumatic for Mother to explain. The way things went, all I did was to deny her the opportunity to grieve because deep down, no matter how she tried to forget, I was still alive.

Inside the card, in mother's sloping, careful handwriting is her birthday message:

At this point in time we can't cope with your chit chat about your personal life. We both find it hard to accept. Life can be difficult at best but for you it will probably be even more troubled. Set goals and do anything you can to achieve them. Best wishes on your birthday. Mom and Dad.

Best wishes. Not *love.* Not *we miss you, call us soon* or *come visit, we got you a great present!* Just *best wishes.*

I used to sign *best wishes* on letters and greeting cards I sent to ex-boyfriends and friends who drifted away and on thank-you letters to relatives I saw once a year for Christmas presents they'd given me, usually socks. It's only awkward when you know the reader knows you don't mean it. *Best wishes* isn't as good as *love* or as mannered as *sincerely. Best wishes* is a discreet way of saying *thanks for nothing* or *you won't ever hear from me again.*

And at the bottom right hand side of the card is a little postscript:

Please don't call us anymore. We don't want to hear from you.

I put the card in the kitchen garbage and watched as it got soaked with a mixture of coffee grinds and the previous night's spaghetti leftovers. Mother's best wishes for me didn't come true. And the boy who fell into the water is just now learning how to swim.

Kitty Tsui

A Femme, A Daddy and Their Dyke

I am fascinated by body parts. There's tits and ass. And ass and thighs. Thighs in particular excite me. Muscular thighs. Thunder thighs. Kind, open thighs. And there are lips. Soft lips. Lips painted a shade of red. Or unpainted but flushed with blood from a session of rough kissing. Lips moving down my inner thigh and up the length of my quadricep. Lips wrapped around the dildo anchored in the crotch of my 501s. Teeth teasing my skin. Teeth sinking into my flesh.

Body parts. There's back and shoulders. Big back. Broad shoulders. Breasts that fill my hand. Firm forearms. An unyielding knee. There's the curve of a stomach. The line of her neck. The bulge of a bicep. There are soft, sweet toes. A gently contoured heel. That look in her eyes. The hint of a smile. The way she holds her chin in an arrogant sort of way.

Let me tell you about my Femme. She has long black hair and stands five foot seven in her stockinged feet. That's tall for a Chinese girl. Her nails are short but perfectly manicured. Sometimes she paints them a shade of red called "Real Ruby," but only when we're going into the bedroom, not out on the town. Her breasts are soft, sweet as a ripe mango.

She wears leather and lace dresses, garter belts and black seamed stockings because she knows I like them. She paints her face and dons high heels. She doesn't bother with panties. She knows that when I get excited, foreplay doesn't exist; I like to get to the core of things.

I force her down onto her hands and knees, play with the breasts that hang down in front of her. I tease her ass with my tongue, torment her cheeks with my knife. I like to enter her slow and make her feel every

269

inch. I grip her hard as I thrust into her and fuck her good and hard the way I know she likes it.

Sometimes I tie her down spread-eagled. With leather restraints lined with sheepskin. Sometimes I tie her with leather thongs that bite. I strap on my biggest dildo and parade in front of her, hefting its weight in my hand. Sometimes I lavish her body with kisses until she begs me to come inside her. Sometimes I'll push into her with no foreplay, knowing she's as wet as ocean spray. I'll thrust my hips into her until she screams and cries out my name. And when her orgasm explodes, I refuse to let her stop.

Other times I tie her up, exposing her back and her ass. I use an assortment of floggers, quirts, single tail whips, and canes. My Femme likes to be beaten. She asks nicely when she wants it. And I love to give it to her. She cries out and gets very wet. I kiss the length of her legs. I take my knife and make a slit from the top of the thigh to the Achilles tendon. The stocking splits, revealing flesh, and a thin line of blood burns into my vision, vivid as neon.

For my Daddy I dress in plain white t-shirts, blue jeans and black boots. She bought me a black motorcycle jacket I always wear. It's a Schott.

Let me tell you about my Daddy's tastes. She likes ass. Mine in particular. But really any ass will do. Spare and hard and tight. Large and round and pliable. In denim or in lace. In leather or a harness. In bikini bottoms or a jockstrap. In silk boxer shorts or cotton jockeys.

My Daddy likes my ass. She often walks steps behind me so she can watch the glutes move in my jeans. My Daddy likes my ass up in the air. She likes my ass in her mouth. She likes the look on my face when I hear the sound of her removing her belt. It's studded and made of heavy leather. I anticipate the pain with great pleasure. Daddy's going to beat my ass until it's blue and red and hot as bread fresh out of the oven.

My Daddy's strong. She's been an iron worker for six years. She stands five feet ten in socks and over six feet tall in boots. Her hair is black, flecked with grey. She wears it in a flat top. She has strong, fleshy fingers and a big fist.

The first thing I noticed about her was the dark moustache growing on her upper lip. The next thing I noticed was the size of her hands.

My Daddy is the first.

"It's going to hurt," she said. "I'm going to open you up, boy, and make you take it."

Now I take my Daddy's fist and her forearm. Hard and driving. Slow and deep.

My Daddy's strong. She takes me without hesitation. In full control. She strokes the core of my pleasure over and over. And she refuses to let me go.

David Watmough

Questions and Answers

Q. I'm Artemis and I live along the Mendocino coast. What's your name?

A. Mine is Davey—and you've reached me in Vancouver, British Columbia.

Q. You mean you're not here in California? But the letters "CA"?

A. Stand for Canada.

Q. Is that so? Do you work these machines for a living? You seem so expert. I'm afraid I'm a hopeless amateur. I'm also a widow.

A. I'm a writer. TV scripts, freelance articles—that kind of thing.

Q. How thrilling! Though a bit hair-raising for your wife I should think. I mean the uncertainty.

A. I'm not married.

Q. Is that so? How very interesting. One meets so few married men on this Internet. I think it is the playground of the young.

A. I am not so young.

Q. But young enough to read these little words on your screen. You sound so sprightly! Are you a man of many tastes?

A. Many tastes. I enjoy meeting strangers—especially those one degree removed from reality. A bit anti-social, I'm afraid.

Q. Oh come! I don't think you are one bit anti-social. A tiny bit laconic perhaps? Do you travel much? Are you familiar with this neck of the woods?

A. You flatter me. Yes, I almost bought a Victorian house some years ago in Mendocino. But last time I visited there I found the township had razed all the buildings that were at the edge of the ocean. I felt part of my life had been bulldozed into oblivion.

272

Q. I live in an area known as The Sea Ranch. We came up here when my husband retired from his optical business. Do you come down here via I-5 or take the coastal route?

A. We drive south as far as Roseburg, Oregon, where we stay overnight. Then we just drive on a few miles south to Coos Bay. The dogs love the beaches.

Q. You speak of "we." Is it a friend who accompanies you and your dogs on these delightful expeditions?

A. Once it was my mother and my aunt. But they are now dead. Usually with someone. Travel is dangerous nowadays.

Q. Which is why we choose this electronic highway, don't you think? I am surprised that there are not more mature people using it in this fashion. It is wasted on the young! Do you live alone as I do, Mr. Davey?

A. I mentioned the dogs, I think. And by the way, "Davey" doesn't take a prefix.

Q. You are so stately with your language! You mentioned dogs but not your entire domestic circumstance. There! I am doing the same as you! I have never used domestic circumstance before. It is rather fun, isn't it? I mean, like wearing masks at a masquerade ball or something.

A. Maybe we use the Internet as a rest from reality.

Q. Oh, I don't think so! We are being very real this evening. I mean two utter strangers talking of their past lives. You cannot know it, but when you mentioned the loss of the house by the sea it brought tears to my eyes.

A. That was certainly not my intention. No need to turn the electronic highway into the via dolorosa!

Q. You are so deft with words! I am quite uneducated. I let my husband do too much of my thinking for me. Now I regret it. But here alone at The Sea Ranch there is so much to regret. Are you a happy man? Or does despondency claim you from time to time?

A. You have so many questions! But "yes" to the last. I cannot claim to be always free of sadness or regret.

Q. That comforts me. Don't you think that sharing is the secret? The way to survive? The opposite is the price of my widowhood. The absence of another's ears or the comfort of his words. You get used to it of course. The original pain fades. But not the hurt of no-one-left-to-listen. That never goes away. I go to great lengths to deal with it. I make common cause with several other widows here but we really have nothing in common. If Basil were alive I would hardly give them the time of day. Does that make me a cynic, Davey?

A. It makes you very human. I know no widows. Only a handful of divorcees —which isn't the same.

Q. We all live in ghettos nowadays, don't you think? I recently heard someone say old people always grumble. I don't want to be labelled like that, do you?

A. I hate labels. If you knew my background you'd understand why. Even my own circle is constantly labelling—which is to say defining and thus confining.

Q. May I ask what kind of circle is that? Is it possible for you to tell me, do you think?

A. We are coming to the limitations of the Internet. If we were physically facing each other I could read your face. There would be icons to tell me if I could go further: a raising of the brow, a down-turning of the mouth.

Q. So this way is perhaps more risky. But where would we be without risk?

A. You have a point. But I'm still not sure I'm courageous enough for major indiscretions.

Q. I am sixty-nine and have "the big C" which has recently metastasised. It is only modesty preventing me from naming the specifics. Now can you understand why I accept risk and want to hold hands with the human race with whatever time I have left?

A. I am seventy-one and homosexual. I have mild diabetes but so far I have escaped AIDS which took my lover. Well, you persistent woman! I have now told a perfect stranger in California things about myself that my mother never knew at her death aged ninety-four.

Q. Those are indeed heavy things we now know about each other. Can we be sure this medium doesn't lead to, well, misuse?

A. I have never doubted it. Then I long ago learned to be prudent—especially with unseen speakers.

Q. I have always wondered about bachelors who chose a childless lifestyle.

A. I would quarrel with the verb "chose." In my life there has been no question of choice. On the other hand, I have always wondered about widows and widowers. My mother claimed that happy marriages invariably led to remarriage.

Q. It is not my view. Perhaps over this and other things we must agree to differ in our computer conversation. Can we not just say that we are just ships passing in the night?

A. Yes indeed, we are ships passing in the night for I can see we are headed for quite different harbours.

Graham Watts

Crossing the Rubicon

Murray throws his comic to the floor, swings his feet off the bed, slumps forward head in hands, and sighs. For several minutes he ignores the pain as his elbows dig into his thighs. He glances at his watch. Almost two. He's late, but still he doesn't move. His father is right. He's a wimp.

No! He is going. He won't deny himself any longer. He jumps up, quickly hand-smoothes his short blond hair and pushes sockless feet into Reeboks. He checks his pockets for wallet and gum and runs downstairs.

Saturday afternoon, his father sits with a bottle of beer watching the sports channel. "Where are you going now?" his father shouts.

Murray hesitates, knowing that he never sounds convincing when he lies. "Downtown. To Comic Cave."

"At your age I was playing football, not wasting my time reading comic books."

"Murray," his mother calls from the kitchen, "Betty wants you to watch videos with her tonight. Is she your girlfriend now?"

"Mum!" At sixteen he feels stifled by his parents. "Look. I'm going. Okay?" Running, he reaches the platform just as the train pulls in.

He sits stiffly, chewing a stick of gum to ease the cramp in his stomach. The train rattles over a bridge. He glances up at the coloured glass towers of the city centre, then down at their reflections in the river. The rattle increases. The train goes underground.

Murray runs out of the station. Crossing the avenue so as not to pass by Comic Cave, he hurries on. Twice before, his courage had failed him here. He had bought a comic, returned to the station fighting back tears of frustration and hating himself.

He reaches an intersection, checks to see that the street is empty, then turns the corner. Near the middle of the block he stops at an opening in a picket fence. Twenty-five feet inside are the steps of a rundown old house. Immobile, he stares at some ants racing along the narrow concrete path. Sweat prickles his upper lip. His resolve evaporates.

A car turns into the street. Heavy metal music pounds his ears in rhythm to the thump in his chest. The car stops. Someone shouts, "Hey! Faggot! My buddy wants his cock sucked." Whistles and laughter assault him.

The ants scatter at the vibrations in the path. Murray bounds up the steps of the Gay Community Centre, bursts through the door, then slams it shut. Leaning his heaving back against it, he struggles to catch his breath.

All twelve heads of the Gay Youth Group turn towards him. Someone comes over and asks, "Are you okay?"

"Yeah," he responds, his attention absorbed by the clear green eyes, the dark curly hair, the smiling face of the inquirer.

This someone thumbs up his name tag. "I'm Paul. What's your name? I'll fix you a tag."

"Murray," he replies, much too loudly.

Jess Wells

Short Term Parking

We were brazen, nearly naked in a parking garage. It was our lunch hour. My business suit was flung over the car seat, her blouse was crumpled over the spare tire. We hoped the windows were steamed opaque. The shoppers scurried around the car. This is just a fling, we said. She hovered over me in her lace bra, studying how my slip clung to the sweat she had brought to my skin.

This is just a fling, we said, silently taking inventory of all the parking ramps where we had been lunching on each other's skin. This is not a challenge to our marriages, we vowed, noting that the lace bra and the slip were not noticed at home. "Chapter One," I said, "Short-Term Parking."

We sat in the rain in her car, in the front seat this time, staring at tracks that took me north to a girlfriend each night. Why couldn't we seem to break it off? We had vowed to do so. Still we found places and ways to have mind-and-spine-bending sex. Waiting for the train, hand in hand, we shared the guilt. The whistle blew. We held our breath. "Chapter Two," I said. "Thank God It's The Southbound Train."

It was wrong. We called it off, we started up. We called it off again. One night beside my wife I woke at 2 a.m. in a sweat, terrified. "Chapter Three," I muttered to myself, "Persistent Truth at 2 a.m." I was in love.

I left my wife. Those I loved had always been tornados. Their words were delivered in storms. Now my life was quiet. She was gentle. "Chapter Four," I whispered to her in the dark, "Tattered Boat, Calm Harbour."

Neither of us were prepared. I couldn't bear another wife. She couldn't speak her mind. We broke up. We fell back into bed, hungry. We deteriorated into friends. We tried to be sex dates. We disintegrated into

278

acquaintances. "Who are we and what is my title?" she moaned. "Who cares about labels!" I shrieked. "Chapter Five," I said, "A Box, A Category, A Question of Which Capacity."

Wounds healed from our previous lives. Some level of faith was restored. We crept towards the trappings of coupledom. My refrigerator held her favourite olives, hers chilled my ice cream. Keys were exchanged, socks mingled in the wash. We were cautious. Money wasn't shared. Moving in was postponed. Time spent apart was guarded. Joint decisions were kept to a minimum. We paced around the ground called marriage, neither of us willing to curl up. "Chapter Six," I told her, "Dogs Circling a Rug."

Dianne Whelan

The Uninvited Guest

It shouldn't be a big deal. The simple act of sitting at a table, passing the butter, the salt, and light conversation about anything but God, politics or my sexuality. I would sit where I always sit, to the left of my father who is always at the head of the table. My mother basically rules the palace but dinner is a sort of figurehead thing for Dad. He never carves the roast, the ham or the turkey. His domestic qualities end with peanut butter on toast. But you would never guess that to see him in his posture at the family dinner table.

Dinner is next Sunday, first one in six months. My girlfriend and I are in town for a few weeks and Mom wants a family dinner. She knows I am here with my girlfriend, but in our phone calls and conversations her name has not come up. They know I travelled in a car with her for three weeks, but when they ask me about the trip, they censor out those parts of the story. It's like walking without a shadow, nothing refracts, everything just passes through.

Whenever I see my parents, I am a wounded animal amongst other wounded animals. I have to walk gently around all the healing scars. I am almost always polite on the phone, but there is a hesitancy in my voice. They know the secret, everybody knows the secret, in fact, it is *not* a secret, but to my parents it is still only *quietly* acknowledged. I find that hard: it's not that I want to talk to my mom about my sex life *per se*, I don't have fantasies of stirring gravy while Mom is mashing potatoes and talking about breast sizes. I just want my girlfriend invited to dinner.

They must know it pisses me off that my sister will quite naturally be bringing her husband to dinner while my partner remains unacknow-ledged. It is all these perks the word *straight* brings to people's lives: the unspoken privileges. It is not bringing my girlfriend to dinner. Every day I phone my mom, who before I say anything tells me how much she is looking forward to dinner. I, of course, am calling to ask her, or actually tell her, that I am bringing my girlfriend. It is a right I suddenly want to seize.

"Hey, Mom, it's me," I want to yell. "I am the spirit of your goddesses, I too hold the hammer, I too pick berries, I too fall in love, you aphrodite crone."

Every day I get up and phone and every day I hang up without taking on the issue. It's just dinner, right? Why do I want to turn something that could be fine for everyone but me into something that will be uncomfortable for everybody?

In seven years I have never brought a girlfriend to dinner. Next week we will drive there and while I am assuring my girlfriend that everything will be fine, my stomach will be break-dancing in my throat. As I walk through the door, I am going to act like nothing is different. Everybody else won't do as good a job hiding the strain. But next week I am going to dinner. Next week I am bringing an uninvited guest to dinner and I am going to demand that place at the table.

Ben Widdicombe

Millennium

There is a man across the street with a tripod. He has closely cropped blond hair and a tight black t-shirt. He is a photographer.

From my room at the top of the house I see him peering through his viewfinder, waiting for a plane. He has explained that he works for a newspaper; that he is photographing planes for a campaign against the new runway. He says the noise is destroying peoples' lives.

Downstairs, a cupboard slams. Jane's voice comes up from the floor-board and hums through my carpet. Scott's voice is clearer, loud and masculine.

" . . . never did," he yells.

"Haven't been," Jane says, before her voice soaks into the walls. I can hear the approach of the plane.

"No!" says Scott.

"Yes!" says Jane.

On my bed, I am reading a magazine. The back pages carry advertise-ments from lonely men.

Me: / Handsome young / Good looking young / Striking / Young / Boy / Bear / Master seek / searching / You: / fit / swimmer's build / non-scene / 'tached / eager slave / and long nights in / discreet / No fats femmes freaks / show me the ropes / genuine first ad / Sydney / Melbourne / Anywhere / people ask me why I'm single / your photo gets mine / all letters answered / send photo in gear.

The photographer tightens a screw on his tripod and crouches behind the camera. I cannot see the plane (it comes from behind), but the air is screaming with noise, filling the street until the gutters run with it and the windows rattle in their sills.

I circle an ad on the page.

Suddenly a shock of shadow on my window and the photographer snaps his camera. I see the plane from the instant it breaks over our roof until it disappears behind tall trees on the other side of the road. Inside my room, the books shudder on their shelves.

When the dogs stop barking the photographer rubs his forehead and frowns. He readjusts his camera and lights a cigarette. He has been there all morning.

The advertisement I have circled says: *If we start now, we'll have been together five years by the year 2000. Twenty-something seeks the real thing. Reply box 5889.*

I don't know why the ad appeals to me. It has a sense of hope, perhaps. Jane slams another cupboard door.

"Liar," she says.

I close the magazine on my bed and go to the top of the stairs. I can hear her feet moving around the kitchen below and things being slammed on the bench. I go down.

Scott is sitting at the kitchen table with his back to the stairs. He is hunched forward, but when he hears my footsteps he leans back in his chair.

Jane is tight-lipped as she transfers boxed food into jars. Kernels of pasta and colourful breakfast cereals are spread across the countertop, and grocery bags are in a pile on the floor. I go to the desk in the next room and get a piece of writing paper from the drawer.

"Paul," she says, "would you come in here for a moment, please?"

I take a stamp and an envelope and move cautiously towards the kitchen.

"I just want to *apologize,*" she says, "for our behaviour." She is speaking to me but her eyes are fixed on her boyfriend.

"No worries," I say. "You guys are allowed to, um . . . you know."

"Fight," she says.

"Yeah. Fight."

"But we all have to live together, and we're sorry." She is still looking at Scott, whose back tenses beneath his shirt.

"Sorry, mate," he says, without turning around.

"No worries. . . . "

I shift on my feet, uneasy at playing Jane's stooge. We have been friends since university, she and I, and I know her tricks better than any boyfriend.

After a respectful pause I go back up the stairs to my room. Behind me, Jane and Scott hiss at each other more quietly.

At my desk, I spread the sheet of writing paper next to the magazine. I reread the ad and select a photograph of myself from a box I keep under my bed. On a notepad I practice the letter.

"Looking for someone to bring in the new century. . . . "

No. I cross the sentence out.

"I am in my late twenties. . . . "

The sound of a cup breaking, and Jane's footsteps toward the front door. Scott's voice says *"Fine,"* and it slams behind her.

" . . . sincere, with a lot of love to give."

Scott turns on his stereo, and as another plane gathers noise he raises the volume to drown it out.

I fold the page in three and put a photograph into the envelope. It's good luck to post the letter immediately.

Downstairs, Scott is sitting in his favourite chair with his eyes closed. When I pass him he is beating the armrests in time with the music.

Sweet Home Alabama.

Outside, the street is empty and bright. The photographer has opened a can of lemonade and is sitting lazily on the curb. On a leather thong around his neck he wears a silver ring, which flashes in the sunlight. I ask him if I can look through his camera.

"Sure," he says.

In the frame of the shot I can see the peak of our roof and my window beneath it. My curtains, I see, are the same colour as the sky.

"Sometimes, the planes come right over the point of your roof," he says. "That's what I'm trying to get."

I look again through his camera, and in the very distance I can see a glint of silver fuselage.

The photographer indicates our street with his hand. "If the airport gets their way," he says, "they'll develop this for a runway."

"Really? They've got plans for that?"

He nods. "Uh-huh. It's all going to go."

"We're just renting," I say. "When's it going to go?"

"All by the year 2000," he says. "The whole lot."

I look at our house on the corner and the others around it. Each one is different.

"But we're fighting it," he says, "every inch. Excuse me."

The curb is broken where Jane backed into the mailbox last year, and I step across the gap to post my letter.

The plane tumbles over our roof in a monsoon of noise, and the moment it's in place the photographer snaps his shutter.

I cannot hear my letter hit the bottom.

Duane Williams

Renovations

the rectum

Now Dale has KS. The cancer is making its debut in his rectum. He's a little sore when Jake picks him up at the hospital in his '69 Bug, shining like an eight ball in the late morning sun. There's a hot pizza in the backseat and the pepperoni smell nearly makes him puke.

"How'd the test go?" Jake asks as he speeds onto the freeway.

"Just fine," he says, rolling down the window. The station wagon in the next lane is packed with pillows, suitcases, hysterical kids waving. One makes fish lips against the glass as he looks away. "The doctor said I'm fine. There wasn't anything wrong after all."

the bathroom

Their voices echo through the empty apartment. The landlord was right—it has potential, lots of potential, not much else. It's a dive but they're fixing it up. They've already painted the walls, *colonial white*, the only colour the landlord would allow. They've built bookshelves with bricks and planks, stolen from the construction site down the street. They've even scraped the paint off the bedroom window (for some reason the previous tenants had blackened it over). Now Jake wants to strip the toilet seat, its floral wallpaper stained a questionable yellow.

"A wooden toilet seat," he insists, "will give the place a country feel." He stands beside the toilet with no shirt on. His nipples are erect and Dale notices that his pecs *are* getting bigger. Lately his thing has been to do pushups over top of him. He says he saw it in a porno.

"You've got to do all that work just to find some kind of cheap fake wood, you know. Take a look at this place, Jake. It was hardly built with an appreciation for quality," he says, taking a seat on the edge of the claw-footed tub. A cockroach crawls from the mouth of a hideous African mask, one of Jake's yard sale discoveries, which he has hung above the toilet. "What the hell?" Dale says, as the thing scales the freshly-painted wall. Jake grabs a piece of toilet paper and scoops up the cockroach. He crushes it between his fingers. There can't be any bones but something cracks. Ugh! Dale steadies himself, grasping the cool porcelain edge with both hands. "You didn't have to kill it," he says. Jake drops it into the toilet and they watch as the spotted paper swirls away. He flushes again and it disappears.

"Wait 'til it's done," Jake says as he puts down the seat. "It's gonna be beautiful."

"You know, you never. . . . "

"What? I never what?" he asks, kneeling beside the toilet.

"Forget it," Dale says.

"Pass me that razor blade, will you?"

"Where?"

"On the sink."

"I don't see any razor blade."

"Dale, I can see it from here," he says, "beside the soap. It's practically biting you in the face."

"Oh yeah. Here it is."

"Dale, is there something wrong?"

"No. Why?"

"You were gonna say something," he says. "You said I never—"

"Oh, I was just thinking out loud," Dale says. He offers him the blade but he doesn't take it. Jake raises an eyebrow at him. "Jake, it was nothing," Dale says, with a smile, so he'll take the blade.

No, he never listens and Dale can't be bothered to convince him about the wood.

He presses his thighs together as he sits there, watching the muscles in Jake's back. They shift and tighten beneath his tan skin. It's been almost two weeks since they moved in; Dale's patience to deal with another mess, especially in the bathroom, is beginning to fail him. He imagines himself having to knock on the irritable old queen's door below to ask, in his very broken French, to use *la toilette*.

Fuzzy dried glue sticks to the seat as Jake peels away the first shred of wallpaper. He's doing it carefully, quietly humming "Amazing Grace," as he usually does to escape a silence. An awkward silence.

Maybe he knows what the doctor said.

"Do we have to wait a while before we do it?" he asks as Dale leaves the room, claustrophobic and sweating like a pig.

the lungs

Dale is on a ladder, hanging a mediaeval chandelier, another of Jake's yard sale discoveries, when Jake comes into the room and turns on the TV. He watches Dale, watches him for the longest time. "You were right," he finally says. "There's no grain in the wood." Dale gives him a look and laughs. Then a cough explodes in his chest and he reaches for Jake's help. On the TV, Oprah is offering a Kleenex to a kid with a hopeless case of acne. The kid has hacked his mother to pieces.

the kitchen

When the previous tenants come to check for mail, just before dinner, Jake invites them in to see the renovations. He would. Dale boils water for tea, using a pot because he still hasn't unpacked the kettle. As Jake shows the couple around the kitchen, they marvel at the changes. The couple especially likes the shiny brass knobs on the cupboard doors. She's a short woman, lipsticked, with very large breasts and hair the colour of beets. He's all teeth. They look like the type who would fuck all day and night in impossible positions.

Jake laughs out the side of his mouth when he says, "And we have a wooden toilet seat. Isn't that right, Dale?"

the bedroom

Dale lies beside him on the mattress, on the floor. Wide awake, again. A wedge of streetlight falls across Jake's body, curled and naked against him, his breath warm against Dale's skin. A semi rumbles by, its tires swishing on the wet road. The whole apartment shakes.

He closes his eyes, extends a breath throughout his body. For the first time since the biopsy he touches himself, moving his finger against the strange tenderness inside him, slowly. Something trickles and he brings his hand into the light.

Blood.

the heart

He hasn't said a word since Dale told him.

Jake pulls up behind an ambulance at the emergency entrance. He turns off the lights but leaves the motor running. They sit there for a while before he looks at Dale. He is looking but it's as though he's staring into space, as though he sees beyond him and further, to the moon.

"I don't understand why you'd lie to me," he says. "I just don't understand."

Jeannie Witkin

A Bad Day

I'd had a bad day the day I contemplated slitting my wrists running into not one but two of my ex-lovers one in front of the canned soup at the grocery store and the other embarrassingly while picking out my Snoopy toothbrush which wouldn't you know she not only noticed but commented on until I became so flustered I knocked over a whole stack of dental floss which unwound its way across the floor stopping in front of the razor blade display at which point I decided fate was subtly sending me a message or rather knocking me over the head with one disposable stainless steel double edged single edged I decided on single edged as I wouldn't want to cut myself while cutting myself if you know what I mean and then self consciously also picking up a can of shaving cream just so the cashier wouldn't assume I was buying razor blades for any other purpose than scraping hair off the tender flesh under my arms realizing luckily at the last minute that not many women use Brut and exchanging it for a more feminine foam packaged in a pink can with a floral pattern so there could be no doubt this was for women the delicate sex to use while pulling sharp metal blades across our bodies so anyway that was it for the personal hygiene aisle and after buying enough food for a week in case I changed my mind and didn't follow through or slipped and just nicked myself or actually used them to shave for the first time since eleventh grade and then wouldn't be able to use them on my wrists since they would be contaminated with shaving cream and microscopic shreds of hair but I would still get hungry so after I had all my purchases in my cart and had made it safely through the check out stand holding my breath as the cashier passed the razor blades over the automatic scanner expecting alarms to sound bells to ring an inquisition as to my motives but she didn't even ask me for ID merely bagging them along with my more mundane items cream of wheat potatoes cheddar cheese all in brown paper bags which I carried home and unloaded cream of wheat in the pantry potatoes in the vegetable bin cheddar cheese on the left hand side of the second shelf Snoopy toothbrush in the bathroom until everything was neatly stowed in its place the pack of razor blades the only item left conspicuous sitting on the counter demanding to be reckoned with challenging me but still I hesitated weighing my bad day against the sharpness of the metal my heavy thoughts against the sleekness of that single edge my angst against the shiny surfaces picturing the long thin cuts I could make carefully following my veins aiming for those buried arteries wondering if I would feel better once I was dead and then decided to at least put off such a major decision 'til later later so I buried the blades in my sock drawer in the very back behind the ones I never wear anymore the ones from my mom that say "Love" all over them but have a hole in the heal yet I refuse to throw away the red pair with flowers around the ankle I've had since the sixth grade which must be made with some indestructible synthetic material the slinky black ones all neatly hide the small box with its horde of single edged razor blades tucked away back there hidden unobtrusive so I can forget all about them if I want to until I have another bad day.

Raymond John Woolfrey

Le Jardin des Merveilles

Never go east of Morgan's," I said.

"What's Morgan's and why shouldn't I go east of it?" Michael asked, impatiently. Michael moved to Montreal from Vancouver two years ago. He's thirty-six, six-foot-one, short dark-brown hair, and he usually wears a big, round earring. His hair and his body are wiry, which also describes his disposition: wired. His face is bony, with thick, dark eyebrows, and black eyes that dart around ceaselessly. We often go to bars together where we yack for hours. This evening we were in Iggy's, and I was trying to explain to him why I'd hardly ever been east of St. Lawrence Street when I was growing up here.

"Morgan's was a department store downtown—now it's The Bay," I explained. "I was quoting my mother. Lots of mothers said that to their kids."

"Really? Why?"

"I never asked. I just lumped it in the same category as 'Never get into a stranger's car.' "

"Wow. Like the East End was full of child molesters, or something," Michael said. "But isn't your mother from the East End?"

"Yeah. But she moved to the Maritimes when she was still a girl. She's pretty anglo."

"You must have gone to the East End sometimes, though—to see her relatives or something."

"We went once when I was small, to one of her aunts in the Plateau. They lived in a triplex with a curving outdoor staircase—I thought it was so neat, I ran up and down it a zillion times, and slid down the railing as well as I could."

I remembered a lot of action around that staircase and in the tiny yard below, with neighbours and relatives coming and going, laughing and having fun with each other—I felt like Maggie Muggins visiting Mr. McGarrity, even though I couldn't understand French back then. I pleaded with my mother for us to move into a place like her aunt's, but she just rolled her eyes and sighed. She'd grown up there, and wasn't going back—a big house in an upper-middle-class suburb was the place to be.

"But when you were older, you must have been curious about the East End," Michael asked.

"Not until I was fourteen. I was a pretty obedient kid—rather a priss, really. So I contented myself with exploring the West End and downtown. I didn't know anybody in the east, anyway, and my mother was an only child—so I had no cousins to visit there."

"Did you find out why anglo boys shouldn't go east of—what is it, Morgan's?"

"Well, sort of."

"What happened?"

"I wanted to go to the zoo. I'd never been to one—my mother said she was too revolted by the animals always 'getting sexy.' Back then there was a children's zoo in Parc La Fontaine called the Garden of Wonders, or *le jardin des merveilles* in French. I was fourteen and I figured I'd better go before I was too old for a children's zoo.

"So I went alone one Sunday afternoon in June. After I'd been there for a while, I saw my math teacher from the past year out with his family. I didn't want him to see me—partly because I was embarrassed at being alone, and partly because I was afraid he knew I used to peek down his shirt to see his chest hair when I went up to his desk."

"I had a teacher I used to do that to," said Michael, shaking his head and smiling.

"I figured I'd had enough of monkeys picking each others' assholes anyway," I continued, "so I headed for the bus stop. As I approached it, the 24 was just pulling away. I ran to the stop ahead to try to catch it, dodging a car that was creeping along the parking lot. Halfway there I realized I wouldn't make it, so I walked back to the other stop, which was closer. On the way I became aware that the same car I had just dodged was cruising back alongside me and at the same pace as my walking. I glanced inside and noticed the driver was looking over at me, leering like.

Once I got to the bus stop, he stopped his car, and gestured with his head ever so slightly that I should come over to him. But the movement was so understated and, well, furtive, I wasn't sure if I imagined it. So I pretended I didn't see, and looked down Sherbrooke Street for the bus."

"Was this across from the library?" asked Michael, suspicious.

"Uh-huh."

"He thought you were a hustler!"

"I had no idea! I didn't even know the concept!" I said.

"On the bus stop sign," I continued, "somebody had written 'once every' over the number '24': I figured I might have a while to wait. From time to time I looked out the corner of my eye at the blue Chevrolet still parked nearby—I didn't dare look at the driver. As time crawled on and the car didn't budge, I was getting rather nervous. Was he a policeman? Had I done something wrong? Was it illegal for English-looking boys from the Town of Mount Royal to venture into the East End?"

"You should have listened to your mother!" Michael joked.

"Yeah," I laughed. "But I wasn't really worried at the time as there were other people waiting for the bus. But I did start wondering if I was getting paranoid when I thought a guy waiting at the bus stop was watching me too. He was kinda weird-looking, with narrow shoulders and a face like a turky vulture—sorta like Robert Bourassa."

Michael made a face: "Eeooh!"

"After a while I realized I wasn't paranoid—he *was* staring at me. So was the guy in the car. I didn't know what was going on. Finally, the turkey-vulture guy spoke: 'Do you want to come with me?' he asked, in English."

"Why in English?" asked Michael.

"You know, everybody speaks to me in English, even before I open my mouth."

"Yeah, you look pretty anglo—a real *tête carrée.*"

"Right. So I looked at him. I wondered if he meant what I thought he meant. No, he's just a little bit weird and he wants a friend, I thought. Besides, I knew that if I left then I'd get home just in time for Bugs Bunny."

Michael laughed. "Yeah, after all, you were still a kid!"

"So being the polite little bourgeois boy that I was, I looked him straight in the eye and replied, 'No thank you, but maybe the man in that car would like to,' indicating the blue Chevrolet to my left."

"You little snot! You knew the score, all right."

"I guess so. It's not as if I knew for sure, though."

"What happened next?"

"The bus came. I got on and went to the back, like all teenagers do, and saw the man at the bus stop through the rear window. I felt a small pang of . . . lost opportunity, I guess. I realized he was offering me something I'd been wanting for so long: sex with a grown man. Surely it would have been some kind of adventure, at least. But as the bus headed west, I looked at him again. He really was unattractive to me, being turkey-like and all. And I really did want to go home in time to see Bugs Bunny."

Kim Yaged

Transmittable

This is just too funny. Ha, what a brother and sister team!"

"Fuck off, Chris."

"No, I mean, is there like something you two want to share?"

April sneered at Chris. Yeah, this would be about the only time she'd be willing to have sex with the little prick. Chris could probably use a nice dose of venereal warts to sober him up. How was her brother friends with him?

"Chris, I said fuck off." Kyle wasn't in the mood for his shit.

"Now, I know you two are into that liberal shit," Chris wasn't letting up. "You can admit it to me. Come on, was there a little hanky-panky going on within the family sheets?"

April, sitting on the couch picking her fingernails, finally looked up.

"Ah! A look of admission," Chris motioned accusingly towards April.

"I don't know which luck is worse—having venereal warts or being told while you happened to be around," Kyle responded.

"Hey, what are friends for but to be around when you need support? I mean, this is not the worst thing in the world. It could have been syphilis or something."

"Thanks for the consolation."

"So, come on. Out with it," Chris urged. "Were the brother and sister team playing together or what? I mean, this is just a bit too coincidental, don't you think?"

"Christ, man, are you really being serious?"

"Admit it, Kyle," Chris circled April. "April here is about the most liberal person either of us will ever lay eyes on, and you'd do anything she asked."

296

April sat there with an expression of indifference. Chris wasn't worthy of a response.

"What'd you guys do," Chris continued, "get a two-fer or something? If you were the same sex, I could understand it, but come on. A guy and a girl? What'd you flip a coin and the loser had to go to the wrong kind of doctor?"

"Cut the shit, man. Venereal warts is one of the most prevalent things these days. Haven't you ever heard of a coincidence?"

"Yeah, yeah, whatever. I ain't buying it."

"Fine, you don't have to. No one asked for your fucking opinion anyway." It was enough already. Kyle was pissed. Couldn't Chris see that? What the fuck was his problem anyway?

"You just got to learn to take a joke," Chris jabbed Kyle in the solar-plexus. "I was just jiving ya."

"Well, I'm not in the mood. I gotta figure out a way to tell Denise about this. I'm sure she's gonna think I've been fooling around."

April reached for the television remote and clicked on the tube. The volume barely audible, she flipped through the channels absent-mind-edly.

"Don't worry about it," Chris responded. "I'll just tell her it's 'all in the family,' man. You know what I mean?"

"Chris, I said I'm not in the mood. Do you not understand English or what?"

"Yeah, yeah, just take a chill. All right?" Chris palmed Kyle's head and shook it back and forth. Kyle pulled away.

"I just can't believe this shit. For the first time in my life I'm being faithful to someone, and this has to happen. For real, man. The woman is gonna flip."

"Don't let that chick hassle you. Who the fuck does she think she is anyway?"

"Chris, you can fuck with me all you want, but don't be calling my woman a chick. You hear me?"

"All's I'm saying is what makes you so sure the broad didn't give it to you?"

The volume on the television rapidly approached excessive. Chris and Kyle turned and stared inquisitively at April. She did not move.

"Girl, will you lower that?" Chris barked.

"Leave her alone, man," Kyle defended his sister. "She's got her own shit to deal with too, you know?"

"Yeah, yeah."

"Let's go shoot some hoop. Maybe that'll clear my head."

"You're right." Chris grabbed his jacket and headed towards the door of the apartment.

"You all right?" Kyle whispered into his sister's ear. She nodded in the affirmative. "I'll be back in a bit, okay?" April nodded again. Kyle kissed his sister on the forehead and caught up to Chris who was already out the door.

As soon as they left, April turned off the television and lay down on the couch. The telephone rang momentarily. April reached over the side of the couch and lifted the receiver, moving as little as possible.

"Hello?"

"April? Hi, it's Denise. Is Kyle around?"

"No."

"Then tell me what happened."

"I've got it," April spoke plainly.

"Does he know?"

"Of course he knows. Our doctors practically called one after the other."

"No, I mean, does he know about us?"

"Of course not." There was a tinge of irritation in April's voice.

"Good."

"Don't you have anything to say to me?" April tried to lead the conversation.

"No."

April was silent.

"Listen, I gotta go," Denise continued. "Would you tell Kyle I called?"

"Sure," April responded tersely.

"I'll see ya."

"Uh-huh."

April hung up the phone and slouched back down on the couch. She stared across the room at a picture of Denise and her brother hanging on the wall. When Kyle came back in from playing ball, he'd probably wonder how it got broken.

Paul Yee

Red

There was once a young man who loved only men. When his work took him to town, he looked about with shy eyes for the males who had taken his heart. He had fallen for four and ten and twenty of them, but not once had words been spoken. He was quiet by nature, and feared the laughter from those he knew.

The young man lived with his parents on a farm flanked by rolling fields. The buildings of stone and wood had stood for many years. He was an only child, and his father and mother hoped for grandchildren to roam and dance around their feet.

After a long day's labour, the young man often became sad and solemn. He frowned and left his dinner cold and uneaten. Alone, he sat outside until late. His parents advised him to attend the country festivals where families gathered for fun. The young farmer donned a clean shirt and pants to go, but he always came home alone.

One day, the mother smiled and said, "My friend four miles away has a daughter who is bright and friendly. Will you marry her?"

The son shook his head and hurried out of the barn.

One day, the father grinned and said, "My friend six miles away has a girl who smiles and sings. Will you marry her?"

The son bolted away and ran through the fields like a rabbit before howling hounds. His face burned from the hot summer sun. He gulped in lungfuls of air and ran and ran.

Finally he reached a grove of shady trees, where songbirds gathered around a small pond. He dropped to the ground and leaned against an ancient trunk. Then he wept bitterly as a breeze rustled the leaves above.

All of a sudden, a bright red bird flew onto his shoulder and asked shrilly, "Why do you cry?"

The young farmer thought he was imagining things and did not answer. But the bird spoke even louder. "Why do you cry?"

Now the young man became afraid and tried to brush the scarlet bird away. But it flew to his other shoulder and called out even more sharply, "Why do you cry?"

Finally the young man took a deep breath and said, "Because I love only men."

"For telling the truth, you shall be rewarded," replied the bird. "Now go home."

And away it flew, high into the bright blue sky.

Late that night, when the world was sound asleep, the young man heard wings flapping outside his window. When he drew aside the curtain, in flew the red bird. It circled three times and landed on the bed. Then, in a burst of blinding light, the bird was transformed into a man. Red hair coated the stranger's lean body and his eyes were at once bold and trusting. Red smiled and drew the young man into his arms.

When morning came, the young man leapt from his bed. He looked for his new friend, but no one was near. For a moment, he thought it had all been a dream. Then he saw on his pillow a small red feather. Gently he slipped it into a safe place.

When he greeted his mother that morning, he ate enough breakfast for two. When he hiked outside with hoe and plough, he bent over and did the work of four.

Thereafter, the young man laughed with his parents when they came together to eat. He sat with them at the front door and watched the sun set. They leaned against one another and listened to the crickets sing through the night. Never again did his parents propose women's names to him.

If the young man felt lonely, he returned to his room, retrieved the feather, and caressed it three times. Red would fly in and embrace him in arms as strong as his own. All night long the young man held his visitor close, kissing every inch of his skin, breathing his sweat, whispering love into his ears.

Then one spring evening, just after the seasons' seeds were sown into the warming soil, the parents became sick. Though a doctor was summoned, it was too late, and they died shortly after. The young man mourned long and hard, for he had loved his parents dearly.

When Red came again to his room, he looked different. "No more will I come," he announced. "Now you are free."

And before the young man could say a word, his friend vanished through the window.

As days and weeks went by, the young man felt alone again. When he went to the fields, the wind whistled across the crops like an angry whip. When he went to town, he traded his produce and departed quickly. He still dared not talk to any man that caught his eye.

At nights, he stroked the feather tenderly, but Red never came back. Over and over, the young man remembered the fine times they had shared and the woolly warmth of Red. Over and over, he recalled those parting words, but he froze at the thought of action.

One day, the young man took his crops to town and noticed a newcomer in the market. A man with glistening hair, thick arms, and a lean face the sun had darkened. The young man felt his heart beat quick and loud, just as it had with Red. But the young man forced himself away and fled for home.

Two miles from town, his snorting horse stopped suddenly on the trail. When the young man came forward, he saw a baby robin lying cold on the ground. It had fallen from its nest.

Startled, he turned and hurried back to town, back to the market where the dark-haired stranger still stood. He went up to him and said, "I need help. Do you need work?"

The stranger stared back. "That depends," he said slowly. "What are you looking for?"

"A man," the young man said loudly, so that everyone could hear. "A man who will love my farm and me as much as he loves himself."

The stranger's face did not change as he said, "Love? What do you know of love?"

The young farmer squared his shoulders and let out a long breath. "I have feared it and found it. No longer will I live without it."

The stranger nodded and they shook hands. Together they headed out to the farm, where they lived and worked and loved for the rest of their lives.

Wayne Yung

Pub Angel

Restless one night, I wanted to go somewhere, anywhere. I found my roommate watching television, and said, "Let's go get some cookies at the Chinese bakery." At the top of the stairs, we put on our boots and jackets before tumbling down into the night.

It was early spring on Pender Street, and the first cherry blossoms blushed pale in the streetlight. We chatted amiably, our footsteps falling lightly as we passed through the locked and shuttered streets of Chinatown. Soon we reached a warm bright oasis in the cool deserted night: the Ho Wah bakery, where plastic food glistened in the window and a neon sign beckoned us inside.

My roommate read out loud the cookie menu, rolling each name in his mouth, tasting every flavour judiciously. "Double chocolate pecan . . . almond cookies . . . peanut butter chocolate chip . . . mmm. . . . " Meanwhile, I mentally recited a few pastry names in Cantonese, precious fragments of a lost childhood language.

The lady behind the counter waited patiently, amused by the odd couple that the night dragged in—a tall skinny banana in a black leather jacket, and a stout white ghost in torn jeans and baseball cap.

After making our purchases, we stepped outside to eat. I pulled him over to a bank machine, grateful for his protection as I cashed my welfare cheque. Afraid of muggers, I folded the money neatly in half and tucked it into my underwear.

On a whim, I suggested we go on to the local gay pub. Shrugging, my roommate agreed. Neither of us drank or smoked, but we didn't feel like going home either.

Upon arrival, we found a drag show in progress, with a fair weeknight crowd. I listened to my roommate with only half-an-ear, distracted by the gaze of a tall young man by the bar.

He had the boyish good looks found in beer commercials, with the tousled hair and dark eyes of a warm happy drunk. I smiled, and his eyes locked with mine. With a deft word, I sent my roommate to go buy drinks, and the young stranger approached. Gently, gravely, he brushed the top of my head with his fingertips. "Nice haircut," he said, grinning, before wandering off.

I told my roommate what had happened, and he rolled his eyes. To save money, he cuts my hair at home: clipper short with a forelock tuft. It's a cut that goes far.

We sat in the corner, watching the crowd. The cute young stranger seemed to know everybody. He made the rounds, sitting on this one's knee, giving that one a sloppy kiss.

I'd never found such warm intimacy in a gay bar before. For the first time, I found myself admiring the courage of drag queens as they risked ridicule on stage. (I remembered that the Québécois word for transvestite was "travestie".) For the first time, I felt warm encouragement from an audience of friends. This was not the most fashionable bar. These were not the most beautiful men. That was not the most fabulous drag show. Nonetheless, there was a great generosity of heart that I had never found before in the usual gay nightclubs, where the arrogant young beauties would have crushed us with their indifference. Maybe it was because these men had nothing to lose, that they had so much to give.

My roommate was admiring an older man who moved with the aid of two aluminum canes. His legs were bent and twisted, but his arms were strong and his face was kind. My companion wanted to approach and compliment the man, even though he was committed to his own lover. I was inspired by the feeling that this was a night when compliments could be given with no strings attached, with genuine admiration and respect.

It was getting late, and we had reached the end of our smoke tolerance. Pulling on my jacket, I screwed up the courage to do something I'd never done before.

The cute young stranger leaned against the bar, watching the show. I tapped him on the shoulder, and whispered in his ear: "I just wanted to say goodnight to the cutest boy in the bar."

He grabbed my crotch and squeezed. "Uh, no, I don't think so," he said, inspecting me through the denim. "No, I think you're the cutest one here."

I grinned and kissed his soft downy cheek before grabbing my roommate to go.

Outside, I laughed out loud, giddy with delight. I told my roommate what had happened, and told him another story:

"When I was a child, I told my friend that I liked this blonde girl. She heard the rumour, and the first thing she said was 'Yuk, a Chinese boy likes me.' After that, I believed that no one wanted the attentions of a Chinese boy." We stopped at a red light. "But just now, a stranger with the face of an angel proved me wrong."

As the light turned green, my hand fell to where he had squeezed me. I was startled to feel the outline of a stiff flat square.

Laughing, I pulled the wad of welfare money out of my crotch, and toasted the night sky.

"Not only the cutest boy in the bar, but for tonight, the richest."

Sarah V Zetlein

The Bath

Sitting propped up amongst White Musk bubbles, it dawned on me that I only had baths when I broke up with my girlfriends.

It seems like I've been running baths quite often lately.

Do you know that you can watch yourself cry in the bath? If it is anything like mine, your belly quivers as your face gushes. If she was really something, the tears roll down your breasts (the very breasts she will never again touch—unless of course you have the post-relationship fuck which always seems to end in another bath) and plop forlornly into the bubbles.

While in the bath you can read the overdue library books which had been piling up on your bedside table as you spent fewer and fewer nights at home in your single bed, and even less of them alert enough to be reading. Detective fiction is particularly helpful. Depending on the severity of the ending you can project alternatively the murderous, investigative or heroic plots inscribed between the pages onto your now ex (but of course you'll remain friends, you'd just hate to ruin a really good friendship).

Music is crucial. Do not—and this is most important—do not play any tape that you may have listened to in her presence, even if it was just the Madonna tape you used to play in the car on the way to the bar on a Friday. Turn on the radio and take pot-luck. Get really annoyed at the sudden realization that every fucking song is about love. Then note that they generally feature boys groaning about love's labour lost to the accompaniment of throbbing guitars and an anxious-sounding drummer. If Juliana Hatfield comes on, sing the chorus line "everybody wants me but you" with her very, very loudly. If it's Me'Shell, sing "if that's your boyfriend he wasn't last night" with her inflection of sarcasm and feel good about it even if it bears no resemblance to your (now defunct) love life. Believe in your own innate sexiness which will no doubt bubble to the surface again soon (once your toes have lost their bath-wrinkliness). Revel in all songs which are cynical but if things are getting really bad, ABC-FM is always a good bet because usually there are no words. Or if it's opera, they're often in Italian. Which is fine. Let it wash over you with the White Musk bubbles. Unless, of course, you speak Italian. Because when you understand what's going on in an opera, they are usually extremely depressing, particularly in the relationship stakes.

When your belly has ceased to quiver, stand up, blast the shower and get out. Slather yourself in lots of moisturiser. Use eye gel, lip balm, your best pyjamas. Yes, you'll start wearing pyjamas to bed again but this can be a good thing. Even buy yourself a new pair. Take your phone to bed and ring your mates. This is therapeutic for two reasons. You get their sympathy and you have the satisfaction of knowing that if she is by any chance trying to ring you, you'll be engaged, unobtainable and necessarily very popular. Don't ring her. Forget her phone number immediately. Note that this last one can be difficult if she is sharing a house with your mates. Avoid this type of relationship right from the beginning.

Go to sleep, even if it is done clutching your pillow (which still bears traces of her perfume, hair and cigarettes). Vow to wash your sheets in the morning but secretly enjoy this final nostalgic and melancholic indulgence. Plan the rest of your life lying there in the dark. Sleep.

P.S. You may wake up in the middle of the night in a real panic. But you really loved her, she made you laugh, what was wrong with you, is she lying awake too? Of course there is only one thing you can do.

Get up, find your bubbles and your chamomile tea, and start running the bath.

And if you still can't sleep, write a story.

Aaron Zyskin

Found Out

The Bronx, 1946

Ira has a new English bike. He wants me to learn to ride his old clunker
so we can get around, but I'm dragging my heels. I don't want to go out
with him in public because he's bound to see me getting heckled sooner
or later. Once he finds out that I'm that big of a sissy, he won't want to
be friends anymore. And now that Hilda and Laura aren't allowed to play
with "boys," which is just a crappy way of saying they can't play with *me*,
I have no one to be with but Ira.

We don't go to the same school because, short as he is, Ira's already in
junior high. Although it's been months that we've been hanging around
together, I've managed to keep us mostly indoors or in the backyards that
run down the hill from his house, where that old lady who throws pails
of water at us is the only person we ever see.

But he's gung-ho about this bike thing. He ambushes me on the street
and coaxes me onto his old bike with the balloon tires. I can't come up
with a reason not to, so I wobble in broken circles on the slope in front of
his house, hitting the pavement with my shoe to keep from falling. I *would*
like to know how to ride this thing.

I'm not learning fast enough for Ira, though. Figuring I'll do better on
the classier bike, he hoists me onto its jacked-up seat and gives me a shove.
Before I know it, I'm rolling downhill, too high off the ground to drag
my feet.

Super! Just like that, I have the hang of it. And right in time too,
because the bike is moving like lightning. I backpedal to brake, but
nothing happens. There's a ton of traffic where our street ends at
Featherbed Lane, but my speed keeps picking up. Before I have time to

blink, I'm in the intersection, steering around a station wagon that's
screeching to a halt. But there's no way I can make it through the line of
cars parked ahead of me.

I make a split-second, right-angle turn, smash sideways into a parked
car, and pitch head first under the delivery truck behind it. I'm scraped
bloody, my right foot hurts like the dickens, and one hand feels like it's
on fire, but I'm alive. A lady helps me to the curb, scolding me all the
way. Some people stop to watch, but move on, along with the crabby
lady, when Ira shows up.

"Nice going," he says, "dumkopf!" His brand-new, beat-up bike is
riding high on his shoulder.

"Did I louse it up real bad?"

"I should've warned you about the handbrakes," he says, setting the
bike down. He studies my eye. "This oughta be a beaut. Let's see your
hand." He spreads my thumb and forefinger to examine the web of skin
between them. Just because he's older, he thinks he's some kind of an
expert.

"Don't *press* on it, birdbrain."

"Boy, are you lucky. If you cut that, your teeth would lock shut. You'd
have to eat through a *straw* for the rest of your life."

"Baloney." I inspect it myself. "That's only if it's real deep."

He turns his bike upside-down and twists the front fender until the
wheel spins free. "Can you walk?" he says.

I stand up. My clothes are splotched with blood. Boy, am I in trouble.
Mom's gonna hit the roof. I can limp, so we start uphill, Ira pushing his
scuffed-up bike and bragging about the handbrakes. Climbing turns out
to be harder on my foot than just walking. As we get near his house, Ira
changes the subject, still talking up a storm.

He'll lend me a change of clothes. We'll slip behind the house and use
the garden hose to wash the blood from my clothes before his mother has
a chance to flip her lid. She'll never notice the bike. He'll replace the
reflector with one from his old bike and retouch the paint before lunch,
if the hardware store has the right colour. We can wrap my ankle in rags.
Bandaging might even take care of the limp. We'll tell my mother I
tripped and scraped my face on the sidewalk. What the heck, we might
as well give it a try.

His sneakiness tickles me, so I don't tell him that you can't get *anything* past my mother—for sure not the biggest accident of my entire life. Instead, I imagine changing clothes in the backyard, washing away blood stains, hiding my limp, and so on. But my daydream ends suddenly when I see a band of boys tramping downhill on both sides of the street.

They're shouting, kicking cans, and firing a ball back and forth. My heart sinks. Getting stuck hobbling with Ira and his broken bike through a gang of rough kids is the worst thing that could possibly happen. There's no way these boys will pass up a chance to hassle me.

I don't hear a word Ira's saying. I correct my step, the only thing I can think to do, but it hurts too much and I go back to limping. The hollering keeps getting louder.

"Cut the crap, asshole."

"Tough shit, you son of a bitch."

Suddenly, they're everywhere, cans clanging, a ball whizzing past my head. I look straight ahead and pretend it's not happening.

"Lookit the little fairies, two on a bike."

"Hey, I didn't know fairies could *bleed*."

A barrage of hoots and wolf whistles, and they're gone. But it was worse than I expected. I never dreamed they'd call *Ira* a sissy, just because he was with me. Now he surely won't want to stay friends.

What's left of our climb is pure torture. Now Ira has found me out. I can't look at him. When we get to his house, I limp off without stopping to say goodbye, pressing the knuckle of my good hand against my teeth. Ira was the only boy on the block who would play with me.

Now what am I gonna do?

Author Biographies

Keith Adamson lives in Glasgow with his partner of twenty years. He has previously contributed work to *Gay Scotland* magazine, as well as to *Oranges and Lemons* and *The Freezer Counter*, anthologies of short stories published by Third House. He works in an architectural practice, and is a volunteer on Strathclyde Lesbian and Gay Switchboard.

Donna Allegra was most recently anthologized in *SportsDykes*, edited by Susan Fox Rogers; *Out of the Class Closet: Lesbians Speak*, edited by Julia Penelope; *Lavender Mansions: 40 Contemporary Gay and Lesbian Short Stories*, edited by Irene Zahava; and *Lesbian Erotics*, edited by Karla Jay.

Alan Alvare is a Vancouver writer and grief counsellor, formerly paid by the Catholic Church to preside in damask on Sundays. His poems, stories and articles have appeared in sundry places, not always on walls. Alan denies any truth to the rumour that he and the Grand Duchess Anastasia are the same person.

Tommi Avicolli Mecca is a writer, performer and queer activist of southern Italian-American descent. His most recent credits include co-editing *Hey Paesan* (a collection of Italian/Sicilian-American and Canadian queer writings to be published in 1996 by Guernica Editions), and *Dagos*, a novel-in-progress. He currently lives in San Francisco.

Damien Barlow is a twenty-one-year-old English/Law student living in "Marvelous" Melbourne (Australia's other queer capital). He is also a wannabe queer theorist who loves deflowering nurses and defrocking stockmen as a pastime.

J.L. Belrose: "I identify as a dyke but otherwise reject labels. I live in the shadow of Blue Mountain in Ontario, Canada. I enjoy conversing with imaginary companions and am therefore either insane or a writer. Lately, I've been opting for the latter."

Michael Bendzela is a fiction writer who has had work pubished in various journals, including *The Chicago Review* and *The North American Review*. He was the recipient of a Pushcart Prize in 1992. He lives in the state of Maine.

Lucy Jane Bledsoe is the author of *Sweat: Stories and a Novella* (Seal Press, 1995) and a children's novel, *The Big Bike Race* (Holiday House, 1995). She is editor of the lesbian erotica anthology *Heatwave: Women in Love and Lust* (Alyson, 1995). Bledsoe writes books for, and teaches creative writing to, adult new readers (literacy students).

Allen Borcherding lives with his partner in Minneapolis, Minnesota, where he works as a nuclear medicine technologist, soon to become a radiation therapist. This is his first published work.

Maureen Brady's books include *Give Me Your Good Ear, Folly, The Question She Put To Herself, Midlife* and *Daybreak.* She lives in New York City, where she teaches writing workshops, and is currently completing a new novel, *Ginger's Fire.*

Beth Brant is a Bay of Quinte Mohawk from Tyendinaga Mohawk Territory in Ontario. She is the editor of *A Gathering of Spirit,* and *I'll Sing Till the Day I Die: Conversations with Tyendinaga Elders,* and the author of *Mohawk Trail, Food & Spirits,* and *Writing As Witness.* She is a mother and grandmother and lives with her partner of nineteen years, Denise Dorsz.

Michael Bronski is the author of *Culture Clash: The Making of Gay Sensibility.* His writings on culture, sex and politics have appeared in numerous anthologies and publications.

David Lyndon Brown was delighted to receive a New Writers' Grant from the Arts Council of New Zealand, Toi Aotearoa, in 1994. He is looking forward to publishing a collection of short stories. He works and plays in Auckland.

Doug Browning: "In the 1968 Bastion Theatre production of *Peter Pan,* wanting to be a lost boy but too old at thirteen, I was cast as a pirate. These days I'm something of an aging amalgam of the two, caught up in a dubious effort to reinvent the past and circumvent the present. 'Helping Hand' is an excerpt from *Drift,* a stalled novel."

Tonia Bryan was born in Barbados and indoctrinated in North America. For fun she watches *Days of Our Lives,* masturbates, and flirts with gay men. The mother of a three-year-old cat, she is also a member of *Fireweed*'s editorial collective, B.A.N.S.H.I.I. and De Poonani Posse.

Grant Campbell was born in Niagara-on-the-Lake, and studied at the University of Toronto and at Queen's University. He lives in Toronto, and has published various short stories and book reviews in *The Downtown Express, Queen's Quarterly, The Evergreen Chronicles* and *The Church-Wellesley Review.*

Julie Varner Catt is a Missourian transplanted to sunny Sydney, Australia, where she writes fiction, news features for the *Sydney Star Observer,* essays for her post-graduate work at Sydney University, and letters to her grandma.

Lawrence W. Cloake was born in Ireland and spent his formative years in Wales. He returned to Ireland and moved to Dublin after graduating from secondary boarding school. He came out at the age of twenty, and at twenty-one met his other half, with whom he still lives in monogamous bliss.

Ailsa Craig lives in Toronto with her life partner and their two cats. She is a regular contributor to *Xtra!* magazine, and has also been published in *Undercurrents* and *Quota Magazine.*

Daniel Curzon is the author of *Something to Do in the Dark* (1971), *The Revolt of the Perverts* (1978) and *The World Can Break Your Heart* (1984). He recently published a companion piece to "Chickens" in the *Kenyon Review*. He teaches English at City College of San Francisco.

tatiana de la tierra is a boss-bitch with a passion for rocks & writing & revolution. Born in Colombia and transplanted to Miami, she zooms the cosmos with bullet-proof vulnerability. tatiana is editor of *conMOCIÓN*, an international bilingual publication for latina lesbians all over.

Dennis Denisoff is the author of a novel, *Dog Years* (Arsenal Pulp, 1991) and a poetry collection, *Tender Agencies* (Arsenal Pulp, 1994). He is also the editor of *Queeries* (Arsenal Pulp, 1993), the first anthology of Canadian gay male prose. He is currently a postdoctoral fellow at Princeton University.

Phillippe H. Doneys is a native of Québec, part-time writer and currently working on a Ph.D. in Southeast Asian studies. He is living and studying in London, England.

Nisa Donnelly is the author of two novels, *The Bar Stories: A Novel After All* (1989), winner of the 1990 Lambda Award for Lesbian Fiction, and *The Love Songs of Phoenix Bay* (1994), both from St. Martin's Press. Her essays and short fiction appear in many anthologies and periodicals. She lives and writes in San Francisco.

Marianne Dresser is a San Francisco-based writer and editor whose work has appeared in *Deneuve, Dykespeak, Girlfriends, Bay Area Reporter, The Lesbian Review of Books,* and *The San Francisco Review of Books.* "A Queer Night in Tokyo" is part of an ongoing series based on various life-experiences.

J.B. Droullard (a pseudonym) is a professor at a Florida university after five years at a university in Montreal. While he has thirty-some scientific publications to his credit, "Contact" represents his first foray into the creative realm. He is presently at work on an autobiographical novel set in Paris.

Annette DuBois is thirty years old and a Scorpio. She was born in New England and has lived in San Francisco, France and the American midwest. She came out at twenty-two and earned a degree in mathematics before realizing she wanted to be Gertrude Stein when she grew up. Her work has been published in *Sinister Wisdom* and *Backspace,* among other interesting places.

Gale "Sky" Edeawo is an African-American freelance writer. She has been writing since 1972, mostly for and about women, and has been published in the U.S. and abroad. Her work consists mainly of poetry, editorials and prose, but she has recently begun to write short stories.

Lois Fine writes, works and plays in Toronto, but dreams of a room with a view.

Luc Frey is the pen-name of a dyke who tells her stories usually only to the seagulls and the seals around the shores of a Scottish isle. In her life she has gone against every possible grain of established society, and taken her fair share of blows. She is now a translator and islander by passion.

Gabrielle Glancy's work has appeared in such publications as *The New Yorker, The Harvard Gay and Lesbian Review,* and *The Paris Review.* Her work has been anthologized in *Sister and Brother: Lesbians and Gay Men Talk About Their Lives Together* and *Lesbians on Love.* "Withholding" is excerpted from a memoir she is currently writing. She was born and raised in New York City, and now lives in San Francisco.

mu groves is a Canadian writer living in Australia. She is currently jumping through the hoops of same-sex immigration policy and working on a feature film script. "What a Drag" was previously published in *Fruit: A Queer Anthology* by the Brisbane Pride Collective (1995).

J.A. Hamilton is the author of the poetry collections *Body Rain* and *Steam-Cleaning Love,* the children's book *Jessica's Elevator* and the fiction collection *July Nights and Other Stories.* She's won numerous awards for her work, including the *Yellow Silk* and *Paragraph* erotic fiction awards and the *Event* non-fiction prize.

Bente Hansen resides in Lethbridge, Alberta with Tracey, her partner of eight years. She has degrees in piano and was working on a Ph.D. in Musicology when she decided to quit school to pursue other interests. Currently, she's working in Lethbridge and contemplating a career in court reporting.

Neil Harris was born in London in 1956. He trained in theatre at the Central School of Speech and Drama, and emigrated to Israel in 1979, where he lives on Kibbutz Tuval with his son Dylan. He works in informal education and journalism and as an AIDS and Safer Sex Counsellor and a facilitator of workshops on issues surrounding gay and lesbian youth.

Wes Hartley is a Vancouver poet and highly invisible Act-Up-style ranter in his fifties, an anarch who dropped-out thirty years ago. He has described his writing as "strong lingo and extreme rhetoric pushed beyond *reducto ad absurdum* towards the hyperbolically sublime."

Matthew R.K. Haynes resides in Boise, Idaho, with his lover of two years, Rhett Tanner, and their paranoia-struck cat, Xochitl. He is attending Boise State University, where he is majoring in English. "Night Soil" is his first published story. He is currently working on a novel.

Jackie Haywood is a West Coast-born and -blossomed, over-50 urban lesbian, also known as Lovie Sizzle, baton-twirling comedy writer and performer. Employed for almost a decade in the frontlines of HIV/AIDS work, Jackie can be found at home in Vancouver immersed in Motown music or behind the wheel of her '61 Ford Falcon.

Christina L. Hulen is a twenty-seven-year-old life-long resident of the San

Francisco Bay Area. While the majority of her fiction writing centres on the lesbian experience, she is also committed to bringing to light the often ignored true stories of courageous women of the past who helped shape the world we live in today. She owes all of her successes to the love and support of her mother, and the encouragement and late night back-rubs from her girlfriend.

Welby Ings was born and grew up in rural New Zealand. He has written a collection of short stories, *Inside from the Rain*, children's books and several plays, which have won numerous literary awards. His gay writing focuses strongly on the lives of rural men, on their visions and experiences and the simple politics of being ordinary.

Kevin Isom is an attorney and writer in Atlanta. He received his B.A. from Vanderbilt University and his J.D. from Emory University. His work has appeared in several newspapers, magazines and anthologies. He is currently at work on a novel.

Faith Jones is a thirty-year-old Jewish femme with a bad back, a good girlfriend, and a useless degree in Women's Studies. She is starting to get published, most recently in *The Femme Mystique*, edited by Lesléa Newman. "True Confessions" first appeared in *Lesbian Contradiction* #44.

M.S. Kershaw's queer-themed works have appeared previously in *Out Magazine: Canada's gay literary/arts journal* and *Queeries: An Anthology of Gay Male Prose*. Originally from the East Kootenays of British Columbia, he now resides in Vancouver, and is completing a novel about technology, desire and decadence.

Mara Kinder is a lesbian single mom student living in east Vancouver. She has a degree in Fine Art and is currently studying philosophy. In her work she attempts to merge family, motherhood and queer issues with critical theory.

Jeff Kirby is the author of *Cock & Soul* and appears in the anthologies *Stallions and Other Studs* and *Queeries*. He lives in Toronto, where he hosts "Queer Sex Stories," a regular evening of erotic readings/performances. He's presently at work on his new play, *Fridge Boys*.

Catherine Lake currently lives and works in Toronto. Her poetry and prose have appeared in a number of literary journals and anthologies. She is presently poetry editor of *Women's Education des femmes* and a member of the Queer Press Collective. Although she yearns to quit her stressful day-to-day job and write full-time, her long-time lover and their dogs continue to give her much joy.

Joe Lavelle lives in Liverpool with his partner John. As well as writing poetry, short fiction, scripts and newspaper articles, he is a paid worker with Merseyside AIDS Support Group and a member of Queer Scribes, Liverpool's lesbian and gay writing group.

Denise Nico Leto is a San Francisco Bay Area poet. Her works have appeared in *Voices in Italian Americana*, *Common Lives/Lesbian Lives* and *Unsettling America:*

An Anthology of Contemporary Multicultural Poetry (Penguin). She co-edited the anthology for *Sinister Wisdom* on Italian-American women entitled *il viaggio delle donne*. Currently she is co-editing an anthology on Italian-descended lesbians and gay men for Guernica Editions.

Shaun Levin is thirty-one, born in South Africa and living in Israel since 1978. He's published several short stories, and has a short play appearing at the 1995 Edinburgh Fringe Festival. He is currently working on his first novel.

Judy Lightwater is a forty-four-year-old Jewish lesbian feminist. She writes, tries to stop violence against women and children, campaigns for gay equality, and consults with non-profit groups in Victoria, B.C. She is currently completing a novel.

L.D. Little lives on a small mixed farm on Nova Scotia's north shore. Her first short story, "Manhandling," was published in *Matrix* magazine.

Michael Lowenthal's fiction and essays have appeared in books including *Men on Men 5*, *Wrestling with the Angel*, and *Sister and Brother*, as well as in periodicals including *The Advocate, Genre, Yellow Silk* and *The Boston Phoenix*. After John Preston's death, he assumed editorship of Preston's final books, *Friends and Lovers, Flesh and the Word 3* and *Winter's Light*. He lives in Boston.

Lori Lyons is a Toronto dyke who spends inordinate amounts of time getting ready to go out.

Judy MacLean is a writer and editor. Her fiction, journalism and commentary have been published in *Out/Look, The Advocate, San Francisco Bay Times, Lesbian Love Stories Vol. II, The San Francisco Chronicle* and *The Washington Post*.

William John Mann is a journalist and fiction writer whose work has appeared in numerous magazines, newspapers, and anthologies, including *Sister and Brother* and *Looking for Mr. Preston*. He is currently working on a biography of queer silent film star William Haines as well as a novel, *Tricking*, from which the story here is excerpted.

David May was a nice boy from a good family who fell in with the wrong crowd. His work has appeared in *Drummer, Mach, Honcho, San Francisco Frontiers, Advocate Men* and *Cat Fancy*. His erotic fiction appears in the anthologies *Rogues of San Francisco, Meltdown!* and *Flesh and the Word 3*. He currently lives in San Francisco with his husband, a dog and three cats.

Tom McDonald currently lives in his home town of New York City, where he is completing his first novel and beginning a full-length play.

Susan B. McIver is a former university professor and research scientist. Her short fiction, mainly humourous, appears widely in Canadian and American magazines and anthologies. She has published in *Tide Lines, The Time of Our Lives, Love's Shadow,* and *Woman in the Window*.

Ian-Andrew McKenzie is managing editor of an international newspaper based in Charlotte, North Carolina. He graduated from the Asheville School and North Carolina State University, where he studied writing and editing. He is currently working on his first novel.

Michael Gregg Michaud was born in Maine and lives in Los Angeles. He is the author of twelve collections of poetry; the most recent is *Giraffes on Horseback Salad*. His work has appeared in *Amelia, Chiron Review, The Harvard Gay and Lesbian Review, James White Review, Northwest Gay and Lesbian Reader* and *Karamu*, among many other publications.

Merril Mushroom lives in rural Tennessee and writes on an old Kaypro CPM. Her work has appeared in numerous periodicals and anthologies.

Adrienne Y. Nelson is an African-American lesbian writer who lives in Los Angeles. She writes poetry, short stories and essays. Her work has appeared in *The Dyke Review, Aché, Coffy Time Blues* and *Words That Matter*, Volumes I and II.

Lesléa Newman is an author and editor with twenty books to her credit, including *Heather Has Two Mommies, A Letter to Harvey Milk, The Femme Mystique, Every Woman's Dream* and *A Loving Testimony: Remembering Loved Ones Lost to AIDS*.

Laura Panter is a graduate of Queen's University in Kingston, Ontario, and is currently living and writing in Toronto.

Christopher Paw's work has appeared in several anthologies as well as numerous magazines. Although he has met at one time or another both RuPaul and Bill Gates, they both refuse to return his phone calls. He lives in Toronto.

Rebekah Perks is a dyke, a writer and a ceramic artist. She lives with her lover in Vermont.

Felice Picano is the author of fifteen books, plays and screenplays. He is a member of the legendary Violet Quill Club, a founder of Seahorse Press and Gay Presses in New York. His most recent books are the novel *Like People In History* and the science fiction novel *Drylands End*. "Matthew's Story—1974" is an excerpt from the novel *Like People In History* (Viking Penguin, 1995).

Victoria Plum writes fiction and feminist theology. She subsidizes these vices with journalism and book reviewing. She lives with her lover in the Shropshire hills in England.

Cynthia J. Price, who is referred to by her two children as "Mother Queerest," lives in a coastal town in Kwa Zulu Natal, South Africa with her wife of thirteen years. After a mixed career of medical technician, mother, part-time student and crocodile-handler, she is now a boring bank clerk who writes to remain sane.

Jim Provenzano's fiction has appeared in *Waves, Whispering Campaign* and other journals and anthologies. He is a contributing editor to *Wilde*, and has written for *The Advocate, Frontiers* and *Ten Percent*. A former staff member of *Outweek*, editor of *Hunt*, and assistant editor of *The Bay Area Reporter*, he also edited *Wanderlust*, a lesbian and gay travel guide. He lives in San Francisco.

Andy Quan is a third-generation Chinese-Canadian, fifth-generation Chinese-American Queer. He has had poems and short fiction published in various literary publications, including *Grain, ARC, Tickle Ace* and *Queeries: An Anthology of Gay Male Prose.* He is currently working for the International Lesbian Gay Association in Brussels, Belgium.

Shelly Rafferty, whose recent work will appear in the *Lesbian Review of Books* and *Contemporary Lesbian Love Poetry*, writes about medical research in upstate New York. She is the co-founder of the Feminist Creative Writers' Retreat and soon to be a new parent.

Faustina Rey is a pseudonym assumed to protect good people in hard times. "The Truth" is a brief excerpt from *The Last Hut on the Mountain*, a novel about growing up lesbian in southern Africa. She welcomes enquiries.

Jeff Richardson is a Toronto-based creativity consultant and leader of workshops in the writing process and in personal development through enhancement of the imagination. In private counselling and in classes, he helps his students to feel safe to explore their unique, innate talents.

Michael Rowe is the author of *Writing Below The Belt: Conversations With Erotic Authors*, and a contributor to *The Harvard Gay & Lesbian Review*, as well as numerous anthologies including, most recently, *Flesh and The Word 3* and *Flashpoint: The Best Gay Male Sexual Writings of 1995.* His first novel *Darkling I Listen* will be published in 1997. He lives in Toronto with his life-partner, Brian, and their adopted nephew, Patrick.

Sandip Roy was born in Calcutta, India and now lives in the U.S. When not busy editing *Trikone Magazine*, the world's oldest magazine for South Asian lesbians and gay men, he likes to take invigorating walks in the park.

Lawrence Schimel is editor of *Switch Hitters: Lesbians Writing Gay Male Erotica and Gay Men Writing Lesbian Erotica* and *Food for Life*, a benefit cookbook, both from Cleis Press. His stories and poems have appeared in over sixty anthologies, including *The Badboy Book of Erotic Poetry, Jewish Girls, Dark Angels, Weird Tales from Shakespeare* and *The Random House Treasury of Light Verse.* He lives in Manhattan.

Craig J. Simmons was raised in northern Québec. After receiving his Bachelor of Fine Arts in Drama from the University of Calgary, he moved to Vancouver in 1991, where he lives with his lover. "Shopping" is his first published piece.

Joe Stamps: "I joined the writer's workshop at the Lesbian and Gay Community Services Center in New York, and continued with the first draft of my short story (when it was nine pages), my novella (when the short story grew to 180 pages), my novel (when it hit 300). And so as a continuing work in progress (hovering around 500 pages with no end in sight), I tell myself there's always the Alexandria Quartet . . . or better yet, Proust. . . . "

Wickie Stamps is a writer whose published works appear in *For Shelter and Beyond: Ending Violence Against Women* (MCBWSG); *Sister and Brother* (HarperCollins San Francisco); *Looking for Mr. Preston* (Masquerade); *Dykescapes* (Alyson); *Doing It For Daddy*; and *Leatherfolks* (Alyson). Forthcoming works: *Best of Brat Attack* and *Flashpoint* (both from Masquerade). She is the editor of *Drummer* magazine.

Christina Starr is an enthusiastic bleached-blonde/lilac/pink lesbian living in downtown Toronto with her five-and-a-half-year-old self-professed lesbian daughter.

Matt Bernstein Sycamore is a faggot, a writer and a whore. He currently lives in Boston.

Sherece Taffe is a fierce black dyke being raised by one energetic goddess-kissed girl child; a poet, writer, lover of her child/spirit, community organizer & founding member of de poonani posse & blackberry; much time is devoted to devising strategies aimed at coaxing her reluctant spirit back into her society-battered body.

Cecilia Tan is a writer, editor and sexuality activist in the Boston area. Her fiction has appeared in anthologies including *Herotica 3, On A Bed of Rice: An Asian American Erotic Feast*, and *Looking for Mr. Preston*. She is the founder/publisher of Circlet Press, specializing in erotic science fiction and fantasy.

Robert Thomson was born in 1964 in Toronto. *SECRET THiNGS*, his first book, was published by Immediate Press in 1994. Robert continues to perform in shows and is currently finishing work on his second book of short fiction, *REVENGE*.

Kitty Tsui loves to write about sex. She is the author of *Breathless*, a collection of erotic short stories forthcoming from Firebrand Books, and the editor of *Wild/Rice: Erotica by Asian Pacific Lesbian and Bisexual Women*. A longer and somewhat different version of "A Femme, a Daddy and Their Dyke" appears as "A Femme in Butch Clothing" in *The Femme Mystique*, edited by Lesléa Newman.

David Watmough was born in Britain and is the author of eleven volumes of novels and short stories, all of them featuring his gay protagonist Davey Bryant, the latest being *The Time of the Kingfishers* (Arsenal Pulp Press, 1994). "Questions & Answers," in modified form, will appear in his collection, *Hunting With Diana*, to be published by Arsenal Pulp Press in 1996. He lives in Vancouver.

Graham Watts, having retired after thirty-eight years as a locksmith, is free to devote his time to gardening and writing. He was born in Australia and is now a Canadian citizen, living in Edmonton, Alberta. "Crossing the Rubicon" is his first published fiction.

Jess Wells is the author of a novel, *AfterShocks*, and three volumes of short stories (*Run; Two Willow Chairs; The Dress/The Sharda Stories*). She is also author of a book of eclectic history and essays (*A Herstory of Prostitution in Western Europe,*), and has had work appear in many literary anthologies within the lesbian, gay and women's movement. She lives in the San Francisco Bay Area.

Dianne Whelan is a photographer/writer presently living in Toronto and working on a new art show that she will tour in the spring of 1996.

Ben Widdicombe moved from London to Sydney, Australia in 1995. Born in Australia in 1970, he inherited rights to Canadian citizenship from his father. He was educated in Queensland, Kent and California, and is currently a staff journalist with the *Sydney Star Observer*.

Duane Williams lives in Hamilton, Ontario. His short stories and poems have appeared in *Queeries: An Anthology of Gay Male Prose*, *The Church-Wellesley Review* and various literary journals.

Jeannie Witkin is a Jewish lesbian living in Berkeley, California. She works with other people's words as a sign language interpreter. Writing lets her speak for herself. She is happiest when climbing tall trees so she can see what is happening in the world around her.

Raymond John Woolfrey grew up in Montreal where he presently works as an editor and translator. He has published short stories in Canada and abroad. His first was included in the 1993 Arsenal Pulp Press anthology *Queeries*. It and "Le Jardin des Mervilles" are part of his collection of Montreal stories (in progress) entitled *East of the Big Q*.

Kim Yaged received the Hopwood Award and the Atanas Ilitch Award for her play *Roomies*. She has written one other stage play and two screenplays. Her poem "DC" will appear in an anthology edited by Lesléa Newman to be published by Ballantine Books in 1996.

Paul Yee writes and works in Toronto, Ontario.

Wayne Yung was born in Edmonton, Alberta in 1971, and published his first short story in 1993. He is currently based in Vancouver as a writer, video artist, performer, sometime cleaning lady and bathhouse temp.

Sarah V Zetlein is twenty-three, and graduated in Politics and Women's Studies from the University of Adelaide, Australia. She currently works as a research assistant and teaches feminist political theory. She writes short fiction and long love letters. Her work has been published in several Australian journals.

Aaron Zyskin grew up in New York City in the 1940s and now lives in California. "Found Out" is a chapter from a larger work-in-progress, *Nobody's Business*, set in The Bronx and spanning the decade 1939-1949, ages four to fourteen in the life of protagonist Melvin Hendler.

James C. Johnstone and *Karen X. Tulchinsky* are writers and editors who co-wrote a piece together in the Lambda Award-winning anthology *Sister & Brother* (HarperCollins San Francisco). James' work has been published in *Prairie Fire, Q Magazine* and the anthology *Flash Points: Best Gay Male Sexual Writing of 1995*. Karen is the author of *In Her Nature*, a short story collection, and the co-editor of the anthology *Tangled Sheets: Stories and Poems of Lesbian Lust*, both published by the Women's Press. James and Karen live in Vancouver.